The King leaned back in his chair. 'You do realise the identity of the woman you spent the night with?'

'Of course I do. Her name is Rosa.'

'Her name is Rosa Corretti!'

Kulal's expression remained unchanged, for he did not care to admit that the brunette's surname was news to him. 'Mmm. That's right. Corretti. She's Italian,' he said, as if imparting some important nugget of information.

'No, she is not Italian,' said Hazail. 'She's Sicilian. And not only is she Sicilian, but she comes from one of the most powerful families on the island.'

'So?'

'So her brothers are probably going to come after you. In fact, the whole damned family is probably going to come after you after you compromised her reputation by spending the night with her.'

Kulal shrugged. 'Then let them come,' he said carelessly. 'For I am afraid of no man!'

SICILY'S CORRETTI DYNASTY

The more powerful the family...the darker the secrets!

Sicily's Most Scandalous Family!
Young, rich, and notoriously handsome, the Correttis' legendary exploits regularly feature in Sicily's tabloid pages!

The Scandal
How long can their reputations withstand the glaring heat of the spotlight before their family's secrets are exposed?

The Legacy
Once nearly destroyed by the secrets cloaking their thirst for power, the new generation of Correttis are riding high again —and no disgrace or scandal will stand in their way...

The Correttis: Sins (May 2013)
A LEGACY OF SECRETS – Carol Marinelli
AN INVITATION TO SIN – Sarah Morgan

The Correttis: Revenge (June 2013)
A SHADOW OF GUILT – Abby Green
AN INHERITANCE OF SHAME – Kate Hewitt

The Correttis: Secrets (July 2013)
A WHISPER OF DISGRACE – Sharon Kendrick
A FAÇADE TO SHATTER – Lynn Raye Harris

The Correttis: Scandals (August 2013)
A SCANDAL IN THE HEADLINES – Caitlin Crews
A HUNGER FOR THE FORBIDDEN – Maisey Yates

THE CORRETTIS
Secrets

SHARON KENDRICK
LYNN RAYE HARRIS

MILLS & BOON

which were rich and warm and red. Or at least, she'd been allowed the occasional half-glassful, topped up with water—watched over by the fiercely protective eyes of her two brothers.

Except that they were not really her brothers, were they? From now on, she had to start thinking of them as her half-brothers.

Rosa gripped the neck of the bottle, a shudder running down her spine as she forced herself to confront the unbelievable truth. That nothing was as it seemed, nor ever would be again. The discovery had been brutal and she'd found out in the worst possible way that she'd been living a lie all her life.

And she was nothing but a fake.

'*Mademoiselle?* You are ready?'

Wordlessly, Rosa nodded as the nightclub attendant gestured towards the podium on which various women had been attempting to pole dance all evening. It would be fair to say that most of them had been making an absolute hash of it, despite the fact that they were slim and blonde and incredibly fit. But then, all the women on this part of the French Riviera looked like that. Rosa was the one who stood out like a sore thumb with her mahogany hair, olive

But Rosa wasn't feeling sensibl
ing…defiant. Because defiance wa
with than heartbreak and loneliness,
ance made you feel alive, instead of
and wondering just where your lif
don't want to be rescued,' she said
lantly as she took another swig of
want to dance.'

'Now that,' he said steadily as he r
tle from her hand and handed it to
ing nearby, who accepted it without
also be arranged.'

He took her hand and led her tov
floor and Rosa was aware of a sud
sense of danger as he took her into h
music began to throb out a sultry b
tall, she thought—taller than any c
ever seen. And his body felt so stron
dry lips. A woman wouldn't stand a
a man like this. The thought thrilled
scared her as she knew it should hav
even know your name,' she shouted

'That's because I haven't told you

'And are you going to tell me?'

'I might—if you're very good.'

skin and the generous curves—which were currently spilling out of her brand-new crimson dress.

She placed one leg rather unsteadily on the podium, wondering if she would be able to dance in the kind of heels she wouldn't have dared wear back home in her native Sicily. But who cared if she stumbled? And who cared if her dress was the shortest thing she'd ever worn? Not her. Tonight she was going to shrug off the old Rosa, who had cared so much about appearances and doing the right thing. Tonight she was going to embrace a brand-new Rosa—one who had grown a tougher skin so that nobody could hurt her ever again. On this privileged strip of French coastline known as the Côte d'Azur, she would emerge from her protective shell into a glittering and unrecognisable creature—and her transformation would be complete.

She took another slug of champagne and put the bottle down, but as she stepped up onto the podium, she found her gaze locked with the man on the other side of the club—the one with the dark hair and the powerful body. He was still watching her—and something in the speculative amusement which glittered in the depths of his eyes made Rosa's stomach perform an odd kind of flip. Hadn't anyone ever

ibly sexy dance a few moments ag...
the whole place in meltdown.'

Rosa's smile became a little glass...
level of flirtation was escalating by...
she was feeling more than a little d...
cause this kind of thing was way o...
rience. Even during her university...
the men she'd fancied had steered c...
they'd discovered who she was. Be...
in their right mind would get invol...
retti woman, a woman they wouldn...
fear that one of her brothers or cous...
after them?

She'd never met anyone who had...
dated by the reputation of her powe...
she wouldn't have been allowed a...
man like this. A man who was sizzl...
sex appeal that she wondered if he...
burn if she reached out and touched...

She knew that the sensible thing to...
turn around and walk away. To go b...
she'd booked into and sleep off the c...
would wake up in the morning—p...
splitting headache—and decide wha...
to do with the rest of her life.

bare neck and she closed her eyes with pleasure. This was…bliss. His arms had tightened around her and she realised that dancing with him was different to dancing with anyone else. He seemed to be making up the rules as he went along, completely ignoring the rhythm of the music and moving them around as if this was a slow waltz instead of a vaguely jumpy beat. And she was letting him. Why wouldn't she let him? Why, he could carry on doing that all night, he was so good at it.

'Do you like that?' he queried softly as the palms of his hands skated possessively over the curve of her bottom.

Her sudden, heady sense of freedom and the sensation of listening to her body's desires made Rosa bold and she didn't shrink away from the way he was pulling her even closer. 'Yes.'

'I thought so. I like it too. I like it very much.'

Kulal closed his eyes as he felt her fingertips move to his shoulders. He could feel the brush of her silken hair against his cheek and the wave of desire which swept over him was so strong that he was filled with an unbearable need to touch her more intimately.

But even though he'd always been known as a mould-breaking prince, Kulal respected his posi-

the time to make the o
ing panties. Or that th
them. 'Just how much
demanded.

That deeply accente
thoughts and Rosa's
air had made her fee
she felt safe in this l
here, she thought. H
nightclub who'd hel
floor. She felt very
he still holding her?
could forget everyth
touching her.

'Come over here a
jet-dark eyes swam
effort of keeping he
and she closed ther

Kulal caught hol
shake as he tried to
hiding his feeling
for having allowed
this. Did she really
when she was in t

'Rosa,' he accu

of her ear as t
your name?'

'Rosa,' she
'Corretti' bit
family or he
that risk. To
recklessly, bu

'Rosa,' he
the thick spi
ing the flank
he felt her wr
you Italian?'

'Yes,' Rosa
to speak whe
her. Who car
ical with the
through, and
rage if they'
But it was ea
her family ar
Not a single

'And do yo
clubs, Rosa?'

She shook
life.'

tion enough not to throw his royal role into jeopardy. Dancing with a woman who was clearly an exhibitionist was one thing, but making love to her in a public place was quite another. So that even though they were shielded by the bobbing crowds around them and even though the flashing lights obscured most of their movements, he did not do what he wanted to do. Which was to play with the tips of her breasts through the thin satin of her minidress. Or to slide his hand up her thigh and touch the undoubtedly moist heat which would be searing its way through her panties.

That's if she was wearing any.

He swallowed, wondering if she could feel the sudden jerk of his erection.

He'd noticed her the moment she'd walked into the nightclub—but then, her shiny red dress had left little to the imagination. She had the type of body which was deeply unfashionable—especially here, in the South of France. She didn't look as if she spent hours at the gym and she didn't look as if she existed on a punishing diet either. The kind of diet which always left women with that furrowed and slightly anxious look—as if they were worried they might pass out from hunger. Instead she was

ripe and lusc
it fell from tl
He'd notic
dark satin a
dress had ski
thighs. Their
he had seen
prised—and
he always kı
was his for tl
soon as poss
kind of sexua
Kulal felt
the duty and
loomed close
days were nu
were to agre
'open' for hi
have to condu
the kind of cı
their husband
with it certai
days of walki
out with a be
He pressed

ridiculously expensive b
hours earlier, along wit
complemented it. It ma
was hanging from her
she didn't remember it
'I don't think so,' sh
The look that Kulal
prehension and, as he s
dance floor, he sudden
ous offer. She might l
come to life, but nov
steady and he began
was. He liked womer
was true, but he liked
His hand resting i
her stagger as they s
caught her and stead
no paparazzi around
levered her into the
and she slumped bac
splayed out in front
a close.
For the first time
tugging down the l
to introduce a moc

'I know I am.' Her head lolled back against the soft leather seat as his unfamiliar words washed over her. 'And it feels fantastic.'

'If you could see yourself you would not think that,' he raged. 'For a drunken woman is never a pretty sight.'

'But a drunken man is okay, I suppose?' she mumbled. Because wasn't this what she'd grown up with? One rule for men and a different one for women. Oh, why was the world so unfair?

'I don't approve of anyone losing control of themselves in such a way as this, no,' he retorted. 'Which is why I'm taking you home.'

The word mocked her enough to make her lips curve into an empty smile. 'Home?' she questioned, and for the first time a trace of bitterness crept into her voice. 'You're going to have a bit of a problem with that one. Because I don't have a home. Not any more.'

Kulal leaned over her, only just managing to avoid the arms which were reaching up in an attempt to snake themselves around his neck. He wasn't interested in this particular alcohol-fuelled sob story. He just needed to get rid of her and he needed to do it quickly. 'Where are you staying?' he questioned urgently.

At this, her eyes snapped open and, blurrily, she looked up at him. She tried to sit up, but somehow the effort of moving was just too much. And he had brought her attention to a much bigger problem. Where *was* she staying?

'I've no idea,' she mumbled, tucking her legs underneath her. It was comfortable here and she didn't want to go anywhere else. She wanted to stay with this man with the dark face and glittering eyes because he made her feel safe and he made her feel excited. She gave a luxurious yawn as she snuggled down against the soft leather seat. 'So I guess I'd better stay with you.'

dignity. And she could be strong. She'd proved that, hadn't she? She had survived her mother scream-ing vitriol at her as she'd made her vile confession. And she'd faced the unbelievable and heartbreak-ing truth, that her beloved father—the single rock in her life—was not her father at all.

She prayed for the right amount of bravado as she stared into Kulal's furious face. 'And did we?'

At this, he smiled, and it was the coldest smile that Rosa had ever seen.

'Believe me, *garbuua*—if you'd had sex with me, you'd remember it, no matter how drunk you were.'

Rosa met the mocking expression in his eyes, tell-ing herself that she wasn't going to be intimidated. She just needed to extricate herself from this regret-table situation—but first of all she must face facts.

'So we didn't?' she questioned flatly.

'No.'

She held the sheet a little tighter. 'Then how come I'm not wearing any clothes?'

'Because I undressed you.'

'You…undressed me? Why?'

'Why do you think?' he snapped. 'Because I wanted to feast my eyes on your delectable body?' And yet Kulal felt the sudden fierce beat of his heart as he tried to subdue the memory of her firm flesh as he had stripped her bare. He'd taken her clothes off on autopilot, averting his eyes when he had slithered that wispy little pair of lace panties down over her knees. In her uninhibited state she had grabbed him and pulled him down towards her—and he'd had the tantalising experience of having his head buried in her magnificent breasts before he had forced himself to move his aching body away. 'If you must know, I removed your clothes because I didn't think you'd want to leave here this morning wearing last night's crumpled dress, or underwear.'

The gap in her memory was making Rosa feel frightened but she wasn't going to let him know that. 'Is that so?' she said.

Kulal heard the disbelief in her voice and felt a slow anger begin to simmer inside him. Didn't she realise how lucky she'd been that someone like him had been the man she'd targeted last night? That somebody completely lacking in moral scruples could have taken her home and... His mouth hardened. 'I'll tell you exactly what happened,' he bit out. 'You couldn't remember where you were staying, and just before you passed out on the back seat of my limousine, you announced that you wanted to stay with me.'

Rosa could do absolutely nothing about the blush which stained her cheeks. 'I said that?'

'You did,' he agreed grimly. 'Leaving me with little choice other than to bring you back here to my hotel. My plan was to get you inside as quietly and as unobtrusively as possible—but unfortunately, that was not on your agenda.'

She saw the furious accusation which had darkened his face. 'It wasn't?' she questioned as a trace of nerves began to creep into her voice.

'Indeed it wasn't. You decided that as many of the people in the immediate vicinity and beyond should know exactly what you wanted—and what you wanted was to go down to the beach and look at the sky….'

Oh, God. It was all coming back to her now. He'd promised to take her somewhere to look at the stars. He'd said that to her in the nightclub as he'd held her in his arms. And in that moment, she felt as if he'd been offering her a slice of paradise. 'What…what happened?' she whispered.

'I decided that an excess of alcohol, a senseless female and close proximity to the Mediterranean were a potentially lethal combination and so I carried you in here, undressed you—and put you to bed.'

'And that's it?'

'That's it.'

'So where did you sleep?' she questioned pointedly.

He gave a short laugh. 'When you rent a hotel villa overlooking the Mediterranean, there tends to be more than one bedroom. In fact, there are three— so I slept in the one next door.'

Rosa's mind was spinning as she listened to his explanation, but the one thought which was uppermost was that her virtue was still intact—and that surprised her. Because she did remember the heady rush of abandonment she'd felt as he'd held her on the dance floor. She wasn't experienced, but she didn't need to be to realise that she'd been putty in his hands last night. That if he hadn't been so moral, then he would have been lying beside her now. Because she had wanted him. Come to think of it, she still wanted him.

He had moved away from the bed and now that he was at a distance it gave her a better opportunity to study him. She wondered where he was from—his rich accent certainly didn't sound Mediterranean and his skin was much too dark.

'Who are you?' she questioned suddenly.

Kulal tensed, realising that he had been expecting this question a whole lot sooner and knowing that his answer would bring with it a whole new set of baggage. Should he lie? Adopt some fictitious identity, knowing that their paths would never cross again? But that might add fuel to a possibly combustive situation. She had already humiliated herself through her drunken behaviour—if she then discovered that he was lying to her, then mightn't she take out her shame on him? He knew women well enough to know that they were impossible when you rejected them. So why not keep her sweet? Why not make her appreciate just how much he had done for her?

'My name is Kulal,' he said.

'I already know that bit. Where are you from—you're not Mediterranean, are you?'

'No, I am not. I come from a country called Zahrastan.' He searched her face for signs of recognition. 'Any idea where that is?'

She shrugged. 'I'm afraid I've never heard of it. Should I have done?'

Kulal told himself that he shouldn't have been

surprised. He wouldn't really expect a pole-dancing socialite to know much about the Arabian principality which produced a vast tranche of the world's oil supply, would he? She probably thought of little else other than which colour she was going to paint her pretty little toenails each day. 'I suggest you try acquainting yourself with a map of the world if you want to find out its exact position.' His voice was dismissive as he slanted her a cool look. 'Now, have I answered all your questions to your satisfaction?'

She wanted to say that no, he hadn't. She wanted to ask him if they couldn't just forget about the disastrous way the evening had ended. If only it was possible to rewind life and stop at the bit you liked best. When she'd been dancing with him it had all felt so...promising. But the repressive note in his voice and the unwelcoming look on his face made her realise that this was not a conversation he was keen on extending. She lifted her fingertips to her temples as if that might help reduce the pounding inside her skull, but it didn't.

'My head hurts,' she said, painfully aware that the first and last hangover of her life should have been conducted in front of such a critical audience.

Kulal nodded as he saw an acceptable exit sign

Angrily, she pushed aside the sheet and headed for the bathroom, recoiling as she caught sight of her reflection in the huge mirror. It was a shock on so many levels, because walking around naked wasn't something she ever did. In Sicily, she always wore a silk nightgown to preserve her modesty because that was how she'd been brought up.

'Imagine if there was a fire in the middle of the night,' her mother had once said, in that tart way she had of speaking to her only daughter. 'And the fireman found you naked and indecent. That is not the way a lady behaves, Rosa.'

As she stood beneath the torrential jets of the shower, Rosa's lips curved with derision. She had just accepted her mother's opinion, hadn't she? The way she always did. Never realising that the woman who had brought her up so strictly was nothing but a cheating hypocrite.

Quickly, she turned on the cold tap—hoping that the shock of the icy water might wash away the memories of the past few days, but it wasn't easy to forget her mother's dramatic confession. She stayed in the shower until she had scrubbed herself clean, and afterwards she found an unused toothbrush and paste and located her clothes and hairbrush. By the time she heard a knock on the bedroom door, she felt a million times better and she psyched herself up to face the judgemental face of Kulal.

'Come in,' she said crisply, her heart beginning to race as he walked in. 'I'm ready.'

'So I see,' Kulal said, reluctantly letting his gaze drift over her. Her feet were bare and the crimson minidress brushed the smooth skin of her thighs. For a moment he felt a powerful wave of temptation as he imagined taking her back to bed, before he swatted it away. She was trouble, he told himself. Last night, he might have been swayed by her beauty and her dancing, but in the cold light of day he knew she was best avoided.

'I've ordered breakfast to be served on the terrace,' he said. 'So why don't we go downstairs?'

Hunger made Rosa nod her head in grudging agreement and she followed him down a wide marble staircase and out onto a terrace, where a table had been laid with croissants, juices and jams, and what looked like a dish of iced mango. The terrace overlooked landscaped gardens and, in the distance, she caught a glimpse of the sapphire sea. It felt as if they were in a self-contained world of their own—a private little bubble which was miles away from the circumspect I have been with you, my beauty,' he said shakily. 'But that all ends as of now. You are no longer drunk and I am no longer angry. This may be one of the most ill-judged decisions of my life, but I want you—and, sweet heaven, I am going to have you. Right now.'

His emphatic statement should have daunted her, but it didn't. She suspected that he didn't particularly like or respect her, but suddenly Rosa didn't care. She didn't care about anything other than the way he was making her feel. Why shouldn't she taste the pleasures which seemed to drive everyone else in the human race, except for her—poor, protected Rosa, who had been shielded from the world for so long? Her lips were dry but somehow she managed to echo his words as she felt his thumb tease its way over one painfully erect nipple.

'I want you, too,' she whispered. 'And right now is fine with me.'

With a hard smile of satisfaction, he bent his head to kiss her again and Rosa never knew what would have happened next had she not heard the sound of an embarrassed cough behind them. With a start, they sprang apart—as if they'd been caught red-handed at the scene of a crime.

And maybe they had, she thought. Because there, standing at the edge of the private garden watching them, was a man as dark-skinned as Kulal himself, though his head was dipped with the faintest degree of subservience.

She watched as a look of anger darkened Kulal's face. 'What the hell is going on?' he demanded. 'Why the hell are you disturbing me, Mutasim—creeping up on me like a spy?'

Rosa thought she'd never seen a man look more embarrassed than Mutasim did as Kulal's words fired into him, and she noticed that the stranger hadn't met her eyes. Not once.

'I beg your indulgence at this untimely intrusion, Your Highness,' said Mutasim softly. 'But your brother, the king, craves your company at the earliest opportunity.'

Rosa's lips parted in shock as the words registered in her befuddled brain. She looked up at Kulal, her bewildered eyes asking him a silent question.

Highness? King?

Were they playing some sort of joke on her? Talking in some kind of code? But her confusion was quickly superseded by shame as Kulal took no notice of her silent plea. Completely ignoring her, he chambermaid's rooms, smoothing down his ruffled robes and smirking all over his face.

Or the time when Kulal had 'borrowed' one of the palace cars for an unauthorised trip into the desert when he was barely sixteen and nobody had known that he could drive. On both those occasions—and, indeed, on many more—righteous anger should surely have come flooding the younger prince's way, but it had not. It was almost as if it had been expected that he should behave wildly—and everyone knew why. Weren't motherless children always indulged?

As two royal princes of a fabulously rich desert kingdom, the two men should have been close but an accident of birth meant that they had grown up living two very different lives. Hazail was the older, the heir to the throne, and the defining factor of his life had always been that he would one day inherit the crown. It had been Hazail's destiny which had occupied most of their father's time as he had tutored his elder son in the art of ruling a powerful desert kingdom.

Kulal had simply been the 'spare'—the extra boy child born as an insurance policy to ensure the line of succession. He had been brought up by a series of amahs—female servants who had adored him but had lacked the strength to discipline the strong-minded little boy. Consequently, he had been given freedom—perhaps a little too much freedom for so strong and so wilful a character. But that had never compensated for the heavy weight which had hung over him since his mother had died—a shocking death which had sent the country spiralling into deep mourning. And Kulal had been marked out by that terrible loss, for she had died saving his life. Deep down he knew that was the reason why his father and his brother had always been so distant towards him. He knew that subconsciously they blamed him for the queen's untimely end, even if logic told them that it was nothing but the cruel intervention of fate. Of two people being in the wrong place at the wrong time.

Perhaps it had been to make up for their emotional distance that they had tended to overlook Kulal's misdemeanours. But it seemed that they were not being overlooked this time. Hazail was pacing the floor like an expectant father, before turning back to his younger brother, still with that exasperated expression on his face.

'She wasn't a pole dancer,' Kulal protested as he

something he could do to remedy a potentially explosive situation?

And then an idea began to form in his mind, an idea so simple that he was surprised it had taken him so long to come up with it.

'I suppose I will have to marry her,' he said.

Hazail stared at him. 'Marry her?'

Kulal shrugged. 'Why not? A short-term marriage would suit both parties very well. It would rescue her "honour," silence any overprotective brothers and it might work in our favour. Think about it, Hazail. We sell the story as some kind of love match and Princess Ayesha will be seen as magnanimous for agreeing to cancel her wedding to me. And just think how the press will seize on it!' He gave a mocking smile. 'The Arabian version of Romeo and Juliet!'

The king's mouth fell open. 'You're serious, aren't you?'

'Entirely serious.' Kulal smiled as he allowed his body to anticipate the pleasure of reuniting with his little Sicilian firecracker. 'I shall go to Rosa Corretti and ask for her hand in marriage.'

There was a pause as the king looked at him. 'This is remarkably good of you, Kulal,' he said quietly.

'Ah, but I am not doing it to be "good,"' Kulal

corrected silkily. 'I am doing it because I can see no feasible alternative. Look on it as an act of supreme patriotism, if you will. Let's just say I'm doing it for the sake of my country.'

haps—for there were enough of them in this part of the South of France. She felt her skin redden. Because hadn't she been one of those drunken revellers herself the other night, when she'd made such an awful fool of herself in front of that arrogant man, Kulal? It was ironic, really. She'd grown up surrounded by arrogant men and seen the heartbreak they could wreak on women, so why hadn't she chosen someone softer and easier as the man she had decided she wanted to take her virginity?

Briefly she shut her eyes because the most humiliating thing of all was that he hadn't wanted her. He'd put her to bed after too much champagne and the disdain on his face the following morning had been clear. It was only when she'd practically thrown herself at him that he had deigned to kiss her. She wondered if they would have gone all the way had the kiss not been interrupted by that other man, the one who'd started talking about a king.

She still couldn't quite believe the words he'd uttered. Something about the king 'craving his company.' Did people really talk like that any more? Perhaps they were some kind of double act who trawled holiday areas pretending to be people they weren't. Operating some kind of cheap scam.

'I know you're in there.'

The terse words carried through the closed door and put a swift halt to Rosa's swirling thoughts. Because that deep voice with the strange accent was horribly familiar and she was unprepared for the wave of desire which made her skin grow heated. A curling expectation began to unfold somewhere deep inside her and it wasn't a feeling she particularly welcomed. She thought of his cruel face and hard body and her heart began to pound. What was the matter with her? He was probably nothing but a weird imposter—some fake sheikh—and she didn't have to answer the door to him.

Oh, why hadn't she turned the lights off?

Because you weren't expecting a late-night visitor, that's why.

'You can try ignoring me if you want, Rosa, but I'm not going anywhere,' persisted the voice. 'And if you stretch my patience too far, then I may be forced to break down this door.'

What a caveman he was! Rosa racked her brain for some kind of response and decided to attempt an audacious piece of bravado. 'And what if I'm not alone?' she demanded. 'Don't you think you might be disturbing something—that I might want a little privacy?'

From the other side of the door, Kulal gritted his teeth as a slow rage began to build inside him. Bad enough that he was being forced to enter a union with this tramp of a woman, but that she should dare to keep him waiting was intolerable!

'Then I'd advise you to tell your paramour to get dressed and to get dressed quickly, since he might not enjoy facing me in my current mood.'

Rosa shivered at the forceful intent behind his words. She should have been shocked by his arrogance, but she was Sicilian and therefore she wasn't a bit shocked. She was used to outrageously chauvinist behaviour within the Corretti clan itself, but this man was making the male members of her own overbearing family seem like absolute pussycats.

Reluctantly, she unlocked the key and opened the door, her senses assailed by the overpowering scent of jasmine from the darkened gardens as she stared at the man who was standing on her doorstep.

He was exactly as she remembered him. No, that wasn't quite true. She'd spent the past two days trying to play him down in her imagination, telling herself that it had been her highly emotional state which had made her react to him in such an uncharacteristic way. Telling herself that he was nothing special, that he was just a man who was aware of his appeal to women and who played on it.

But she had been wrong. More than wrong. Because tonight, his undeniable sexiness was edged with something potent—something which suddenly made her feel innocent and fragile. He looked as if he meant business—and it wasn't just the way he was dressed, in a dark and sombre suit, which emphasised his powerful physique. He looked as if he hadn't shaved that day so that his dark jaw was faintly shadowed with stubble. It was a look which was essentially masculine and subtly modern, yet it didn't match the expression in his black eyes. Because that was the antithesis of modern—it was darkly glittering and almost primitive.

She swallowed. 'What do you want?'

'A little courtesy might be a good place to start. I'd like to come in.'

To Rosa's disbelief he didn't bother waiting for her assent, just walked straight past her. 'You can't just barge in here like that!' she protested.

'Too late. I just did. So let's not waste any more

time with futile protestations. Shut the door like a good girl, will you? I want to talk to you.'

Fury came in many forms and the form which was visiting Rosa right then was making her speechless with a growing anger. Like a good girl, he had said—and hadn't she run away from Sicily to escape precisely that type of patronising attitude? It took a moment or two before she could compose herself enough to suck in a deep breath and manage to turn it into an outraged question.

'What are you doing here?' she demanded.

'Are you going to shut the door, or am I?'

She kicked it shut before she could ask herself why she wasn't calling hotel security—if such a thing existed in this place—to have him ejected. Maybe because there seemed something distinctly unfinished between them—something which still needed to be said. But she wasn't going to let him think that she was a pushover, even though her heart was now racing for a very different reason. She had behaved like a stupid fool the other night and she didn't intend to do so again. 'I didn't think we had anything left to say to each other, after that man Mutasim bundled me into a taxi the other day.'

He didn't appear to be listening to her for his eyes

were trained on the closed door in the far corner of the room. 'So is there some thwarted lover in there?' he questioned softly. 'Cowering in fear as he puts his clothes back on?'

For a moment Rosa was tempted to say yes, wondering if he would have the bravado to actually go in and confront some fictitious man. But deep down she knew the answer. Of course he would. She could tell from the tension in his powerful body that he was afraid of nothing. Or no one.

But then, neither was she, she reminded herself. Not any more. She'd spent her whole life being bossed around by autocratic men and being reined in by old-fashioned rules, and the new Rosa Corretti had no intention of continuing with that repressive tradition. So this Kulal—whoever he was—had better understand that, before she kicked him out of here for good.

'No, I haven't got anyone cowering in the bedroom—not that it's any of your business if I had,' she snapped. 'I was about to go to bed myself when I was rudely interrupted by your unwanted appearance.'

Kulal felt his pulse quicken. So she was alone, was she? Alone and probably as hungry for him as she'd been the other night. And wouldn't that be the easiest way to get her to agree to his proposition—by getting her horizontal? His lips curved with the hint of an expectant smile. Because a woman would agree to pretty much anything when a man was making love to her.

Now that he was safely in her hotel room, he allowed himself to study her closely—thinking that she looked very different to the sexy strumpet who had writhed around the pole in her tiny crimson dress the other night. Her dark hair was tied over one shoulder in a single plait and she wore a heavy, silken robe, which shimmered to the ground as she moved. A classy kind of garment, he thought approvingly. And even though it covered every inch of her body, the delicate fabric still clung to every delicious curve, reminding him all too vividly of what lay beneath.

'You are looking very beautiful tonight,' he murmured.

Rosa stiffened because the calculating look she'd seen hardening his eyes was completely at odds with the silken caress of his voice. And yet stupidly, her body couldn't seem to stop reacting to him. She wanted him to pull her into his hard body and she wanted him to kiss her again. But he was trouble. She knew that. He might exude an undeniable appeal which was clawing away at something deep inside her, but she sensed an undeniable danger about him.

'I asked what you were doing here,' she said quietly. 'And so far you haven't come up with a satisfactory answer.'

Kulal frowned. She was certainly behaving very differently this evening. She wasn't coming on to him at all, or making any indication that she wanted to continue the delicious kiss which had been abruptly terminated by the appearance of his brother's aide.

'We need to have a conversation,' he said.

'At this time of night?'

He nodded. The concealing cloak of nighttime was infinitely preferable to a meeting conducted in the harsh light of the Mediterranean sunshine. And even though this rather humble hotel was not the kind of place which usually attracted the paparazzi, his striking looks always made him the subject of prying eyes. 'I'm afraid so.'

'Then you'd better hurry up and get on with it, Mr...?'

He met the challenge in her voice, thinking how spectacular her eyes were, as they looked at him with impertinent challenge. 'I think you were made perfectly aware by the interruption which took place yesterday that I am not a "Mr," he said shortly. 'In fact, I am a prince.'

'A prince?' she echoed, like someone waiting for the punchline to a joke.

He nodded. 'Although I prefer to think of myself as a sheikh first and a prince second. I am Sheikh Kulal Al-Dimashqi, the second son of the royal house of Zahrastan.' He elevated his dark brows in careless question. 'But perhaps you have found out a little more about me since we were parted so abruptly. Was your interest not piqued by the stranger you almost had sex with?' He gave a mocking smile. 'Especially when you discovered that his brother was a king.'

Rosa glared at him, trying to ignore his crude taunt. 'If you must know—I thought that you might be involved in some kind of scam.'

'A scam?' he echoed.

'Yes. That man turning up and announcing that the "king" wanted to see you.' She gave him a scornful look. 'People pretend to be aristocrats all the time! It helps them get into expensive hotels without paying.'

He gave the room a deprecating glance. 'Then I don't imagine they'd be targeting a place like this, do you?'

Rosa didn't rise to the taunt. Why should she, when it was true? She'd chosen the hotel precisely because it hadn't been expensive. Because it was the last place on earth that you would ever expect to find a Corretti staying and therefore it was unlikely that any of her family would come looking for her here. But the Hotel Jasmin was exactly what she needed in her troubled state. She liked the peace of the place. The laid-back attitude and the old-fashioned gardens. There were mostly French people staying here and the service was simple and unobtrusive. There were no tourists, no dull international menu or any Wi-Fi connection which might have encouraged people to sit around, tapping away on their computers so that you felt as if you'd walked into a giant office.

'If you don't like it, then leave,' she said quietly. 'I'm not stopping you.'

Kulal hesitated—and for him, such hesitation was rare. But this conversation was not going according to plan. For a start, she had not fallen on him with lust in her eyes and a body impatient for the pleasure he could give her. He had thought that he would be in her bed by now and yet he was nowhere near it. She seemed completely different to the woman who had begged him to kiss her and he began to wonder why.

'I know who you are,' he said suddenly.

Rosa didn't react. It had been one of the first lessons she had been taught—never show a stranger what you are thinking. She had broken that rule the other night, under the influence of the unaccustomed champagne, but she would not be repeating such a fundamental mistake tonight.

'And who am I?' she questioned lightly, thinking that perhaps he could provide a better answer than any she could come up with. Because she didn't seem to know who she was herself any more.

He sucked in a deep breath. 'Your name is Rosa Corretti and you are a member of the prestigious Sicilian family of that name.'

Rosa nodded. At least he hadn't come out with the usual accusatory stereotype, as people usually did. They discovered that you came from a powerful family with a sometimes questionable past, and assumed that you were all gangsters. Hadn't that been one of the reasons why she'd been so protected during her upbringing—to keep her away from the judgement of the outside world, as well as to protect her innocence?

'Bravo, Sheikh Kulal Al-Dimashqi,' she said softly. 'And what else have you found out about me?'

He stared at her. 'Nothing,' he said, his words edged with frustration.

'Nothing?'

He shook his head. He had some of the best intelligence sources in the world, but when it came to finding out more about the daughter of Carlo Corretti, it seemed that they had come up against a brick wall. There was plenty about her two brothers and a whole bunch of colourful cousins, but Rosa might as well not have existed for all the information they'd been able to provide. 'Absolutely nothing. Oh, I know which schools you went to and that you studied linguistics at the University of Palermo, but other than that, not a thing. No lists of lovers and no recorded misdemeanours. No earlier experimentations with pole dancing. You come from a society which seems expert in keeping secrets,' he observed caustically.

Somehow Rosa suppressed a bitter laugh. He didn't know the half of it. Not just a society which was good at keeping secrets, but a family which was riddled with them. 'I think I would agree with that,' she said coolly.

Kulal was starting to feel confused and it was not a feeling he was used to. Because Rosa Corretti was perplexing him. The other night, her sexuality had shimmered off her half-clothed frame like the bright haloes of light which gleamed around the planet Saturn. But tonight, she seemed proud and untouchable. And why was the daughter of such a wealthy dynasty staying in a humble hotel room like this?

'So what brings you to the French Riviera?' he questioned.

Rosa wondered what he would say if she told him. How he would react if she explained that her identity crisis was very real and not the characteristic angst of some spoiled little rich girl. And for a second she was tempted to tell him. To unburden herself to someone who didn't know the Corretti family, and who didn't particularly care about them. Wouldn't it be liberating to share her terrible story with someone else and to free herself from the resulting poison which had flooded through her veins?

But old habits died hard and Rosa was too well-taught in the art of keeping secrets to dare divulge the darkest one of all to this man who was dominating the small room. She could tell him something, yes—she just could not tell him everything.

'I wanted to get away,' she said, giving a careless shrug of her shoulders as if to add credence to her statement. 'To escape from home and see a little of the world. Lots of women my age do that. It's perfectly normal.'

But a trip to see the world did not tend to make a person look so haunted, Kulal thought. His eyes narrowed. 'So it's a temporary trip?'

'I guess.'

'And when are you planning to go back?'

His question was unexpected and it made her confront what she had been doing her best not to confront. Rosa shuddered. Back to what? To a home she no longer recognised and a family who had changed beyond recognition as the result of a few spilled and deadly words?

'I'm not,' she said forcefully. 'I'm never going back to Sicily!'

CHAPTER FIVE

KULAL WATCHED ROSA closely as she bit out her heartfelt words—more closely than he usually bothered to watch any woman, but by now she was beginning to perplex him. He had seen the play of emotions which had crossed her beautiful face when he'd asked her about her native Sicily. He had seen wariness and fear. Disgust too. Yes, he had definitely seen disgust when she had declared that she was never going back home. Someone more curious might have wondered what had caused such an extreme reaction, but he had never been a man to delve too deeply. He was more interested in the facts than in what lay behind them.

'So you will find employment here?' he mused.

'Or perhaps you are wealthy enough to live comfortably without any need to go out to work?'

If he hadn't hit on such a raw nerve, then Rosa might have told him to keep his intrusive questions to himself. Because there always had been money whenever she'd wanted it and plenty of it too. A trust fund had been put in place for her from the moment she'd been born and she'd been able to access it any time she liked. Sometimes she'd wondered what life might have been like if she'd had to save up in order to buy the latest expensive pair of shoes she'd coveted, but that was something she'd never experienced. At least, not until now. Because quickly following the text summoning her home had come another, informing her that all access to her funds had been frozen. That there was no more money to be had.

She knew exactly what her family were trying to do.

They were trying to force her to go back to Sicily by starving her out!

She'd known that they could be ruthless. She'd seen them dispose of enemies and workers—even husbands and wives—she just hadn't realised that the same ruthlessness could be directed at her.

She stared at Kulal as his question lodged in her mind, suddenly realising that even if she did try to go out to work that her options open to her were very limited. She had a respectable degree in languages, but she wasn't actually trained in anything, was she?

'Actually, I'm not wealthy,' she said. 'Not any more.'

'So what are you going to do?' he persisted.

Frustration made her turn on him again. Was he getting some kind of kick by watching her squirm? 'What I do or I don't do is none of your business.'

'But I could make it my business.'

His tone had softened and instinctively Rosa stiffened, for she suspected that this was a man who didn't really do soft. She looked at him suspiciously. 'Why would you do that?'

'Because I think we could offer each other mutual help in a time of mutual need.'

She looked at him suspiciously. 'I'm not sure I understand.'

He took a step forward, closing some of the space between them, and he saw from the sudden tension in her body that she was acutely aware of that fact. As was he... 'I think you're running from something, Rosa,' he said as he stared down into her big, dark eyes. 'Something or someone. I also think that you're hiding—that you don't want anyone to know you're here. And that you're broke. Or at least, if not broke, then rapidly running out of funds.'

Rosa swallowed because his proximity was making her feel as unsettled as his perception. And how spooky was that, when pretty much everything he'd guessed had been true? Soon after she'd found out that her funds had been frozen, she had sold a bracelet to a second-hand jeweller in nearby Nice, but had received much less for it than she'd been expecting. And wasn't it funny how money didn't seem to go anywhere, especially when you weren't used to living frugally? Especially when she'd blown most of her budget on a tiny crimson dress which had got her into all this trouble.

'Why are you so interested in me?' she whispered.

Kulal's mouth flattened into an uncompromising line. Time to destroy any emerging fantasies which might destabilise what he was about to say. 'I'm not interested in you, *habeebi*,' he said softly. 'But more in what we can offer each other.'

Beneath the slippery fabric of her gown, Rosa felt the prickling of her skin and she wasn't sure if it was excitement or fear. Was he going to suggest that they continue where they'd left off the other day, when they were so rudely interrupted in the garden of his hotel villa? And if he did say that… if he pulled her in his arms and kissed her with the same kind of hungry passion she'd tasted the other day, would she honestly be able to push him away?

The words seemed to be having difficulty leaving her mouth, but she knew she had to say them. 'What kind of offer?'

Kulal's lips curved into a smile of satisfaction as he read the unmistakable signs of sexual desire on her face, and knew he was home and dry.

'My offer of marriage,' he said.

His words echoed around the room and a feeling of unreality began to wash over Rosa as she stared into his black eyes. She tried to wonder what it would be like if he'd made his suggestion with some degree of affection, rather than with that cruel and calculating expression. But she was a Corretti, wasn't she? And therefore ideally equipped to deal with his proposal in the same businesslike way as he'd made it.

'Marry you?' she said drily. 'Don't you have someone more suitable you could ask? Perhaps somebody you've known longer than five minutes, in a relationship which is founded on more than lust and insults?'

Briefly, Kulal thought of Ayesha and wondered whether now was the time to reveal his broken engagement. In terms of getting the Corretti girl to agree to his plan, surely it would be better to keep it secret? But he remembered the bitterness on her face as she'd spoken disparagingly about 'secrets' and figured that she was bound to find out some time. Far better it came from him than from some mischievous news source.

'Actually, I had a fiancée,' he said. 'Until very recently.'

Rosa's eyes narrowed. 'How recently?'

There was a pause. 'Until yesterday.'

The brutal time scale meant that no mental calculations were necessary and she stared at him in disbelief. 'You mean you...you made love to me when you were engaged to another woman?'

He gave a short laugh. 'I don't classify kissing someone who has just hurled themselves into my arms as "making love."'

'You bastard,' she said quietly. 'You complete and utter bastard. You know damned well that if I hadn't been drunk then, you would have ended up in my bed that night.'

Kulal only just managed to repress a shudder. It was outrageous that he was going to have to marry a woman like this. A woman who showed no shame about spreading her favours so widely. Yes, he liked his lovers to be liberated—of course he did—but a wife was something completely different. That a royal prince should take such a tramp as his bride was unthinkable! Until he reminded himself that this was intended to be nothing but a temporary marriage and that her virtue was irrelevant. He remembered the way she'd kissed him. The way she'd pressed her delicious body into his so her magnificent breasts had flattened against his chest. At least she would come to the bridal chamber with a satisfying degree of sexual knowledge.

'I was behaving no differently to how men have always behaved,' he drawled.

'You mean you expected your fiancée to ignore your outrageous behaviour?'

'I expected my fiancée to know nothing about what I was doing,' he said. 'But it seems I was wrong. And it also seems she didn't understand that a man owes it to his future bride to gain as much experience as possible before he takes her innocence on their wedding night.'

Rosa almost laughed at his insolence. 'Is that supposed to be a joke?'

'What's funny about it?'

'You're making it sound as if you were doing her a favour by sleeping with as many women as possible.'

'That is one way of looking at it,' he agreed seriously. 'And it is certainly a valid point. Generations of men from all cultures have taken a comprehensive amount of lovers before tying themselves down to marriage. For no woman wants a man who is a novice in the art of lovemaking.'

'And no woman wants a man who is so arrogant that he doesn't realise what a jerk he's being!'

'A jerk?' he ground out. 'You dare to call the sheikh of Zahrastan a jerk?'

'I do when it happens to be true.'

His eyes narrowed, but he could not deny the rush of blood to his groin, because her unprecedented insolence was inexplicably turning him on. 'And tell me this, Rosa Corretti—are you always so outspoken?'

In truth, no—she wasn't. The old Rosa was often button-lipped and uptight. She never voiced the scandalous thoughts which sometimes plagued her because that was the way she'd been brought up. To be serene and calm and ladylike. To hide her feelings behind a polished exterior. But what had been the point of playing her obedient role to perfection when everyone else had been deceiving her?

This man Kulal had deceived her too. He hadn't bothered telling her he was engaged to be married when he had practically glued himself to her on the dance floor, so why on earth would she tread carefully to spare his feelings? She doubted whether he had any!

'My outspokenness is irrelevant,' she snapped. 'And you haven't explained why you've made this astonishing proposal of marriage.'

'To protect my reputation,' he said.

She gave a short laugh. So he was self-serving as well as arrogant. 'Surprise, surprise.'

'And to protect yours.'

'I don't know what you're talking about.'

There was a pause while he chose his words, though he was finding it difficult to keep the irritation from his voice. 'My brother has found out that we spent the night together, so the information is out there. From what I understand, your own family is pretty good at information gathering.' He glanced at her from beneath the half-shuttered lids of his eyes as he watched her body tense. 'How do you think they might react if they discover you've been sleeping with an Arabian prince?'

She shuddered to think how they'd react if she'd been sleeping with anyone. 'But we didn't sleep together!' she hissed. 'You know we didn't.'

'And you think anyone is likely to believe that?'

Distractedly, Rosa rubbed the palm of her hand back and forth over her lips as his words hit home. With a shudder, she tried to imagine Alessandro and Santo's reaction to the news that their baby sister had been behaving like a *puttana*. The family would still be reeling from her mother's shocking disclosure—which would probably make their reaction even harsher than normal. She was still a Corretti, wasn't she? And a female Corretti, to boot. Bottom line was that her innocence would be seen as having been compromised, and all hell would be let loose. She could imagine them sending out a gang of heavies to bring her back again. Even worse— they might come and get her themselves.

'Mannaggia,' she whispered unthinkingly. 'What a fool I have been.'

It occurred to Kulal that not once during the entire conversation had she made any attempt to flirt with him, nor to show any kind of gratitude that he was offering a solution to her predicament. Why, she barely seemed aware of the bed in one corner of the room—a fact which was now beginning to dominate his thoughts. If it had been anyone else, he would have taken her into his arms and started to kiss her, but her face was so full of a simmering rage that he thought it unwise to try. He was beginning to realise that the situation was balanced on a knife edge, and that now he wanted her to agree to a plan which had initially repulsed him.

Because Kulal was an expert at finding the good in a bad situation. It was what had sustained him during his lonely childhood. He had refused to dwell on the fact that his mother's love had been brutally torn from him, and to focus instead on the unparalleled freedom which he had enjoyed within the palace walls. He had learnt to be utterly self-sufficient and hit out at anyone who should ever dare to pity him.

Now he looked at Rosa Corretti and thought about the benefits of having her as his wife. He thought about what enjoyment her curvaceous beauty would afford him. A body which he had touched only briefly would become his to play with as he pleased! And once his passion for her had worn off, he could send her on her way.

'A short marriage which can be dissolved once the dust has settled,' he elaborated. 'A marriage which could be beneficial to us both.'

She had lifted her head and was staring at him as if she was seeing him for the first time and didn't very much like what she saw.

'Beneficial?' she snorted. 'I think not. I think that marriage to you would be something of a nightmare.'

'Are you so sure?' he mocked.

'Absolutely positive!' she asserted, until she forced herself to confront an alternative which was even worse. She couldn't go home and yet she couldn't stay here with rapidly dwindling resources. Even if she ran to somewhere else and found herself a humble job, her family would surely come after her and find her. She forced herself to smile. 'But I can see that it would have some advantages.'

'You mean you're now agreeing to my proposition?'

'Only on certain conditions.'

'I'm afraid that won't be possible,' he stated softly. 'You don't get to bargain with a sheikh.'

'Oh, but I do!' she said firmly. 'Because you need this marriage more than I do!'

'You think so?'

'I know so.' She shot him a look of pure challenge. 'You're afraid of what my brothers might do when they find out about our liaison, aren't you?'

'Are you out of your mind?' His lips curled with derision. 'Kulal Al-Dimashqi is afraid of no one, Rosa. Not now and not ever. But I love my country and the fallout from our ill-advised night together could bring shame on our royal house.' There was a pause. 'You have no need to worry about tying yourself to me for a lifetime if that is what gives you cause for hesitation, for I will happily give you a divorce once a suitable time has elapsed.'

Rosa mulled over his words, aware that he was offering her a way out. It might not have been the way she would have chosen, but she wasn't exactly being dazzled by choice, was she? 'How long?' she questioned. 'Will we have to be married?'

He glimmered her a cool smile. 'How does a year sound?'

'Like eleven months too long?'

'I can assure you that it will fly by,' he said smoothly. 'Because time always does. Before you know it, the year will be up and I will send you on your way with a fortune big enough to guarantee your independence and a lifetime's memories of sexual bliss.'

Rosa met the gleam of his ebony eyes. His sexual boast was shocking and his arrogance was second to none, and yet... It seemed such a stupid thing to feel, but in the midst of all her confused emotions, she was aware only of a feeling of safety when she looked at him. Because whatever faults he possessed, she felt sure he would protect her. Nobody would dare come near her if Sheikh Kulal Al-Dimashqi was fighting in her corner.

Even if she could wave a magic wand—which is what she'd originally wanted—she knew now that her old life was over. She couldn't go back. She'd fled to France and booked into a cheap hotel and sold an old family bracelet and nearly got herself laid. For the first time in her life, she'd felt as if she was really living—the way her brothers were allowed to live—instead of existing in the pampered little bubble they'd created for her.

She'd tasted freedom and found it a heady brew

and she could never return to the life she'd known before. All those eyes watching her. All those unspoken codes she'd grown up with, and the expectation which came with them. That Rosa was a good girl and that one day she'd marry some suitable Sicilian who had been picked for her.

If she was going to have to endure the ignominy of an arranged marriage, then why shouldn't she arrange it herself? Especially as this particular marriage had a get-out clause. She wanted independence and Kulal had offered it to her. He had offered her a generous pay-out too. For the first time in her life she would be independent! Imagine being able to do as she wanted, without having to run to someone else for permission. Her traditional family could not object once she'd got that all-important band of gold on her finger.

'It's a very tempting offer,' she said.

'I find it's always wise to make your offers tempting. It usually gets people to agree to them.' A smile slid across his lips as he slanted her a quizzical look. 'And your "conditions" are?'

Rosa hesitated. She had been about to tell him that it would have to be a celibate marriage. That she would not have sex with a man who thought so little of women—a man who had been prepared to cheat on his ex-fiancée without a flicker of conscience. But she could see now that such a demand would be impossible to enforce. Could she really imagine saying no to the sexual advances of a man like Kulal Al-Dimashqi? Could she really picture herself trying to resist him? She felt the sudden lurch of her heart.

Not in a million years.

She looked at the black eyes which glittered in his hawk-like face and in that moment she suspected he knew exactly what she was thinking. She could feel her skin tightening as their gazes clashed in recognition—as if her body was silently acknowledging the sizzling connection which blazed between them. She might not like what he stood for and she might disapprove of his views on women, but she wasn't stupid enough to deny that she wanted him.

The fact that he could treat his ex-fiancée so badly told her he wasn't a man to be trusted, but what man was? Even her own uncle had cold-bloodedly bedded her mother! She wasn't looking for trust, or softness—or any of the things which most women wanted when they took a husband. And with her family background, she certainly wasn't looking for love. Her mouth flattened. Definitely not love.

She wanted someone to show her how to become a woman in the fullest sense of the word—and Kulal would be the ideal candidate. She would take from him everything he was prepared to give and then she would walk away.

'I've decided to waive my conditions,' she said, her airy tone matching the careless shrug of her shoulders.

Kulal saw the way her colour had heightened and again he smiled. 'I rather thought you might,' he murmured, his gaze drifting down to where her luscious breasts were jutting against the satin of her robe. He could see the nipples hardening as he watched them and he felt the responding jerk of desire. 'And that pleases me.'

'But I don't want my brothers finding out,' she continued. 'Because they'll try and put a stop to this wedding, if they do.'

For a moment he contemplated the idea of challenging her brothers—or laughing aloud at the very idea that their supremacy could challenge his. But why fight a battle which was ultimately pointless? They would get their precious Rosa back when the year was up. 'There are things we need to decide, but we can easily put them on hold.' His voice was husky as his gaze drifted once more to her nipples. 'And start occupying ourselves a little more pleasurably.'

She looked at him. 'Meaning?'

'You know very well what I mean, Rosa. Your body certainly gives every indication of doing so. And there's a bed right over there, just waiting.'

Rosa flinched as she crossed her arms over the betraying tightening of her breasts. 'Don't treat me like a whore, Kulal,' she said quietly. 'Or I'll walk away from this proposed union right now.'

He saw the way she had lifted her chin. Saw the glint of steel which had entered her dark eyes—and in that moment she looked very proud and very Sicilian. A formidable woman, he recognised as he inclined his head in a gesture of grudging acknowledgement. 'Very well,' he said softly. 'If such games amuse you, then we will obey convention and wait a little longer—and the anticipation will add spice to my growing hunger. I shall send a car for you in the morning. And in the meantime, you might want to give some thought to some appropriate attire.'

Her fingers touched the slippery silk lapel of her robe. 'What do you mean—appropriate?'

He wanted to say that stark naked would be his

first choice and the skimpy crimson dress which had done such dangerous things to his blood pressure would be a close second. But not in public. In public she was going to have to play the part expected of her. They both were.

'Something which a future princess might wear on the way to meet her prince.'

She thought about the few clothes she had flung into her suitcase just before her impetuous flight from Sicily. 'I'll try.'

'And make sure you bring all your belongings with you.'

She looked at him warily. 'Why, where am I going?'

'To Paris.' He gave the ghost of a smile. 'To begin your new life.'

CHAPTER SIX

A NEW LIFE.

Kulal's words played repeatedly in Rosa's mind the following morning as she crammed down the lid of her suitcase. Was it possible to just shrug off your old life and emerge without any traces of it clinging to your skin? She snapped the suitcase closed. All she knew was that she was going to try—she was going to lose her troubled past and step out into a new and unknown future as the sheikh's bride.

Remembering Kulal's directive about appropriate attire, she chose a silk chiffon dress the colour of raspberry sorbet and black shoes which made her feel very tall—but she wore no jewellery, not even the ring her father had given her for her sixteenth birthday. Platinum bright and studded with emeralds, her hand felt strangely bare without it for she was never without it glittering on her little finger. But now it seemed to mock her and the relationship she'd enjoyed with her father. It made her question whether that, too, had been false, like everything else around her.

Had he known? she wondered. Had he realised before his own violent death that the daughter he'd so adored had been the child of the brother he detested? Had he been broken-hearted and careless as a result—dropping a match in that cavernous old warehouse which he and his brother had owned so that they had burned to death, their tortured cries carrying out on the hot, Sicilian breeze?

She was grateful for the loud knock which broke into her troubled thoughts and she opened the door to find Kulal's driver standing there. Wordlessly, he took her suitcase from her, leaving Rosa to follow him. But her questions about Kulal's whereabouts were met with a polite shrug. As if he didn't understand what she was saying—even when she spoke to him in French—and Rosa got the feeling that he understood her very well.

Her feeling of isolation grew as the car headed out towards the airport and she peered out of the window at the upmarket holidaymakers. Against the azure backdrop of the sea, there were women in tiny shorts, big sun hats and even bigger pairs of sunglasses as they hung around the harbour areas, as if waiting for an owner of one of the luxury yachts to pluck them up and sail them away to paradise. She thought how carefree they all looked as they fished around in their giant leather bags. As if they had nothing more taxing on their minds than when their next coat of lipstick needed to be applied. She wondered if they even noticed her—the woman in the expensive limousine being taken to marry a man who was little more than a stranger.

The powerful car slid to a halt at the Nice airport and she was escorted straight out onto one of the airstrips, where a large plane stood waiting on the tarmac. Its gleaming jade-and-rose bodywork reminded her of some oversize exotic bird and a steward wearing matching livery ushered her on board. The light in the cabin was dim and it took a moment or two for her eyes to adjust to the sight of Kulal reclining on one of the seats, reading through what looked like a pile of official paperwork. He looked utterly relaxed, with his long legs stretched out in front of him and one arm pillowing his ebony head.

Reluctantly, she ran her eyes over him in unwilling appraisal, unable to deny the sheer physical perfection of the man.

Did he hear her quiet intake of breath? Was that the reason for his enigmatic smile as his gaze flicked upwards?

'Don't look so frightened, Rosa,' he said softly, his eyes making their own leisurely journey down over the entire length of her body.

'I'm not frightened,' she answered, trying to convince herself it was true, even though that lazy scrutiny was making her skin tingle in a very distracting way. She told herself that she'd met enough powerful men in her twenty-three years to make her impervious to them. But she'd never met anyone who had looked at her quite like that before. He had removed his jacket and was wearing dark trousers and a white shirt with the sleeves rolled up. She could see the crisp sprinkling of hairs on his powerful forearms and, despite his relaxed pose, she was very aware of all the latent strength in his muscular body.

'Come over here and sit down,' he said, patting the elongated seat beside him.

She approached with the caution of someone walking towards an unexploded bomb, knowing it would sound naive if she complained that the angle of the seat made it look more like a bed. Yet a couple of days ago she'd wanted more than anything to find herself in bed with him. She wondered what had happened to that new and confident Rosa Corretti, who had looked at this man and decided that she wanted him.

Was it because this morning he was exuding a sex appeal which seemed intimidating and for the first time she realised that he was planning to deliver? That things had moved beyond the hypothetical and sex had become a reality. She was aware that his initial relaxed pose had gone and been replaced by a sudden tension—as if he, too, had suddenly acknowledged the close confinement of the aircraft cabin as the outer doors slammed shut.

She slid into the seat beside him, aware that he was still watching her, his dark eyes seeming to drink in every move she made. She told herself that she mustn't be intimidated. That she needed to be more like the woman who had pole danced her way into his line of vision, rather than the one whose heart was now beating out a thready tattoo. 'I hope that what I'm wearing is "appropriate,"' she said.

'Utterly.' He watched as she smoothed the delicate material of her dress over her bare knees. 'You will need an entirely new wardrobe to cope with the demands of life as a princess, of course—though I don't imagine you'll have much of a problem with that. I've yet to meet a woman who doesn't salivate at the thought of buying new clothes, especially when someone else is picking up the bill.'

Levelly, she met his gaze. 'Are you going to spend all your time denigrating women?'

'Not all my time, no.' His smile was edged with pure danger. 'I'm sure we'll be able to come up with something more exciting to fill our time.'

'Because…' She didn't want to let this go. She didn't want him to keep making comparisons—because wouldn't that just tap into her crippling certainty that she was going to disappoint him? That he had signed up for something and was going to get something completely different. 'I'm sure your knowledge of women is comprehensive—it's just a little off-putting if you're going to keep reminding me of the fact.'

'I'm sure your knowledge of men is equally comprehensive, Rosa.'

'You'd be surprised.'

'I doubt it. I've yet to meet a woman who surprises me.'

Rosa gave a little shake of her head. What a cynic he was. Shouldn't she have tried to hook up with someone softer—and kinder? Someone who wouldn't have whirled into her life like a very sexy tornado. The plane engines began to flare into life and suddenly she started to laugh—the unexpected sound taking her by surprise because it seemed a long time since she'd laughed at anything.

He raised his eyebrows. 'What's so funny?'

'Everything.' She looked at him. 'Within the space of a few short hours I've become the kind of person who steps onto a private jet with a man I don't really know—a man I'm going to marry. I'm going to be a princess and I'm going to live in Paris and I don't have a clue what my life will be like. It just doesn't...' Her voice trailed off as she met his eyes and shrugged. 'It just doesn't feel real, that's all.'

Once again, Kulal saw that fleeting look of vulnerability—the one which didn't match the sensual lips and hedonist's body. The one which was making his gut twist with an inexplicable unease. 'If it's any consolation, it feels pretty bizarre to me too,' he said flatly as the irony of the situation hit him—not for the first time.

He should have been contemplating matrimony

with a high-born royal from a neighbouring country but instead he found himself with Rosa Corretti,
the daughter of a nefarious Sicilian family with a
terrifying reputation. One who flaunted her body
like a hooker, but who had since denied him all but
the briefest kiss.

His mouth twisted into a hard smile. He could feel
the exquisite hardening of an erection beneath the
fine cloth of his Italian trousers and he shifted his
body a little. Why should he have to wait a second
longer to enjoy all the sensual possibilities which
her beautiful body offered?

From the galley, the steward appeared with a tray
and Kulal said something terse in his own language,
so that the man set the drinks down on the table and
then quickly disappeared.

Rosa saw the way that Kulal's knuckles had suddenly clenched against the hard outline of his thighs.
'Is something wrong?' she asked.

'Something is very wrong.' Turning to her, he
lifted his hand to touch her face, his finger slowly
tracing the outline of her lips. 'You are driving me
crazy, Rosa. I am aching to possess you and I cannot wait much longer.'

Rosa swallowed as he moved his hand downwards

so that it was now lying directly over her breast and she wondered if he could feel the wild beat of her heart. His words were so…brazen. He made sex sound so straightforward—as if doing it and wanting it was perfectly natural—but she had no idea how to answer him, because she had been brought up to think that it was wrong and forbidden.

'You are silent,' he observed, his fingers now drifting down over her belly before coming at last to rest on her knee. 'That is good. So often a woman destroys the mood of love with her inane chatter.'

Part of her wanted to scream at him for his arrogance, but no scream came—and how could it, when his hand had now drifted beneath the hem of her dress and she was holding her breath to see what he would do next?

His fingers began to slide upwards and Rosa's eyes closed as desire began to flicker over her skin—a desire which was powerful enough to obliterate any lingering feelings of guilt. He was drawing little circles just above her knee and, while it was exciting her, it was also frustrating the hell out of her. She began to wish that he would touch her somewhere else—touch her where she was beginning to ache like crazy. And maybe her restless little wriggle told him that, because his fingers had now crept up to reach the bare skin of her thigh. The warmth coiling somewhere deep inside her began to spread over her whole body and she could hear the loud thunder of her heart. Her thighs seemed to be parting without any conscious action on her part, and she expelled a breath of disbelieving pleasure as his fingers brushed intimately against the searing heat of her sex.

'Mmm,' was all he said.

'Kulal,' she breathed.

Waves of shock and excitement washed over her as he pushed aside the moist panel of her panties and began to move his finger against her aroused flesh and Rosa thought that nothing had ever felt this good. Nothing. She could hear strange, gasping little sounds echoing around the cabin, which she realised must be hers. She could feel the tension as her body strained towards something tantalising which seemed just out of reach. Something which surely promised more than it could ever deliver. And then it happened—almost without warning—like a shower of fireworks exploding unexpectedly in the sky. She found her body contracting with the most exquisite sensations, the force of them taking her by surprise. It felt like flying—and then afterwards it felt like floating down into some dreamy place, all boneless with the pleasure which was still washing over her. She gasped aloud as her head fell back. Her tongue snaked out to touch her mouth and even that made her sensitive lips tremble and for count-less minutes she just lay there, drifting in and out of the most incredible daydreams.

'Unzip me,' he whispered.

His words broke into her dreamy thoughts and Rosa's lashes flew open to meet the opaque smoul-der in his eyes. But there was no softness in them—nothing but hard-edged desire. Her gaze flickered to his groin and her nerve failed her.

'I can't,' she whispered.

'Why not?' He frowned. 'What's wrong?'

Rosa bit her lip and felt the sharp indentation of her teeth. A million things were wrong and, stu-pidly, the one which seemed to bother her most was the fact that he hadn't even kissed her. She realised that she had just had her first orgasm but Kulal had made it happen with all the cold-bloodedness of a scientist performing an experiment in a laboratory. She might want to learn all about sex but she hadn't intended her first real lesson to take place on an aircraft, and she certainly didn't want to be treated like some sort of faceless puppet.

She felt like someone who'd never skated before being put on an ice rink and told to dance. The other night when she'd been drinking, she'd been filled with an unfamiliar bravado as she had flung herself at him. Even the next morning, she'd still been disorientated enough to make an uninhibited pass at him. But now that the moment of truth had arrived, she was scared.

So why not tell him? Why not be upfront with him? Surely even someone as hard-hearted as Kulal might be gentle if he realised the true depth of her inexperience.

She drew in a deep breath and let the words out slowly. 'I'm a virgin.'

'Sure. And I'm Peter Pan,' he murmured, guiding her hand towards his groin.

'No,' she said weakly as she snatched her fingers away. 'I'm serious.'

He drew back from her and she couldn't quite make out the expression on his face. Surely that wasn't boredom she could read there?

'So am I, *habeebi*, so am I. So why don't we leave the role play until our appetites have grown a little more jaded? I know the fantasies which turn women on and we can do the "innocent virgin being ravished by the big, bad sheikh" to your heart's content, but for this first time, shall we just stick to what nature intended and adjourn to the bedroom?'

Rosa stared at him as his harsh words registered themselves in her befuddled brain. He didn't believe her! He didn't believe she'd never had sex with a man!

A wave of shame washed over her. Why should he believe her, after the way she'd behaved? He had signed up for a woman who shimmied around in a revealing dress, not an overprotected Sicilian girl who'd never felt the intimate caress of a man's hands on her body until now. And mightn't he be disappointed if he knew how naive she was?

Her mind began to race. This was supposed to be a marriage of convenience, for her convenience as much as his, but it wouldn't be very convenient for him if his new wife was a hopeless novice, would it? Maybe it would be better if he discovered the truth on their wedding night—when it was too late to turn around and tell her he'd changed his mind about marriage?

She tugged her dress back down.

'What do you think you're doing?' he demanded.

She met his incredulous look, trying to imagine what a more experienced woman might say in such a situation. 'You're planning to have sex with me?'

'What do you think—that I want to discuss the state of the world's economy?' He glared at her. 'Of course I'm planning on having sex with you. Isn't that what you've been practically begging me to do since we first met?'

Rosa pursed her lips together, although she conceded that he did have a point. 'You want this to be our first time together?' she questioned. 'When any number of your crew could walk in and discover us?'

'I don't think so,' he snapped. 'My crew have strict instructions not to disturb me whenever I have a woman on board. No one will dare to come in.'

Rosa felt sick. Was he setting out to humiliate her, as she had seen men humiliate women so often before? 'You make a habit of having sex on this plane, do you?'

'No, Rosa, you're the first,' he drawled sarcastically. 'What do you think?'

'I think that as your fiancée, I should be shown a little respect.'

'Having sex with you doesn't show a lack of re-spect.'

She shook her head, because how could you shake off a lifetime's indoctrination in a couple of min-utes? 'And what if I told you that it would make me feel cheap?'

He leaned back and surveyed her, one finger slowly tapping his lip. 'But acting cheap didn't par-ticularly bother you when I made you come just a few minutes ago, did it?' He saw her blush with what looked like intense embarrassment but he did not heed it, his own intense frustration making him want to drive his argument home. 'Nor did you seem to feel cheap the other night, when you shamelessly flaunted your body at the club for all to see.'

She swallowed. 'I was drunk.'

'And do you make a habit of getting drunk? Is this something I should know?'

She met the accusation in his eyes and shook her head. 'No, I don't make a habit of it,' she said quietly. 'In fact, I've never been drunk before that night.'

His gaze grew thoughtful. 'So something led you to drink from the champagne bottle, like a work-man slaking his thirst in the heat of the midday sun?

Something which disturbed you enough to behave in a way which you say was uncharacteristic?'

His perception was appealing and Rosa wondered how much to tell him. She'd never been close enough to a man to even think about admitting what was on her mind before, though come to think of it, she hadn't known real intimacy with anyone. Her relationship with her mother had always been strained— and her two brothers would have run a mile if she'd started talking to them about feelings. They were Corretti men and they did that Corretti thing of buttoning up all their emotions—that was, if they even had any emotions.

Rosa had never known what it was like to speak from the heart, and as she looked into Kulal's cool black eyes she wondered if she could trust him enough to dare.

Yet what did she have to lose?

'I had just discovered something about my family,' she said.

Kulal forced himself to look interested in what she was about to say, even if the last thing he was interested in was talking about her family. But he had learnt much about women during an extensive career spent seducing them, and had discovered that a little patience shown at the beginning paid dividends in the long run. He injected just the right amount of curiosity into his voice. 'And what might that have been?'

Rosa hesitated, knowing that she risked making her mother sound like some sort of slut if she told him the truth—and that women were inevitably compared to their mothers. But she had to remember that she wasn't trying to impress him. It didn't matter what he thought of her, not when her place in his life was so temporary.

Even so, she felt the painful twist of her heart as she said the words out loud and the bitter memories came flooding back. 'I discovered that my father was not really my father.'

Kulal shrugged. 'I imagine that must have been disturbing.'

'Yes, Kulal, it was disturbing,' she said drily.

'But you must realise that such a situation as yours is not terribly unusual. Don't they say that one in twenty-five children in the west are brought up by a man who is not their biological father?'

She blinked, because the last thing she had expected from him was a careless kind of acceptance.

'How strange that you should know something like that.'

'Not strange at all.' He shrugged. 'I happen to be something of an expert on these matters, since I've been the subject of several paternity claims.'

Her eyes opened wide and she felt the sudden anxious beat of her heart. 'You mean, you've got... children?'

He gave a short laugh, because she might as well have asked him if he had ever taken a trip to the moon. 'No, Rosa, I do not have any children— though one of the downsides to being a sheikh is that women have tried in the past to get themselves impregnated, in order to secure themselves a place in my life.'

Rosa stared at him in horrified fascination. He came out with the most outrageously chauvinistic statements—worse than her own brothers' at times—and yet somehow he managed to get away with it. Was that because his sophisticated exterior didn't necessarily reflect the true man underneath?

Because on the surface he might look like a modern playboy, with his sleek designer suit and his private jet, but beneath all the trappings he was nothing short of primitive. He was powerful and wealthy, yet he certainly wasn't predictable. His matter-of-fact response to her admission about her paternity had surprised her, and had removed some of the emotional sting from its tail—something she hadn't thought possible. And wasn't part of her grateful to him for that? Just as she was grateful for the almost effortless way he had just given her an orgasm.

Her cheeks grew pink as she remembered the way she'd let him touch her and the way that had made her feel. She couldn't carry on feeling daunted by his sexuality, could she? Despite what she suspected was a very selfish nature, he had just proved to be the most generous of lovers. And surely she should be generous back. How difficult could it be to give a man pleasure? Why not get it over with, so that it was out of the way and that she wouldn't have to dread it any more?

She lifted her hand to his face, letting her fingers slide over his sensual mouth, and even that brief touch felt electric. As she let her hand drift to the unopened neck of his silk shirt, she could see the suspicion which narrowed his eyes and her words of explanation came out in a breathy rush. 'Maybe I've changed my mind,' she whispered. 'Maybe we could make love after all—if you say that your staff would be sure to leave us alone.'

There was a split-second pause. A moment when she saw anger and frustration darken his face, before he swiftly removed her hand from his neck.

'You think you can play with me, as a cat would a mouse?' he demanded. 'That I am a man who can be picked up and put down? Are you nothing more than a tease, Rosa?'

'No!' she protested. 'I never meant to tease you. I was nervous, that's all—but I think I'm over that now.'

'Well, that's too bad,' he responded acidly, shifting his aching body away from her. Maybe it was time he showed her who she was dealing with— that he was not the kind of man to tolerate a spoiled little girl's sexual games. His smile was cold. 'It's not going to happen. At least, not right now. The flight to Paris only takes fifty minutes and I'm afraid we've wasted most of them talking.'

Rosa felt her heart clench. Wasted them? When she'd opened up to him like she'd never done to anyone else? When she'd let him touch her body as nobody had ever touched it before. When she'd decided that maybe she could trust him enough to tell him the truth about her parentage, only now it seemed that he was throwing it all back in her face. When would she ever learn that the only person she could really trust was herself?

'How silly of me,' she said lightly.

'Very silly,' he agreed, though the tremble of her lips made him briefly wonder whether it was worth telling the pilot to circle the plane so that he could indeed seduce her. Wouldn't ridding himself of this terrible ache make such an indulgent breach worthwhile?

And yet, hadn't he been partially responsible for this very unsatisfactory turn of events? He had been leaning forward, about to kiss her, when he had been arrested by the look on her face as he had touched her so intimately. He had never seen a reaction so instant nor so rapturous and hadn't he just watched her with a kind of dazed voyeurism, instead of undressing her and starting to make love to her?

He shifted his body as he decided against a delayed landing. Maybe it was better this way. The fantasies he had been building about his feisty little Sicilian should be enjoyed in slow time—not in some rushed explosion of need in the rather limited confines of an aircraft.

He snapped shut his seat belt and subjected her to a cool stare. 'In life, I find that timing is everything. Maybe that's something you should bear in mind for the future, Rosa.'

CHAPTER SEVEN

KULAL'S BREATH CAUGHT in his throat as Rosa entered the Damask reception room of the Zahrastanian Embassy, looking like a vision in her bridal finery. He stared at her, finding it hard to reconcile the pole-dancing temptress with the woman walking slowly towards him. By necessity, the white gown she wore was modest, covering her entire body so that only her hands and her neck were left bare. Her dark hair was coiled on top of her head and the lace-trimmed veil was held in place by a priceless diamond-and-ruby tiara from the Al-Dimashqi collection.

Inexplicably, he felt the sudden twist of his heart, for she looked… His gaze drifted over her and he gave a small shake of his head. She looked beautiful.

More beautiful than any woman he'd ever seen and he wondered if his senses were inevitably heightened by the significance of the ceremony which was about to take place.

They had been apart ever since his car had dropped her off at the Plaza Athénée Hotel yesterday, after a tense and silent journey from the airport. He had spent the night alone at his own apartment, simmering with a sexual frustration which was completely new to him. Naked, he had tossed and turned in his vast bed while the events of that bizarre flight to Paris had taunted him. Rosa had refused to have sex with him, and had then inexplicably changed her mind, just before coming in to land. He had never met such a capricious woman before!

The wedding had been scheduled—without fanfare—to take place within hours of their arriving in the French capital because he didn't want the world's press to get wind of it. Inevitably, word would get out sooner or later and then the palace's slick PR machine could whirr into action. But someone must have talked—the way they always did—which had meant that he'd been forced to clear a path through the waiting photographers who'd been standing outside the embassy when he had arrived earlier.

But now his bride was here and any lingering mis-
givings he might have been harbouring were dissolved by that tentative look she was slanting at him
from behind the misty cover of her veil. How well
she played the part, he thought approvingly. That
faux shyness was remarkably convincing and he
knew that the embassy officials would approve of
her demure appearance.

'Rosa,' he said as he stepped forward and raised
her hand to his lips.

Rosa could feel his warm breath on her fingertips and the tantalising promise of his touch only
added to her general feeling of disorientation. Even
discounting the fact that she was standing in an exquisite bridal gown in the middle of the Zahrastanian Embassy, the man she had agreed to marry now
looked like a stranger. Today, his playboy reputation and urbane appearance were nothing but distant memories. The immaculately cut suit had been
replaced by a flowing garment of white silk and his
hair was covered with a headdress of the same colour, held in place by an intricately knotted band of
golden thread. He looked dark and indomitable, and
the starkness of his robes seemed to emphasise the
chiselled contours of his face.

Rosa swallowed down a feeling of nerves. 'The place is swarming with press,' she said.

Kulal shrugged. 'Weddings are news, I'm afraid.'

'Particularly a wedding involving a sheikh who was recently engaged to someone else and particularly if he's marrying a woman from a notorious family,' she answered drily. Rosa stared down at the sparkle of her brand-new ruby-and-diamond ring, which had been hastily despatched to her hotel by motorcycle courier late last night. She supposed there might have been less romantic ways for a man to give a woman an engagement ring, but right now she couldn't think of one. She looked up into his face and once again she couldn't help herself from being stirred by his proud, dark beauty. 'I can't imagine how my family are going to react when they find out what I've done.'

'They're going to have to accept it because they'll have no choice. And you'll no longer have to fear their influence, Rosa, since from now on you will come under my protection.'

Protection. It was a word which meant different things to different people, but it had particular resonance for someone from Sicily and Rosa gave him an ironic smile. 'One cage exchanged for another, you mean?' she questioned lightly, glancing up at the high, moulded ceilings of the exquisite embassy room. 'Even if this cage is considerably more gilded than the one I knew at home.'

'You seem to forget that this marriage is nothing but a temporary arrangement,' he said softly. 'One which has been manufactured to satisfy our critics. It's not as if it's going to be a lifetime commitment.'

Kulal's words nagged at her conscience throughout the short service which followed and Rosa thought about the woman he'd previously been engaged to. Had she heard about this wedding and was she lying and sobbing her heart out on some faraway pillow, thinking about the man who got away?

And then, rather more selfishly, Rosa thought about herself, knowing that she was here on false pretences, in more ways than one. She held out her hand so that Kulal could slip on the glittering diamond wedding band, knowing that he'd be expecting great things from her in the bedroom and she wondered how he was going to react when he discovered the truth. What was he going to say when he discovered that the only thing she knew about sex was that amazing orgasm she'd had on the plane?

'You may now kiss the bride,' said the celebrant.

Rosa stared up into the gleam of Kulal's eyes and held her breath as she waited, but the swift, almost perfunctory graze of his mouth over hers left her feeling oddly rejected.

Her disappointment was so great that she summoned up the courage to rise up on tiptoe to put her lips close to his ear. 'That wasn't much of a kiss.'

'I agree that it was briefer than any kiss I have ever given any woman, but I fear that once I start kissing you, I may not be able to stop.' He linked his fingers in hers and gave them a squeeze, putting his lips to her ear so that nobody else could hear. 'And perhaps it would be inappropriate for me to ruck up that pretty dress and take you unceremoniously against the wall, which is what I feel like doing.'

'Kulal!' The word trembled from her lips. 'That's the kind of thing a savage would say!'

'But perhaps my "savage" words turn you on, my beauty.' His black eyes gleamed with challenge as he observed the sudden flush of colour in her cheeks. 'Am I right?'

And although she shook her head to halt his erotic line of questioning, the truth was that he was turning her on. Turning her on in a way she wouldn't have thought possible, especially when all he was doing was holding her hand. Rosa could feel her breasts pushing against the bodice of her gown, as if they were anxious to be freed from their lacy confinement. Her mouth was drying and her skin was tightening with anticipation, so that she felt almost dizzy. But even though she felt a little daunted by this rush of unfamiliar sensations, she met his eyes with a sudden fearlessness, recognising that this was her opportunity, her time to grow. She had married Kulal to be free and independent, not to cower in the corner just because he was making her body respond to him in a way which was perfectly natural.

'Yes,' she said softly. 'Your words turn me on. They turn me on very much, if you must know.'

She saw the sudden tension which passed over his face before he nodded. 'Then let's get this next bit over with,' he said, sliding his arm around her waist. 'Let's go outside and give the press exactly what they want.'

But despite his warning, Rosa was unprepared for the wall of blinding light as the embassy doors were opened onto the street, where the small number of photographers had grown into a jostling crowd.

'Rosa!' someone yelled as the flashlights flared.

'What do your family think about you marrying a sheikh?'

'Rosa, how do you think Kulal's ex-fiancée is feeling today?'

Rosa could feel herself stiffen, but Kulal pressed his fingers into the flesh at her waist.

'Smile,' he instructed softly. 'Look like you're having fun.'

But she felt almost paralysed by the flashbulbs and the damning nature of the questions and maybe Kulal realised that, for suddenly he turned her towards him, his lips parting so that she could see the gleam of his teeth.

'Seems like I'm going to have to kiss you properly after all,' he said.

'And is that such a hardship?' she whispered.

'Everything about me is hard at the moment,' he commented drily as he lowered his mouth onto hers.

For a moment, the only thing Rosa was aware of was the press going crazy, but then the outside world blurred and faded and she was aware of nothing, other than the sensation of his lips exploring hers. Desire raced through her, as if he'd turned on some powerful current. As if she was on fire. She pressed the palms of her hands against his chest, revelling in the feel of his powerful torso, until she realised that he was pulling away from her and that the kiss had come to an abrupt end.

His eyes were impossible to read as he stared down into her upturned face, as if he was seeing something there which he had not expected to see. 'That's the first time I've ever kissed a woman in public and I don't think it's an experiment which needs repeating. I think I'd better get you back to my apartment as quickly as possible,' he said, his mouth barely moving for fear that some clever lip-reader in the press corps could pick up on what he was saying. 'Before we're hauled up on a charge of public indecency.'

Rosa could feel herself blushing as his bodyguards began to clear a way through the press, but she was surprised when Kulal waved a dismissive hand at the driver, who was opening the door of his official car. 'No. We'll walk,' he said. 'It isn't far.'

'But, Highness—'

'I said we'll walk.' And with that, he took her hand in his and began to lead her along the street, his mood unexpectedly buoyant as they began to walk along the wide boulevard. He stared down at their interlocked fingers, suddenly aware of the fact that he'd never held hands with a woman in public before. Her skin was the delicious honeyed shade which denoted her Sicilian upbringing, but his own was very much darker and there seemed to be a certain erotic association about the contrast between the differing hues. 'And smile,' he added softly.

It was the most bizarre experience of Rosa's life, walking in her lace wedding dress through the exclusive streets of the sixteenth *arrondissement*, her new husband beside her in his flowing white robes. Bodyguards speaking furiously into earpieces shadowed them all the way and people stopped what they were doing to turn and stare. She saw cars slowing down and drivers leaning out of their windows to capture their image on cellphones, and there were yet more press waiting outside his upmarket apartment block. She wondered if there would have been quite so much fuss if Kulal hadn't been wearing his traditional robes—and that only added to her sense of unreality. As if he was some kind of fantasy figure, rather than an ordinary man. But he isn't an ordinary man, she reminded herself, and this whole marriage was the stuff of fantasy.

He gripped her hand tightly as yet more flashbulbs exploded in her face, but this time she felt much less intimidated. She waved away the question of what her family would think or how her brothers would respond. Sustained exposure to something meant that you could get used to it and Rosa found she was even able to smile at one of the more persistent lens men. She felt breathless with nerves and a growing excitement as they walked into the foyer and took the elevator up to the penthouse suite, with Kulal watching her in speculative silence all the while, as if he didn't quite trust himself to speak. She kept telling herself that she wasn't going to be scared by what was about to happen. She had wanted adventure, hadn't she? Well, she had certainly found it!

Still silent, he opened the door to his apartment and Rosa stepped into a huge entrance hall. She had been prepared for luxury and she wasn't disappointed. Impressionist paintings adorned the walls and she'd never seen so much antique furniture outside of a museum. On dark, wooden floors lay faded silk rugs which looked centuries old and she wondered how many different pairs of feet had walked over them. She thought that a place like this could never really feel like home—or more specifically her home, until she remembered that it was never intended to be.

She found herself trained in the spotlight of his dark eyes as he watched her, like a hunter silently following the progress of its quarry.

'Drink?' he questioned.

'Just…some water would be fine.'

He led her into an incongruously modern kitchen of steel and granite and poured her a glass of ice water which she drank standing up, still in her wedding dress. She noticed that he didn't drink anything himself, and when she'd put her empty glass down, it was to find him still watching her.

'I want you in my bed,' he said simply.

She held her breath for a long moment before she expelled it. 'Then take me there.'

She could sense the growing tension in his body as he led her through a maze of corridors straight into the biggest bedroom she had ever seen, where vases of crimson roses stood on every available surface, their powerful perfume scenting the air. Tall windows overlooked a perfect vista of Paris, where the Seine was glittering in the afternoon sunlight, and beyond that she could see the arching fretwork of the Eiffel Tower.

'As you see,' he said. 'I have made every preparation for our honeymoon. I have even arranged for the sun to shine.'

Rosa glanced around the room, thinking that it looked gorgeous, but slightly unreal—as if a magazine shoot was about to take place. A vast four-poster bed played host to banks of pillows and shiny cushions and a bottle of champagne stood in an ice bucket on a small table nearby. And now there was nothing to stop them. No curious air crew or officials or intrusive cameras hovering nearby. Now she could give herself up to what she had been aching to experience for so long. She was going to start living the way other people lived, and for the first time in her life she was going to have sex.

She saw that he was staring at her and the pounding in her heart increased.

'Do you know, I have never seen a woman look more beautiful,' he said, swallowing down an inexplicable lump in his throat and finding himself surprised by his reaction. Was that because she had resisted him? Because she had not let him have her on the plane? He had never waited so long to have sex with a woman and the postponement of pleasure was making him ache. With a commanding finger, he beckoned to her. 'Come here.'

The look in his eyes was so irresistible and the yearning inside her so strong that Rosa went straight into his arms.

'I think it's time that I undressed you,' he said unsteadily. 'Don't you?'

'Yes,' she answered, with shy assent.

First he removed the ruby-and-diamond tiara and put it down on a nearby table and then he unclipped her veil with dextrous fingers and let it slither to the ground.

She closed her eyes as he lowered his head to kiss her and she honestly thought she might pass out with the sheer pleasure of that kiss. She was aware of the powerful scent of the roses and the way his hands were moving over her body, caressing her curves as if he was determined to explore every inch of her. She scarcely noticed him sliding down the long zip of her dress until it had pooled in a circle of lace around her ankles and she was left standing in nothing but her underwear. The cool air rushed onto her skin as he dragged his mouth away to study her and she should have felt nervous, but the expression in his gaze was making her feel anything but nervous. This felt right, she thought exultantly. Like what she had been created for.

'You look...' But Kulal's voice trailed off because, once again, the sight of her had taken his breath away. Her breasts were spilling out of a low-cut white bra and the matching high-cut panties were digging slightly into the soft curve of her hips. He'd never seen a woman who looked so fleshy before and it took a moment before he could compose himself enough to speak again. 'Exquisite,' he finished raggedly. 'The most beautiful thing I have ever seen.'

Rosa reached her hand up to touch his face, his words filling her with confidence as she reminded herself of the woman he had been attracted to—the one who had danced so provocatively on that podium. She had not been shy. So she began to tug at the white silken headdress as if undressing a man was something she did every day of the week. 'Why are you wearing this?' she asked as she removed the whole contraption, including the woven golden headband. 'I've only ever seen you in a suit before.'

He took the headdress from her and threw it on top of the tiara. 'Because usually I prefer to blend in. I find that people are much more accommodating when they think you're just like them.'

'But you're not?'

He laughed. 'Of course I'm not. I am like few

other men—for how can I be? I was born in a pal-ace and reared as a son of the desert. People always see me as a playboy and I can act that role to per-fection. But in my heart I am a sheikh.' There was a pause as he looked at her. 'And for once I wanted to look like one.'

'Why?'

There was a pause as Kulal considered her ques-tion but the truth was he didn't know what had mo-tivated him to reach for his thawb this morning, instead of a sleek designer suit. He frowned as he forced himself to remember that this was all for show. That the symbolism of the ceremony meant nothing. 'For the press, of course.' He traced his finger over the centre of her cushioned lips. 'It will make a great picture in tomorrow's papers.'

Rosa nodded but she could feel a sinking sensa-tion of disappointment. So he had been playing up for the cameras all along. Was that the reason for the kiss on the steps of the embassy, the one which had felt so electric—because it provided a great photo opportunity, rather than because he'd been longing to kiss her as she had him?

But this was what she had signed up for, wasn't

it? An expedient marriage which they could both walk away from.

'It will make a fantastic picture,' she agreed, stepping out of the discarded dress and staring up at him, her heart now beating very fast. She was just going to have to forget about her feelings and be the woman he thought she was. That woman would have listened to nothing but the desire which was rising up inside her, making her want to rip off his silken robe and feel his skin beneath her fingertips. And maybe he'd read her mind, for he kicked off his shoes before suddenly peeling the garment from his body in one swift movement, and Rosa gasped when she realised that he was completely naked underneath.

Kulal smiled, for her gasp pleased him—though it was certainly not the first time he had been greeted with such a reaction when a woman saw his body for the first time. He reached down to touch the hard ridge of his erection as he met her startled eyes and gave a lazy smile. 'Worth waiting for?'

Rosa swallowed down a mixture of excitement and fear because she'd never actually seen a naked man before, but she mustn't beat herself up about it. She reminded herself that generations of women had started their wedding night in a similar state of ignorance. It might be old-fashioned, but it certainly wasn't a crime.

'Definitely,' she said truthfully, and it was obviously the right thing to say, for he gave a satisfied nod before picking her up in his arms and carrying her over to the bed.

She felt the soft mattress dip beneath their combined weight, and as he lowered his head to kiss her, she was aware of his practised fingers removing her underclothes until she was as naked as he was. He kissed her with a passion which left her breathless—as if he was making up for lost time, and under the sweet and relentless torment of his tongue, Rosa moaned with pleasure.

His hand was on her breast, his fingers tiptoeing their way down over her belly, and suddenly her own hands were exploring him and it felt like the most natural thing in the world. She revelled in the hard planes and muscular lines of his body, which were so different to the fleshy contours of her own. She thought about what had happened on the plane and she wasn't sure how fast these things were supposed to move, but they seemed to be happening very fast indeed. For a moment Kulal pulled away from her to tear open a little foil packet which was lying on top of a cabinet next to the bed—and maybe he saw her confusion because in the midst of stroking it on, he gave a satisfied smile.

'I told you that I had everything prepared for our honeymoon.'

He moved over her and she could feel the wetness between her thighs and the slight resistance as he started to push inside her. For a moment he stilled and she prayed that he wasn't going to stop, so she sank her lips against his shoulder and grazed at his skin with her teeth. And the simple gesture seemed to flick a switch somewhere deep inside him as, with a low growl, he began to move.

It wasn't anything like how she'd thought it would be. She hadn't realised that it would feel so...intimate. That the joining of their flesh would make her feel so incredibly close to him. She was pliant in his arms, content to let him lead and to learn from him, so that when he lifted up her thighs she wrapped them around his back. And when his hands slid beneath her buttocks to pull her even closer, she gasped aloud at the sensation of his deeper penetration.

She knew what an orgasm felt like, but the one she experienced now was magnified by the sensation of

Kulal deep inside her body and his mouth exploring hers in the most sensual of kisses, his fingers tangling luxuriously in her hair. Sensation ripped through her like a forest fire as every pore of her body seemed alive with a blissful kind of awareness. She felt her back arching helplessly beneath him and dug her nails into his back as the incredible spasms ripped through her. It took a while before she opened her eyes to find him watching her, black eyes narrowed with every sweet thrust he made. And then those eyes became wild and hectic, his movements increasing before he made a guttural cry and slowly came to a shuddering rest on top of her.

For a while she felt dizzy and overcome by the most delicious wave of torpor. Her fingers crept up to his shoulders and began lazily to knead at the flesh there. She wished that she could capture that moment and bottle it, knowing that if she could it would sustain her for the rest of her life.

'You were a virgin,' he said at last, breaking the silence.

'Yes.' A pause. She prayed that would be enough because she didn't want to break this delectable mood, but his dark eyes were hard and questioning and, reluctantly, she shrugged. 'I told you that on the plane.'

Kulal rolled away from the cushioned curves of her body and shook his head. He remembered the first time he'd ever had sex, at the age of sixteen—and afterwards the palace maid had given him a hand-rolled cigarette. He remembered the way the rough tobacco had scorched its way down into his lungs and he had never smoked since, but now he found himself wishing that he could inhale some of that sickly sweet smoke and make himself dizzy.

'I didn't believe you,' he said slowly. 'You certainly didn't act like an innocent.'

'Blame the drink.'

'And what else do I blame, Rosa? Or should that be "who"?' He lifted her chin with his finger and the green and gold flecks in the depths of her eyes looked bright and vivid. He saw the uncertainty which flickered across her face, that strange vulnerability which appeared when you least expected it, and he shook his head in disbelief. 'You're twenty-three years old and you've never had sex with a man before today?'

'I thought we'd just established that.'

'I'm asking why.'

'And do you always subject your lovers to questioning, straight after…' She thought about how best to phrase it. She knew that people called it 'making love,' but there'd been no love involved in what had just happened, had there? 'Straight after having sex with them?' she finished baldly.

'Up until now, no. But then up until today I've never had a virgin—or a wife, come to that.'

'Bit of a double whammy?' she questioned flippantly.

'You can wisecrack until the sun comes up, but I'm not going to be satisfied until you've answered a few of my questions.'

Rosa wriggled uncomfortably, because she didn't want to think about it. She didn't want to think about anything. All she wanted was to hang on to this delicious warmth which was still pulsing through her body. She wanted to cling on to the amazing memory of what had just happened until it happened again, but she could see from the hard glint in his eyes that he had no intention of letting her avoid his questions. Why was he so damned persistent? she thought.

'I lived a very restrictive life in Sicily,' she explained. 'It's not unusual there, even these days, for a female to be wrapped in cotton wool until she is married. I was the only girl and I had two fiercely overprotective brothers, except that they...'

Rosa's words trailed off and Kulal heard the sudden bitterness which had crept into her voice. 'They what?'

Rosa pursed her lips together, her first instinct to come up with some fabrication about her past, but what was the point of telling lies? If she shocked him with the ultimate truth, then maybe the marriage would be even shorter than either of them had intended. Except that suddenly she realised she didn't want it to be. She felt as if they'd only just started on their own particular journey and she wanted more of it. Even if it wasn't real, she wanted more of that stuff which felt like intimacy.

'They're not my brothers. I've just discovered that they're actually my...half-brothers.'

He frowned. 'I don't understand.'

How could he possibly understand when she was still having difficulty grasping the facts herself? So that now she would be forced to say out loud the words which still made her want to retch. 'That's why I ran away from Sicily,' she said, and drew in a ragged breath. 'Because I found out something which rocked my whole world.'

'Go on,' he said.

She stared at him, wishing more than anything else that what she was about to tell him wasn't true. But it was. True and horrible and irreversible. She swallowed. 'There was a huge family gathering— a wedding which never happened—and my mother got drunk. Very drunk. I could hear her shouting, even above the sound of the music, but I couldn't quite make out what was being said. And when I did, well—' She swallowed down the bitterness which had taken up residence in her throat. 'I couldn't be-lieve it.'

She remembered her mother's face looking flushed and contorted. She remembered the sudden lull in the music as Carmela's slurred words had echoed around the room. Awful, shocking words which had chilled her to the bone. They still did. Rosa tried to stop her lips from trembling as she stared into Kulal's face, but it seemed that this was something else which was beyond her control. She took another deep breath. 'I discovered that my father was not my father,' she said.

'You already told me that on the plane.'

'I discovered that my father was in fact my uncle,' she finished painfully, just so that there could be no misunderstanding. 'My mother slept with my uncle.'

She was unprepared for the violence of his reaction. She saw his face darken as if some kind of violent storm was brewing there. She sensed that he was about to move away from her even before he actually did. He unpeeled himself from her warm body and got off the bed, walking to the other side of the vast room where he stood there surveying her, as if she was an alien species who had just dropped into his life from another world.

CHAPTER EIGHT

SHIVERING FROM HIS sudden departure from the bed and from the new coldness in his eyes, Rosa met Kulal's accusing gaze.

'Your mother slept with your uncle?' he demanded in a voice which was icy with disbelief.

'Yes.' She tried not to flinch, thinking that it sounded even worse when it came from someone else's lips. And Kulal clearly thought so too, because his face had frozen into a sombre mask. 'But this is terrible!' he flared. 'I have rarely heard anything more shocking.'

'You think I don't know that?' she questioned. 'You think I wouldn't give everything I owned for it not to be so?'

'Is this not incest?' he questioned, almost as if he was speaking to himself.

'No! No!' And to Rosa's horror, she burst into tears. All the tears she'd been bottling up ever since her mother had blurted out the horrible truth now came spilling out. She hadn't dared to give in to the danger of crying before, terrified that once she started she might never stop. She had needed all her energy and her strength to get away from Sicily and the dark web of deceit which had been woven into her life for all these years. But now that the tears had begun, they seemed unstoppable. They slid down her cheeks and onto her breasts, dripping from the prominent curves to fall in a growing damp mark on the pristine linen sheet. 'I d-don't know what it is, but it's not that,' she declared raggedly. 'My mother and my uncle were not related by blood.'

'But they were related by honour!'

'Yes, they were!' She glared at him, wiping away the falling tears with a clenched fist. 'Don't you think this has been difficult enough, without you, a complete stranger, getting on your high horse and taking the moral high ground?'

'But I am not a "complete stranger," Rosa. I am your husband!'

His words seemed to bring her to her senses and she shook her head. 'But only as a symbol,' she whispered. 'As an expedient measure which suits us both. You're not a real husband, Kulal—and a marriage of convenience doesn't give you the right to stand in judgement of me, especially when this was something which was completely out of my control.'

For a moment there was a silence. Kulal stared at the fierce set of her lips, as if she was determined not to cry again. And he saw something in her which he recognised with a painful twist of his heart. Something he had buried so deep that he had almost forgotten its existence but which was now reflected in Rosa's tearstained eyes. It was powerlessness, yes, but it was anger too—that in a single moment, your life could change for ever. For him, it had happened when his mother had scrambled up a rock to go to the aid of her trapped child. For Rosa it had happened when her mother had looked at her husband's brother with lust in her eyes.

Damn the past, he thought viciously. And damn the never-ending repercussions of that past.

He walked across the room towards her and sat down on the edge of the bed, watching her gaze slide briefly to the roughness of his naked thighs before she turned her head to stare into his face instead. He could see the wariness which had frozen her features and he took one of her cold hands in his. 'You should have told me all this before,' he said.

'And would you have still married me?'

There was a pause as he imagined the reaction of the press, if ever this were to get out. He could read the desperate question in her eyes and he knew it would be the easiest thing in the world to tell her what she wanted to hear. But wasn't it about time that people stopped lying to Rosa Corretti?

'I don't know,' he said heavily.

It was not the answer she wanted, but strangely enough it comforted her. Much better to hear the harsh truth than honeyed words which meant nothing. And this was an honest relationship, wasn't it? That's what it had been from the very beginning. They hadn't pretended to feel things they didn't feel and they didn't need to say things they didn't mean. 'You think it's an easy thing to tell someone something like that?' she questioned. 'That I'm not burning up with shame having to admit it to you now?'

He heard the guilt which had distorted her voice and once again he felt the simmer of anger. 'Of course it's not easy. But this is not your shame. You are nothing but a victim in all this, Rosa.'

'And I don't want to be a victim! I'm fed up with being a damned victim!' she declared, shaking her head so that her dark hair flew wildly about her bare shoulders. 'But what would someone like you know about that?'

He heard the resentment in her voice and usually he would have brushed away her question, with all its inquisitive undertones. He didn't tell women things about his feelings or his past because there was no need to. He kept his secrets hidden from everyone, even from himself. But her admission had made him feel uncomfortable—more than that, it had ignited painful memories which had lain dormant inside his own heart for so long. What could you say to a woman like Rosa Corretti, who had been forced to face such an intolerable situation? Wouldn't it only be human kindness to open the door on his own suffering?

'I know more than you would ever guess,' he said slowly. 'And at least you can rest assured that the dark secret in your life and the consequences of that secret were outside your control. At least you are not responsible for what happened to you.'

She could hear the terrible pain which laced his words and saw the way that his face had frozen into a forbidding mask. The hard gleam in his eyes was piercing through her—as if daring her to ask him more—and she suspected that a look like that might put most people off. But Rosa did dare, because what did she have left to lose? 'What happened?'

Kulal shook his head, but that did nothing to keep the memories at bay. He remembered a story that his English tutor used to tell him. The story of a man called Orpheus, who had been told never to look back. But Orpheus had looked back and had been left broken-hearted as a result. Kulal had never forgotten the moral of that story—that looking back could destroy you, and going forward was the only way that you could survive. 'It doesn't matter,' he said bitterly.

'Oh, but I think it does,' said Rosa softly. 'And I think you want to tell me.'

He turned on her then, his face dark with the deepest sorrow Rosa had ever seen, and she held her breath as she waited.

'I caused the death of my mother,' he said bitterly.

For a moment she didn't speak. She wanted to brush away the bald statement like unwanted dust,

but the suffering she saw on his face warned her not
to make light of it. 'How?'

Kulal glowered. He had been expecting her to respond with a placatory 'Of course you didn't!' because that was what everyone always said, even if
their accusatory eyes carried an entirely different
message. 'You want to hear how?' he demanded.
'Then I'll tell you.'

Rosa leaned back against the pillows and shiny
cushions and nodded. 'Go on, then.'

There was something so unexpectedly calm about
her that Kulal did something he'd never done before. He completely disregarded the fact that she
was naked and that her cushioned breasts were just
crying out to have him lay his head on them. Instead
he opened his mouth and let out the words which
had been smouldering away inside him for so long
that they seemed to taint the air with their darkness.
'I was six years old,' he said. 'And a very naughty
child, apparently.'

She nodded. 'Most six-year-old boys are naughty.'

'I don't need you to try and reassure me, Rosa!'

'I was merely pointing out a fact.'

'Well, don't!'

She shrugged. The fury in his voice would have

been off-putting to a lot of people, but she had grown up with furious men whose word was law and she knew how to deal with it. She lay very still and watched him.

Kulal picked his next words carefully; he felt like someone plunging his hand into a basket of fruit, knowing that angry wasps were buzzing inside. 'It had been a hot summer, piteously hot—with the worst drought our country had ever known. Sand-storms had been raging in the desert for weeks and we had all been confined to the palace. We were going stir-crazy. I remember feeling that so vividly. I remember the constant drip of sweat, despite the fans that whirred overhead. My older brother was away in Europe, and I missed his company. But my mother said we would go on a picnic as soon as the weather improved and one morning the storm just died down, as if it had never happened. There was a strange calm to the air—and even though my mother complained of a slight headache, I was eager to leave.'

He was silent for a moment. How eccentric the memory could be, he thought. How was it that some-thing which you'd blocked for over thirty years could suddenly reappear in your mind, as crystal clear as if it had happened the day before? Were these things he remembered himself, or things he had been told? Or maybe they were just a combination of things he had pieced together after the event.

'We were driven out to Saxrasahl—a very famous dried-out plain which was once an oasis and is surrounded by intricate rock formations.'

Rosa nodded. She wanted to say that it sounded beautiful, but this was something she could never say, for his voice was leaden with the sound of approaching doom and she knew he would never associate such a place with beauty.

'We ate our food, but I was eager to play and there was nobody to play with. My mother's headache had grown worse and the driver and the bodyguards were too hot to join in with me. My mother told me to stay within eyeshot, but I remember being engrossed in my game. I remember climbing to the top of a rock, but the dryness of the terrain meant that it started to crumble. I...screamed.' He closed his eyes and his heart began to pound. 'And I heard my mother's voice calling my name—and soon after that, I saw her face appear, for she had climbed the rock to find me.'

He stared down at his hands, as if he might find

some comfort in those tight, clenched fists. The silence seemed to go on and on until Rosa reached out and touched one shoulder which was so hard and unyielding that he might as well have been carved from stone.

'And then?'

He lifted his head and it was as much as she could do not to recoil from the heartbreak written in his eyes. 'Her foot slipped. The bodyguard yelled—for he was only feet away from her—but it was too late. She fell.'

She forced herself to ask the painful question, because what else could she have said in the circumstances? 'And she died?'

He shook his head. 'Not straightaway. She was airlifted to hospital but she never came out of the coma. She slipped away two nights later, with my father holding her hand.' A father who had never really forgiven him and a brother who had returned from Europe to accuse him of putting their beloved mother in danger. Later, both men had done their best to try to make up for the words which they'd uttered in the depths of their own grief, but it had been too late. And no blame or accusation had ever been more condemnatory than that which Kulal had directed at himself.

As his voice died away, Rosa stared at him, wondering what on earth she could say to a tortured man who had just bared his soul. What words could possibly bring him comfort? She thought about everything he had missed—all the cuddles and the warmth and knowing that somebody who loved you more than anyone else in the world would always be there for you. And then she felt a sharp and bitter pang of understanding, because she'd never had a mother like that, had she? She moved closer, her arms slipping around his neck as she offered him all the comfort in her heart.

'I'm sorry,' she whispered. 'So very sorry.'

He tried not to flinch but the warmth of her body was irresistible. He had told her more than he'd ever told anyone. His playboy mask had slipped and she had glimpsed the real and ravaged face behind. He felt raw and he felt vulnerable. He felt all the things he had vowed never to feel again.

'It doesn't matter,' he said unevenly.

'Of course it matters.' She saw the bleakness etched onto his features as she dared to bring up the one glaring omission from his story. 'When your mother died, did you never think that perhaps her headaches might have been contributory? Was a post-mortem ever done?'

'No!' Her questions only added an extra layer of pain to his bitter memories and, pulling away from her, he steeled himself against her look of concern. Did she think that he was regularly going to bare his heart to her and subject himself to this kind of pain? And if that was the case, then surely it was his duty to enlighten her.

'That's it, Rosa,' he said flatly. 'We've had this conversation because maybe it was necessary, but we won't be having it again. We've looked inside our individual wardrobes and seen all the skeletons hanging there, but now we're closing the door on them. Do you understand?'

She heard the finality in his voice. 'If that's what you want.'

His eyes narrowed. 'Yes, it's what I want, but maybe it's not what you want. Because this wasn't what you signed up for, is it?'

'I don't think either of us really knew what we were signing up for.'

'Which is why I'm giving you the opportunity to walk away.'

'Walk away?' Rosa blinked at him. 'What are you talking about?'

'Leave. Go on. Leave now. Why not? It makes perfect sense. You'll still get your pay-off—only you'll get it sooner than you ever anticipated. Because I think I've done rather better out of this marriage deal than you.' He forced himself to say the words—wanting her to hate him, because if she hated him, then she would go. She would go and he wouldn't have to look into her eyes and realise that she knew his secret and that she had seen his pain. 'Just think, Rosa—all that money I'm prepared to pay for having taken your virginity. You can walk away now—free and independent, just like you wanted.'

But Rosa didn't move because she knew exactly what he was doing. He was regretting having confided in her and now he was trying to drive her away. He was offering her money and trying to make her sound like some kind of whore in the process—something she'd emphatically told him she would not tolerate. Hoping that she'd leave here in some kind of rage.

A few hours ago and she might have been tempted, but that had been before he'd taken her to his bed. Before he'd shown her what she was capable of feeling. There was a reason it was called sexual awakening, she realised. Something had happened to her, and it was all down to him. It felt as if she'd been existing in a shadowy place before Kulal had brought her senses to life. And she didn't want to lose this feeling.

'Going is the last thing I want,' she said, and knew she hadn't imagined the long breath which escaped from his lips.

'Then what do you want?'

She took the edge of the linen sheet and began to pleat it between her fingers, because that was easier than looking into those piercing black eyes. She recognised that she wasn't ready to go it alone—at least, not yet. Not when the world outside Sicily still seemed such a big and frightening place. Wasn't the whole point of this bizarre marriage that Kulal could give her something which nobody else could? Not just the money which was going to buy her independence, but a sexual education which had only just begun. And why should anything be allowed to spoil the best thing that had ever happened to her?

Looking up, she pushed the heavy fall of hair back from her face and the movement caused her heavy breasts to sway. She saw him shift a little and her attention was caught by the growing erection between his thighs and in that moment she felt shy and powerful, all at the same time. 'I want you to teach me everything you know.'

He stared at her, knowing that he should distance himself from her and yet how could he when she looked so damned gorgeous? How could he force her to leave when he wanted her so much that he felt he could explode with need? He could smell the lingering scent of sex on the air and could feel the erratic beat of his heart as he leaned forward and bent his lips to her neck. 'Anything specific you have in mind?' he questioned unevenly. 'The history of Zahrastan, maybe? Or the new energy proposals I'm setting out next week?'

She tipped her head back. 'About pleasure,' she whispered through dry lips. 'Teach me everything you know about pleasure. I'll be your wife and one day I will walk out of your life. But in the meantime...'

'What?

She wriggled again, more impatiently this time. 'Please?'

He drew back to see the sudden rush of colour to her cheeks and something made him want to show her who was in charge. To show her that, ultimately, he was the one who called all the shots. And perhaps the first lesson she needed to learn was how to articulate her own desires, instead of expecting him to second-guess them. Because only that way would she ever be truly independent. 'Please, what?' he prompted softly.

Rosa met the dark gleam of his eyes, and swallowed. 'Please will you do it to me again?'

CHAPTER NINE

KULAL STROKED HIS fingertips over the silken curtain of dark hair which lay spread all over the pillow and felt the inevitable hardening of his body.

'I know you're awake, Rosa,' he said softly. 'So why don't you open your eyes and kiss me?'

Rosa stirred as the sheikh's voice penetrated her dreamy thoughts and, obediently, she let her eyelashes flutter open. He was lying next to her, propped up on one elbow—deliciously naked and gloriously virile, studying her body as if it was the most beautiful body he'd ever seen, which was what he had told her in the early hours of this morning as he had pulled her hungrily into his arms. Each morning she woke up to a similarly appreciative reaction, but it still took some getting used to.

She pushed the blanket of mussed hair away from her face and yawned. 'But I might have been asleep,' she objected.

He glanced at his wristwatch. 'It's nearly midday.'

'And it's Saturday. Or are you saying that it's impossible for someone to be asleep if it's nearly lunch-time?'

'I knew you weren't asleep because you've been wriggling that delicious bottom—' he smiled as his arm snaked around her waist and he turned her around, so that his erection was pressing hard against her belly '—against me for the past half-hour. So it was a toss between going for a cold shower, or seeing if I might be able to get you to do something more interesting than sleeping.'

She leaned forward, brushing her mouth against his and feeling the instant shimmer of lust which flamed over her skin. 'You can always get me to do that,' she said, her voice sounding almost shy as he cupped her buttocks to pull her closer. But wasn't it insane to feel shy, when in the few short weeks since their marriage Kulal had stripped her bare in just about every way there was?

He had taught her so much. He had shown her that sex was something to be enjoyed and savoured, not something furtive and shameful. In short, he had liberated her from a lot of her own hang-ups and all she was trying to do now was avoid getting too dependent on a man who was never intended to be anything other than a temporary fixture. 'In fact, you can get me to do just about anything,' she finished softly, and saw his eyes darken.

'I know,' he said. 'And I'd be happy with pretty much anything you'd care to do to me right now.'

'Oh, Kulal.'

'Oh, Rosa,' he murmured back, and lowered his head to kiss her. He thought that her lips felt cool and tasted of the peppermint tea she'd brought back to bed when they'd first woken. Her arms tightened around him and the desire he felt grew stronger— his heart beating out a crazy rhythm as he pushed one hard thigh against the fleshy softness of hers. He thought how perfect she was in his arms, how their lovemaking just got better and better and pretty much took his breath away every time. And he thought how their honeymoon had surprised him in all kinds of ways.

At first, they had barely left the apartment—with only the occasional trip to a theatre or a restaurant punctuating their lazy days and long nights of sexual exploration. For the first time in his life he had cleared his diary and turned off his phone—because he never took a holiday. Never. He told himself that it would be a useful experiment to see if his charitable foundation could function well without him, but deep down he knew that wasn't the real reason. The truth was that he didn't want to leave Rosa's side. He couldn't get enough of her; he couldn't seem to keep his hands off her. And when they had ventured out, he had felt like a tourist in his adopted city. She'd made him do things he would normally never have dreamt of doing, like climbing as far as it was possible up the Eiffel Tower—with his bodyguards trailing behind them. And when he had remonstrated that he did not wish to join in with other sightseers, she had halted his objections simply by kissing him.

'You're never too cool to see the whole of Paris from the top of the Eiffel Tower,' she'd giggled against his lips. And later that week they had taken a riverboat down the Seine and she had looked up the name of all the bridges in her guidebook and recited them to him. They'd sat and drunk coffee incognito at the famous Café de Flore and made two similarly unrecorded trips to the theatre. In fact, they'd managed to avoid a single press photographer capturing any honeymoon images and to Kulal this had felt like a small triumph—especially when he'd realised that she actually hadn't been interested in being photographed with him.

He'd even taken her shopping—something he'd never done before, although he'd picked up plenty of inflated bills in his time. But with Rosa it was different. She didn't seem bothered about the cost of things and he enjoyed dressing his new wife with clothes which befitted a princess. Just as he enjoyed buying—and removing—the outrageous scraps of silken underwear which could barely contain her luscious curves.

He still couldn't get his head around it. What was the appeal of lying next to her and just watching her—as if the sight of the slow inhalation and exhalation of her breath was the single most fascinating spectacle in the world? Usually he absented himself pretty early, because he didn't like women hanging around him in the morning. He liked his space and his privacy. He liked the feeling of being alone— the way he'd always been.

But not with Rosa—and he was still trying to work out why.

Was it because she gave herself to him so completely? Because she was all his and only his—like a newly minted coin which had been held by no other person? With her, he felt primeval. Something possessive and powerful gripped him whenever he held her, something which battered at his senses like a raging storm. Perhaps that was the ancient power of the marriage vows—that no matter how carelessly the words had been spoken, they still managed to convey a profound significance to the couple involved.

He moved his head down between her thighs, hearing her breathless little gasp of anticipation as he began to lick her. He revelled in the taste of her sweet-sharp stickiness and the way that his fingers sank into her soft hips—just as he revelled in her orgasm as she bucked helplessly beneath his tongue. He stayed there for a while, his lips pressed hard against her until at last she grew still and then he moved over her, and into her. He closed his eyes as he lost himself in her slick heat. Allowed the urgent rhythm to spiral them both up to a place so high that the slow and incredible fall back to earth left him breathless, and spent.

He must have fallen asleep, because when he

opened his eyes it was to the smell of strong coffee and the sight of Rosa sitting on the window seat in a silken robe the colour of claret, with the glory of Paris framing her like an Impressionist painting.

'I've made you some coffee,' she said.

'I can smell it.' He sat up as she placed it on the table beside the bed. 'You make the best coffee in the world.'

'This is true,' she said seriously. 'Because I'm Sicilian and we do the best of everything.' But as Rosa lifted the pot to pour her own coffee, she was aware of how hollow her words sounded. She used to revel in her Sicilian roots and identity, with the fierce pride which had been drummed into her ever since she could remember. Being born and raised on the beautiful Mediterranean island had always given her a feeling of belonging. She'd felt part of her family and also part of the bigger island community, which had always existed there. But not any more. Her mother's betrayal seemed to have had even wider-reaching repercussions than she'd originally anticipated. Not only had her relationships within the family been dramatically altered, but a wall of silence seemed to have descended since Rosa's dramatic flight from her homeland.

'Have you heard anything from your family?' he questioned softly.

Had he read her thoughts, or had her wistfulness shown on her face? She didn't want to show him she was hurt because she was trying very hard not to be. But it did hurt that neither of her brothers had been in touch, even though she'd emailed them her new phone number and told them she was now married and living in Paris.

'I've heard from Lia,' she said slowly. 'She's the half-sister I never knew I had. The one I insulted after my mother had dropped her bombshell. I wrote and apologised for the way I lashed out at her and she was so sweet. She said she understood. She also said she'd always wanted a sister—she just hadn't been expecting to find one quite so dramatically! But I guess we'll never get to know each other now.'

Kulal frowned. 'There's nothing stopping you going back to Sicily, you know—if you wanted to speak to them face to face,' he said. 'I could take you there, if it would help.'

Rosa shook her head. And have everyone cluster round and want to find out about her glamorous new husband? She wasn't that good an actress and some-how she couldn't bear the pity she'd have to endure when her family discovered the truth of why they'd married. 'I told you—I can't imagine me ever wanting to go back. There's no place for me there now. The person I used to be doesn't exist any more.'

Because the new Rosa was now a princess, even if it was only a very temporary role. She didn't get to wear a crown but she got to share the bed of a man who was a real-life prince. A desert sheikh—a man who couldn't seem to get enough of her…and much as she revelled in his attention, she knew it was getting dangerous. She'd been feeling that for days now. It happened every time she opened her eyes and saw him lying next to her and it continued throughout the day. She hugged the memory of their lovemaking to her like a delicious present. She'd never felt so contented—nor ecstatic—in her whole life and she knew that it would be madness to allow her feelings for Kulal to grow.

But how did you stop yourself feeling something when your heart was determined to do the opposite? She picked up her cup and sipped her coffee. She could not afford to get too attached to her husband, because one day they were going to split. She knew that. She'd signed that damned pre-nup, hadn't she? The one which offered her a massively generous amount of money, in exchange for a 'clean break' settlement? She just needed to train herself to get used to that bald fact and to maintain some kind of emotional distance.

She tried telling herself she was okay with it, when Kulal announced that their honeymoon was over and that he was planning to return to work at his foundation the following Monday. But the reality was that she'd wanted to cling to him and beg him not to go and that feeling had scared her more than her very real dilemma—about how to usefully spend her days while he was working.

'I'm not sure what I'm going to do all day in Paris, with you back at the office full-time,' she said.

He glittered her a smile. 'Do more of what you did in Sicily. You were a lady of leisure there, weren't you?'

Rosa didn't let her smile slip, even though it wasn't the most flattering way to describe her former life. It was true she hadn't had a career, though she'd been awarded a respectable languages degree from the University of Palermo. But it had been difficult to find a job which hadn't been vetoed by her controlling family. She'd done bits of interpreting work whenever she could, but opportunities were scarce. So she'd ended up with a part-time administrative job at the university where she'd studied—and it had felt a bit like stepping back in time. As if she hadn't progressed much beyond the student she'd once been.

'I wasn't exactly a lady of leisure,' she defended. 'I did have a part-time job—'

'Well, there's no need for you to have a part-time job now,' he said, a touch impatiently. 'Just enjoy your days and let me pick up the bill.'

Rosa tried not to feel offended by his dismissive words just as she tried to throw herself into her new life as a stay-at-home Parisian wife. She explored more of Paris and the many attractions it had to offer. She walked everywhere—always tailed by the ubiquitous bodyguard—and began to gain the confidence which came from learning the geography of a once-strange city. In the mornings she took in a gallery or an exhibition, and in the afternoons she went to see a film and her once-fluent French began to improve as a consequence.

But she got a distinct sense that she was simply filling in time, that she was becoming like many of the other rich expatriates who counted away their hours with culture. She began to look forward to

Kulal's homecoming with more enthusiasm than she told herself was wise. He didn't want an eager woman throwing herself at him like an underexercised puppy whenever he came home from work, did he? He wanted a woman who'd had an interesting day, because surely that way she'd be more interesting herself.

One evening, he came back late from the office and went straight into the shower, and when he walked into the bedroom, Rosa was sitting in front of the dressing table in her bra and pants, blow drying her hair.

'You haven't forgotten we're out to dinner tonight?' he questioned, momentarily distracted by the sight of the lace-covered globes of her breasts.

'No, of course I haven't.' She put the hairdryer down and watched his reflection as he began to rub a towel over his damp body. 'We're seeing someone from a TV company, am I right?'

'You are. Actually, the executive producer of one of France's most successful independent companies, who wants to make a documentary about Zahrastan.'

She met his eyes in the mirror. 'Maybe that's a good thing—to place it in the minds of the public.'

She leaned forward and slicked some lipstick over her mouth. 'I'd never heard of Zahrastan until I met you.'

'Precisely.' Roughly, he rubbed at his hair. 'We need to let the world see that we're not some big, bad oppressive dictatorship. The biggest problem was persuading my brother to allow a foreign crew to enter the country in order to film.'

'And he was agreeable?'

Kulal laughed. 'Oddly enough, he was very agreeable—since he's notoriously prickly about foreign opinion. But I think he's decided that Zahrastan has to be seen as embracing the modern world.'

'And do you…' She hesitated, because since that first night, when he'd poured out the blame and guilt he'd felt about his mother's death, he'd barely mentioned his brother. In fact, the frankness of that night had not been repeated, even though she had tentatively tried to get him to open up on more than one occasion. But he had blocked her moves with the skill of a seasoned chess player. She got the feeling that he had allowed her to see a rare chink in his armour and had no intention of repeating it and it frustrated the hell out of her. Because wasn't it natural to want to chip away at that armour and see more of the real man beneath? Didn't that kind of intimacy feel just as profound—maybe even more profound—as anything which they shared during sex? She sucked in a breath as she watched him pull on a white shirt. 'Do you talk to your brother much?'

He raised his eyebrows, as if she had somehow overstepped the mark. 'Obviously we've spoken about the film crew. How else would I know his feelings on the subject?'

The faint sarcasm which edged his words was new but Rosa wasn't going to give up, because this was the first opportunity she'd had in ages. 'I don't mean about that. I mean, about…about what happened to your mother.'

She saw him stiffen before his eyes suddenly became cool and watchful. Like a snake's eyes, she found herself thinking as a little flutter of trepidation whispered over her skin.

'Sorry?'

'I just thought—'

'Well, don't,' he snapped. 'Because there's nothing left to say on the subject, Rosa. I thought we'd already decided that.'

His words were steely—they sounded like a metal door being slammed—but Rosa wasn't going to give up. She knew the danger of locking away painful things. You locked them away and they festered and then one day they all came bubbling out in a horrible mess. Wasn't that what her own mother had done? 'I just get the feeling that there's so much between you which isn't resolved. That maybe—'

'Maybe nothing,' he clipped out, and now his words were coated with ice. 'I told you those things because...' Kulal felt a brief flicker of anger, but it was directed at himself as much as at her. What the hell had possessed him to tell her all those things? To open up his heart in a way which was unheard of? 'Because you'd given me a brief glimpse into your own sorry family saga and I decided it was only fair to try to redress the balance. But I didn't tell you so that you could suddenly decide to "fix me."' He stared at her. 'You have enough things to worry you, Rosa—and if you feel the need for some sort of redemptive programme in your life, then I suggest you might try working on your own stuff first.'

His attack had come out of nowhere and it startled her. Rosa stared into his hawk-like face and thought that his expression looked cruel and almost...unrecognisable. Except that wasn't strictly true, was it? He had looked at her that way when she'd woken up in his villa. When she'd found herself alone in his bed and discovered him staring at her as if he didn't like her very much....

She fished around for something to say. Something which wouldn't involve bursting into tears and demanding to know why he'd felt the need to spoil everything with his cruel words. But instead, she fixed him with a questioning look which was very polite and utterly shallow. 'What kind of documentary?'

He nodded, as if approving her sudden change of subject. 'A groundbreaking one, with not a camel in sight.'

She gave the smile she knew was expected of her before walking into her dressing room to choose something to wear. Her hands were shaking as she pulled open the closet door, but she tried to tell herself that she couldn't heap all the blame on Kulal.

Because in a way he was right, wasn't he? She hadn't worked out any of her own stuff. She still felt bitter and hurt by what she had learnt about her parentage. She had run away from her family, but it seemed that her family had been happy to let her go—and she was surprised by the sharp pain she felt as a result. Had she thought she was still their precious Rosa who could do no wrong? That they'd come seeking some kind of reconciliation or to comfort her, when the reality was that they would have been furious and humiliated by her desertion?

She began to riffle her way through her clothes, picking out an ankle-length dress, which Kulal had chosen for her himself. It was a simple red dress, but the beauty was in the fabric which clung like molten syrup to her curves. Skyscraper heels in ebony leather and loose hair completed the look, though impulsively she clipped a scarlet silk flower behind her ear at the last minute.

Kulal's reaction to her appearance was gratifying, although she had to reapply her lipstick after he'd kissed it all away, and still glowing from the sweetness of that kiss, she decided that she was going to forget the bitter words he'd spoken. What was the point of ruining the evening ahead, especially when he looked so…gorgeous. His dark, sculpted features were highlighted by the fact that he was newly shaved and his ebony hair gleamed in the early-evening sunshine as they stepped into the official car.

Was it normal to feel this way? she wondered. To want to touch him at every given moment and run her fingers over each inch of his body? But she didn't give in to her desire—just sat serenely beside him on the back seat of the large car, asking him intelligent questions about the proposed documentary, so that by the time they arrived in the trendy Marais area of the city she felt composed. As if she had been born to walk into swish restaurants by the side of a man who had caught the attention of every person in the room.

The TV executive was called Arnaud Bertrand, and if she'd been with anyone other than Kulal, Rosa might have found him attractive. His chiselled jaw and sensual mouth hinted at his earlier career as an underwear model, before he'd realised that it was far better to rely on his brains, rather than his beauty. Or so he told Rosa, during a lull in the conversation, when Kulal was busy talking to the location manager about the practicalities of taking a film crew to Zahrastan.

'Whilst you,' he mused, his eyes moving to the bright flower she wore in her hair, 'could rely on both, I think. Brains and beauty.'

'I'm not beautiful,' she said quickly.

'You don't think so?' Arnaud narrowed his eyes. 'With that lustrous hair and perfect skin, you remind me of Monica Bellucci. And you are the wife of one of the world's most powerful men, a man who could have any woman he chooses. That in itself speaks volumes about you.'

Rosa bit back a wry smile. If only he knew why Kulal had ended up with this too-curvy Sicilian with a complicated past! 'And I'm certainly no academic,' she said, swiftly changing the subject and wondering if he paid such lavish compliments to every woman who entered his radar.

'But you're a linguist, right? You speak French and English—and Italian, of course.'

Rosa shrugged. 'Plenty of people do.'

'But plenty of people do not look like you, Rosa. You have a freshness about you—and a vibrancy too.' Arnaud lifted his wine glass to his lips, and over his shoulder Rosa thought she could see a faint frown appearing on Kulal's brow. 'Tell me, would you be interested in taking a screen test?'

Rosa blinked. 'You mean for television?'

'Of course for television—that's my medium.'

'I don't act,' said Rosa bluntly. 'And don't they say that the camera adds ten pounds? I'm completely the wrong shape for the small screen—I'd fill it!'

'Ah, but I believe in smashing stereotypes,' said Arnaud softly. 'I'm trained to recognise that certain *je ne sais quoi* which the camera loves and I think you have it. I'm not expecting you to act, just do a brief test. Would you be interested?'

Telling herself that it would be rude to refuse his offer—or maybe that it would simply be easier to go along with it—Rosa took his card and slipped it into her handbag.

'Ring me,' he said, and then turned back to talk to Kulal.

The dinner was delicious and the wines kept on coming and Rosa felt wonderfully replete as their car arrived to take them home. But even though she made a few predictable comments about how well the evening had gone, Kulal merely answered her in clipped monosyllables. His powerful body seemed tense and forbidding, but she was feeling expansive—and more than a little bit randy—so she trickled her fingertips over his forearm. But he didn't react and, feeling foolish, she quickly removed her hand as if it had been contaminated. He didn't say another word until they were back at the apartment and the lights which bounced nightly off the Eiffel Tower were flickering over the huge sitting room, making it seem as if they were standing in the centre of a silent fireworks display.

'You seemed to hit it off very well with Arnaud,' he said slowly.

'That was the whole point, surely?' She clicked on one of the lamps, telling herself she was imagining the scowl of accusation on his face. 'I was there as your wife, to support you—and the best way I could do that was to be friendly.'

His black eyes bored into her. 'Did being friendly involve thrusting your breasts in the face of the executive producer?'

Rosa tensed as she heard an ugly and unmistakable note in his voice. It was a note she knew too well from having grown up in a family of powerful men. Men who had an overabundance of male testosterone and an overinflated sense of their own importance. It was possession—pure and simple—and it made her skin turn to ice.

She tried to keep the tremble of outrage from her voice. 'That's a completely unreasonable thing to say.'

'You think so? Then why did he give you his card? You think I didn't notice that?'

The card was buried at the bottom of her handbag and Rosa honestly didn't think she would have given it another thought if Kulal hadn't challenged her, but his attitude was riling her. More than riling her—it was making rebellion stir up inside her. Because hadn't she fled Sicily precisely to avoid this kind of domineering attitude? To stop people treating her as if she was some puppet whose strings they could pull at will.

'He asked me if I was interested in taking a screen test.'

'You?'

'Yes, me, Kulal—is that such a bizarre thing for him to have said?' she demanded, pushing aside the nagging voice which reminded her that he was only echoing her own initial reaction.

'And you told him no?'

She heard the certainty in his voice and drew in a breath as her emotions began to wage a sudden and dramatic war. She knew what he wanted and she knew she could please him by telling him exactly what he wanted to hear—but then what? You caved into a bully once and that was giving him carte blanche to bully you all over again. She had planned to do nothing about Arnaud's offer of a screen test, but now she was beginning to have second thoughts. She stared at her husband, not liking the Kulal she was seeing tonight, knowing that he had no right to dictate what she should or shouldn't do. Because surely he hadn't forgotten that this marriage wasn't real?

'I haven't told him anything,' she said. 'At least, not yet.'

There was a pause as Kulal stared at her. 'But you're going to tell him that you're not interested,' he said.

Rosa's mouth dried as she felt the sudden tension in the room. Because that had been a statement, not a question. Or rather, it had bordered on being an order.

Rebellion flared up inside her once more. 'I'm going to hear what he has to say,' she answered stubbornly.

Kulal could feel a tight knot of anger but he could feel something else too. A flicker of something which burned beneath the anger and which was growing like a weed inside him. Something painful and intolerable. Something unfamiliar and yet horribly recognisable. He rammed his hands deep into the pockets of his trousers—something he couldn't remember doing since he'd been a schoolboy and had been sent to that terrible prep school in England. But he didn't want her to see the bunched tension of his knotted fists. Because wouldn't that reveal the fact that he was in pain—and he didn't want to be in pain!

He gave a tight shrug of his shoulders. 'Suit yourself,' he said coolly. 'I'm going to bed.'

Rosa watched him go. He'd sounded so dismissive, as if he didn't want her to share his bed that night. She licked her lips. So was she going to let herself be intimidated? Crawl off to sleep in one of the empty bedrooms as if she'd done something wrong, when all she'd done was to consider a perfectly reasonable offer which had been made to her.

Like hell she was!

She went to the bathroom and stripped off her dress, then brushed her hair and washed her face—and when she had removed every trace of the evening, she heard something behind her and glanced into the mirror.

Not something.

Someone.

Kulal stood behind her—completely naked and completely aroused by the look of him. On his face burned an expression she'd never seen there before. Was it anger or desire, she wondered, or a potent mixture of both? She saw the heat in his black eyes and instinct was telling her that maybe sleeping in one of the spare rooms was a better idea than slipping into the marital bed when he was in this kind of mood. Anything would be better than having to face that undiluted rage on Kulal's face.

But that was before he put his arms around her. Before he dropped his lips to her shoulder and traced a line there—the words he uttered made indistinct by his kiss. But they were not tender words. They were words of want, not words of need. They were graphic words about what he wanted to do to her, and although the baldness of his erotic wish list made her feel that she should beg for sleep and ask him to wait until morning, Rosa did no such thing.

His hands were far too clever to let her escape. His fingers made her weak with longing and so did his lips, so that by the time he entered her from behind, she was as turned on as he was. Turned on enough to watch their dual reflections in the mirror when he urged her to do so. Turned on by the sight of her own orgasm—and just as turned on by the sight of his.

But even though the kiss he gave her afterwards was lazy and sticky, he disentangled himself sooner than she wanted him to. She wanted him to stroke her and comfort her; to tell her to forget about the hurtful things he'd said. But he didn't. The only thing he told her was that he needed to do some work before he slept.

And he didn't follow her to bed.

CHAPTER TEN

ROSA AWOKE TO an empty space beside her and when she blinked open her heavy eyelids it was to see Kulal pulling on a jacket. He was dressed for the office in dark trousers and a pristine white shirt and she shifted a little to get a better look at him, but she noticed that he made no acknowledgement as she stirred.

She sat up in bed, a chill creeping over her skin as she remembered the angry words of the previous evening which had culminated in that cold, almost anatomical sex in the bathroom. She shivered. At the time it had turned her on like mad to see the wild passion flaring in their eyes, as they'd watched their reflected images bucking their way to fulfilment with all the guilty pleasure of voyeurs. But now it all seemed curiously empty. Vividly, she recalled those big, dark hands cupping her breasts and the look of fierce intensity which had shadowed his face as he'd thrust into her. It was like watching a rerun of a porn show and felt like the emotional equivalent of a hangover and her cheeks began to burn with shame. How could she have let herself do that, when in the previous few moments he had been damning her with his snide accusations about flaunting her body? Accusations which hadn't even been true.

Which left the question of how she was going to handle the situation this morning. Did she bring up the whole painful subject and risk one of those dreadful circular arguments which went nowhere? Or should she just be grown up about what had happened? Forget what had been said the night before and start the new day on a new and positive note.

She sat up in bed. 'Morning!' she said cheerfully.

He turned round then and Rosa could see the shuttering of his dark eyes.

'I didn't want to wake you,' he said.

Suddenly, she felt self-conscious. He was dressed in that immaculate suit, while beneath the sheet she felt naked and vulnerable. She wondered if he, too, was remembering last night's erotic scene in the bathroom, and some unknown instinct made her pull the sheet a little higher. 'I didn't realise you were going to work so early.'

He shrugged. 'There are things I need to do.'

The smile she attempted was more difficult than she'd thought—especially when he was talking to her in that polite, cool tone, as if she was someone he'd just met at a party. No, maybe not at a party— because then he would be smiling back at her. He wouldn't be looking at her with that flat expression in his eyes. 'Surely as the boss, you can be excluded a crack-of-dawn start!' she said, her voice just a little too bright.

'It's not a question of being excused, Rosa—more that I have plenty of ongoing projects which need my attention.' Kulal buttoned his jacket, acknowledging how false her words sounded. And suddenly he realised that the honeymoon was over; it had ended last night when those dark feelings had taken him to a place he hadn't wanted to go. When he'd looked at her and experienced a blinding jealousy at the way she'd flirted with the Frenchman throughout dinner. He remembered the painful pounding of his heart as he'd stared into an abyss which had seemed uncomfortably familiar—and it had taken all his energy to regain his usual clarity of mind.

He wondered if she was feeling more reasonable today. If she'd woken up and realised that Arnaud Bertrand had simply been using her as a means to try to get closer to him. He surveyed her curvaceous body which was outlined by the white sheet. 'So what are you planning to do today?'

For a moment she hesitated, because she knew the most acceptable way to answer his question. She could fake a light excitement about visiting some art gallery or exhibition, or recount the synopsis of a film she was intending to see.

But Kulal's behaviour last night had scared her. It had shown her the ruthlessness he was capable of. It had painted a dark picture of what he could be like if things didn't go his way, and it had served as a timely warning that she needed to protect herself. She needed to guard against her own stupid emotions—the ones which had started tricking her into thinking that Kulal had started to care for her. Because he hadn't. She didn't have a special place in his heart just because the sexual chemistry between them was so hot.

It was important to remember something else

too—something she hadn't dared admit until now. That if she let herself start to care for him, then she would get hurt. Badly hurt. She'd go back to being a victim—the kind of woman who things happened to, instead of making them happen for herself. And he wasn't exactly falling over himself this morning to tell her that he had spoken impulsively and out of turn, was he? He wasn't apologising for all those insults he'd thrown at her last night.

She remembered the way she'd capitulated to her controlling family for all those years and she twisted a strand of hair around her finger. 'I thought I'd give Arnaud a ring.'

'Arnaud Bertrand?'

'He's the only Arnaud I know.'

He could feel the rapid flare of rage, but somehow he kept his expression neutral. 'I thought you'd decided that wasn't a good idea?'

'I don't remember saying that.'

'Maybe not in so many words.' His eyes narrowed as he tried not to dwell on the area of her breasts which was not concealed by the sheet. 'But in the cold light of morning, perhaps you've considered the general unsuitability of a sheikh's wife flaunting herself on television.'

'I wasn't planning to do anything to bring your name into disrepute, Kulal.'

'No pole dancing, then?'

'That's unfair.'

'You think so? You wish to deny the past, perhaps?'

She met the accusation in his eyes and she wanted to tell him to stop doing this. To stop it right now before he did irreparable harm to what they had. She wanted to rewind the clock back to yesterday morning, when his words had been tender, not harsh. 'You know why I pole danced,' she said quietly. 'I was drunk and I was running away from an impossible situation. You know that.'

His black eyes continued to bore into her. 'So what are you running away from this time, Rosa?'

She could feel the hammering of her heart as she clutched at the sheet. 'I'm not running from anything,' she said. 'I'm just trying to find out what talents I have. I want to grab every opportunity which comes my way, because I'm aware that the clock on this marriage is ticking away. And that when we part, I want to know who the real Rosa Corretti is and what she's capable of.' She stared at him in appeal, wanting him to understand. Praying that he would understand.

He picked up a file of papers. 'Then I must wish you well,' he said.

His words were dismissive and Rosa could feel her fingernails digging into the palms of her hands as he headed out of the room without even bothering to kiss her goodbye. Damn him and his prissy attitude, she raged silently as she heard the front door slam behind him.

Defiantly, she showered and dressed—and although she always felt at her thinnest in black, she remembered reading somewhere that you should never wear black in front of the camera. So she put on a green silk dress which brought out the emerald flecks in her eyes, and after a couple of cups of strong coffee she rang Arnaud Bertrand.

'Madame de la Désert,' he said slowly. 'This is a surprise.'

Rosa sucked in a deep breath, wondering if his offer had just been something meaningless which he'd tossed out during a lull in the dinner party conversation. 'Did you mean it when you suggested the screen test?'

There was a pause. 'But of course I meant it,' he

said smoothly. 'I never say anything I don't mean. Can you come in for a test this afternoon?'

She thought afterwards that if he'd scheduled the test for the following week, then she might never have taken it. Maybe that was why he did it so quickly. All Rosa knew was that later that day she had the car drop her off at the TV studio, which was situated on the Avenue de la Grande Armée. The building overlooked the Arc de Triomphe and Arnaud told her that the iconic backdrop was often hired out to visiting foreign broadcasters.

'You don't seem too nervous,' he observed as he ran his eyes over her silky green dress.

Rosa gave an automatic smile. My husband doesn't want me to be here, she found herself wanting to say. I keep thinking about him, instead of the reason I'm here—and that's the reason why I'm not nervous. But she forced herself to push the memory of Kulal's face from her mind and to flash a bright smile at the TV executive instead. 'Surely nerves in front of the camera are a bad thing?'

'They certainly are.' Arnaud smiled back as he led her into the studio, where the lights were belting out a heat as fierce as a tropical sun. 'How good are you at ad-libbing?'

Rosa shrugged. 'I have no idea.'

They stood her in front of a giant green screen and explained that the weather report was one of the few things on television which didn't require an autocue. They told her that Paris was going to have sunny spells throughout the day, but that there would be scattered showers overnight. And then they asked her to talk about it on camera for thirty seconds, without a script.

She was a natural. Or at least, that's what they said afterwards, when she'd finished her slot. Just as the last few seconds were ticking away, she had turned to the camera and said, 'Sometimes I wish I was back in Sicily, where the sun always shines.' She'd heard shouts of laughter in her earpiece, and when Arnaud came to collect her from the studio floor, he'd been grinning—as if he'd just done something very clever.

He took her for coffee afterwards and told her that he'd been entirely correct and she did have that certain *je ne sais quoi* which made the camera love her. That it was a rare commodity but television gold. They couldn't offer her much at the moment, but they thought she'd be perfect for a daily 'novelty slot,' just after the lunchtime news.

She received the news with the enthusiasm she knew was expected of her, but when she left the café to slide into the back of the waiting limousine, all she could think of was how she was going to break it to Kulal. And wasn't that crazy? Because this was the chance of a lifetime—and wasn't this marriage supposed to be about freedom?

She had to start taking control. She was legally contracted to be Kulal's wife for another ten months and she certainly couldn't spend it moping around the place, wishing he felt stuff for her which he clearly didn't. If she didn't like something, then she needed to change it. And if she couldn't change him, then she needed to change herself. Couldn't she show her sheikh husband that it was possible to live in harmony, if they both made the effort? That they could compromise if they wanted to, just like any other modern couple.

She felt filled with a new sense of purpose as she took the elevator up to the apartment, and when Kulal arrived home she was waiting for him out on the terrace. She had mixed a drink of his favourite rosewater and pomegranate juice and his eyebrows rose speculatively as she held up the frosted pink jug. 'Drink?'

'A drink would be perfect,' he said, pulling off his jacket as he went out onto the terrace and joined her. He had thought that he would arrive home to an atmosphere, that she might be sulking in response to his obvious disapproval of her intention to ring Bertrand. But it seemed he had been wrong, for he'd never seen her looking quite so relaxed.

Sinking into one of the chairs, he watched as she bent to drop ice into the glass, his gaze resting on the curve of her bottom, and his heart began to accelerate as she handed him the drink. She was wearing her hair loose, just the way he liked it, and her flame-coloured dress accentuated her exotic colouring. Not only did she look good, but she was behaving in a way which pleased him since her attitude towards him was undeniably accommodating. Did this mean that she had reconsidered her rash statements of this morning? His gaze was approving as he took a sip of his drink and let out a rare sigh of contentment. 'I must applaud you, Rosa,' he said. 'For this is exactly how a man likes to be greeted after a hard day at the office.'

She waited until he'd put his drink down before she walked over and sat on his lap, looping her arms around his neck. 'And have you had a good day?'

'When you wriggle on my lap like that, it makes me forget—other than to say that it's getting better by the minute.'

She dipped her head forward and brushed her mouth over his. 'Is it?' she whispered.

He didn't answer, just put his hand up to anchor her head so that he could kiss her, and Rosa felt the shimmering of desire as if whispered over her skin. Her hands reached out to frame his face, her fingertips tracing the hard outline of his jaw and feeling the faint rasp of new growth there. Her fingers crept upwards, so that they could feel the hard slant of his cheekbones beneath the silken skin. And all during her tactile survey of his face, he continued to subject her to that sweetly drugging kiss so she was startled when, abruptly, he terminated it, pushing her away by a fraction so that he could look directly into her eyes.

'What's the matter?' she managed through dry lips. 'D-don't you want to make love?'

'You mean here?'

She wondered how best to respond. Up until now, Kulal had been the dominant one—not surprising given his vast experience and her complete lack of it. But she'd had a pretty intensive introduction to sex, hadn't she? Surely she'd had enough tuition for her to take the lead for once. Maybe that was what he wanted her to do.

'Of course here,' she whispered as she drifted her hand down to his groin, where he felt as hard as steel, and began to stroke him through the straining material of his trousers. 'I want you now. I can lift up my skirt and you can just slip inside me. No one need know a thing.'

The explicitness of her words excited yet shocked him and Kulal recognised a subtle shift in power between them as his body responded instantly to her touch. For a moment he allowed himself the fantasy of following through. Of allowing her floaty dress to conceal what was going on underneath. Of unzipping himself and pushing deep inside her honeyed heat. Gripping her wrist to arrest the movement of her captivating fingers, he put his face very close to hers. 'You don't think we can be seen?'

Rosa swallowed. 'This terrace is completely private.'

'Nowhere is completely private. There are long-range lenses and buildings all around which offer perfect vantage points.' His black eyes shot out black fire which blazed over her. 'Unless you are turned on by the thought that someone might be watching? Perhaps deep down you are longing for the kind of notoriety which would come from being the first woman to be photographed having sex with the sheikh?'

She stared at him, her heart beginning to pound painfully in her chest as she heard his unjust and harsh accusation. 'Is that what you think?' she whispered. 'Is that what you really think?'

'I don't know what to think. You are a constant series of surprises to me, Rosa—surprises which are becoming more apparent by the day. I had no idea, for example, that you were a frustrated television star.'

Shaking her head with indignation, she jumped off his lap and ran back inside the apartment but she quickly realised that he was following her. She could see his huge shadow dwarfing her and could hear him pressing a button so that the blinds floated silently down, leeching the room of all brightness and colour. She turned, seeing the look on his face.

'Don't,' she said, her heart quickening.

'Don't what?' he questioned. 'Don't continue what you started outside, only without the possibility of some paparazzi salivating over his camera? I thought that was what you were angling for, Rosa.'

The prospect of sex when he was looking as aroused as that made Rosa's body tremble for his touch, but pride made her shake her head with a sudden fury. 'Don't keep treating me like some mindless puppet who can't think for herself,' she said fiercely.

Her unexpected words made him halt in his tracks and he deliberately made his voice grow silky. 'But I'm just acting in your best interests. Surely you can see that it was unwise for us to be intimate outside, with the possibility that we could be seen by the paparazzi?'

'Yes, I can see that,' she said impatiently. 'But there are more diplomatic ways to tell me than by making me sound like some little tart who is seeking a crude kind of notoriety.'

There was a pause for a moment as he considered her words, his eyes travelling over her hurt and angry face before, slowly, he nodded. 'I'm sorry,' he said.

For a moment she thought she'd imagined it. She stared at him in disbelief. Had Kulal actually said *sorry*? 'You are?' she questioned cautiously.

'Of course I am.' He gave a heavy sigh. 'You've just given me what is probably the best homecoming I've ever had and all I've done is throw it back in your face.'

For a moment Rosa was too overcome to respond. Because Kulal had used an emotive word which could mean so much, especially to someone like him. Homecoming. Coming from a man whose own home life had been shattered by the death of his mother—wasn't that the greatest compliment he had ever paid her?

'It's okay,' she managed, but she was shaking with emotion all the same.

'I can be an ungrateful bastard at times,' he admitted as he stepped forward and took her in his arms. 'I guess part of me was still worried that you'd gone ahead and allowed yourself to take Bertrand's ridiculous suggestion seriously.'

Rosa stilled as the truth dawned on her. He thought she'd changed her mind. That she'd opted for the docile role of compliant wife—the role he obviously expected of her. That she was doing what he wanted her to do. She bit her lip. So what did she tell him? She could play safe by phoning Arnaud in the morning and telling him she'd changed her mind, thus guaranteeing harmony in her marriage. But at what cost? Was she going to have to subjugate everything about herself which didn't please this demanding sheikh? And for what? For him to turn around and leave her when the year was up, no matter what she did.

'You think it was a ridiculous suggestion?' she said carefully.

His lips gave the flicker of a smile. 'I'm afraid it was. I know what these people are like, Rosa. He wants to make sure that I give him permission to film in Zahrastan, which is why he chose to flatter you. People often try to target powerful men through their wives. Though if he was a little more discerning, he might have realised that his behaviour has angered me and that I dislike men fawning over you in such a way.'

For a moment Rosa was so outraged that she couldn't speak, even though his attitude was one she was used to. One she'd grown up with… He was making her sound like a racehorse, or a fancy car which another man was attempting to joyride. How dare he speak of her in such dismissive tones? She stared up at him, trying to stop her voice from trembling as she spoke. 'You think that's the only reason he showed interest in me—to get close to you?'

'Not the only reason, no. Any man with a pulse would want to get close to you in an altogether different way.'

Rosa nodded. 'So you wouldn't approve of me taking a screen test to appear on French TV?'

He gave a cynical smile. 'What do you think?'

'I think you'd better get your head around the fact that I've done exactly that.'

His eyes narrowed as she wrenched herself out of his arms. 'What are you talking about?'

'It's quite simple, Kulal. I went into the studios this afternoon and they gave me a try-out. They said I was very telegenic and so they've given me a slot.'

'They've given you a slot?' he repeated dangerously. 'On national television?'

'The very same. Only a tiny slot—it's true. But at least that means it won't be too disruptive to our lives.' She stared into the steely gleam of his black eyes. 'And next week I start presenting the weather report on the lunchtime news.'

CHAPTER ELEVEN

THE INTENSE LIGHT felt hot on her cheeks, but Rosa didn't mind. The brightness of the studio made some of the other presenters grow overheated, but not her. She was used to the glaring blaze of the Sicilian sun, so a few television lights weren't going to make her sweat! She flashed a wide smile as she finished her segment, reminding viewers to remember to pack an umbrella 'if you don't want your nice Parisian clothes to get wet!'

As always, her final comment made the crew smile, just as it would make the nation smile. In the instantly accessible world of television, Rosa had become a bit of a star, which was something she'd never envisaged.

Her rise to prominence in the national consciousness had all happened so quickly—and her popularity had been picked up by the press, during a quiet summer when there wasn't very much news. Newspaper analysts had been quick to question 'Why Rosa?' because she wasn't an obvious choice to be a pin-up. France had a recognised template for beauty, and Rosa didn't fit it. She was curvy and she didn't wear black. Her clothes were the colours of an exotic bird's plumage and she wore flowers in her hair. She should have been invisible in a place where thinness reigned supreme and women worshiped at the altar of high fashion. But people liked her. Men liked her because she was the stuff of forbidden fantasy, and their wives liked her because they didn't perceive her as a threat. French department stores had reported an increased demand for colour-blocked clothes. A glossy magazine had even urged its readers to throw away their diet books and 'channel your inner Rosa.'

Then had come the discovery that before her marriage to one of the world's most powerful men, Rosa had been a Corretti—and all hell had broken loose. Suddenly, she had become even more sought-after. The studio bosses asked her to do an extra weather slot on the highly prestigious breakfast show, but she'd said no, because who in their right mind would want to get up at three in the morning? Even farmers slept for longer than that! Requests for interviews began to pour in but she told Arnaud to refuse them all. She knew her family would go ballistic if journalists started to pry into its chequered history. And she knew that any more exposure would make Kulal even angrier than he already was....

'Just why are you doing this, Rosa?' he had demanded one morning, just before he'd stormed off to his office. 'Pursuing a useless career as a weather announcer? Telling people what they can already read on their cellphones!'

Those had been his actual words—words which had been intended to wound and which had hit their target full-on. Rosa had swallowed down the hurt she'd felt. If only he had given her a few crumbs of praise, then she might have refused the offer of the Friday teatime slot in addition to her regular lunchtime one. If he'd told her that her French accent was flawless—which was what everyone else said—or that she'd managed to make women who felt bad about their bodies feel better about themselves, then she might have cut back or even deferred her fledgling career until after the marriage had ended.

But Kulal wasn't in the business of praising. He was in the business of making her feel like she had overstepped the mark. As if she had no right to do anything with her life if it dared to interfere with his.

She arrived home late one Friday after a meeting with Arnaud, and when she rushed into the apartment Kulal was standing waiting for her. His gaze ran over her, his black eyes lingering on the rose in her hair, and she saw the almost imperceptible twist of his lips. The fresh flower had become her 'trademark' and was provided by the studio before every show, but she'd forgotten she was wearing it and it was now probably wilting.

'You're late,' he observed caustically. 'And your face is covered in make-up.'

She touched her fingertips to her cheek and they came away the deep bronze colour of the heavy studio foundation. 'I wanted to get away as quickly as possible.' She drew in a deep breath and smiled. 'To get home to you.'

'That's very considerate of you, but have you forgotten that we were supposed to have been going out tonight?'

'Out?' She looked at him blankly, and then clapped her hand over her mouth in horror. 'Cocktails at the French Embassy!' she breathed. 'Oh, Kulal—it slipped my mind completely. But it's not too late, is it? We can still go.'

'It is too late, and the sheikh is never late,' he snapped. 'It would be an unspeakable diplomatic breach!'

'I'm sorry.'

With a growing feeling of frustration, Kulal stared at her, wanting to kiss her and yet wanting to rail against her all at the same time. Did she think that this situation she had manufactured was in any way acceptable to him? That he would ever tolerate being consigned to second place in her life? 'Obviously you're having difficulty fitting me into your busy schedule, Rosa.'

'That's not fair. My work hardly impacts on your life at all. Why didn't you remind me this morning?'

'Because it is not my place to remind you!' he bit out as he found himself longing for the days when she'd always been there, waiting. When he'd needed to do nothing but open the front door before she would be nestling in his arms—a package of curvaceous warmth and eager kisses. He remembered the way they used to sit on the terrace and watch the sun going down, before the lights of the city brought it to vivid life once more. 'You think I have nothing better to do than to act as your social secretary?'

'No, Kulal,' she said tiredly. 'I don't think that.'

She went into the bathroom to shower away the heavy make-up, and when she returned she thought that his mood was better. But maybe that was because she was wearing a light summer dress which came to just above the knee. She could see the instinctive gleam of his black eyes as he pulled her into his arms and kissed her. One kiss led to another, and then another—and sex always made Kulal feel better. Actually, it usually did the same for her, but today she was left feeling strangely empty as she lay in his arms afterwards.

The weather that weekend was amazing—the sky a clear and vaulted blue and the sunshine bright and golden as it shone down on one of the world's most beautiful cities. They spent Saturday morning in one of the flea markets, followed by a stroll around the Tuileries after lunch. Most of Sunday took place in bed.

'Doesn't this feel fantastic?' murmured Kulal as he traced lazy circles all over her stomach. 'And don't you feel fantastic—all soft and sensual?'

Sensation shivered over her. Yes, it felt fantastic. It

always did. Rosa felt her heart clench, knowing that she was going to miss this when the year was up. Could she ever imagine being physically intimate with another man like this? She shuddered. Never in a million years! Could she imagine a life without Kulal full stop? A sudden darkness crept into her heart as she nestled closer to his naked body. 'Do you ever think about what's going to happen when we dissolve the marriage?' she questioned.

'There's no point,' Kulal said, but her question had destroyed the mood and he rolled away from her. He had learnt never to project—even though sometimes he saw the dark wings of the future flapping ominously on the periphery of his vision. 'We made a decision and we're sticking to it. What's to think about?'

Rosa watched as he got out of bed and headed for the door, returning a few minutes later with two glasses of white wine. She took hers and began to sip at it, but her thoughts were troubled and she couldn't seem to shake them off. She'd told herself right from the beginning that she didn't believe in love. That she wasn't looking for love—but wasn't it peculiar how sometimes love seemed to come looking for you? How it could creep up on you and wrap its velvet fingers around your heart without you realising—even when the man in question could be stubborn, demanding and autocratic? Reason seemed to have no effect on her volatile emotions and she knew why.

She had fallen in love with her sheikh husband even though that was the last thing which either of them wanted.

No further mention was made of the future which meant that by Monday morning the atmosphere between them was serene. The missed party at the embassy was long forgotten and the goodbye kiss they shared as Kulal left for the office was lingering.

'I wish you didn't have to go,' she said.

'I wish that too.'

She wriggled her body against him. 'And I promise I won't ever be late again.'

Kulal gave an odd kind of smile before brushing his lips over hers one final time. 'Let's hope not.'

Rosa went to the studios, but as the crew began to mike her up for her segment, she thought that they didn't seem as chatty as usual. And afterwards, when she went to the dressing room to wipe off her make-up, there was a knock at the door.

It was Arnaud Bertrand and she raised her eyebrows in surprise, because he didn't usually come to her dressing room.

'Have you got a minute?' he said awkwardly. 'I need to talk to you.'

'Talk away.' She smiled at him in the mirror. 'Do you mean here, or would you rather go next door and we can get some coffee?'

'No, here is fine.' He looked slightly uncomfortable, his hands digging deep into the pockets of his trousers. 'Rosa, there's no easy way to say this, but I'm afraid we're pulling your slot.'

She turned round. 'What do you mean?'

'The bosses have decided that it's no longer working.'

She gazed at him blankly. 'But…I don't understand. You told me that everyone loved the feature. You said that you hadn't had so much fan mail since Johnny Depp gave that interview.'

He didn't quite meet her eyes. 'I'm afraid it's out of my hands.'

Rosa frowned as her heart began to pound loudly in her chest. 'Something's happened, hasn't it?'

Arnaud looked even more uncomfortable. 'Nothing has happened.'

'You're not a very good liar, Arnaud.' Her eyes

narrowed. 'Has this got something to do with my husband?'

'I can't—'

'Oh, I think you can. Tell me!' she said, and then softened her voice. 'Please.'

There was a moment of silence before he gave a sigh of resignation. 'Okay, I'll tell you—but you didn't hear it from me. It does have something to do with your husband. In fact, it has everything to do with him. He's threatened to pull out of the documentary if we don't stop...' He shrugged his shoulders. '"Monopolising my wife" was how I think he phrased it.'

Rosa flinched to think that any man could be old-fashioned and chauvinistic enough to march up to a bunch of TV executives and tell them something like that. 'And you're willing to just cave in?' she questioned heatedly. 'To let this go just because you want to make some damned documentary about his country?'

Arnaud shook his head. 'It's not just the documentary!' he said. 'It's everything else. Your husband is a powerful man, Rosa—not just in Paris, but pretty much everywhere else. And you don't make enemies of men like that.'

The realisation of what Kulal had done suddenly hit her and Rosa felt sick. Her heart was pounding and her chest felt so tight that Arnaud reached out towards her in alarm.

'Mon dieu!' he exclaimed. 'But your face is like chalk! Sit down, and I will fetch you some water.'

But she shook her head. 'I don't want anything,' she said fiercely. But that wasn't quite true, was it? She wanted to regain her honour and her pride and there was only one way she was going to do that.

She flipped through her address book before going outside, ignoring Kulal's official limousine which was waiting for her just as it always was. Quickly, she darted down one of the side streets and felt a flash of triumph as she gave her bodyguard the slip, before clicking onto the map section of her phone. Her footsteps were rapid as she walked to the sixteenth *arrondissement* until she had reached the ornate nineteenth-century building which housed Kulal's foundation.

She realised that it was the first time she'd ever been inside the building and she saw the reception-ist's look of shock as she walked in.

'I'm Rosa,' she said automatically, knowing how

hot and dishevelled she must look after her dash across the city.

'You are the sheikh's wife,' breathed the receptionist, her look of shock deepening. 'And I have seen you on the television.'

'Where is he?' Rosa asked quietly. 'Where is the sheikh?'

'I'm afraid he is in a meeting, and I'll have to—'

'Where is he?' Rosa repeated, and then spotted the staircase on the opposite side of the lobby. He would be at the top of the building—of course he would—because powerful people always chose their vantage points up high, so that they could look down on the rest of the world. She ran up the stairs, two at a time, until there was nowhere left to go and she passed another receptionist who had clearly been warned that trouble was on the way. The woman shot a horrified glance in the direction of a set of double doors and that look told Rosa everything she needed to know.

She burst in through the doors to see a huge table with lots of men in suits sitting around it and they all looked up as she appeared. But only one man dominated the room with his powerful presence. A man with black eyes and dark skin and the demeanour of a desert warrior, despite the sleek outlines of his Italian suit. He was getting to his feet and all the men were looking up at him in alarm, before staring at her again.

'Rosa,' he said in a voice she'd never heard him use before. 'What an unexpected pleasure.'

'I want to talk to you.'

'Can't this wait until later?' he questioned. 'Because as you can see, I'm in the middle of a meeting which has taken some time and trouble to organise.'

'No, it can't wait!' she flared, hearing the onlookers draw in a collective shocked breath and she recognised then that people spent their lives appeasing Kulal and giving him exactly what he wanted. And how could that be good for him? 'So either you get rid of them now, or we're going to have an audience while I put to you a few very pertinent questions!'

'Gentlemen, looks like we're done here,' said Kulal, but Rosa couldn't miss the unmistakable glint of anger in his eyes.

They stood in silence while all the men filed out, and when the door had been closed, Kulal looked at her and she saw that the glint had become a quietly smouldering blaze.

'So, are you going to give me some sort of explanation for this unwarranted intrusion?'

'Are you?' she retorted.

'I'm not in the mood for riddles, Rosa!'

'Aren't you? Well then, let me spell this one out for you! Did you...' She gripped on to the back of a chair to steady herself, aware that her voice sounded all croaky. Kulal gestured towards the water jug on the table but she shook her head furiously, as if he was offering her a beaker of poison. 'Did you put a stop to my weather slot?'

There was a moment of silence.

'I want the truth, Kulal! Did you?'

He shrugged. 'I'm no television executive,' he said. 'It's not within my power to do something like that.'

'But it's certainly within your power to threaten to withdraw permission for filming to begin in Zahrastan, isn't it? And it's certainly within your power to lean heavily on investors, if that's what it takes. Is that what you did, Kulal?'

He looked at her for a long moment and then he gave a curt nod, as if he had just come to a decision. 'Yes, I did it—and you want to know why? Because I don't think it's such a heinous crime for a husband to want to see more of his wife. A wife who is only mine for a year! Why should I wish to share her with millions of viewers and the people who read those dreadful magazines?'

Rosa's throat was so tight that it felt as if it had an invisible cord clenched around it and it took a moment or two before she could respond with any degree of clarity. 'So you just stormed in and took control? You decided that because you didn't like it, that you would change it. Because even if it is only for a year, you don't really want a wife, do you, Kulal? What you want is a doll—a doll you can play with whenever you want. Someone that you can dress and undress and put to bed. Something you can walk away from in the morning, knowing exactly where your little doll has been all day, because one of your damned bodyguards has been tracking her.'

At this moment, an urgent-sounding buzzer on his desk began to go off and Kulal leaned over to press his finger on it. 'Yes…?'

Rosa recognised the frantic tones of the bodyguard who had been assigned to her that day. 'Boss, I've lost the princess.'

'Don't worry, I've found her.'

'You see!' She glared at him as he clicked off the

connection. 'You even make me sound like a doll— or a package which has inadvertently gone missing.'

'As my wife you require a security issue!' he flared. 'You cannot deny that, Rosa!'

'I'm not here to talk about my security!' she flared back. 'I'm here to talk about the fact that you heavy-handedly put an end to my burgeoning TV career and you didn't even have the courtesy to tell me!'

His mouth tightened. 'And is this television slot really so important to you?'

She shook her head as hot, infuriating tears began to spring to her eyes. 'You're missing the point,' she said. 'I left one life because people expected me to behave a certain way. I was trapped and controlled and told what to do every minute of the day. And you're doing exactly the same thing! You promised me freedom and independence and you've given me the opposite.'

'You'll get your freedom and independence when the marriage is over,' he said, his hands clenching into tight fists.

'And it'll be too late by then,' she said, and now her voice was trembling. 'Kulal, you're making this very difficult for me. You don't want a wife with a career, but neither do you want a wife who you'll let close enough to love you. Can't you see that I'm between a rock and a hard place here?'

His eyes flicked over her and he steeled himself against the tears which were sparking so brightly in her eyes. He remembered the night of their honeymoon when she'd sobbed against his bare chest as she'd told him about her mother's betrayal and a shiver of something dark and empathetic had whispered over his skin. But the intensity of those feelings had made him feel raw and vulnerable—and hadn't he vowed that he would never allow himself to feel that way again? He drew a deep breath as he stared at the flyaway mess of her dark hair and the flushed sheen of her face. 'Can we discuss this later?' he said. 'When you've calmed down a little, and maybe had a chance to brush your hair?'

Rosa almost choked with frustration, until she realised that maybe this was exactly what she needed—to hear him utter the truth in all its stark brutality. Get out of his life, she told herself. Get out now while you still can—before he sees just how much he has hurt you. She sucked in a deep breath. 'I'd like that drink now, if you don't mind.'

He poured her a glass of water. 'I can ring for some ice, if you like.'

'No, thanks.' Her smile was wan as she gulped down the tepid liquid. 'Tell me, Kulal, do you always get exactly what it is you want?'

Her words took him back. He thought about what they used to say about him in Zahrastan. *What Kulal wants, Kulal gets.* But not always. Not the one time when it really mattered, when his heart had been shattered into a thousand little pieces—and he was damned if he was going to risk that happening again. 'You're talking in riddles again,' he said.

'Am I? Yet you're a highly intelligent man. I'm sure you can understand exactly what I'm talking about, if only you'd let yourself. But there's no need to look so worried. The discussion's over and I'm going now.'

'And we'll talk about it some more tonight.'

'Of course we will.' The lie came easily to her lips, just as it had come to his. Because Kulal had no intention of talking about this any more. She knew that. The decision had been made—his decision—and he would just expect her to get used to it. To go along with it, like a good little girl. She could imagine the scene which would enfold tonight. The hungry kiss, heightened by all the tension, and then a session of lovemaking powerful enough to push any nagging doubts from her mind. Well, not any more. Because Rosa Corretti was through with being manipulated. She was going to start taking control of her life, as of now.

She looked up at him, but it felt as if her face might split in two with the effort it took to smile. 'I'll see you later.'

CHAPTER TWELVE

KULAL SHOULD HAVE felt better after Rosa had gone, leaving him alone in his vast office. He told himself that she needed to understand that they'd made a deal and that he wasn't prepared for her to start reneging on it. He hadn't signed up for someone who wouldn't be there when he needed her. Until he reminded himself fiercely that he didn't actually need anybody—because need was dangerous. It made you dependent and it made you weak.

He pulled a pile of papers towards him and started to read them, but the afternoon passed by much too slowly. He knew that he could have left the office any time he pleased, since he didn't have any more meetings planned, and even if he did, he could always cancel them. But he didn't go home. Why should he go home early to a woman who didn't appreciate him?

What Kulal wanted, Kulal got.

The words stayed irritatingly in his head, like an advertising jingle which wouldn't go away, and his temple was throbbing by the time he took the elevator up to the apartment. As the doors slid open he wondered what was the best way to handle what had happened earlier. He could quietly take Rosa aside and tell her that he wouldn't tolerate a repeat of such a hysterical scene but mightn't that make her stubborn? Mightn't the argument then continue into the evening, when he had plenty of other things he'd rather be doing with her than arguing?

And he had made his point, hadn't he? He had won. There would be no more missed cocktail parties, nor would they be disturbed by any phone calls from the infernal Bertrand. There would be no more business colleagues telling him that their wives had seen a picture of his wife in a magazine.

The apartment was strangely silent—there wasn't even any music playing—and Kulal walked through to the drawing room to see if Rosa was out on the terrace. But the French windows were closed and there was no sign of her with a forgiving smile on her beautiful lips as she sashayed towards him in one of her vibrant dresses.

'Rosa?' The word echoed around the vast rooms like something shouted into a tunnel. 'Rosa!' he called once more, but there was no reply.

He told himself that she must have just gone out for a while. But she didn't do that, did she—because where would she go? The galleries were shut for the day and there was no need for her to perform the multiple tasks which fell to other, less exalted women. She didn't need to shop or to cook or to clean. She was a princess and that was why she needed to behave like a princess!

A faint frown creased his brow as he remembered the frustration on her face when she'd confronted him today. The anger spitting green and golden sparks from her dark eyes. He remembered the messy spill of her hair and her shiny face—a look which was worlds apart from the usual sleek grooming of his former lovers. He thought about the wilted rose tucked behind her ear, and a wave of lust so strong washed over him that for a moment he just stood very still and closed his eyes.

He was just about to phone her, when he walked past the dining room and saw the cream-coloured envelope which was lying on the oak table and his heart missed a beat. He stared at it for a moment, and when he walked over and picked it up, he noticed almost impartially that his fingers weren't quite steady.

It was the first thing she'd ever written to him and, judging by the tone, she intended it to be her last.

'Kulal,' it read. Not 'dear' Kulal or 'darling' Kulal—or any of the other sweet things she had sometimes whispered to him when he was deep inside her body—but just his name, stark and emotionless, just like the words which followed.

I imagine you'll be pleased to discover that I've gone, especially after that rather unfortunate scene at your office today. I'm sorry if I embarrassed you in front of your colleagues, but please be assured that it won't ever happen again, because I'm leaving and I think you'll agree that's best.

Since I won't be honouring our marriage

contract, you can tear up the pre-nup. All I'm taking are my wedding and engagement rings, which you told me were mine to keep. I'll probably sell them and set myself up with somewhere to rent, before I look for a job. And one day—who knows?—I may be able to pay you back for them, in full.

Thank you for all that you have taught me, which turns out to have been a lot more than just about sex.

I hope you can find it in yourself to be happy and I wish you nothing but good things.

Yours ever,

Rosa.

'No!' He felt a dry and tearing pain as he crumpled the piece of paper tightly in his hand and it fell in a ball and bounced soundlessly on the table while Kulal dug his phone from his pocket.

He punched out her number, unsurprised when it went straight to voicemail and a curiously flat-sounding Rosa said that she would return the call as quickly as possible. Which was clearly not going to happen. He left two messages before letting out another howl of rage, tempted to hurl the damned phone against the wall. And he remembered Rosa telling him she'd done just that when she'd run from Sicily, when she'd wanted to cut off all communication with her family. And now she was running from him. He had gone from his privileged position as her husband and her lover to being cast out in the cold. And he had no one to blame but himself. He had convinced himself that he was fearless and strong and yet he had been so scared of dealing with his emotions that he had built a wall around them. He had allowed a tragedy in his past to blight any possibility of a future and he had pushed away the woman he loved.

A wave of pain hit him. A pain so intense that it felt like an iron fist clenching its way around his heart. Where was she?

He dialled his chief bodyguard. 'I want you to find someone for me,' he clipped out.

'Anyone you like, boss. Who is it?'

There was a pause as, for one brief moment, Kulal confronted his own fierce pride and knew that he was going to have to let it go. Who cared if his bodyguards discovered that his wife had left him?

Who cared about anything other than getting Rosa back again?

'My wife.'

'The princess has gone?' questioned the bodyguard in surprise.

'Yes, the princess has gone!' snapped Kulal. 'Because your people weren't doing their job properly. They let her leave the studios unguarded and now she's managed to give everyone the slip. And if you value your future you'll find out where she is by sunset tomorrow.'

They did better than that—they had located Rosa by the following afternoon and Kulal was astonished to discover that she'd flown back to Sicily.

Sicily?

She'd told him she'd never go back there! She'd told him that no way was she going to get involved with her dysfunctional family ever again.

'Is she staying with her family?'

'No, boss. She's all alone in a beach house on the eastern side of the island.'

Kulal nodded. 'Prepare the plane,' he said grimly.

It occurred to him when his jet touched down several hours later that her powerful family might have attempted to try to stop him from entering the country, but he was wrong. It also occurred to him that maybe he should have waited until the next morning to see her, for the sun was already beginning to sink in the sky as his waiting car drove away from the airfield. But for the first time in his life he couldn't bear the thought of waiting—no matter how much bigger a psychological advantage that would be.

Eventually, the car bumped to a halt and the driver pointed to a solitary beach house in the distance, barely visible through all the trees and shrubbery. It was in part of a nature reserve and the area was impassable to all cars. Kulal found himself thinking that the gleaming limousine wouldn't have stood a chance of negotiating that narrow path. He told his driver to go and he told the car containing the accompanying bodyguards to follow, waving aside their protests with a flat and implacable movement of his hand.

'I don't want anyone else here,' he said fiercely. 'Now go.'

'But, boss—'

'Go!'

He stood and watched the powerful vehicles roar

away to make sure they obeyed him. Large clouds of dust puffed around their gleaming paintwork as the two cars became little black dots in the distance. And suddenly, he felt an unexpected wave of liberation. It was, he realised, a long time since he'd gone anywhere without being shadowed by one of the guards who had been part of his life for as long as he could remember.

For the first time, he allowed himself to look properly at his surroundings, taking in a deep breath of the scented air. It smelt of lemon and pine and he could hear the massed choir of the cicadas echoing over the hills. The baked vegetation was surprisingly green—with flowers dotted here and there—and in the distance he could see the deep cobalt of the sea. He stared down at his feet and some instinct made him slip off his loafers and carry them.

The warm sand was gritty between his toes and as he walked along the narrow path he felt that sense of freedom again. Was that because for the first time in his life he was following his heart? Because in this moment he was no longer a royal prince and sheikh, but simply a man who had come to make amends with his woman.

The beach house which lay ahead of him was modest, just a one-storey building with a wide, wooden veranda looking out to sea. The beauty lay in its position—the matchless view and the solitude—and suddenly Kulal wondered what he was going to do if Rosa wasn't there. How would she react if she came back later to find him waiting for her? Would she turn the might of the Corretti family against an estranged husband she could rightly accuse of stalking her?

He didn't care. Let the Correttis come. Let them all come. He wasn't going anywhere until he'd looked into Rosa's eyes and told her what she needed to hear.

He moved silently, for at heart he was a child of the desert, taught how to blend into whichever landscape he inhabited. He thought fleetingly that Sicily was as beautiful as everything he'd ever heard about it, and that he'd like the chance to explore it further. And then he saw her and his footsteps halted, so that he stood perfectly still.

Sitting at the far end of the veranda, her legs dangling over the side, she was shaded by an umbrella pine tree but was wearing a sun hat as an extra precaution. The hat looked new and was made of straw—its crown festooned with a bright mass of orange and pink silk flowers, which matched her sundress. He could feel a lump forming in his throat as he watched her staring intently out at the sea. He wanted to stand there all day watching her but he thought that she might turn around and be startled. More than startled.

'Rosa,' he said softly.

For a moment Rosa didn't move, telling herself it was like one of those fantasies which schoolgirls sometimes concocted. The ones where the object of their affections would suddenly be spirited in front of them, no matter how unlikely that scenario would be.

'Rosa,' said the voice again.

Her fingernails dug into her thighs. Bad enough that she should be without him—but did she also have to suffer auditory hallucinations which were designed to torment her?

Slowly, she turned her head and her breath froze in her throat. She could hear the loud thunder of her heart as he held up the palms of his hands, like someone in an old cowboy film, admitting surrender.

'I didn't mean to startle you,' he said.

'Well, you did.' She tried not to feast her eyes on him, but it was impossible. How could you not look at him and keep on looking, when he seemed like a dark and sculpted god who had just been planted in the Sicilian landscape? He was wearing pale linen trousers and a pale silk shirt—the sleeves rolled up to reveal his dark, hair-roughened arms. From this distance she couldn't really see his expression, but as he grew nearer she noticed that his feet were bare. Kulal walking in public in bare feet? She looked over his shoulder to the landscape behind. And where were his bodyguards?

It didn't matter. None of those questions were relevant because he was no longer part of her life. She'd escaped from him and his controlling ways. Nothing had changed. Only the externals. She had left him and his home in Paris and she was starting a new life for herself. It wasn't going to be easy because she still wanted him, but she was going to do it. She needed to do it.

He was closer now. He was stepping down onto the veranda so that she could see the dark gleam of his eyes and she knew she ought to tell him to just go away and leave her alone, but in that moment she discovered that her sense of curiosity was stronger than her sense of self-preservation.

'What are you doing here?' she questioned, trying to inject just the right note of careless sarcasm into her voice. 'No, don't tell me—you've come to try to bring your little doll back to Paris. Is it time to brush her hair and put her back into her shiny box?'

Kulal stood looking down at her, reading the hurt and anger on her upturned face as he thought of all the inducements he could use to get her to return to Paris with him. He thought of all the things he could say to try to persuade her. Things she probably wouldn't believe—and who could blame her? And he didn't know where to begin, because this was all new to him. He clenched his fists as all his buttoned-up feelings demanded to be set free, but habit made him want to resist. Damn it, why shouldn't he resist? There was a reason why he had put all his emotions into cold storage and it was a good reason. If you didn't allow yourself to feel things, then you couldn't get hurt.

But suddenly, it was no longer working. Whatever had protected him in the past was failing to protect him now for the pain in his heart was very real and very raw. He moved across the terrace and sat down beside her and he saw her body tense. For a moment there was silence.

'I miss you,' he said.

She shook her head. 'No, you don't. You just think you do. It's because I was the one who walked away and your pride is hurt. You'll get over it.'

'No, I won't get over it,' he said. 'I don't think I could, even if I wanted to. And I don't. I just want you back in my life because I love you, Rosa.' The words left his mouth in a breathless rush, but his voice was shaking with emotion as he finished his quiet declaration. 'I love you in a way I never thought I could love anyone, and that's the truth.'

Rosa could feel a horrible lump forming in her throat and the betraying flavour of salt in her mouth but she wasn't going to cry. Damn him—she wasn't going to cry. And she wasn't going to listen to his empty words either. He might have all the real power—the social and the economic power which came with his royal title—but she had power too. She had the power to live her life as she wanted to.

Without pain and without heartbreak. She shook her head. 'It's too late, Kulal.'

'No!' In the growing darkness his word was fervent as it rang out on the still, Sicilian air. 'Don't tell me that we don't all deserve a second chance when we screw up so spectacularly. And I recognise that I've behaved like a fool. You said in my office that you wanted to love me but that I wouldn't let you close enough. But I'm letting you close now. Are you telling me that your feelings for me have changed, Rosa? That twenty-four hours have altered the situation so radically?'

She tried not to be affected by the look of raw pain on his face as he spoke, but it was the hardest thing she'd ever had to do. Because of course she hadn't stopped loving him. Love wasn't something you could just turn on and off, like a tap. She wanted to take him into her arms and cradle him. She wanted to lose her heartache in the sweetness of his kiss—but what good would that do? This is short-term pain for long-term gain, she told herself fiercely. He just needs to win at everything and that's why he wants you back.

'I'm not the kind of woman you need, Kulal,' she

said quietly. 'You need someone you can dominate. Someone who will do exactly what you want her to do. Some women might call that being masterful but I call it being a control freak and I'm afraid that I can't live like that. Not any more.'

His body tensed. 'You can have your TV slot back!'

'No!' Frustratedly, she shook her hands in the air. 'You don't understand! This is nothing to do with my TV slot.'

'But isn't that what drove you away?'

She stared at him. 'That was the final straw, yes. But what really drove me away was the fundamental inequality of our relationship. I don't want to live with someone who won't let me do something—so that only when I push and push will he change his mind and give me his permission. I'm a grown-up, Kulal. I don't need anyone's permission to live my life. Not yours, nor my family's. I've had that for too many years and I don't want it any more.'

He saw the sudden fierceness on her face. 'Why did you come back to Sicily?' he questioned suddenly. 'When you told me you would never return.'

There was silence for a moment as Rosa mulled

over his question. 'Because I thought about something you said and realised that you were right. That I had no right to try to fix you, when my own life was so unresolved,' she said. 'I knew I needed to speak to my brothers and to my mother. Especially my mother. I needed to hear her side of the story. I needed to hear what made her betray my dad with his own brother, but then I had to let it go. Because it's her life, not mine.'

'And what did she say?'

'I'm meeting her for coffee tomorrow morning.' She nearly said, 'I'll let you know,' until she realised that she wouldn't, because tomorrow he would be gone from here. She wanted him gone from here. She needed him gone from here.

He saw the new strain on her face and his heart twisted. 'I'm sorry for what you've been through with your family, Rosa—'

'Yes, I know that,' she put in, hating the betraying little crack which seemed to have crept into her voice. 'And that was one of the things I first loved about you—that you defied all my expectations. That once you'd got over the shock of my parentage, you supported me. And I was so grateful to you for that, Kulal. I thought you would judge me negatively, but you didn't. And then, when you opened up to me on the night of our wedding, I felt something like hope about the future. It felt as if two people who had been damaged could find comfort and solace in each other. But then you clammed up—and even though there were moments when I felt as if a real passion and friendship was there, it was as if you wanted to keep it locked away from me.'

'And I did,' he said slowly, her words unlocking a conundrum he'd never really understood until now. He stared at her. 'I guess I was terrified of getting too close to anyone. It felt like too much of a risk. Can you understand that, Rosa?'

She nodded as she heard the flicker of uncertainty in his voice and suddenly her man of steel seemed soft and vulnerable and she couldn't seem to stop her heart from reaching out to him. 'Of course I can understand,' she said. 'Your mother was torn away from you in a way which left you heartbroken. Worse still was that you blamed yourself. You still do.'

'You know why I blame myself,' he said quietly. 'You know what happened that day.'

'But you're not even sure about the facts, are you?' she whispered. 'You've refused to look at the post-mortem report or speak to the doctors.' She saw him flinch but she knew she had to carry on. Because even though Kulal was no longer a small boy locked in a nightmare of guilt and loss, he was a man still suffering as a consequence of that day, and he would continue to suffer unless he confronted it. 'I think you should go back to Zahrastan and find out the truth. You told me that your mother was suffering from headaches prior to the picnic. Well, maybe the fall was a result of that. Maybe she would have died anyway—or maybe she wouldn't. You have to know, Kulal. You can't keep living your life burdened by guilt and neither can you keep avoiding risk, just because it's safer that way. You have to learn to take a chance—on me, yes, but more importantly, on yourself.'

He swallowed, struggling to cope with the new and very powerful feelings which were beginning to emerge. And he wondered if it really was too late. 'I'll go,' he said. 'And I'll face whatever truth awaits me there—but before I do, there's something you need to know. Something I never told you before, but which I should have done.' There was a pause as he looked down at the soft parting of her lips. 'That the first time I saw you, you spoke to something in my heart. I looked across that crowded nightclub, little realising that I was about to meet a woman who would change just about everything.'

'Kulal—'

'And that is why I am asking you—with all the earnestness at my command—can we please try again? Because I love you, Rosa, and I want to be a real husband to you—in every sense of the word.'

She was swallowing frantically but it was no good, because the tears which had begun welling up in her eyes had begun to trickle down her cheeks. And she saw from the sudden darkening of his features that he was in danger of misinterpreting those tears and that's when she stopped fighting her own feelings. She gave in to what she'd been wanting to do all along and flung her arms around his neck, her face wet as she pressed her lips to his.

'Yes,' she said, whispering the words directly into his mouth. 'Yes in every language that I speak—and in yours too, which I have yet to learn. Yes, because I love you too—even though I tried to tell myself that I was crazy to love you. But I couldn't stop my-self, no matter how hard I tried. And I want to spend the rest of my life loving you back, but only if you promise never to lock me out of your heart again.'

'I promise,' he said fiercely. 'Now will you please just kiss me properly before I go out of my mind?'

Her lips were pressing hard against his almost before he'd finished the sentence but the kiss felt different. It felt like a statement—and a seal. It felt almost life-changing. And maybe it was. She smiled as if she'd suddenly understood the world's best-kept secret as Kulal stood up and lifted her into his arms, before carrying her into the small, wooden house.

Because didn't everyone always say that true love had the power to transform?

EPILOGUE

THE AL-DIMASHQI PALACE shone in the late-afternoon light, rising up from the stark landscape like a beautiful fairy-tale castle in the distance and Rosa peered out of the car window with a fast-growing feeling of excitement. She had been longing to visit the desert kingdom of Zahrastan and now the moment was here at last. She could see turrets and domes and the tantalising glimmer of water in among the rose gardens and she gave a little sigh of anticipation.

Kulal squeezed her hand. 'Nervous?' he questioned.

'A bit.' She turned to look at him. 'I'm terrified your brother won't like me.'

'What's not to like?' His eyes were soft as he studied her. 'You are the woman who has tamed the tear-away sheikh. The proud Sicilian beauty my people are longing to meet.' He lifted her hand to his lips and kissed it. 'And the woman who has captured my heart so completely.'

'Well, when you put it like that.' She brushed her fingertips over his mouth, but her next words were hesitant. 'And how do you feel about coming back, Kulal? I mean, really.'

Kulal was quiet for a moment while he considered her question. This was his second trip to Zahrastan in as many months. The first time he had come alone and it had been a trip of necessity, not of pleasure. He had gone to the hospital in the capital, where his mother had been taken following her fall. Assiduously, he had forced himself to read through all the records and then had spoken to the medical director, who'd been a very junior doctor at the time.

Vividly, Kulal remembered flying back to Paris. He remembered the hopeful expression on Rosa's face and the way it had become wary when he told her that the tests had proved inconclusive. That he still didn't know whether his mother's death had been caused by the fall or by some pre-existing condition. But that it was okay. He'd told her that too. It was all okay. The past had happened and there was nothing he could do to change it. All he had was the present—the glorious present, with his loving wife, who had taught him so much, by his side.

'I feel joy,' he said simply. 'And gratitude. That in finding you, I could find myself and learn to live in a way I never thought possible. And I'm looking forward to the celebrations.'

'Me too,' she said. 'Though I've had my reservations about the guest list.'

'Well, don't. I utterly forbid it. And I don't know why you're giggling like that, Rosa—because I do!'

He tightened his hand around hers. They were here in Zahrastan because the king wanted to throw a big party for his brother and his Sicilian bride. Kulal's former fiancée, Ayesha, would be there, with the Tuscan nobleman she had surprised everyone by marrying after Kulal had 'freed' her from their engagement. His lips curved. How life could constantly surprise! Rosa's family had also been invited and most of them were coming. There would doubtless be friction, though hopefully the august surroundings of the Al-Dimashqi palace might inject a little calm into the sometimes overexuberant nature of the Corretti clan.

And if it didn't? If there were noisy scenes and

tears, and make-ups and break-ups? So what. What would be, would be. Kulal had learnt that there was much in life he couldn't control. He'd learnt that taking a risk was sometimes as necessary to life as breathing itself. He touched his hand to the gleaming crown of his wife's dark hair and smiled as he bent to kiss her.

And he'd learnt that love was the most necessary thing of all.

* * * * *

*Read on for an exclusive interview
with Sharon Kendrick!*

BEHIND THE SCENES OF
SICILY'S CORRETTI DYNASTY
with Sharon Kendrick

It's such a huge world to create—an entire Sicilian dynasty. Did you discuss parts of it with the other writers?

My story (which features an unbelievably sexy sheikh!) takes place mainly in Paris and the South of France, so my hero and heroine don't spend much time in Sicily. However, before my story starts, Rosa (my heroine) has a row with Lia (Lynn Raye Harris's heroine) and we discussed exactly what was said during this altercation.

How does being part of the continuity differ from when you are writing your own stories?

It's pretty fabulous to have a plot handed to you on a golden platter!

What was the biggest challenge? And what did you most enjoy about it?

My biggest challenge was making my hero able to

respect a woman who started out by behaving like a bit of a tramp!

As you wrote your hero and heroine was there anything about them that surprised you?

I was surprised at how dark Kulal became once he'd married Rosa—even though the marriage was never meant to be anything but temporary.

What was your favourite part of creating the world of Sicily's most famous dynasty?

I liked Rosa's battle for independence and Kulal's courage in facing up to his demons.

If you could have given your heroine one piece of advice before the opening pages of the book, what would it be?

He's nothing but trouble!

What was your hero's biggest secret?

I don't think I can tell you Kulal's big secret, because it might spoil your enjoyment of the book.

What does your hero love most about your heroine?

He loves her spirit and her self-belief (which grows out of adversity).

What does your heroine love most about your hero?

sighs How long have you got? He's powerful, successful and super-confident, plus he also has a (deserved) reputation as a ladies' man. But Rosa can see through all the layers to the complex man beneath and it is that man she falls in love with.

Which of the Correttis would you most like to meet and why?

I'd like to meet all of Rosa's immediate and extended family because something tells me that it would be one hell of a party!

'Congratulations, Lia,' he said, his voice chilling her. 'You've won the jackpot after all.

'You're about to become a Scott.'

'This is not how I wanted this to happen,' she said, on a throat-aching whisper. Tears pressed the backs of her eyes. She couldn't let them fall.

'You came here,' he said, his voice hard. 'What did you expect? Did you think I would be happy?'

She dropped her gaze. A single tear spilled free and she dashed it away, determined not to cry in front of him. Not to be weak.

'I had hoped you might be, yes.' She lifted her chin and sucked back her tears. 'Clearly, I was mistaken.'

'We'll marry,' he said. 'Because we must. But it's an arrangement, do you understand? We'll do it for as long as necessary to protect our families and then we'll end it when the time comes.'

A Façade to Shatter

LYNN RAYE HARRIS

First published in Great Britain 2013
Mills & Boon, an imprint of Harlequin (UK) Limited,
Eton House, 18-24 Paradise Road, Richmond, Surrey TW9 1SR

THE CORRETTIS: SECRETS
© Harlequin Enterprises II B.V./S.à.r.l. 2013

A Façade to Shatter © Harlequin Books S.A. 2013

Special thanks and acknowledgement are given to Lynn Raye Harris for her contribution to Sicily's Corretti Dynasty series

ISBN: 978 0 263 90619 6

53-0713

Harlequin (UK) policy is to use papers that are natural, renewable and recyclable products and made from wood grown in sustainable forests. The logging and manufacturing processes conform to the legal environmental regulations of the country of origin.

Printed and bound
by CPI Group (UK) Ltd, Croydon, CR0 4YY

Lynn Raye Harris read her first Mills & Boon® romance when her grandmother carted home a box from a yard sale. She didn't know she wanted to be a writer then, but she definitely knew she wanted to marry a sheikh or a prince and live the glamorous life she read about in the pages. Instead, she married a military man and moved around the world. These days she makes her home in North Alabama, with her handsome husband and two crazy cats. Writing for Mills & Boon is a dream come true. You can visit her at www.lynnrayeharris.com

For all those who serve in the armed forces,
thank you for your service.

CHAPTER ONE

ZACH SCOTT DIDN'T do parties. Not anymore.

Once, he'd been the life of the party. But everything
had changed a little over a year ago. Zach shoved his
hands into his tuxedo trouser pockets and frowned.
He'd thought coming to Sicily with a friend, in order
to attend a wedding, would be an easy thing to do.
There'd been no wedding, it had turned out, but the
reception was taking place anyway. And he stood on
the edge of the ballroom, wondering where Taylor
Carmichael had got to. Wondering if he could slip
away and text his regrets to her.

His head was pounding after a rough night. He'd
been dreaming again. Dreaming of guns and explo-
sions and planes plummeting from the sky.

There was nothing like a fight for survival to rear-
range a man's priorities. Since his plane had been shot
down in enemy territory, the kinds of things he'd once

done—fund-raisers, public appearances, speeches, political dinners—were now a kind of torture he'd prefer to live without.

Except it was more impossible to get out of those things now than ever before. Not only was he Zachariah James Scott IV, son of an eminent United States senator and heir to a pharmaceuticals fortune, he was also a returning military hero.

Zach's frown deepened.

Since his rescue—in which every single marine sent to extract him had perished—he'd been in demand as a sort of all-American poster boy. The media couldn't get enough of him, and he knew a big part of that was his father's continual use of his story in his public appearances.

Zachariah J. Scott III wasn't about to let the story die. Not when it could do him a world of political good.

His son had done his duty when he could have chosen an easier path. *His* son had chosen to serve his country instead of himself. It was true that Zach could have sat on the Scott Pharmaceuticals board and moved mountains of money instead of flying jets into a war zone. But the jets were a part of him.

Or had been a part of him until the crash had left him with crushing, unpredictable headaches that made it too dangerous to fly.

Yes, everyone loved that he'd bravely gone to war and survived.

Except he didn't feel brave, and he damn sure didn't feel like he'd done anything extraordinary. He didn't want the attention, didn't deserve the accolades. He'd failed pretty spectacularly, in his opinion.

But he couldn't make them stop. So he stood stiffly and smiled for the cameras like a dutiful military man should, and he felt dead inside. And the deader he felt, the more interested the media seemed to get.

It wasn't all bad, though. He'd taken over the stewardship of the Scott Foundation, his family's charitable arm, and he worked tirelessly to promote military veterans' causes. They often came back with so little, and with their lives shattered. The government tried to take care of them, but it was a huge job—and sometimes they fell through the cracks.

It was Zach's goal to save as many of them as he could. He owed it to them, by God.

He made a visual sweep of the room. At least the media attention wasn't directed at him right now. The Sicilian media was far more interested in the fact the bride had jilted the groom at the altar. Zach was of no interest whatsoever to this crowd. That, at least, was a bonus.

It wasn't often he could move anonymously through a gathering like this one.

Still, he was on edge, as if he were being followed. He prowled the edges of the crowd in the darkened ballroom, his headache barely under control as he searched for Taylor. She wasn't answering his texts, and he was growing concerned. She'd been so worried about this trip, about her return to acting, and about the director's opinion of her.

But Taylor was tough, and he knew she would have gone into the press event with her head held high. She wanted this film badly, wanted the money and respectability for the veterans' clinic back in Washington, D.C., where she'd spent so much time working to help others. He thought of the soldiers, sailors, airmen and marines—most suffering the debilitating effects of posttraumatic stress—the clinic helped, thought of the constant need for funding, and knew that Taylor would have entered that room determined to succeed.

What he didn't know was how it had turned out.

He stepped into a quiet corner—if there was such a thing—and reached into his breast pocket for his phone. A small medal hanging from a ribbon came out with it, and he blinked as he realized what it was. The Distinguished Flying Cross he'd been awarded after returning from the high Afghan desert. Taylor must have put it in there when she'd picked up the tux from the cleaners for him. He fingered the starburst, squeezed it in his palm before putting it back into his pocket.

He hadn't wanted the medal, but he hadn't had a choice. There were other medals, too, which his father never failed to mention in his speeches, but Zach just wanted to forget them all.

Taylor insisted he had to realize he deserved them. She meant well, damn her, but she drove him crazier than any sister ever could have.

He dialed Taylor's number impatiently. No answer. Frustration hammered into him. He wanted to know she was all right, and he wanted to escape this room. The crowd was swelling—never let it be said that Sicilians let a chance to party go to waste—and the noise level was growing louder.

He was in no mood.

He turned toward the exit just as the DJ blared the first track and the crowd cheered. The lights went completely out and strobe lights flashed. Zach's heart began to thud painfully. Against his will, he shrank into the wall, breathing hard.

It's just a party, just a party. But the flashes didn't stop, people started to shout, and he couldn't fight the panic dragging him down any longer.

No, no, no...

Suddenly he was back in the trench, in the pitch of night, the bursts of gunfire and explosives all around him, the thrumming of their bass boom ricocheting into his breastbone, making his body ache with the pressure. He closed his eyes, swallowed hard, his throat full of sand and dust and grit.

Violence and frustration bloomed inside his gut. He wanted to fight, wanted to surge upright and grab a gun, wanted to help the marines hold off the enemy. But they'd drugged him, because he'd broken his leg, and he couldn't move.

He lay helpless, his eyes squeezed tight—and then he felt a soft hand on his arm. The hand moved along his upper arm, ghosted over his cheek. The touch of skin on skin broke his paralysis.

He reacted with the instincts of a warrior, grabbing the hand and twisting it until the owner cried out. The cry was soft, feminine, not at all that of a terrorist bent on destroying him. Vaguely, he realized the body pressed against his was not rough. It was clad in something satiny that slid against the fabric of his own clothing.

He forced his eyes open after long moments. The lights still flashed, and his heart still pumped adrenaline into his body. He blinked and shook his head. Was he not in the desert? Was he not the last one alive in the trench?

The sounds began to separate themselves until he could pick out music, laughter and loud conversation.

He focused on the elegant paneled wall in front of him—and realized he held a woman against it, her hand high up behind her back. He could hear her panting softly.

"Please," she said, her voice calmer than he expected it to be. "I don't think I am who you think I am."

Who he thought she was? Zach blinked. Who did he think she was?

A terrorist. Someone bent on killing him.

But she wasn't, was she? He was in Sicily, at the infamous Corretti wedding, and this woman was a guest. Her blue-green eyes were set in a pretty face. Dark hair was piled on top of her head, and her breasts strained against the fabric of her gown, threatening to pop free at any moment. He hadn't spun her around, but instead held her against the wall with his body practically wrapped around hers.

One hand held hers behind her back, nearly between her shoulder blades, while the other gripped her jaw and forced her head back against the paneling. Her soft curves melded against him, filling all the hard angles of his body in ways he hadn't experienced in a very long time.

He'd had no room for softness in his life since returning from the war. He'd viewed it as something of a regret, but a necessary one. Now, he found that he was starving for the contact. His body began to stir, the telltale thrum of blood in his groin taking him by surprise.

Zach let the woman go as if she'd burned him and took a hasty step backward. What the hell was wrong with him? This was why he didn't like public appearances anymore—what if he lost his mind the way he just had? What would the media say then?

Son of a bitch.

"Forgive me," he said tightly.

"Are you all right?" she asked.

It was such a normal question, in response to an abnormal situation, and yet he couldn't formulate an answer. He simply wanted to escape. For once, instead of standing stoically and enduring whatever was flung at him, he wanted out.

There was no one here to stop him, no reporters or cameras, no duty pressing him to remain where he was and endure.

He turned blindly, seeking an exit. Somehow, he found a door and burst through it, into the cool and quiet hallway. Behind him, he heard movement. He didn't know why he turned, but he did.

She was there, watching him. Her hair was dark red and her dress a shocking shade of pink that looked as if it was about to split across her generous breasts.

"Are you all right?" she asked again.

"Fine," he replied in crisp Italian. "I apologize. You startled me."

She came forward then, hesitantly, her hands clasped together in front of her. She was lovely, he decided, in spite of the horrible dress. Her shape was imprinted on his mind, her curves still burning into his body. His hands itched to explore her, but he kept them clenched into fists at his sides. He used to take whatever women offered him, as often as they offered it, but that man had ceased to exist in the months after he'd returned from the war.

At first, he'd indulged in sex because he'd thought it would help him forget. It hadn't. It had only sharpened the contrast between life and death, only made him feel worse instead of better.

Now, denying himself was a matter of routine. Not to mention safer for all involved. His dreams were too unpredictable to sleep with a woman at his side.

Worse, they seemed to be sliding into his waking life if what had just happened was any indication.

The woman was still looking at him. Blue-green eyes fringed in dark lashes blinked up at him as a line formed on her forehead. "You really don't look well."

He glanced down at her hands, at the way she rubbed the thumb of one hand into her wrist. He'd hurt her, and it sickened him. What kind of man had he become? He was coming unglued inside, and no one could help him.

"I'm fine," he clipped out. "I'm sorry I hurt you."

Her eyes dropped. "You didn't really. You just surprised me."

"You're lying," he said, and her head snapped up, her eyes searching his. Something in those eyes called to him, but he shut it off and backed away.

"You don't know that," she replied, her chin lifting. "You don't know me."

He almost believed her. But her lip trembled, ruining her brave façade, and Zach loathed himself. "You should go," he said. "Walk away. It's safer."

She blinked. "Safer? Are you so dangerous, then?"

He swallowed. "Perhaps."

Her gaze was steady. Penetrating. "I'm not afraid," she said softly. "And I don't think you're dangerous to anyone but yourself."

Her words hit him like a punch to the gut. No one had ever said that to him before. The truth of it was sharper than any blade.

More frightening.

Anger and despair flowed over him in waves. He wanted to be normal again, wanted to be what he'd once been. But he couldn't seem to dig out of the morass, and he hated himself for it. He simply didn't know what normal was anymore.

"I'm sorry," he said again, because there was nothing else he could say. And then he turned and strode away.

Lia Corretti sucked in a disappointed breath as she watched the tall, dark American striding down the hall away from her. Something fell from his hand and bounced on the plush carpet. Lia hurried forward, calling to him.

He did not turn back. She stooped to pick up the small object on the floor. It was some kind of military medal suspended from a red, white and blue ribbon. She clutched it in her hand and looked down the long corridor at his retreating back. He walked so precisely, so stiffly, with the bearing of a soldier.

Of course he did.

She looked at the medal again. He'd dropped it on purpose. She did not doubt that. She'd seen his fingers open, seen the shiny object tumble to the floor, but he hadn't stopped to retrieve it.

Why?

Her wrist still smarted where he'd twisted it behind her back. She didn't think he'd been aware of what he'd been doing. He'd seemed...distant, as if he were somewhere else. It's what had made her go to him, what had made her touch him and ask if he was all right. He'd been plastered against that wall, his eyes squeezed tight shut, and she'd thought he'd been ill.

Lia closed her fingers around the medal. It was warm from his skin, and her heart skipped. She could still see the raw look on his face when he'd realized what he was doing to her.

She knew that look. It was one of self-loathing, one of relief and one of confusion all rolled into one. She knew it because she'd lived with those feelings her entire life.

In that moment, she'd felt a kinship with him. It was so strange. After a lifetime of isolation, one moment of looking into a stranger's eyes had made her feel less alone than she'd ever felt before.

She turned to go back into the ballroom, though she'd rather be anywhere else, and caught a glimpse of her reflection in one of the full-length mirrors lining the corridor. Revulsion shuddered through her.

No wonder he'd wanted to get away.

She was a whale. A giant pink whale bursting at the seams. She'd been so excited when she'd been asked to be a bridesmaid. She'd finally thought she might be accepted by the sleek, beautiful Corretti family, but instead she'd been forced into a blazing pink dress at least two sizes too small for her bust. Carmela Corretti had laughed when she'd walked out of the fitting room, but she'd promised to have the dress fixed.

She hadn't, of course.

Lia's grandmother was the only one who'd seemed to sympathize. When Lia put the dress on today, despair and humiliation rolling through her in giant waves, her grandmother had hugged her tight and told her she was beautiful.

Tears pricked Lia's eyes. Teresa Corretti was the only one in the family who had ever been kind to her. Her grandfather hadn't been unkind, precisely, but he'd always frightened her. She still couldn't believe he was gone. He'd loomed so large in her life that she'd started to think him immortal. He'd been intense, driven, the kind of man no one crossed. But now he was dead, and the family wasn't any closer than they'd ever been. Not only that, but Lia wasn't certain that her cousin Alessandro wasn't to be more feared as the new head of the family.

Lia screwed up her courage and reentered the ballroom. A glance at her watch told her she'd put in enough time to call it an evening. She was going to find her grandmother and tell her she was leaving. No one would care that she was gone anyway.

The music pumped and thumped as it had before, and the crowd surged. But then another sound lifted over the din. It took Lia a minute to realize it was Carmela, shrieking drunkenly.

Lia despised her late uncle's wife, but thankfully

she hardly ever had to be around the woman. She didn't care what Carmela's problem was tonight. She just wanted to go back to her room and get out of this awful dress. She'd curl up with a book or something inane on television and try to forget the humiliations of the day.

But, before she could find her grandmother, the music suddenly died and the crowd parted as if Moses himself were standing there.

Everyone turned to look at Lia. She shrank instinctively under the scrutiny, her heart pounding. Was this yet another ploy of Carmela's to embarrass her? Did she really have to endure another scene? What had she ever done to the woman?

But it wasn't Carmela who caught her attention. It was Rosa. Carmela's daughter stood there, her face pale, her eyes fixed on her mother's face.

"That's right," Carmela said gleefully, her voice rising over the sudden silence of the gathered crowd, "Benito Corretti is your father, not Carlo! That one is your sister," she spat, pointing a red-tipped finger at Lia as if she were a particularly loathsome bug. "Be thankful you did not turn out like her. She's useless— fat and mousy and weak!"

Rosa looked stricken. Lia's heart stuttered in her chest. She had a sister? She wasn't close with her three half-brothers. She wasn't close with anyone. But a sister?

She'd never had anyone, not really. She'd often longed for a sister, someone she might get to know in a way she couldn't get to know brothers. Her three half-brothers had one another. Plus they were men. A sister, however—that felt different somehow.

A surge of hope flooded her then. Perhaps she wasn't really alone in this family, after all. She had a sister.

A sister who was every bit as lost at this moment as Lia had been her entire life. She could see it on Rosa's face, and she wanted to help. It was the one thing she had to offer that she knew was valuable. But suddenly, Rosa was storming away from Carmela, coming across the room straight for Lia. She reached out instinctively to comfort her when she came near. But Rosa didn't stop. The look she gave Lia could have frozen lava. Lia's heart cracked as Rosa shoved her hands away with a growled, "Don't!"

A throb of pain ricocheted through her chest where her heart had been. Rejection was nothing new to her, but the freshness of it in the face of her hope was almost too much. She stood there for long moments after Rosa had gone, aware of the eyes upon her.

Aware of the pity.

Soon, before she could think of a single pithy re-

mark, the crowd turned away, their attention wan-
ing. Self-loathing flooded her. No wonder Rosa hadn't
wanted her comfort. She was so pitiful. So naive.

How many times had she let her heart open? How
many times had she had the door slammed in her face?
When was she going to learn to guard herself better?

Shame and anger coiled together inside her belly.
Why couldn't she be decisive? Brave? Why did she
care how they treated her?

Why couldn't she just tell them all to go to hell the
way her mother would have done?

Grace Hart had been beautiful, perfect, a gorgeous
movie star who'd been swept off her feet by Benito
Corretti. She'd had no problem handling the Correttis, until she'd accidentally driven her car off a cliff
and left Benito a lonely widower with a baby. Soon
after that, Benito had sent Lia to live with Salvatore
and Teresa.

She knew why he'd done it. Because she wasn't
beautiful and perfect like her mother. Because she
was shy and awkward and lacking in the most basic
graces. She'd grown up on the periphery, watching her
cousins and half-siblings from a distance. Wanting her
father's love but getting only cool silence.

No, she wasn't beautiful and perfect, and she wasn't
decisive. She hated crowds, and she hated pretending

she fit in when everyone knew she didn't. She was a failure.

She wanted to go home, back to her small cottage at Salvatore and Teresa's country estate, back to her books and her garden. She loved getting her fingers in the dirt, loved creating something beautiful from nothing more than soil and water and seeds. It gave her hope somehow that she wasn't as inconsequential as she always felt.

Useless. Fat and mousy and weak.

Lia turned and fled through the same door Rosa had stormed out of. This was it. The final straw in her long, tortured life as a Corretti. She was finished pretending to fit in.

She meant to go to her room, but instead she marched out through the courtyard and found herself standing in front of the swimming pool.

There was no one in it tonight. The hotel had been overrun with wedding guests, and they were all at the reception. The air was hot, and the blue water was so clear, the pool lit from below with soft lights. For a moment Lia thought of jumping in with her dress on. It would ruin the stupid thing, but she hardly cared.

She stood there for a long time, hot feelings swelling within her. She wanted to be decisive. Brave. She wanted to make her own decisions, and she didn't want to let anyone make her feel inferior or unneeded ever again.

She took a step closer to the edge of the pool, staring down into the depths of the water. It would ruin her dress, her shoes, her hair.

So what?

For the first time in a long time, she was going to do what she wanted. She was going to step into the pool and ruin her dress, and she damn well didn't care. She was going to wash away the pain of the day and emerge clean. A new, determined Lia.

Before she could change her mind, she kicked off her shoes and stepped over the edge, letting the water take her down. It closed over her head so peacefully, shutting out all the sounds from above. Shutting out the pain and anger, the humiliation of this day.

She didn't fight it, didn't kick or struggle. She was a strong swimmer, and she wasn't afraid. She just let the water take her down to the bottom, where everything was still. She'd only sit here a moment, and then she'd kick to the top again.

Above her, she heard some kind of noise. And then the water rippled as someone leaped into the pool with her. It annoyed her. She wasn't finished being quiet and still.

Guests from the reception, no doubt. Drunk and looking for a good time.

Lia started to kick upward again, her solace interrupted now. She would get out of the pool and drag her sodden body back to her room. But her dress was heavier than she'd thought, twisting around her legs and pulling her back down again.

She kicked harder, but got nowhere. And then she realized with a sinking feeling that the suction of the drain had trapped part of her skirt. Panic bloomed inside her as she kicked harder.

Stupid, stupid, stupid.

She couldn't cry for help, couldn't do anything but try to rip herself out of the pink mess.

The dress didn't want to come off. Her lungs ached. Any minute and they would burst.

She kicked harder—but she was caught by her own folly.

No, by Carmela's folly, she thought numbly. Carmela's folly of a dress. Wouldn't everyone laugh when they discovered her bloated body in the pool tomorrow?

Poor, pitiful, stupid Lia. She'd been decisive, all right. She'd made a decision that was going to kill her. She wondered if her mother had thought the same thing in those seconds when her car had hung suspended over the cliffs before plunging onto the rocks below....

CHAPTER TWO

LIA WOKE SLOWLY. She coughed, her throat and chest aching as she did so. She remembered being in the pool, remembered her dress getting caught. She pushed herself up on an elbow. She was in a darkened room. She sat upright, and the sheet slid down her body. How had she gotten out of the pool? And why was she naked? She didn't remember going back to her room, didn't remember anything but that last moment where she'd thought of the Correttis finding her pink-clad body trapped at the bottom of the pool.

She pushed the sheet back, intending to get out of the bed, but a movement in the darkness arrested her.

"I wouldn't do that if I were you," a deep male voice said.

Lia grabbed the sheet and yanked it back up. How long had he been standing there?

"Who are you? And why are you in my room?"

His laugh was dry. "I'm Zach. And you're in my room, sugar."

Sugar. "You're American," she said, her heart thumping steadily. The same American as earlier?

"I'm sorry," he said.

"For what?"

"You sound disappointed."

She shook her head, stopping when her brain couldn't quite keep up. She felt light-headed, as if she'd been drinking, when she hadn't had more than a single glass of champagne all evening.

"How did I get here?"

"I carried you."

"Impossible," she scoffed. She was tall and awkward and fat. He couldn't have done it without a cart and a team of horses to pull her.

"Clearly not," he told her. "Because you're here."

"But why?" The last thing she remembered was water and darkness.

Wait, that wasn't right. There'd also been light, a hard surface under her back and the scalding taste of chlorine in her throat.

"Because you begged me not to call anyone when I pulled you out of the pool."

She vaguely recalled it. She remembered that she'd been worried about anyone seeing her, about them laughing and pointing. About Carmela standing there, slim arms folded, evil face twisted in a smirk, nodding and laughing...fat and mousy and weak.

"It was the only thing you said. Repeatedly," he added, and Lia wanted to hide.

She put a hand to her head. Her hair was still damp, though not soaked. And she was naked. Utterly, completely naked. Her face flamed.

He sat beside her on the bed, holding out a glass of water. "Here, take this," he said, his voice gentle.

She looked up, met his gaze—and her heart skipped several beats in a row. It was the same man. He had dark eyes, a hard jaw and the beginnings of a scruff where he hadn't shaved in hours. His hair was cropped short, almost military style, and his lips were just about the sexiest thing she'd ever seen in her life.

She took the water and drank deeply, choking when she'd had too much. He grabbed the glass and set it aside, no doubt ready to pound her on the back if she needed it. She held a hand up, stopping him before he could do so.

"I'm fine," she squeaked out. "Thank you."

He sat back and watched her carefully. "Are you certain?"

She looked at him again—and realized his expression was full of pity. Pity! It was almost more than she could bear to have one more person look at her like that tonight.

"Yes."

"You were lucky tonight," he said, his voice hardening. "Next time, there might not be anyone to pull you out."

She knew he was trying to say something important, but she was too weary to figure out what it was. And then his meaning hit her.

"I wasn't trying to kill myself," she protested. "It was an accident."

He raised an eyebrow. "I saw you step into the water. You just decided to go swimming while fully dressed?"

She dropped her gaze from his. "Something like that." What would he know of it if she told him the real reason? He was beautiful, perfect. She'd thought they had something in common earlier tonight, but she'd been wrong.

Of course.

She usually was. It disappointed her more than she could say. And made her feel lonelier than ever. This man, whatever his flaws, had nothing in common with her. How could he?

"What's your name?" he asked, his voice turning soft.

"Lia. And I hated my dress, if you must know. That's why I jumped in the pool."

His bark of laughter surprised her. "Then why did you buy it in the first place?"

"I didn't. It was a bridesmaid dress, and it was hideous."

"Pink is not your color, I'm sorry to say." His voice was too warm to take offense. "Definitely not." She was slightly confused, given his reaction to her earlier, and more than a little curious about him. It occurred to her she should be apprehensive to be alone with a strange man, in his room, while she was naked beneath his sheets.

But she wasn't. Paradoxically, he made her feel safe. As if he would stand between her and the world if she asked him to. It wasn't true, of course, but it was a nice feeling for the moment.

"I'm afraid I couldn't save the dress," he said. "It tore in the drain, and the rest rather disintegrated once I tried to remove it."

She felt heat creeping into her cheeks again. "You removed everything, I see."

"Yes, sorry, but I didn't want you soaking my sheets. Or getting sick from lying around in cold, clammy clothing."

What did she say to that? *Did you like what you saw? Thank you? I hope you weren't terribly inconvenienced?*

Lia cleared her throat and hoped she didn't look as embarrassed as she felt. "Did you find your medal?"

It was the most benign thing she could think of. She'd tucked it into her cleavage when she'd returned to the ballroom. She would regret it if it were lost. Something about it had seemed important to her, even if he'd cast it aside so easily.

"I did."

"Why did you drop it?" It seemed a harmless topic. Far safer than the subject of her body, no doubt.

"I have my reasons," he said coolly.

Lia waited, but he didn't say anything else. "If you intend to throw it away again, I'll keep it." She didn't know where that had come from, but she meant it. It seemed wrong to throw something like that away.

"It's yours if you want it," he said after a taut moment in which she thought she saw regret and anger scud across his handsome face.

She sensed there were currents swirling beneath the surface that she just didn't understand. But she wanted to. "What did you get it for?"

He shoved a hand through his hair. She watched the muscles bunch in his forearm, swallowed. He'd been in a tuxedo the last time she'd seen him, but now he wore a dark T-shirt that clung to the well-defined muscles of his chest and arms, and a pair of faded jeans. His feet, she noted, were bare.

So sexy.

"Flying," he said.

"Flying? You are a pilot?"

"I was."

"What happened?" His face clouded, and she realized she'd gone too far. She wanted to know why he'd reacted the way he had in the ballroom, but she could tell she'd crossed a line with her question. Whatever it was caused him pain, and it was not her right to know anything more than she already did.

"Never mind. Don't answer that," she told him before he could speak.

He shrugged, as if it were nothing. She sensed it was everything. "It's no secret. I went to war. I got shot down. My flying days are over."

He said it with such finality, such bittersweet grace, that it made her ache for him. "I'm sorry."

"Why?" His dark eyes gleamed as he watched her.

"Because you seem sad about it," she said truthfully. And haunted, if his reaction in the ballroom earlier was any indication. What could happen to make a man react that way? She didn't understand it, but she imagined he'd been through something terrible. And that made her hurt for him.

He sighed. "I wish I could still fly, yes. But we don't always get to do what we want, do we?"

Lia shook her head. "Definitely not."

He leaned forward until she could smell him—warm spice, a hint of chlorine. "What's your story, Lia?"

She licked her lips. "Story?"

"Why are you here? What do you regret?"

She didn't want to tell him she was a Corretti. Not yet. If he were here at the wedding, he was someone's guest. She just didn't know whose guest he was. And she didn't want to know. Somehow, it would spoil everything.

"I was a bridesmaid," she said, shrugging.

"And what do you regret?" His dark eyes were intent on hers, and she felt as if her blood had turned to hot syrup in her veins.

"I regret that I agreed to wear that dress," she said, trying to lighten the mood.

He laughed in response, and answering warmth rolled through her. "You'll never have to wear it again, I assure you."

"Then I owe you an even bigger debt of gratitude than I thought."

His gaze dropped, lingered on her mouth. Her breath shortened as if he'd caressed her lips with a finger instead of with his eyes. She found herself wishing he would kiss her more than she'd ever wished for anything.

He sat there for a long minute, his body leaning toward hers even as she leaned toward him. Her heart thrummed as the distance between them closed inch by tiny inch.

Suddenly, he swore and shot up from the bed. A light switched on, and she realized he'd gone to the desk nearby. The light was low, but it still made her blink against the sudden intrusion into her retinas.

"You don't owe me anything." His voice was rough, and it scraped over her nerve endings. Made her shiver.

She blinked up at him. He stood there with his hands shoved in his pockets, watching her. A lock of hair fell across her face, and she pushed it back, tucking it behind her ear.

Zach's gaze sharpened. He watched her with such an intense expression on his face. But she couldn't decide what he was feeling. Desire? Irritation? Disdain?

Dio, she was naive. She hated it. She imagined Rosa would have known what to do with this man. Lia wished she could talk to her sister, ask her advice— but how silly was that? Rosa was as estranged from her as she'd ever been. This new connection between them meant nothing to Rosa.

Lia's hair fell across her face again and she combed her fingers through it, wincing at how tangled it was. She would need a lot of conditioner to get this mess sorted.

She looked up at Zach, and her heart stopped beating. His expression was stark, focused—and she realized that the sheet had slipped down to reveal the curve of a breast. Her first instinct was to yank the fabric up again.

But she didn't.

She couldn't.

The air seemed to grow thicker between them. He didn't move or speak. Neither did she. It was as if time sat still, waiting for them.

"Are you staying in the hotel?" Zach asked abruptly, and the bubble of yearning pulsing between them seemed to pop.

Lia closed her eyes and tried to slow her reckless heart. "I am," she told him.

What did she know of desire, other than what she'd read in romance novels? Her experience of men was limited to a few awkward dates to please her grandmother. She'd been kissed—groped on one memorable occasion—but that was the sum total of her sexual experience. Whatever had been going on here, she was certain she had it wrong. Zach did not want her.

Which he proved in the next few seconds. He turned away and pulled open a drawer. Then he threw something at her.

"Get dressed. I'll take you back to your room."

Embarrassment warred with anger as her fingers

curled into the fabric of a white T-shirt. "This will hardly do the job," she said, turning to self-deprecation when what she really wanted to do was run back to her room and hide beneath the covers. *Fat and mousy and weak.*

"Put it on and I'll get a robe from the closet."

Lia snorted in spite of herself. "The walk of shame without the shame. How droll."

He moved closer, his gaze sharpening again, and her heart pounded. "And is that what you want, Lia? Shame?"

Between the horrendous dress she'd had to wear while people stared and pointed, to the very public brush-off she'd had from Rosa, she'd had enough shame today to last her for a while.

Lia shrugged lightly, though inside she felt anything but light. She was wound tight, ready to scream, but she wouldn't. Not until she was back in her room and could bury her face in the pillow first.

"A figure of speech," she said. "Now turn around if you want me to put this on."

He hesitated for a long moment. But then he did as she said, and she dropped the sheet and tugged the shirt into place. It was bigger than she'd thought, but she still had her doubts it would cover her bottom when she stood. She scooted to the edge of the bed and put her legs over the side.

She stood gingerly. Her head swam a little, but she was mostly fine. The shirt barely covered her bottom, but it managed.

"I'll take that robe now," she said imperiously.

Zach walked over to the closet and pulled out a white, fluffy Corretti Hotel robe. Then he turned and brought it back to her, his gaze unreadable as he handed it over. He did a good job of keeping his eyes locked on hers—

But then they dropped, skimming over her breasts— which tingled in response, the nipples tightening beneath his gaze—then farther down to the tops of her naked thighs, before snapping back to her face. His eyes glittered darkly, and a sharp feeling knifed into her.

If she were a brave woman, a more experienced woman, she'd close the distance between them and put her arms around his neck.

But she wasn't, and she didn't. She was just a silly virgin standing here in a man's T-shirt and wishing he would take her in his arms and kiss her.

Lia shrugged into the robe and tied it tight around her waist. "Thank you for your help, but there's no need for you to come with me. I can find my own way back to my room."

"I insist," he said, taking her elbow in a light but firm grip.

She pulled away. "And I'd rather you didn't."

"It's nonnegotiable, sugar."

Something snapped inside her then. Lia lifted her chin. She was so very tired of people telling her what to do. Of not being taken seriously or respected in any way. She was tired enough of it that she was done putting up with it.

This day, as they say, had been the last straw.

Lia plopped down on the edge of the bed and performed her first overt act of defiance as she crossed one leg over the other and said, "I suppose I'm staying here, then."

Zach fought the urge to grind his teeth. It was everything he could do not to push her back on the bed and untie that robe. His body was painfully hard. Lia tossed her hair again—that hot, tangled mess that was somehow sexier than any polished style could have been—and Zach suppressed the groan that wanted to climb up his throat.

Nothing about this woman was typical. She wasn't afraid of him, she didn't seem to want to impress him and she'd jumped into a pool fully clothed because she hated her dress. And now she sat there glaring at him because he was trying to be a gentleman—for once in his life—and make sure she got back to her room safely.

She crossed her arms beneath her breasts and he fought the urge to go to her, to tunnel his fingers into the thick mass of her auburn hair and lift her mouth to his.

That was what she needed, damn it—a hot, thorough, commanding kiss.

Hell, she needed more than that, but he wasn't going to do any of it. No matter that she seemed to want him to.

And why not?

Tonight, he was a man who'd dragged a drowning woman from a pool, a man who hadn't had sex in so long he'd nearly forgotten what it was like. He wasn't a senator's son or an all-American hero. He wasn't a broken and battered war vet. He was just a man who was interested in a woman for the first time in a long time.

More than interested. His body had been hard from the moment he'd stripped her out of that sodden pink dress, her creamy golden skin and dusky pink nipples firing his blood. He'd tried not to look, tried to view the task with ruthless efficiency, but her body was so lush and beautiful that it would take a man made of stone not to react.

Holy hell.

She stared at him defiantly, her chin lifting, and he had an overwhelming urge to master her. To push her back on the bed, peel open that robe and take what he wanted. Would she be as hot as those smoldering eyes seemed to say she would? Would she burn him to a crisp if he dared to give in to this urgent need?

"If you stay, you might get more than you bargained for," he growled. Because he was primed, on edge, ready to explode. It had been so long since he'd felt desire that to feel it now was a huge adrenaline rush.

Like flying.

"I've already had more than I bargained for today," she said hotly, color flooding her cheeks. "I've had to parade around in front of everyone in a hideous dress that made me look even fatter than I am. I've had to endure the whispers and stares, the laughter, the humiliation."

Zach blinked. Fat? No way. But of course she would think so. Women always did, unless they happened to be about five-six and weighed one hundred pounds. This one was taller than that, about five eight or so, and stacked with curves. She wasn't willowy. And she damn sure wasn't fat.

She choked out a laugh. "I also found out I have a sister—of course, she wants nothing to do with me—and on top of all of that, I finally did something daring and jumped in the pool fully clothed, only to nearly drown."

She sucked in a sharp breath, and he knew she was hovering on the edge of tears. "And then I wake up here, with you, completely naked—"

He thought she was going to cry, but she got to her feet suddenly, her eyes blazing, her chin thrusting in the air, though he could see that it still trembled. Her hands were fists at her sides.

"Even then, the only reaction I arouse in you is pity. I'm naked in front of a man and all he thinks about is the quickest way to get rid of me—so you will excuse me if I fail to cower before this latest pronouncement!"

Zach could only stare at her, mesmerized. He'd have sworn she was going to cry, sworn she would blubber and fall apart—but she hadn't. She was staring at him now, two high red spots on her cheeks, her dark auburn hair tumbling over her shoulders, her eyes flashing fire. The robe had slipped open a bit, exposing the inside of a creamy thigh.

Lust flooded him until he had to react or explode. He meant to turn away, meant to put distance between them. Hell, he meant to walk out of the room and not come back—

But instead, he closed the distance between them, gripped her shoulders as he bent toward her.

"Pity is the last thing I feel for you, Lia," he grated, still determined in some part of his brain to push her away before it was too late.

But then he tugged her closer, until she pressed against him, until she'd have to be stupid not to know what he was thinking about right now.

She gasped, and a skein of hot need uncoiled within him.

"Does this feel like pity?" he growled, his hands sliding down to grip her hips and pull her fully into him.

Her eyes grew large in her lovely face, liquid. For the barest of moments, he thought she seemed too innocent, too sweet. But then she reached up and put a palm to his cheek. Her thumb ghosted over his lips. He couldn't suppress a shudder of longing.

"No," she said, her voice barely more than a whisper. "It doesn't."

He thought there was a note of wonder in her voice, but he ignored it and pressed on, sliding a hand around to cup her round bottom. She wasn't fat, the stupid woman. She was curvaceous, with generously proportioned boobs and hips that other women could only envy.

"Is this what you want, Lia?" he asked, dipping his head, sliding his lips along her cheek in surrender to the hot feelings pounding through him.

Her only answer was a soft gasp. Desire scorched into him, hammered in his veins. He'd wanted her to go back to her room, wanted to remove the temptation when he had no idea what might happen if he had sex with her, but now that she was in his arms, sending her away had suddenly become impossible.

Her arms went around his neck, and he shuddered. She should be frightened of him after what had happened in the ballroom, but she showed no fear whatsoever. Then again, he had been the one to pull her from the water. Perhaps that redeemed him somewhat in her eyes.

"Why aren't you afraid of me?" he asked against the soft skin of her throat.

"I'm only afraid you'll stop," she said, and he squeezed her to him in reaction as emotions overwhelmed him.

He wanted to tell her not to trust him, wanted to tell her to run far and fast, that he could give her nothing more than a night of passion. He wanted to, but he couldn't find the voice right now. Not when what he so desperately wanted to do was slide his tongue into her mouth and see if she tasted as sweet as she looked.

Zach drew back just enough to see her face. Her eyes were closed, dark lashes fanning her cheekbones, and her pink lips parted on a sigh. She arched her body into his and heat streaked through him. It had been so long. Too long…

He shouldn't do this. He really shouldn't. He didn't know this woman at all.

But it felt like he did. Like he'd known her for ages. With a groan, Zach fell headlong into temptation.

CHAPTER THREE

As Zach's mouth came down on hers, Lia's first thought was to freeze. Her second was to melt into his kiss. She'd been kissed before, but nothing like this. Nothing with this kind of heat or raw passion. He wanted her. He *really* wanted her. This was not a dream, or a fever, or an illusion. This was a man—a hot, mysterious, dangerous man—and he wanted her, Lia Corretti.

His tongue slid against hers, and she shivered with longing. She didn't really know what she was doing—but she knew how it was supposed to feel, how she was supposed to react.

And she had no problem reacting. Lia arched into him, met his tongue eagerly, if somewhat inexpertly. She just hoped he didn't realize it.

The kiss was hot, thrilling, stomach-churning in a

good way. Her body ached with the sudden need to feel more than this. To feel everything.

She knew she shouldn't be doing this with him. Wanting this. But she did.

Oh, how she did.

To hell with what she was supposed to do. To hell with feeling unwanted and unloved and unattractive. What was she waiting for? *Who* was she waiting for?

Zach made her feel beautiful, desirable. She wanted to keep feeling that way.

When Zach loosened the robe, her heartbeat spiked. But she didn't stop him. She had no intention of stopping him. When would she ever get another chance to feel this way? Eligible men weren't exactly thick on the ground in her grandparents' village.

And even if they were, they'd have been unlikely to risk Salvatore Corretti's wrath by sleeping with his granddaughter out of wedlock.

Zach's warm hand slid along her bare thigh, up beneath the T-shirt he'd loaned her. His touch felt like silk and heat and she only wanted more. She shifted against him, felt the evidence of his arousal. He was hard, thick, and her body reacted with a surge of moisture between her thighs.

A sliver of fear wormed its way through her happiness. Was she really going to do this? Was she really going to have sex for the first time with an American whose last name she didn't even know? Was she going to keep pretending like she knew what she was doing even though she didn't?

Yes.

Yes, most definitely. Today was a new day for Lia Corretti. She was finally going to be brave and decisive and in control of her own destiny. No one would force her to wear an ugly pink dress—or call her fat, mousy and weak—in front of hundreds of people ever again.

The robe fell from her shoulders and then Zach swept her up into his arms. She gasped at his strength as he put a knee on the bed and laid her back on the mattress. And then she froze as he came down on top of her, his jeans-clad body so much bigger than hers.

He must have felt her hesitation because he lifted his head, his dark eyes searching hers. "If you don't want this, Lia—"

She put her fingers over his mouth to stop him from uttering another word. "I do," she said. And then she told a lie. "But it's been a long time and I—I…"

The words died on her lips. Surely he would see right through her, see to the heart of her deception. She had no experience at all, and he would be angry when he figured that out. And then he would send her away.

He pulled her hand from his mouth and pressed a kiss to her palm. "It's been a long time for me, as well." She must have looked doubtful, because he laughed softly. "Cross my heart, Lia. It's the truth."

She lifted a trembling hand to trace her fingers over his firm, sensuous lips. She barely knew him, and yet she felt as if she'd known him forever. But what if she disappointed him somehow? What if this was nothing like she'd read in novels?

"But you are so beautiful," she said.

He laughed, and she realized she'd spoken aloud. Heat flooded her. Oh, how simple she was sometimes!

"And so are you," he said, dipping his head to drop kisses along the column of her throat.

"You don't have to say that." She gasped as his tongue swirled in the hollow at the base of her throat. "I'm already in your bed."

"I never say things I don't mean." He lifted his head, his mouth curling in a wicked grin. "Besides, you're forgetting that I've already seen everything. And I approve, Lia. I definitely approve."

She didn't get a chance to reply because his hands spanned her hips and pushed the T-shirt upward, over her breasts, baring her to his sight.

"Still perfect," he said, and then he took one of her nipples in his mouth, his tongue swirling around the hard little point while she worked so hard not to scream.

She'd had no idea it would feel like this. No idea

that a man's mouth on her breast could send such sweet, aching pleasure shooting into her core. Her sex throbbed with heat and want, and her hands clutched his head, held him to her when she feared he would leave.

He did not. He only moved his attentions to her other breast, and Lia thought she would die from the sensations streaking through her. How had she missed out on this for so many years? How had she missed so much living?

Zach's tongue traced the underside of her breast, and then he was moving down, kissing a hot trail over her stomach. She was torn between anticipation and embarrassment that he could see the soft jiggle of her flesh. Why hadn't she insisted on turning out the light?

But then his tongue slid along the seam of her sex and she forgot everything but him. Lia cried out, unable to help herself. Never had she imagined how good this could feel, how perfect.

He circled her clitoris with his tongue, growing ever closer, until he finally touched her right where all those nerves concentrated. Lia stopped breathing. Her body clenched tighter and tighter as he focused his attention on that single spot. She wanted to reach the peak so badly, and she never wanted it to end, either.

She tried to hold out, tried to make it last, but Zach

was far too skilled at making her body sing for him. Lia exploded in a shower of molten sparks, his name on her lips.

She turned her head into the pillow, embarrassed, gasping, trying to gather the shards of herself back together again. What had he done to her? How had he made her lose control so quickly, so thoroughly?

She felt Zach move and she turned to look at him. He stood beside the bed, tugging off his clothes. He looked fierce, and her heart thrummed at the intensity on his face. She had no idea what she should be doing, but she didn't think she could go wrong by trying to help him remove his clothes. She sat up and started unbuckling his belt while he ripped his shirt over his head.

"Just a minute," he said, turning and disappearing into the adjoining bathroom for a second. When he returned, he was holding a condom package that bore the Corretti Hotel logo. She nearly laughed. Leave it to Matteo to think of everything in his hotels.

Zach's jeans disappeared, and Lia's breath caught at the sheer beauty of his body. He was hard, muscular—but he was also scarred. There was a long red scar that ran along his thigh, and a smaller round scar near his rib cage. Emotion welled inside her as she realized what it was: a bullet wound. She wanted to ask him what had happened, but he knelt between her thighs and rolled on the condom—and all thoughts of bullet wounds fled from her head as her breath shortened at the knowledge of what came next.

He bent and took her mouth with his, stoking the fire inside her instantaneously. When he stretched out over the top of her, she could think of nothing but how perfect this felt, how amazing to be naked beneath a man, his body stretched over hers, dominating hers in all the right ways.

Lia wrapped her legs around his waist, arched her body into him, her hands sliding down his back until she could grip his buttocks. It was natural, instinctual, and she gloried in the sound of approval he made in his throat.

She wanted to explore him, wanted to remember this night forever. But the fire between them was too urgent to go slowly. Lia gasped as she felt the head of his penis at her entrance. She knew this would hurt. What she didn't know was how badly.

Zach reached between them and stroked her. "Are you ready, Lia?" he whispered. "Or have you changed your mind? Last chance to say so."

Lia loved that he would ask. Now, like this, with his body poised to enter hers, he stopped to ask if she still wanted him. Part of her wanted him to stop. Part of her was terrified.

Brave. She nibbled his earlobe between her teeth,

felt a ribbon of satisfaction wind through her at the soft growl he emitted. She was brave.

There was no other answer she could give except yes. Her body was on fire, humming from the way he touched her, the way he made her ache for more.

"Please," she said, the only word she could manage. It came out sounding like a sob. Zach stilled for the briefest second—and then he was sliding forward, his body entering hers.

She tensed when there was a slight resistance, but it didn't last. Zach's eyes clouded as he looked down at her, as if he were thinking, but then she shifted her hips, and he groaned softly. He was fully inside her now, his length stretching her in ways she'd never experienced before.

It was the most astonishing feeling. She arched her hips upward, gasping as sensation streaked through her.

"Lia, you make me forget—" She didn't know what else he planned to say because he took her mouth then, kissing her hard, urgently, his tongue sliding against hers so hotly.

They lay like that for a long moment, kissing deeply, their bodies connected and still.

Then he began to move, slowly at first, and then faster as she took everything he had to give and asked for more. The air between them shimmered with heat, with power.

Everything about making love was foreign to her—and yet it wasn't. She felt as if she'd always known how it would be, as if she'd only been waiting for him to take her on this sensual journey.

As they moved together, as their bodies lifted and separated and came together again, she could feel something just out of reach, something wonderful and shattering and necessary. She strained toward it, needing it, trying to catch it—

And then, with a gasp of wonder, she did.

"Yes," he told her, his breath hot in her ear as he threaded his fingers through hers and held her hands over her head, "like that. Just like that, Lia."

Lia sobbed as she flew out over the abyss. And then her breath caught hard in her chest before it burst from her again in a long, loud cry, her senses splintering on the rocks below. Zach captured her mouth, swallowed her cries as she moaned and gasped again and again.

Soon, he followed her over the edge, gripping her hips and lifting her to him as he found his own release. He gave her cries back to her then, and she drank them in greedily, until the only thing that remained was the sound of their breathing.

Zach moved first, lifting himself up and rolling away from her. Lia lay stunned at the intensity of the experience. Like a slow drip from a faucet, uncertainty began to erode the surface of her languor.

What happened now? Did she thank him for the good time, put on the robe and leave? Or did she roll over and run her fingers over the smooth muscle of his abdomen?

She knew what she wanted to do. She wanted to touch him again. Explore him when her body was calm and still.

But she was paralyzed with indecision. And then Zach decided for her. He didn't say anything as he got up and walked into the bathroom. Lia's heart performed a slow dive into her belly. They'd had sex, and he was finished.

She scrambled up and grabbed the robe, slipping it on and swinging her legs over the side of the bed before he returned. Before she'd gone three steps, he walked out again.

Both of them crashed to a halt, staring at each other.

He was, she thought with a pang, beyond gorgeous. Beautifully, unconsciously naked. Tall and dark, packed with muscle that flexed and popped with his every movement. He looked like something she'd dreamed up instead of a flesh-and-blood man she'd really just had sex with.

Dio, she'd just had sex….

"Zach—"

"Lia—"

They spoke at the same time, their voices clashing. Lia dropped her gaze to the floor.

"Are you hungry?" Zach asked, and she looked up to see him watching her, a half smile on his handsome face. She couldn't keep her eyes from roaming his perfect body, no matter how she tried to focus solely on his face.

"Not that kind of hungry," he added with a laugh. "Though I'm definitely game for another round later."

Another round. Oh, my… Her insides thrummed with electricity at the thought.

"I haven't eaten since breakfast," she managed, her pulse thumping at the idea of doing it all again. And again.

Zach walked over to the desk and picked up the menu there. "Any suggestions?" he asked.

She had to struggle to concentrate. She knew what was on the menu without looking, but she could hardly think of food when Zach stood naked before her.

"Some antipasti, a little pasta alla Norma, some wine. It is all good," she finally managed, knowing that her brother would serve nothing but the best in his hotel.

"And dessert," Zach said, grinning. "Let's not forget dessert." He picked up the phone and ordered in flawless Italian—adding cannoli and fresh strawberries to the list—while Lia went into the bathroom to freshen up.

Her reflection surprised her. She'd thought she would look different—and, indeed, she did in a way. She looked like the cat that'd gotten into the cream. Yes, it was a terrible cliché, but it was truly the best way to describe that look of supreme satisfaction. Her skin glowed and her eyes were bright. Her lips were shockingly rosy and plump.

From kissing Zach. Her stomach flipped hard, and she wondered if she'd be able to eat a bite when he sat there with her, looking so tempting and yummy.

Lia forced herself to focus. She used the comb on the vanity to smooth her wild tangle of hair—as much as possible anyway—and wiped away the mascara that had smudged beneath her eyes. Then, heart pounding, she returned to Zach's suite. He'd pulled on his jeans and sat in a chair by the window, staring at the screen of his smart phone. When he realized she was there, he put the phone on the table.

His gaze was sharp, hot, and her skin began to prickle.

"Your Italian is perfect," she said, casting about for something innocuous to say. Something that would give these butterflies in her belly a chance to settle again. "Where did you learn it?"

"My grandfather was from Sicily," he said. "And I

learned it from my mother. She refused to teach me the Sicilian dialect her father spoke, but she did teach me Italian."

Her gaze slid over him again. Now that she knew he had Sicilian blood in him, she could see it. He had the hot, dark eyes of a Sicilian. "Then you have been to Sicily before, yes?"

He inclined his head. "But not for many years."

She went and perched on the edge of the sofa, facing him. His gaze slid over her, warmed her in ways she hadn't known were possible before tonight. "You are friends with the bride's family or the groom's?"

He laughed. "Neither. I came with a friend." He picked up the phone again and frowned as he glanced at the screen. "I can't seem to find her, though."

Her. Lia swallowed as her stomach turned inside out. Of course a man who looked like this one was not alone. But where was his girlfriend, and why hadn't she come searching for him? If it were Lia, she wouldn't let him out of her sight.

But now she needed to do just that. Lia stood. "I should go," she said. "It's late, and you must be tired…."

Words failed her. She turned away, blindly, fighting a sudden rush of ridiculous tears. But then he was there, a hand wrapping around her arm, pulling her back against him so that she could feel the hot press of his body through the robe.

"Forgive me."

"There's nothing to forgive," she said stiffly.

His mouth was on her hair, her temple. "I'm not here with another woman, Lia. Not like that. Taylor is a friend, and she's here to work."

"Taylor Carmichael?" Lia knew of only one Taylor who would be in Sicily to work right now, and that was the gorgeous former child star. She'd heard her grandmother talking about Santo's film, and the troubled woman who was slated to star in it.

She heard Zach sigh. And then he turned her in his arms, put his hands on either side of her face and held her so he could look into her eyes. "Yes, Taylor Carmichael. Yes, she's beautiful and desirable—but not to me. We've only ever been friends. She's the sister I never had."

Lia bit her lip. It was almost impossible to believe that two such gorgeous creatures weren't sleeping together. "I think you need glasses, Zach."

He laughed. "Hardly. I know when I have a beautiful woman in my arms."

Lia flushed with pleasure. She'd never felt beautiful. Until tonight. Oh, she still worried that she was too fat and too awkward, but she could hardly deny the evidence of his desire for her. She was quite a good dreamer, but she had definitely not dreamed what had happened in his bed only minutes ago.

What she hoped would happen again.

She closed her eyes. One time with him, and she was already becoming a woman of questionable morals.

He tipped her chin up with a long finger and pressed his lips to hers. Desire, so recently sated, still managed to lift a head and send a finger of need sliding down the pathways of her nervous system.

She stepped closer, her lips parting beneath his… and the kiss slid over the edge of polite and into the realm of hot and amazing. He was in the process of shoving the robe off her shoulders when there was a knock on the door.

He took a step back, breaking the kiss, and tugged the robe into place with a sigh of regret. "Food first," he said with a wicked smile. "And then we play."

Lia could only shudder in response.

They spent the night entangled together, their bodies craving the pleasure they found in each other. Lia learned more about sex, about her own body, than she'd dreamed possible.

They showered together in the morning, and then spent the day walking around Palermo, ducking into churches and restaurants, stopping in ancient alleys to kiss and touch, drinking espresso and eating pasta.

It was a perfect day, followed by another perfect evening. They were strangers, and not strangers. It was as if they'd known each other forever. Zach's smile made her heart throb painfully whenever he turned it on her. His laugh had the power to make her ache with raw hunger.

They talked, in Italian and in English, about endless things. She confessed that she was a Corretti. Zach didn't seem to care, other than a brief lifting of the eyebrows as he connected her to the hotel owners.

She discovered that Zach lived in Washington, D.C., and that he'd met Taylor Carmichael at a clinic for military veterans. She didn't ask about his scars because he'd grown tight-lipped when he'd told her that much.

They returned to the hotel, to his room, and spent the entire night wrapped in each other once more. He left the balcony doors open so that a breeze from the sea blew in. Church bells chimed the hour, every hour, but sanctuary was in this room, this bed.

And yet it was ending. They both knew it. Lia had to return to her grandparents' estate, and Zach was going back to the States. He'd heard from Taylor, finally, and she'd told him everything was fine, though she was somehow now engaged to Lia's brother Luca.

Zach didn't seem too happy about that, but he'd accepted it after they'd talked a bit longer.

He did not, Lia noticed, tell Taylor about her.

Yet she kept hoping for more, for some sign this meant more to him than simply sex. It had to. She couldn't be the only one affected by this thing between them. Could she?

But when she awoke early the next morning, Zach was gone. She hadn't heard a thing. His suitcase was gone, everything in the bathroom, everything that indicated he'd once been here.

All that remained was a single rose in a vase and a hastily scribbled note propped beside it. She snatched it up and opened it. The military medal fell out and hit the floor with a plink.

Lia's pulse throbbed as she read the note.

Be well, Lia.

Her heart crumpled beneath the weight of those words. Words that meant well, but ultimately meant nothing. She retrieved the medal, and then sank onto the bed and lifted his pillow to her face. It still smelled like him and she breathed it in, seeking calm.

Zach was gone, and she was alone once more. Like always.

CHAPTER FOUR

THE EVENING WAS hot and muggy, and Zach stood off to one side of the crowd gathered at the country club. He took a sip from his water glass, cleverly disguised as a mixed drink by the addition of a lime slice and a cocktail stirrer, and then set it on a passing tray.

He never drank at functions like this. It was something he'd learned growing up. Always keep your head and always be prepared for any eventuality. His father hadn't made a career in politics out of being imprudent, and Zach had learned the lesson well.

These days, however, he was less concerned with the good impression than he was with the opportunity to escape. Once he'd done his duty—made the speech, shook the hands, accepted the honor, cut the ribbon, got the promised funding for the Scott Foundation's causes—he was gone.

Tonight, he'd had to give a speech. And right now,

his father was holding court with a group of people he no doubt hoped would become campaign donors. His mother was circulating with the skill of a career politician's wife, smiling and making polite small talk.

There were reporters in the room—there were always reporters—but the cameras were thankfully stowed at the moment. They'd come out during his speech, of course, and he'd had to work hard to concentrate on the crowd and not the flashes. A matron came over and started to talk to him. He nodded politely, spoke when necessary and kept his eye on the exit. The second he could excuse himself, he was gone. He'd already been here too long, and he was beginning to feel as if the walls were closing in.

He scanned the crowd out of habit, his gaze landing on a woman who made him think of Sicily. She was standing near the door, her head bowed so he couldn't see her face. The crowd moved, closing off his view of her. His pulse started to thrum, but of course, she wasn't Lia Corretti. Lia was in Sicily, no doubt making love to some other lucky bastard. A current of heat slid through him as he remembered her lush body arrayed before him.

If he'd been a different man, he'd have stayed in Sicily and kept her in his bed until they'd grown tired of each other. It's what the old Zach would have done.

But the man he was now couldn't take that chance.

He'd spent two nights with her and she'd made him feel almost normal again. Yet it was a lie, and he'd known it.

He didn't know Lia at all, really, but he knew she deserved better than that. Better than him.

"Zach?"

His head whipped around, his gaze clashing with the woman's who'd moved through the crowd unseen and now stood before him. Shock coursed through him. It was as if he'd blinked and found himself whisked back to a different party. Almost against his will, his body responded to the stimulus of seeing her again. He wasn't so inexperienced as to allow an unwanted erection, but a tingle of excitement buzzed in his veins nevertheless.

Lia Corretti gazed up at him, her blue-green eyes filled with some emotion he couldn't place. Her dark red hair was twisted on her head, a few strands falling free to dangle over one shoulder. She was wearing a black dress with high heels and a simple pair of diamond earrings.

She wasn't dripping in jewels like so many of the women in this room, yet she looked as if she belonged. The woman who'd been talking to him had thankfully melted away, her attention caught by someone else.

"Hello, Lia," he said, covering his shock with a blandness that belied the turmoil raging inside him.

He spoke as if it hadn't been a month, as if they'd never spent two blissful nights together. As if he didn't care that she was standing before him when what he really wanted to ask her was what the hell she was doing here.

But he was afraid he knew. It wouldn't be the first time a woman he'd slept with had gotten the wrong idea. He was a Scott, and Scotts were accustomed to dealing with fortune hunters. She hadn't seemed to be that type of woman, but clearly he'd been wrong.

He noticed that her golden skin somehow managed to look pale in the ballroom lights. Tight. There were lines around her lips, her eyes. She looked as if she'd been sick. And then she closed her eyes, her skin growing even paler. Instinctively, Zach reached for her arm.

He didn't count on the electricity sizzling through him at that single touch, or at the way she jerked in response.

"I'm sorry," she said in English, her accent sliding over the words. "I shouldn't have come here. I should have found another way."

"Why are you here?" he demanded, his voice more abrupt than he'd intended it to be.

She looked up at him, her eyes wide and earnest. Innocent. Why did he think of innocence when he thought of Lia? They'd had a one-night—correction, two-night—stand, but he couldn't shake the idea that the woman he'd made love to had somehow been innocent before he'd corrupted her.

"I—I need to tell you something."

"You could have called," he said coolly.

She shook her head. "Even if you had given me your number..." She seemed to stiffen, her chin coming up defiantly. "It is not the kind of thing one can say over the phone."

Zach took her by the elbow, firmly but gently, and steered her toward the nearest exit. She didn't resist. They emerged from the crowded ballroom onto a terrace that overlooked the golf course. It was dark, but the putting green was lit and there were still players practicing their swings.

He let her go and moved out of her orbit, his entire body tight with anger and restlessness. "And what do you wish to say to me, Lia?"

He sounded cold and in control. Inhuman. It was precisely what he needed to be in order to deal with her. He'd let himself feel softer emotions when he'd been with her before, and look where that had gotten him. If he'd been more direct, she wouldn't be here now. She would know that her chances of anything besides sex from him were nonexistent.

He would not make that mistake again.

Lia blinked. Her tongue darted out over her lower

lip, and a bolt of sensation shot through him at that singular movement. His body wanted to react, but he refused to let it. She was a woman like any other, he reminded himself. If sex was what he wanted, he had only to walk back in that ballroom and select a partner.

Her gaze flicked to the door. "Perhaps we should go somewhere more private."

"No. Tell me what you came to say, and then go back to your hotel."

She seemed taken aback at the intensity of his tone. She ran a hand down her dress nervously, and then lifted it to tuck one of the dangling locks of hair behind her ear. "You've changed," she said.

He shook his head. "I'd think, rather, that you do not know me." He spread his hands wide. "This is who I am, Lia. What I am."

She looked hurt, and he felt an uncharacteristic pinch in his heart. But he knew how to handle this. He knew the words to say because he'd said a variation of them countless times before.

"Palermo was fun. But there can be nothing more between us. I'm sorry you came all this way."

He'd expected her to crumple beneath the weight of his words. She didn't. For a long moment, she only stared at him. And then she drew herself up, her eyes flashing. It was not the response he expected, and it surprised him. Intrigued him, too, if he were willing to admit it.

"There can be more," she said firmly. "There *must* be more."

Zach cursed himself. Why, of all the possible women in the world, had he chosen this one to break his long sexual fast with? He'd known there was something innocent about her, something naive. He should have sent her back to her room. Unfortunately, his brain had short-circuited the instant all the blood that should have powered it started flowing south.

"I'm sorry if you got the wrong idea, sugar," he began.

She didn't let him finish. Her brows drew down angrily as she closed the distance between them and poked him hard in the chest with a manicured finger. He was too stunned to react. "The wrong idea?" she demanded.

She swore in Italian, curses that somehow sounded so pretty but were actually quite rude if translated. Zach was bemused in spite of himself.

"There were consequences to those two days," she flashed. "For both of us, *bello.*"

Ice shot down his spine, sobering him right up again.

"What are you talking about?" he snapped.

Her lips tightened. And then she said the words that sliced through him like a sword thrust to the heart.

"I'm pregnant, Zach. With *your* baby."

Lia watched the play of emotions over his face. There was disbelief, of course. Anger. Denial.

She understood all those feelings. She'd experienced each one in the past few days, many times over. But she'd also experienced joy and happiness. And fear. She couldn't forget the fear.

"That's impossible," he said tightly. His handsome face was hard and cold, his eyes like chips of dark, burning ice as they bored into her.

Lia wanted to sit down. She was beginning to regret coming here tonight. She'd only just arrived in Washington today, and she'd hardly rested. She was suffering from the effects of too much air travel, too much stress and too many crazy hormones zinging through her system.

This was not at all how she'd pictured this happening. She hadn't thought beyond seeing him, hadn't thought he would force her to tell him her news standing in the darkness and watching men tap golf balls toward a little hole in the ground.

She also hadn't expected him to be so hostile. So cold.

Lia swallowed against the fear clogging her throat.

She had to be brave. She'd already endured so much just to get to this point. There was no going back now.

"Apparently not," she said, imbuing her voice with iron. "Because I am most assuredly pregnant."

"How do you know it's mine?"

His voice was a whip in the darkness, his words piercing her. "Because there has been no one else," she shot back, fury and hurt roiling like a storm-tossed sea in her belly.

"We spent two nights together, Lia. And we used condoms." His eyes were hard, furious.

"There was once," she said, her skin warming. "Once when you, um, when we—"

She couldn't finish the thought. But he knew. He looked stunned. And then he closed his eyes, and she knew he remembered.

"Christ."

There'd been one time when they'd been sleeping and he'd grown hard against her as they slowly wakened. He'd slipped inside her, stroked into her lazily a few times, and then withdrew and put on a condom. It had been so random, so instinctive, that neither of them thought about it afterward.

"Exactly," she said softly, exhaustion creeping into her limbs. Why hadn't she just stayed at the hotel and slept? Her plan had always been to see him privately, but when she'd seen the announcement in the paper about his speech tonight, she'd become focused on getting here and telling him the news. On sharing this burden with someone who could help her.

But that wasn't the only reason.

For an entire month, she'd missed him. Missed his warm skin, the scent of soap and man, the way he skimmed his fingers over her body, the silky glide of his lips against hers.

The erotic pulse of his body inside hers, taking her to heights she'd never before experienced.

Lia shivered, though it was not cold. A drop of sweat trickled between her breasts. She felt...moist. And she definitely needed to sit down.

Zach stood ramrod straight on the terrace before her. "You may be pregnant, but that doesn't make the baby mine," he said. She swallowed down the nausea that had been her constant companion—it was lessening thanks to medication the doctor had prescribed—and tried to bring him into focus. "We were together two nights. How do I know you didn't have another lover?"

Lia's heart ached. She'd known he might not take the news well—what man would when a spontaneous encounter with a stranger turned life-altering in such a huge way?—but she hadn't expected him to accuse her of having another lover. Of basically coming all this way to lie to him.

"I need to get out of this heat," she choked out, turning blindly. She couldn't stand here and defend herself when she just wanted to sit down somewhere cool. When her heart hurt and her stomach churned and she wanted to cry.

She'd only taken a few steps toward the door when she felt as if the bottom was dropping out from under her. Lia shot a hand out and braced herself on the railing near the door as nausea threatened to overwhelm her. She turned to lean against it, grateful for the solid barrier holding her up.

"What's wrong?"

She looked up to find Zach standing over her, his stern face showing concern where moments ago it had only been anger.

Lia put a shaky hand to her forehead. "I'm hormonal, Zach. And you aren't helping matters."

He blew out a breath. And then his hand wrapped around her elbow as he pulled her to his side. "Come on."

He led her away from the door and then in through another door farther down. It led into a dark bar with tables and chairs and only a few patrons. Zach steered her to a table in the corner, far from anyone, and sat her down.

"Wait here."

She was too tired to argue so she did as he ordered,

propping her head against one palm as she fought her queasy stomach.

He returned with a glass and a bottle of San Pellegrino, opening it and pouring it for her. She took a grateful sip, let the cold bubbly water slide down her throat and extinguish the fire in her belly.

Zach sank into the chair across from her. His arms were folded over what she remembered was an impressive chest when it was bare. His stare was not in the least bit friendly as he watched her. She thought of the military medal she'd tucked into her purse and pictured him in a flight suit, standing tall and proud beside a sleek fighter jet.

"Better?" he asked shortly.

She nodded. "Somewhat, yes."

"Good." His eyes narrowed. "Why should I believe this baby is mine, Lia?"

Her heart thudded. There was no reason she could actually give him. *Because I was a virgin. Because you are the only man I've ever been with.* "A paternity test should clear it up," she said coolly, though inside she was anything but cool. "I will submit the first moment it is safe to do so."

He turned his head and stared off into space. His profile was sharp, handsome. His hair was still cut in that military style, short and cropped close. On him, it was perfect. Not for the first time, she wondered what he'd seen in her. No doubt he was wondering the same thing.

"You seem to have it all thought out," he said evenly. Coldly.

Lia clutched the glass in her hands. "Not really. All I know is we created a baby together. And our baby deserves to have both parents in his or her life."

It was the one thought that had sustained her on the long trip from Sicily. The one thing she'd had to cling to when everything else was falling apart.

Zach would want his child. She'd told herself that over and over.

But she didn't really know if it was true.

What if he was exactly like her father and just didn't care about the life he'd helped to create? Despair rose up inside her soul. How could this be the same man she'd lain in bed with? That man had been warm, mysterious, considerate. He wouldn't abandon a helpless baby.

But this man…

She shivered. This one was cold and hard and mean.

He looked at her evenly. Across the room, a few people sat at tables or lounged at the bar. One woman leaned in toward the man across from her and said something that made him laugh. How Lia envied that woman. She was with a man who wanted her, a man who was happy she was there.

"I don't know what you expect, Lia, but I'm not the father type. Or the husband type." His voice was low and icy, his emotions so carefully controlled she had no idea if he felt anything at all.

"You don't have a choice about being a father," she said, her throat aching.

His dark eyes glittered. And then he smiled. A cruel smile. "There is always a choice. This is the twenty-first century, not the dark ages. You don't have to have this child. You don't have to keep this child."

His words seared into her. Lia shot to her feet and clutched her tiny purse to her like a shield. Her hands were trembling. Her body was trembling.

"I want this baby, Zach. I intend to give my child the best life possible. With or without you," she added, her throat tightening over the words. Though she didn't know how she was going to do that. She had nothing. The money she had from her mother wasn't in her control. She didn't even know how much there was; her grandfather had always managed it. Now, she supposed, Alessandro was managing it.

She didn't really know Alessandro, but he was her grandfather's handpicked successor. And if he was anything like Salvatore had been, then he was not a man you demanded anything from.

When she walked out of here, she had nothing more than she'd walked in with. The bit of cash she'd saved

from her allowance and the credit card on her grandmother's account. She kept hoping her grandmother
wouldn't notice the charges, though she had no idea
how much longer that could last. She'd fled while her
grandmother was out of town, but Teresa would return any day and find Lia gone.

Then what? The family would shut down her ability to spend a dime other than her cash. Then someone would come for her. Lia shuddered.

Her heart thundered while Zach stared her down.
Please, she silently begged. *Please don't reject us.
Please don't send us back there.*

His eyes did not change. There was no warmth, no
sympathy. No feeling at all. She'd been too hasty with
that ultimatum. Too stupid.

"Without me," he said, his voice low and measured.

She considered him for a long moment, her eyes
pricking with tears, her breath whooshing in and out
of her chest as she fought to maintain control. He was
a bastard. A horrible, rotten bastard.

What had happened to the man who'd been frightened and alone in that ballroom back in Palermo?
The man who'd been vulnerable, and who'd dropped
his military medal because he must believe, on some
level, that he didn't deserve it?

She'd come here with such hope for the future.

She'd come here expecting to find the man who had charmed her and made her feel special.

But this man was not the same man. She despised him in that moment. Despised herself for being so weak and needy that she'd had sex with a stranger—not once, but many times over two days. It was as if she'd wanted to challenge fate, as if she'd been laughing and daring life to knock her in the teeth one more time.

Well, it certainly had, hadn't it? She'd let herself feel something for a man she didn't know, let herself believe there was more to it than simple biology. Not love, certainly not, but…something. Some feeling that was somehow more than she should have felt for a man she'd only just met.

She was so naive.

The pain sliced into her heart. "I spoke with Taylor Carmichael after you left Sicily. She thinks you are a good man," Lia told him. Something flickered in his gaze, yet he said nothing. "But I think she doesn't really know you the way she thinks she does."

She turned and headed for the exit, though the door was a blur through her tears. One of the patrons in the bar looked up as she passed. He grinned at her, an eyebrow lifting, but she kept walking, her entire world crumbling apart. She hoped Zach would stop her. Prayed he would.

Prayed that she was wrong and he was just very surprised and not reacting well.

But she reached the door and tugged it open, and still he wasn't behind her. Lia stepped into the corridor and hurried down it, her heels sinking into the plush carpet. And then she was outside, nodding to the doorman's query if she would like a taxi. Here, the world moved as it had before. Nothing had changed. Inside her soul, however, everything was different.

She was pregnant. She was alone.

She wished she had someone to talk to—a friend, a sister, anyone who would listen—but that was wishful thinking. She'd never had anyone to talk to.

A taxi glided up the rounded drive and the doorman opened it with a flourish. Lia handed him a few dollars and then slid inside and turned her head away from the elegant building as the taxi drove away. She refused to look back. That part of her life was over.

CHAPTER FIVE

LIA DIDN'T SLEEP WELL. She'd returned to her hotel, ordered room service—soup and crackers—and then taken a hot bath and climbed into bed with the television remote. She'd fallen asleep almost instantly, but then she'd awakened when it was still dark out. She lay there and stared at the ceiling.

Her entire life was crashing around her ears, and there was nothing she could do about it. Zach had rejected her. She had no choice but to return to Sicily. No choice but to tell her grandmother everything that had happened. She could only pray that Alessandro was a better man than her grandfather had been, and that he wouldn't force her to marry someone she didn't love simply for the sake of protecting the family reputation

She didn't hold out much hope, actually.

She put her hand over her still-flat belly. What was she going to do? Where was she going to go? If she tried to keep running, the Correttis would find her. She couldn't melt away and become anonymous. She couldn't find a job and raise her child alone. She had no idea how to begin. She had no skills, no advanced education. She'd never worked a day in her life.

But she would. She would, damn it, if that's what it took. She wasn't half-bad with plants. Maybe she could get a job in a nursery, or in someone's garden. She could prune plants, coax forth blooms, mulch and pot and plan seasonal beds.

It wasn't much, but it was something.

Tears filled her eyes and she dashed them away angrily. Eventually, she fell asleep again. When she woke this time, it was full daylight. She got up and dressed. She thought about ordering room service again, but she needed to be careful with her expenses. She would go and find a diner somewhere, a place she could eat cheaply.

And then she would figure out what to do.

Lia swept her long hair into a ponytail and grabbed her purse. She was just about to open the door when someone knocked on it. The housekeeper, no doubt. She pulled open the door.

Except it wasn't the housekeeper.

Lia's heart dipped into her toes at the sight of Zach on the threshold. But then it rose hotly as anger beat a pulse through her veins. He'd been so cruel to her last night.

"What do you want?" she asked, holding the door tight with one hand. Ready to slam it on him.

"To talk to you."

He was so handsome he made her ache. And that only made her madder. Was she really such a push-over for a pretty face? Was that how she'd found her-self in this predicament? The first man to ever pay any real attention to her had the body of a god and the face of an angel—was it any wonder she'd fallen beneath his spell?

This time she would be strong. She gripped the door hard, her knuckles whitening. "I understood you the first time. What more can you have to say?"

He blew out a breath, focused on the wall of win-dows behind her head. "I called Taylor."

Her heart throbbed with a new emotion. Jealousy. "And this concerns me how?"

"You know how, Lia. Let me in so we can talk."

She wanted to say no, wanted to slam the door in his face—but she couldn't do it. Wordlessly, she pulled the door open. Then she turned her back on him and went over to the couch to sit and wait. He came in-side and stood a few feet away, his hands shoved into his jeans pockets.

"You went to see Taylor," he said. "To find out where I lived."

She lifted her chin. "I knew you lived in Washington, D.C. You told me so."

"Yes, but it's a big city. And you needed an address."

She toyed with the edge of her sleeve. "I'd have found you. You did tell me about your father, if you recall."

But it would have been much harder, which was why she'd gone to see Taylor. And how embarrassing that had been. She'd had to explain to a complete stranger that she needed to find Zach because she had something to tell him.

Taylor hadn't accepted that excuse. She'd demanded to know more. Lia hadn't blamed her, since she was Zach's friend, but it was still a humiliating experience. Taylor hadn't actually believed her—until she'd produced the medal. Lia still wasn't certain that Taylor believed everything, but she'd relented at that point because she'd believed enough.

"You've gone to a lot of trouble," he said.

Lia swallowed. What could she say? *I had no choice? My family will be furious? I'm afraid?*

"A baby needs two parents," she said. "And a man should know if he's going to be a father."

"And just what did you expect me to do about it, sugar?"

Irritation zipped through her like a lash. *Sugar* wasn't an endearment, spoken like this; it was a way of keeping her at a distance. Of objectifying her. "You know my name. I'd prefer you use it."

His eyes flashed. "Lia, then. Answer the question."

She folded her arms and looked toward the windows. She could see the white dome of the Capitol building sitting on the hill. Why had she chosen this hotel? It was far too expensive. If her grandmother cut off her credit cards, she'd be doing dishes in the hotel kitchen for the next ten years just to pay for one night.

"I thought you would want to know."

"You could have called."

She swung back to look at him. "Are you serious? Would you want this kind of news over the phone?"

He didn't answer. Instead, he pulled something from his rear pocket and tapped it on his palm. "How much money do you want, Lia?"

Her heart turned to stone in her chest as she realized he was holding a checkbook. And though she needed money—desperately—it hurt that he thought all he needed to do was buy her off.

And it hurt that he didn't want this child growing inside her. That he could so easily shove aside that connection and have nothing to do with a person who was one half of him.

My God, she'd really chosen well, hadn't she?

"You think I came here for money?" It would solve her most immediate problem, but it wouldn't really solve anything. She'd still be single and pregnant, and her family would still be furious—and the Correttis had a long arm.

"Didn't you?"

Lia stood. She had to fold her arms over her middle to hide their trembling. "Get out," she said, fighting the wave of hysteria bubbling up inside her.

He took a step toward her and then stopped. The checkbook disappeared in his jeans again. He looked dark and broody and so full of secrets he frightened her. And yet a part of her wanted, desperately, to slide into his arms and experience that same exhilaration she had back in Sicily.

"You expect marriage," he said, almost to himself. "That's why you came."

It seemed so silly when spoken aloud like that, but she couldn't deny the truth of it. She had thought she would race to D.C., tell Zach she was pregnant and he would be so happy he'd want to take care of her and the baby forever.

Lia closed her eyes. What was wrong with her? Why was she always looking for acceptance and affection where there was none? Why did she think she needed a man, any man, in her life anyway?

"This is your baby in here," she said, spreading her hand over her abdomen. "How can you not want it?"

He raked a hand through his hair and turned away from her. Once more, she was studying his beautiful, angry profile.

"Assuming what you say is true, I'm not good father material." He said it quietly, with conviction, and her heart twisted in her chest.

Still, she couldn't allow sympathy for the pain in his voice to deflect her from the other part of what he'd said. "If you don't believe me, why are you here? Do you usually offer to pay women to get them to go away?"

He turned back to her, his expression cool. "I've encountered this situation before, yes. It has never been true, by the way." He spread his hands wide. "But my family name encourages the deception."

Lia stiffened. "I really don't care who your family is," she said tightly. "I did not come here for them."

"Then what do you want, Lia?"

She swallowed. She'd thought—naively, of course—there had been something between them in Palermo. Something more than just simple animal attraction. She'd thought he might be glad to see her. God, she was such a fool.

The only thing she had was the truth.

"My family will be very angry when they find out," she said softly. "And Alessandro will likely marry me off to one of his business associates to prevent a scandal." She dropped her gaze and smoothed her hand over her belly again. "I suppose I could deal with that if it were only me. But I'm afraid for my baby. A Sicilian man won't appreciate a wife who is pregnant with another man's child."

She could feel his gaze on her and she lifted her head, met the tortured darkness of his eyes. And the heat. It surprised her to find heat there, but it was indisputable. The heat of anger, no doubt.

"You know this to be true," she said. "You are part Sicilian yourself."

"A small part, but yes, I know what you mean."

She could have breathed a sigh of relief—except she didn't think he'd changed his mind about anything. "Then you will not want your child raised by another man. A man who will not love him or her, and who will resent the baby's presence in his household."

Zach was still. "You should have chosen better," he said.

She blinked. It was not at all the response she'd anticipated. "I beg your pardon?"

"That night. You should have chosen to leave instead of stay."

She'd bared her fears to him and this was what he had to say. Anger spiked in her belly. "It takes two, Zach. You were there, too."

He took a step toward her, stopped. His hands flexed at his sides. "Yes, and I tried to send you away, if you will recall. Considering how we first met, you should have run far and fast."

Her skin was hot—with shame, with anger, with self-recrimination. "It's not all my fault. Perhaps you should have tried harder."

As if anything would have induced her to leave after the way he'd looked at her: as if he wanted to devour her. It had been such a novel experience that she'd only wanted more.

"I should have," he said. "But I was weak."

"This baby is yours," she said, a thread of desperation weaving through her. If he walked out now, if he sent her back to Sicily, what would become of her and the baby? She couldn't face her cousin's wrath. Her grandmother would do what she could, but even Teresa Corretti would do what the head of the family dictated in the end. And he would dictate that she not have a child out of wedlock. Or he would throw her out and cut her off without a cent.

For a moment, she contemplated that option. It would be…heavenly, in a way. She would be free of the Correttis, free of the pain and anger that went along with being the outsider in her family.

Except she knew it wouldn't happen that way. Salvatore Corretti had ruled his family with an iron fist. And no wayward granddaughter would have ever brought shame on the family name in such a way. A Corretti grandson could father illegitimate children all day long, and he would not have cared. Let one of his granddaughters get pregnant, with no man in sight, and he most certainly would have come unglued.

Alessandro was a Corretti male and would be no different. He'd learned at their grandfather's knee how to run this family and she could not take the risk he was somehow more enlightened. He'd never been enlightened enough to pay attention to her in all these years, which told her a lot about how he already felt about her. Add in the humiliation of his aborted wedding, and she was certain he was in no mood to be sympathetic.

"How can you be sure, Lia?"

She had to give herself a mental shake to retrieve the thread of the conversation. He wanted to know how she could be sure the baby was his, as if she was the kind of woman who had a different sexual partner every night.

"Because I am. Because I've been with no one else."

He swore softly.

Her cheeks heated. Hot emotion whipped through her. She was tired of feeling guilty, tired of feeling as if she was the one who'd done something wrong. She felt snappish.

"This isn't ideal for me, either, you know. I didn't ask to get pregnant, especially not my first time ever having sex—"

She broke off as she realized what she'd said. His face grew thunderous. He closed the distance between them, stopped just short of grabbing her. His hands were clenched into fists at his sides. "What did you say?"

Lia's heart pounded. Adrenaline roared through her veins. She felt light-headed. "Nothing," she whispered as his eyes darkened. "It was nothing."

"You told me that night it had been a long time…." His voice was diamond-edged.

"I thought if I told you the truth, you'd send me away."

He swallowed, hard. "I would have. I should have anyway." His gaze dropped, his dark lashes dipping to cover his beautiful eyes. "I thought something was… different with you. But it had been so long since I'd been with anyone that I dismissed my intuition. You didn't act like a virgin, but you felt like one when I…"

He swore again, his eyes meeting hers once more.

"I'd have done things differently if I'd known. Been more gentle. You should have told me."

Lia couldn't stop herself from lifting a hand and sliding it along the bare skin of his arm. It was the first time she'd touched him, really touched him, in a month. And the electric sizzle ricocheting through her body told her just how little had changed for her.

"I should have. I know it. But everything was so surreal, and I was afraid it would end. You were the first person to make me feel wanted in a very long time. I liked that feeling."

He moved away from her, went over and sank down on a chair. Then he sat forward and put his head in his hands. Lia didn't say anything. She didn't move, though her heart throbbed at the sight of him looking so overwhelmed.

"This is not what I expected to happen at this point in my life," he said to the floor.

"I don't think either of us did," she replied, swallowing. "And though I could make it all go away with a visit to a doctor, as you intimated earlier, I can't do that. It's not who I am or what I want."

He lifted his head. "No, I know that." He blew out a breath, swore. And then he stood again, his presence nearly overwhelming her as his eyes flashed fire. "The press will have a field day with this."

Lia bit the inside of her lip. In all the drama, she'd

never considered the press. It was true the paparazzi flocked around her family like piranha. But she'd never been their target, probably because she was so humdrum and uninteresting in her family of brilliant swans.

But this baby was a game changer, especially considering who Zach was. His family was even more famous than hers. American royalty, if there was such a thing. A family with incredible wealth and power. She'd read all about the Scotts on her way across the Atlantic.

And she'd read about their heroic son, a man who'd returned from the war after a dramatic plane crash behind enemy lines. Her gaze drifted to where she'd set her purse. Inside, in a little zippered pocket, she still had Zach's medal. A medal he hadn't cared about.

She thought of him flat against the ballroom wall in the Corretti Hotel, his eyes tightly closed as he fought against something, and knew there was more to the story than had been reported.

"We're the only ones who know," she said. "And I have no plans to inform them. I think the secret is safe for now."

His gaze was steady, cool, and she realized he didn't entirely trust her. It stung.

"There are always leaks." He shoved a hand through his hair. "There's only one way to deal with this. One way to keep everything from exploding into an even bigger problem than it already is."

Her heart thundered in her chest. And it hurt, too. Hurt because he'd called her—and their baby—a problem.

"Congratulations, Lia," he said, his voice chilling her. "You've won the jackpot, after all. You're about to become a Scott."

"This is not how I wanted this to happen," she said on a throat-aching whisper. Tears pressed the backs of her eyes. She couldn't let them fall.

"You came here," he said, his voice hard. "What did you expect? Did you think I would be happy?"

She dropped her gaze. A single tear spilled free and she dashed it away, determined not to cry in front of him. Not to be weak.

"I had hoped you might be, yes." She lifted her chin and sucked back her tears. "Clearly, I was mistaken."

"We'll marry," he said. "Because we must. But it's an arrangement, do you understand? We'll do it for as long as necessary to protect our families, and then we'll end it when the time comes."

Anger started to burn in her, scouring her insides. He was no better than her father had been. He didn't care about his child any more than Benito Corretti had cared about her. He was making a deal, nothing more. It made her sick. And furious.

"Fine," she said tightly. "I accept. But if we are having an arrangement, as you so nicely put it, then I want it understood that this arrangement is in name only."

She didn't know what made her say that, but once she said it she knew it was right. Because this situation was so out of her power that she needed something she could control. Something she could have a say about.

He stared at her for a long moment. And then his sexy lips curled up in a smile, surprising her after he'd been so hard and cold. "I can't guarantee that, sugar. But we'll try it your way to start. Just know that when you do surrender to me, I won't be saying no."

Lia pulled herself erect and looked at him with all the haughtiness she could muster. Which wasn't much, she was sure. But damn if he hadn't infuriated her. "There will be no surrender, Zach. Not ever again."

"We'll see," he said with all the arrogant surety of a man who was accustomed to getting his way. And then he headed toward the door. "I'll let you know when the arrangements are made."

"How long will this take?" she asked as he opened the door.

He turned back to her. "Eager, Lia?"

She sucked in a breath. No, she was just worried about her ability to stay in this hotel. And about her family sending someone to fetch her if they figured out where she was. "No, but I have no idea how long these things take in America. I can't stay in this hotel for weeks, Zach."

His eyes slipped over her. "No, you can't. The media will descend soon enough. You'll move in with me. I'll send someone for you later."

He closed the door before she could say another word. She stood there for a long time, uncertain whether she'd found salvation by coming to D.C.

Or whether she'd damned herself instead.

CHAPTER SIX

ZACH LIVED IN a sprawling house in Virginia. It was gated, with manicured green lawns and a view of the Potomac River. Here, the Potomac was still close to the source and was wilder and freer than it had been in Washington. It tumbled over huge boulders, rushing and gurgling toward the city where it would become wide, placid and subject to Chesapeake tides.

Lia stood in a room that overlooked the backyard and the cliffs of the Potomac. Glass doors opened onto a wide stone balcony that ran the length of the house. Immediately outside was a small seating area, with a chair and a table. Perfect for reading.

The gardens weren't overly ornate, but there were a lot of gorgeous flowering plants in manicured beds. Roses bloomed in profusion along two stone walls, red and pink and white. Fat flowering hydrangeas, blue and pink, sat in the shade beneath tall trees, and a host of bright annuals bloomed in beds that ran down toward the river.

Lia's fingers itched. She wanted to lose herself in the garden, to go dig into the dirt and forget all about Zach Scott and the Correttis for a while.

But that was impossible right now.

She hadn't seen Zach since she'd arrived. A chauffeur had come to get her at the hotel earlier, after a terse call from Zach informing her to be ready. Once she'd arrived, a uniformed maid had showed her to this room and offered to put her things away. Lia only had one suitcase and a carry-on, so she didn't really have much with her. She'd declined and hung everything herself.

Now she felt like she was in stasis. Just waiting for something to happen. The garden called to her, but she resisted. What would Zach think if he came looking for her and she was on her knees in the dirt?

As the minutes dragged by, she resolved to go out on the balcony and run her fingers through the potted geraniums and lavender, just for something to do, but a knock at her door stopped her. "Yes?" she called.

The door opened and Zach stood there, tall, handsome and brooding as ever. Lia folded her arms over her chest and waited.

"If you've no objection, I've brought a doctor who is going to take a blood sample."

"Why?"

Zach came into the room, his hands shoved into the pockets of his faded jeans. *Dio*, he was sexy. Lia shook herself and tried not to think about him that way. She failed, naturally. Her heart thumped and pumped and her bones loosened in the shell of her skin.

"There is a paternity test that will isolate the baby's DNA from your blood. Just to be certain, you realize."

Lia lifted her chin. "I have nothing to hide."

It hurt, of course, that he didn't believe her. But if a test would erase all doubt, she was for it. Not only that, but she also looked forward to the apology he would have to make when the test proved he was this baby's father.

"I'll bring her up, then."

"Yes, do."

He left and then returned a few minutes later with a smiling woman who took Lia's blood and asked her questions about how she was feeling. Once it was over, and the woman was gone, Lia was left with Zach.

"I have an important dinner to attend tonight," he told her. "You will accompany me."

Lia swallowed. She wasn't accustomed to large gatherings. Aside from the wedding-that-wasn't, and a few family things that happened once a year, she spent most of her time alone or with her grandmother.

"I don't have anything to wear," she said. She didn't

even know what kind of dinner it was, but if it was anything like that gathering she'd crashed last night, she knew she didn't have anything appropriate. She'd put on the nicest thing she had for that event.

Zach didn't look perturbed. "There is time. I'll send you to my mother's personal shopper."

"That is not necessary," she said, though in truth she wouldn't begin to know where to start in this city.

"I think it is, Lia. It'll go much faster if you simply let her help you pick out what you need. For tonight, you'll need formal wear. But select a range of clothing appropriate for various events."

"And do you attend many events?" she asked, her heartbeat spiking at the thought of being out among so many people so frequently.

Plants she understood. People not so much.

His eyes were flat. "I am a Scott. And a returning war hero. My presence is in demand quite often, I'm afraid."

She didn't miss the way his voice slid over the words *war hero*. It was like they were oily, evil words for some reason. As if he hated them.

"You don't sound as if you enjoy it."

One corner of his mouth lifted. "No, I don't. Not anymore."

She wanted to ask what had changed, but she didn't. "Then why do it?"

"Because I am a Scott. Because people depend on me. And if you are going to be a Scott, too, then you'd better get used to doing things because you have to instead of want to."

Lia nibbled the inside of her lip. She was no good at the social thing. She had no practice at it. But, for tonight, she would have to try and be something she wasn't. She would have to navigate the social waters without falling flat on her metaphorical face.

"I'm no good at this, Zach," she told him truthfully. "I don't have any experience."

Not to mention she was awkward and grew tongue-tied around too many people. She'd always been so self-conscious, so worried about whether or not others liked her.

Because she'd never felt very wanted and she didn't know how to fix it.

"Then you'll learn," he said. "Because you have no choice."

Zach slipped into his tuxedo jacket and tugged the cuffs of his shirt until they were straight beneath the jacket arms. Tonight was another event, another speech, where he would be speaking to some of Washington's elite about the need for funding for veterans' causes. Everyone tended to think, because the military worked for the government, that returning vets' care was assured. It was to a point. Where that point ended was where Zach stepped in.

But tonight was different in a way he had not expected. For the first time since he'd returned from the war, he was taking a woman with him. A woman who was his date.

His fiancée, for God's sake. An unsettled feeling swirled in his gut at the notion, but it was too late to back out now. He'd had the call from the doctor. They'd rushed the results—because he'd paid them a great deal of money to do so—and he knew the truth.

Lia Corretti was pregnant with his child.

He wasn't quite sure how that made him feel. He was still stunned at his reaction to her earlier today, in her hotel room, when he'd suddenly decided that marrying her was the thing to do. It had been a preemptive strike, because though he'd fully intended to get an answer to the child's paternity before proceeding, he'd also known on a gut level that she was telling him the truth.

She'd been a virgin. He'd realized something was different about her that night in Palermo, but she'd distracted him before he'd puzzled out precisely what it was. Not that being a virgin made someone truthful, but he imagined it was highly unlikely she'd turned around and taken a new lover so quickly.

His gut had known what his head hadn't wanted to

admit. And now he had a fiancée. A fiancée he didn't quite know how to fit into this life of his. She hadn't wanted to accompany him tonight, but he'd insisted she would anyway.

He'd been angry and resentful toward her all day. But now he felt a twinge of guilt over his reaction. Still, he'd told her the truth. She would learn to deal with her responsibilities as his wife because she had no choice.

They had appearances to maintain and commitments to keep. If he was going to have a wife, then she was going to be at his side. It's the way it worked in his world. The way it had always worked.

He went downstairs and into his office, where he opened the wall safe and extracted a box. He'd told Lia to shop for clothing, but he'd not thought of jewelry. He had no idea what she would wear tonight, but he knew what would look good with her coloring. He opened the box and slid a finger over the art deco rubies and diamonds. These had belonged to his grandmother. She'd left them to him on her death and he'd put them away, certain it would be years before he found a woman to give them to.

He flipped the box closed after a long moment and held it tight. His life was changing in ways he hadn't expected. Ways he wasn't quite sure how to cope with. He resented the changes, but he would deal with them the way he dealt with everything else in his life these days.

By hiding his feelings beneath a mountain of duty and honor.

She was learning, or trying to. Lia stood beside Zach at a posh gathering being held in the National Gallery of Art. It was past closing time, and the museum was only open for this exclusive party.

She'd chosen a gown in a rich cream color, and swept her dark hair off her shoulders and pinned it up. She'd applied her makeup carefully, slid into her heels—not too high because she was already self-conscious about her height—and wrapped a shawl around her shoulders. Her jewelry had consisted of her simple diamonds, until she'd arrived downstairs and found Zach waiting for her in the foyer of the big house.

His gaze had flicked over her appreciatively, and she'd felt warmth spread through her limbs. She liked the way he looked at her. And she wasn't happy about that. After the way he'd behaved since she'd arrived, she didn't want to like anything about him. She kept telling herself that the man she'd spent two days with was gone—except she couldn't quite convince herself when he looked at her the way he had earlier.

"Wear these," he'd said, flipping open a box that held a ruby-and-diamond necklace and matching earrings. It was ornate, but somehow simple, too. An impressive feat for an expensive necklace.

"I shouldn't," she said. "I'm too clumsy—"

"Nonsense." His tone had been firm. "You're a beautiful woman, Lia. And you are about to be my wife."

He'd taken the necklace from the box and clasped it on her once he'd removed her small pendant. Then he placed her necklace carefully in the box he'd taken the larger necklace from. She was grateful for that, considering it was the only jewelry she had that had belonged to her mother. It might be small and unimpressive, but Zach didn't treat it that way, and that touched her even though she did not want it to. He held out his hand for her earrings, which she handed over, and then she put the diamonds and rubies on.

When she was finished, he gave a satisfactory smile. "Excellent. You look lovely."

They'd climbed into the Mercedes, and the chauffeur—Raoul—had driven them here, where Zach had been greeted like the political royalty he was. Now, they were sipping cocktails and waiting for the dinner to begin.

She didn't miss that women slanted their gazes toward her. Some were appraising while others were downright hostile. Zach kept her at her side. Periodically, he would drape an arm around her, or slide his hand into the small of her back to guide her through the crowd. His touches made her jumpy yet she found herself craving them.

Soon they were seated at a large round table toward the front of the gathering. Lia wasn't intimidated by the array of cutlery and plates before her. She might not be any good at the socializing part of this, but she'd been brought up by Teresa Corretti, the most elegant woman in all of Sicily. Lia knew which fork to use, and which bread plate was hers. She also knew how to sit through a multicourse meal and how to pace herself so that she wasn't too full before the last course arrived.

But tonight she was finding it hard to concentrate on her food. She was still tired from the trip, and the stress of everything was starting to overwhelm her. She'd left Sicily on impulse, and now she was here with Zach, and he wasn't the man she'd thought he was.

He was an automaton, an aristocrat, a man who did what he had to do because he cared about things like social standing and reputation. While it wasn't a foreign concept to her, coming from the Corretti family, it wasn't what she'd thought she was fleeing toward when leaving Sicily.

She could hardly reconcile the man he was here—dressed in a bespoke tuxedo and sporting an expensive watch—with the stiff military man who'd thrown a medal at her feet. The two did not seem to go together, and it confused her.

"You aren't eating."

His breath ghosted over her ear and a shiver of something slid down her backbone. She turned her head, discovered that he was frowning down at her, his dark eyes intense.

"I'm tired," she said. "My schedule is all messed up. In a couple of hours, I would be waking up and having breakfast, were I still home."

"You need to eat something. For your health."

She knew what he meant. And why he didn't say it. "I've eaten the soup and some of the bread."

"Beef is good for you. There's iron in there."

"I've had a bite of it."

"Eat more, Lia."

"I can't eat just because you order me to," she snapped quietly.

Zach glanced at someone across the table and smiled. Then he lifted his hand and slid it along her jaw, turning her head as he did so. To anyone else, the gesture looked loving and attentive. But she knew what it really was. He was attempting to keep her in line.

His eyes held hers. She couldn't look away. His mouth was only inches away, and she found herself wanting to stretch toward him, wanting to tilt her face up and press her lips to his.

His gaze dropped to her mouth, and one corner of his beautiful, sensual lips lifted. "Yes, precisely," he murmured. She felt her face flood with heat. "And I am not ordering you to eat, Lia. I'm concerned about your health."

She dropped her gaze from his. "*Grazie.* But I will not let my health suffer, I assure you."

"Excellent," he said. "Because you are mine now, and I take care of what is mine."

A shiver slid through her. And a flash of anger. "Are you certain about that? What if the test results aren't what you want them to be?"

His eyes sparkled with humor that she sensed was at her expense. "I've already had the result. And it is precisely what you said it was."

Lia wanted to jerk herself out of his grip, but she knew this was not the place to show a bit of temper. "You could not have told me this earlier?"

He shrugged. "Why? You already knew the answer."

"Perhaps I would like an apology. You did suggest I was lying, as well as exceedingly promiscuous."

"My mistake."

"You consider that an apology?"

"I do. You must realize, sugar, that you aren't the

first to try and trap me this way. You're just the first to succeed."

Lia shoved her chair back, uncaring how it looked to the other guests at their table. The murmur of conversation ceased and all eyes were on her. She swallowed and stood, hoping the trembling didn't show.

"If you will excuse me, ladies and gentlemen," she said. "I believe I must freshen up."

Then she turned and marched away without waiting for a response. She was certain the fashionable ladies were appalled with her. The gentlemen probably shrugged it off as foreign eccentricity. Nevertheless, she didn't quite care what they thought. She wasn't about to sit there and let Zach talk to her like that.

She found the ladies' room and went inside to perch on one of the settees and calm down. She refreshed her lipstick in the mirror and smoothed a few stray hairs into place. As she gazed at her reflection, it hit her how unusual her reaction just now had been. She'd sat through enough humiliating Corretti functions in her life to know how to be invisible for the duration.

She also knew how to be a lady whenever any attention happened to turn on her, and she knew that marching away in a huff was not a part of the training her grandmother had instilled in her. Teresa Corretti would be disappointed at that display of temper just now.

Lia curled her hands into fists on her lap and took a deep breath. Damn Zach, he had a way of getting beneath her skin and irritating her so much that she simply reacted without thinking. It wasn't like her to draw attention to herself, or to argue, but she couldn't help it with him.

Still, she should not have let him get to her like that. But he'd suggested she'd purposely set out to trap him into marriage, and it made her furious. What kind of God's gift to women did he think he was anyway? It was ludicrous. And she planned to tell him so just as soon as they were alone and she could give him a proper piece of her mind.

Lia stood and smoothed her dress. She studied herself in the mirror and was pleased with what she saw. Oh, she was still too plump—and too tall—but she cleaned up quite nicely when she was able to wear designer dresses someone had picked out specifically for her shape and coloring.

When she left the ladies' room, Zach was standing across from the door, leaning against the wall in a sexy slouch that made her heart kick up. He really was spectacular. Tall, broad and intensely handsome. The kind of man that, yes, would have women falling all over him.

"You've been gone awhile," he said.

Lia tilted her chin up. "Yes. I needed to get my temper under control."

Zach laughed. She didn't like the way the sound slid beneath her skin. Curled around her heart. Warmed her from the inside out.

"I wasn't aware you had a temper, Lia."

"Of course I do. And you know just how to aggravate it." She'd never really realized precisely how furious another person could make her until she'd met Zach. He had an ability to make her feel things she'd never quite felt before—and to say things she would have never said to another person. Usually, she hid her emotions down deep.

Except with him. With him, she couldn't help but say what she was feeling.

It was that or burst.

She crossed the hall and stood right in front of him, nearly toe to toe. She was tall in her heels, five-eleven, but she still had to tilt her head back to look up at him. "You might think you are some sort of priceless gift to womankind, Zach Scott, but I'll have you know that I would much prefer to be back home and for none of this to have happened."

It wasn't quite true, but she wasn't going to tell him that. She wasn't sorry for the two nights they'd spent together. She wasn't even sorry about her baby. She was sorry for the way it had happened, and for the man it had happened with. Why couldn't she have chosen a good Sicilian man for her night of rebellion? A single, sexy Sicilian who had no hang-ups about women and their motives.

Even as she thought it, she knew she didn't really want that, either.

"For your information," she continued, "I did not set out to 'trap' you. That is the most arrogant, conceited, unbelievable thing you have said yet. No one forced you to do what you did in Palermo. No one forced you to take that risk."

His expression was dark. "No, you're right about that. No one forced me. It was a mistake, and I was stupid enough to make it." His eyes slid over her, came to rest on her face again. "Everything about those two days was a mistake."

Lia tried not to let that hurt her, but she didn't quite succeed. It stung her in places she'd thought she'd locked away long ago. "Well, now that we have that out of the way, I think it must be time for the dessert course."

She turned her back on him and started down the hall, back toward the dinner. Tears pricked her eyes. Angry tears, she told herself.

Zach's hand on her elbow brought her up short. She whirled around and jerked out of his grip.

He was a dark, brooding presence. "Look, I didn't

mean that the way it sounded." He shoved a hand through his hair, blew out a breath.

Lia glared at him steadily. "I did not trap you, Zach. I'd like you to admit that."

His expression remained dark. "Fine. You didn't trap me."

"And what about not believing I was telling the truth? Are you going to admit you were wrong about that, too?"

His eyes gleamed. "No."

She stiffened. "Of all the rude, arrogant—"

"What reason did I have to believe you?" he said heatedly. "We're strangers, Lia, regardless of what happened in Palermo."

She swallowed against the knot of anger and pain clogging her throat. But she knew what he said was true. Would she have believed a story like hers if she were Zach? Considering his previous experience of women, perhaps not.

"I will concede that point," she said coolly, though her heart beat hot at the admission. "But I don't like it."

He reached for her hand, slipped it into his. Her entire body went on red alert just from that simple touch. She wanted more of him, more of what they'd had in Palermo. And yet she knew that was the last thing she should want. The very last. They had an arrangement in name only, to protect their families, until such time as they could go their separate ways and not cause a scandal.

She had to remember he didn't truly want this child. Or her.

She tried to pull her hand away, but he held it tight.

"Darling, we're returning to the event," he chided her. "We have to look happy together if they are to believe our whirlwind romance."

"I'm not very good at pretending," she said stiffly.

He tugged her closer. "Then I will have to give you a reason to smile," he said, slipping his hand around to the small of her back and pressing her against him. He pulled the hand he'd trapped up to his chest, pressed her palm against the smooth fabric of his tuxedo.

"There is nothing you can do to make me smile, Zach," she said, though her heart beat harder and faster as the look in his eyes changed. Heat flared in their dark depths and her body responded by softening, melting. She held herself rigid, unwilling to give in to the feelings swirling inside her. Feelings that wanted her to tilt her head back and offer her lips up for him to claim. "I want you to let me go."

His eyes were hooded as they dropped to her mouth, and a shot of adrenaline pulsed into her veins.

"I will," he murmured. "But not quite yet."

CHAPTER SEVEN

ZACH WAS ON the edge of control. Not in a way that made him sweat as helpless panic rose in his throat and threatened to squeeze the life from him. But he had a need to dominate. A need to take this infuriating woman to his bed and not let her out of it for several hours.

Not until she sighed her pleasure into his ear. Not until she gasped out his name the way she had in Palermo. Sweet, innocent Lia. He wanted to taste her again. Wanted to know if she was as sweet as he remembered. As intoxicating.

She stood very still in his grasp. He didn't hold her tight. She could have broken free with a single tug. Oh, not when he'd first gripped her hand. Definitely not then. At that moment, he'd been intending to saunter back into the gathering with his woman at his side, looking happy and enraptured for the world to see.

He knew how this game was played. He could have a fast romance and marriage, but first he had to be seen with Lia. And they needed to appear as if they couldn't keep their hands off each other. So far, they'd looked as if they might prefer to touch anyone else rather than each other.

He had to change that perception, especially since there were at least three reporters circulating at this party tonight. Tomorrow, on the society pages of the local papers, they'd mention his date. By tomorrow evening, they'd know everything about Lia Corretti.

And what he wanted them to know was that she was mad for him.

Except she didn't look so much mad for him as mad at him at the moment. Furious, with her snapping blue-green eyes and dark auburn hair that caught the light like a flame. Her lips parted slightly as he stared at them. Her breathing grew shallow, her creamy breasts rising and falling more rapidly.

He could see the pulse thrumming in her neck. A very male sort of satisfaction slid through him. Lia was not immune, no matter how she bristled and glared.

Zach reached up and ran his thumb over the pulse at her throat. She gasped, but she didn't pull away.

"We were good together," he purred. "We could be again."

Her eyes were wide as she gazed up at him. "This is an arrangement, Zach," she said, her voice hardly more than a whisper. "An arrangement that does not include sex."

He was beginning to regret that he'd used that word with her. She was intent on keeping it strictly business since he'd told her this was a temporary solution to protect their families from the media.

He'd fully intended it to be temporary when he'd said it. It had seemed the perfect solution. He didn't know the first thing about being a father, wasn't sure he could even do it. If he married Lia, gave their child a name and a legacy, they could go their separate ways in a few months and everything would be fine.

Except, strangely, since the moment the doctor had given him the test results earlier, he'd felt a sense of duty that warred with those thoughts.

And more than duty. When Lia had come downstairs tonight, he'd felt the same shot of lust he'd experienced in his room in Palermo. The same hard knot of desire had coiled inside his gut and refused to let go.

He bent toward her, breathed in her scent. "What is your perfume, Lia?" he asked, his breath against her ear. A shudder rolled through her. He could feel it in his fingertips where they pressed into her back and throat.

"It's my own," she said, her voice husky. "I went to a perfumer in the village. She made it for me."

Zach breathed again. "Vanilla. A hint of lavender. Perhaps even a shot of lemon. For tartness," he finished.

"I—I don't know," she said quickly. "I didn't ask."

Zach couldn't stop himself from what he did next. He touched his tongue to her throat, glided to the sweet spot beneath her ear. The sound that came out of her made him hard.

Her hands were on his lapels, clutching him. "Zach, stop…"

"Do you really want me to?" he said against her sweet flesh.

She shuddered again, and he reacted with animal instinct, pushing her into an alcove where they were hidden from prying eyes. Unless someone was standing right in front of the opening, they would not be visible from down the corridor.

It was appalling behavior for a public event, but right now Zach was operating on a pure shot of desire.

"I definitely taste lemon," he said, tilting her chin up and back until her eyes were on his. "You are so beautiful, Lia. So hot."

"You are trying to seduce me," she said, closing her eyes. "You would say anything to further your purpose."

His hand slid around her back, up her rib cage. He shaped her breast, his thumb caressing her nipple beneath the fabric. He was gratified when it pebbled beneath his touch.

"Why do you say such things? Why don't you want to believe the truth? If you weren't hot, I wouldn't be unable to control myself with you. Don't you remember how it felt? How we burned together?"

"I remember it every day," she said, still not looking at him. "I carry a reminder."

He let his hand fall to her belly, pressed gently against her there. She uttered a little protest, but he didn't take his hand away. He knew it bothered her that her belly wasn't hard and lean. No, she was soft and pliable, womanly. Her body was curvy, not angular and hard from exercise. He liked it just the way it was.

"Maybe we should alter the arrangement," he said, his tongue suddenly feeling thick in his mouth. As if he didn't know the right thing to say. As if he were so new at this game of seducing a woman that the outcome could be in doubt.

She turned her head toward him, as if she was going to speak, and he knew the answer wouldn't be what he wanted to hear from the way she stiffened at his words.

But he wasn't going to give her a chance to say a thing. He brought his mouth down on hers, trapping her body between him and the wall. His heart was thundering in his chest, the way it did when he'd gotten that adrenaline rush after he'd aimed his jet straight up and climbed the sky like it was a mountain. Once he'd stopped climbing and starting racing toward earth again, only to pull up before it was too late, the g-forces holding him tight to his seat, he'd gotten another huge rush that made him laugh out loud at the sheer joy of flight.

Kissing Lia was similar to that feeling. Her lips were soft beneath his, though he sensed she didn't want them to be. Her hands curled into fists on his lapels—but she didn't push him away. He ghosted a thumb over her nipple and she gasped, letting his tongue inside her mouth.

Another shot of unfiltered desire ricocheted into his groin, making him painfully hard. He'd not been with a woman since he'd been with her. And before that, he'd not been with a woman in months. Lia had been the one to break the drought—and, strangely, he still desired her the way a man desired cool water after a hot trek in the desert.

Zach slid his tongue along hers, coaxed her into responding. She made a little noise in her throat—desire, frustration, he didn't know which—but she stroked him in return. He tightened his grip on her, pulled her in closer to his body.

And then he assaulted her mouth more precisely, more urgently, taking everything she had to give him and demanding yet more. Her arms went around his neck, and then her body was arching into his, her hips pressing ever closer to that hardness at the core of him.

He cupped her ass with both hands, pulled her tightly to him, so tightly there could be no doubt what he wanted from her. He flexed his hips, pressing his hardness into her, finding that precise spot that made her gasp and moan.

He could make her come this way. He *would* make her come this way. He needed to hear her pleasure, needed to be the one to make her feel it.

Dimly, the click of heels against tile registered in his brain. The sound was coming closer, closer. With a frustrated groan, Zach broke away from the sweet taste of Lia. She looked up at him, blinking dazedly, her eyes slightly unfocused and distant, her lips moist and shiny. By degrees, her features changed, set, hardened into a cool mask.

"I'm sorry," he said right before the heels clicked to a stop in front of the alcove. Except he didn't know what he was sorry for.

"Mr. Scott?"

Zach closed his eyes for a brief moment. Then he turned to greet the socialite who stood there. "Yes, Mrs. Cunningham?"

Elizabeth Cunningham's gaze darted past him to Lia, then back again. He didn't miss the tightening of Elizabeth's mouth, or the disapproving gleam in her eye. It pissed him off. Royally. Elizabeth Cunningham was thirty years younger than her husband, and much too judgmental for one who'd reached the pinnacle of society by marrying into it.

Zach reached for Lia's hand, pulled her to his side. Claimed her. He thought she might move away from him, but she didn't. She seemed to grasp the importance of appearances, after all.

"It's time for your speech," the other woman said, her gaze settling on his face once more.

Zach made a show of looking at his watch. "Ah, yes, so it is. I lose track of time when I'm with my lovely fiancée, I'm afraid."

Elizabeth's eyes widened. They darted to Lia. To Lia's credit, she didn't flinch or give away by look or gesture that she was anything other than what he'd said she was.

"Come, darling," he told her, tucking her hand into his arm and leading her back toward the gathered crowd. Another speech, another event to tick off his social calendar.

Afterward, he would take Lia home…and then he'd finish what he'd started here tonight.

* * *

Lia was shell-shocked. She sat through the rest of the evening in a daze. Her mouth still tingled where Zach had kissed her. Her body throbbed with tension and need. She'd been so furious with him, so convinced she would never, ever be susceptible to his charms again.

She'd been wrong. Woefully, pitifully wrong.

She was still the same lonely girl she'd always been, the same girl looking for acceptance and affection. She despised herself for that weakness, despised Zach for taking advantage of it. She took a sip of her water and let her gaze slide over the crowd before turning back to Zach.

He stood at a podium close to their table, talking about his father, about the war, about the night he was shot down over enemy territory. He said the words, but she wasn't convinced he felt any of them.

He was detached. Cold. The crowd was not. They sat rapt. And Lia couldn't help herself. She was rapt with them. She learned about how his plane took a hit and he'd had to bail out. How he'd broken his leg in the landing, and how he'd had to drag himself to shelter before the enemy found him.

Then she listened to him talk about the six marines who'd been sent in to extract him after several days.

They had all died trying to save him. He was the only survivor. It sent a chill down her spine and raised the hairs on the back of her neck.

He'd suffered much, she thought. So much that she couldn't even begin to understand. She wanted to go to him, wanted to wrap her arms around him and lower his head to her shoulder. And then she just wanted to hold him tight and listen to him breathe.

Toward the end of his speech, a photographer started to take photos. His flash snapped again and again. Zach seemed to stiffen slightly, but he kept talking, kept the crowd in the grip of his oratory. The photographer moved in closer. No one seemed to think anything of it, but Lia remembered that night in Palermo and her palms started to sweat.

Zach gripped the sides of the podium, his knuckles white. The flash went off again and again and she didn't miss the way he flinched in reaction. It was so subtle as to seem a natural tic, but something told Lia it was not. Then he seemed to stumble over his thoughts, repeating something he'd just said. Panic rose up in Lia's chest, gripped her by the throat.

She couldn't watch him lose his way like he had in Palermo. She couldn't let him suffer that kind of public meltdown. She didn't know that he would, but she couldn't get past the memory of the way she'd met him, plastered against that wall with his eyes tight shut and the flashing and booming of lights and bass all around.

She didn't have to look at this crowd any longer to know it would be disastrous if he did.

Right now, everyone seemed to be paying attention to Zach. She didn't quite know what to do, or how to deflect their attention—and then she did. She coughed. Loudly. After a moment, Zach's gaze slid in her direction. She kept coughing, and then she reached for the water, took a swallow as if she were having trouble. Zach's attention was firmly on her now. He darted his eyes over the crowd, but they inevitably came back to her.

She coughed again, sipped more water. The photographer seemed satisfied enough with his photos thus far that he lowered his camera and melted toward the back of the crowd.

Lia stopped coughing. A few minutes later, Zach wound up his speech. The room erupted in applause. Lia breathed deeply, relieved. Though, perhaps Zach had been in control the whole time. Perhaps he'd never needed her intervention, lame though it was.

She watched him walk toward her. People stopped him, talked to him, making his progress back to her side take quite a long time. But then he was there, and she was gazing up at him, searching his face for signs of stress.

There were none.

He gazed over her head, his attention caught by something. Just for a moment, his mouth tightened. The flash went off again and Lia whirled toward the source.

"Come, darling," Zach said, holding out his hand. "Let's get you home."

Several of the Washington elite slid sideways glances at them, but Lia didn't care. She gave Zach a big smile and put her hand in his. He helped her from her chair and then they were moving toward the exit. They were waylaid a few more times, but soon they were on the street and Lia sucked in a relieved breath. They were facing the National Mall and the street was far quieter here since it fronted the museums instead of busy Constitution Avenue.

Raoul pulled up in the Mercedes on cue. Zach didn't wait for him to come around and open the door. He yanked it open and motioned Lia inside. Then he joined her and they were speeding off into the night. Zach leaned back against the seat and closed his eyes. His palms were steepled together in his lap.

She found herself wanting to trace a finger along the hard line of his jaw. She would not do it, of course.

"Are you all right?" she asked presently.

His eyes opened. "Fine. Why?"

She fiddled with the beading on her gown. "I thought the photographer might have disturbed you."

Zach was very still. "Not at all," he said after a moment's hesitation. "It goes with the territory. I am accustomed to it."

His answer disappointed her, but she decided not to push him further. She remembered how angry he'd been in Palermo, how disgusted with himself. She'd hoped he might confide in her tonight, but she had to understand why he did not.

Still, she ached for him.

"I'm sorry those things happened to you," she said. "In the war."

He shrugged. "That's what war is, Lia. Brutal, inhumane. People get hurt and people die. I'm one of the lucky ones."

Lucky ones. He didn't sound as if he believed those words at all. And yet he was lucky. He was here, alive—and she was suddenly very thankful for that. Her chest squeezed tight as she thought of what he'd said tonight—and how very close she'd come to never knowing him at all.

"Why don't you fly anymore, Zach?" She remembered that he'd said he couldn't but she didn't know why. She'd asked him that night in Palermo, but then she'd told him not to answer when she'd thought she'd crossed a line into something too personal.

Now, however, she wanted to know. She felt like she needed to know in order to understand him better. Her heart beat harder as she waited.

He sighed. And then he tapped his temple. "Head trauma. Unpredictable headaches accompanied by vision loss. Definitely not a good idea when flying a fighter jet at thirty thousand feet."

He sounded so nonchalant about it, but she knew how much it must hurt him. "I'm sorry."

His eyes gleamed as he looked at her. "Me, too. I loved flying."

"I don't like to fly," she said. "I find it scary."

He grinned, and it warmed her. "That's because you don't understand how it works. By that, I mean the noises the plane makes, the process of flight—not to mention the fact you aren't in control. It's some unseen person up there, holding your life in his or her hands. But it's all very basic, I assure you."

"I know it's mostly safe," she said. "But you're right. I haven't flown much, and the sounds and bumps and lack of control scare me."

She'd longed for a sedative on the long flight from Sicily, but she hadn't dared take one because of the baby.

His laugh made a little tendril of flame lick through her. "A fighter jet is so much more intense. The engines scream, the thrust is incredible and the only thing keeping you from blacking out is the G suit."

Lia blinked. "What is a G suit?"

"An antigravity suit," he said. "It has sensors that tell it when to inflate. It fits tight around the abdomen and legs in order to prevent the blood draining from the brain during quick acceleration."

Lia shivered. "That sounds frightening."

He shrugged. "Blacking out would be frightening. The suit not so much. You get used to it."

"You miss flying, don't you?"

He nodded. "Every damn day."

"Then I'm sorry you can't do it anymore."

"Me, too." He put his head back on the seat and closed his eyes. She wanted to reach out and touch him, wanted to run her fingers along his jaw and into his hair. But she didn't.

She couldn't breach that barrier, no matter how much she wanted to. She didn't know what she really meant by such a gesture, what she expected. And she couldn't bear it if he turned away from her. If he rejected her.

Lia clasped her hands in her lap and turned to look at the White House as they glided by on Constitution Avenue, heading toward the Lincoln Memorial and the bridge across the Potomac. The monuments were brightly lit, glowing white in the night. Traffic wasn't heavy and they moved swiftly past the sites, across the bridge and toward Zach's house in Virginia.

Lia racked her brain for something to say, something basic and innocuous. No matter what he'd said about the photographer, she was certain he'd had trouble with the intrusiveness of the flash.

But she didn't feel she could push the subject. He'd already shared something with her when he'd told her why he could no longer fly, and how much he missed it. He had not said those things during his speech. He'd said them to her, privately, and she knew it bothered him a great deal.

She was still trying to think of something to say when Zach's phone rang. He opened his eyes and drew it from his pocket, answering only once he'd looked at the display. He spent the next fifteen minutes discussing his schedule with someone, and then the car was sliding between the gates and pulling up in front of the house.

Zach helped her out of the car and they passed inside as a uniformed maid opened the door. It was dark and quiet inside. The maid disappeared once Zach told her they needed nothing else this evening.

The grand staircase loomed before them, subtly lit with wall sconces that went up to the landing. Zach took Lia's elbow and guided her up the stairs. His touch was like a brand, sizzling into her, and her breath shortened as all her attention seemed to focus on that one spot. She didn't want to feel this heat, this curl of excitement and fear that rolled in her belly, but she couldn't seem to help it.

The way he'd touched her earlier, kissed her—

Lia swallowed. She shouldn't want him to do it again, and yet a part of her did. A lonely, traitorous part of her. She wanted him to need her, wanted him to share his loneliness with her.

He escorted her to the room she'd been shown to earlier. But he didn't push her against the wall the way he had in the museum. His hand fell away from her elbow and he took a step back.

Disappointment swirled in her belly, left her feeling hot and achy and empty. After that blazing kiss in the art museum, she'd expected something far different. And after his speech tonight, she'd wanted something far different. That was the Zach she wanted to know—the one who hid his feelings beneath a veneer of coldness, who'd watched six marines die and who would never fly again, though he loved it.

That was the Zach he buried deep, the one he'd let out in Palermo. The one she wanted again.

"You did well tonight," he said. Still so cool, so indifferent.

Lia dropped her gaze as another emotion flared to life inside her. Confusion. Maybe she was wrong. Maybe he was just very good at being what the situation required. War hero. Senator's son. Fiery lover. "Thank you."

"Good night, Lia." He leaned forward and kissed her cheek. The touch was light, almost imperceptible. His hands were in his pockets.

She blinked up at him. "Good night, Zach."

He didn't make a move to leave so she opened her door and went inside her room because she thought that was what he wanted her to do. Then she turned and pressed her ear against the door, straining to hear him as he walked away. Her heart pounded in her chest.

What if he didn't go? What if he knocked on her door instead? What if she opened it and he took her in his arms and said he needed her?

What would she do?

Maybe she should open the door. Just yank it open and confront him. Ask him why he'd kissed her like that earlier. Why he'd mentioned altering the arrangement and then acted like it never happened.

Her fingers tightened on the knob. She would do it. She would jerk it open. She would demand an answer and she wouldn't fear rejection—

Footsteps moved away down the hall. A door opened and closed.

Lia wanted to cry out in frustration. She'd waited too long.

The moment was gone.

CHAPTER EIGHT

IT WAS STILL DARK when Lia woke. She lay in bed, uncertain for the first few moments where she was. And then she remembered. She was in Zach's house, in a guest room. She reached for her phone to check the time—2:00 a.m.

Lia yawned and pressed the button to open her mail. Four new messages popped into her inbox, but only one caught her attention.

From: Rosa Corretti
To: Lia Corretti
Subject: Hi

Lia's pulse thrummed as she clicked on the message. She read through it quickly, and then went back to the beginning to make sure she'd read it right the first time. Rosa was actually writing to her. There wasn't a snarky word or single insult in the entire missive. In fact, there was a word Lia had never expected to see: *Sorry.*

Rosa was sorry for snapping at her after Carmela's outburst. Not only that, but her half sister said she'd been thinking about many things and that she realized how rotten it must have been for Lia to live with Teresa and Salvatore once her father remarried and had a new family.

Rosa wouldn't know that Lia had actually been sent away long before Benito remarried. Why would she? Until just now, Lia was pretty sure Rosa barely remembered her existence, much less thought about her in any capacity.

Still, it was nice to hear from her. Surprising, but nice.

Lia would answer her, most definitely, but she wasn't about to get her hopes up for what their relationship could be. She'd spent her entire life mostly forgotten, and she wasn't planning to stick her neck out now. She didn't really know Rosa, but she knew what kind of woman Carmela was. Hopefully her daughter was nothing like her, but Lia intended to proceed with caution.

She got out of bed and slipped on her robe. Even thinking about Carmela had the power to make her feel badly about herself. When she remembered the way Zach had left her at her door tonight, the feeling intensified. It had taken her some time, but she'd figured out what he'd been doing at the museum when he'd kissed her.

He'd been getting her under control after she'd broken out of the box he'd put her in for the night. She'd dared to show temper, and he'd managed to smooth it over and make her forget for a while. He'd tugged her into the corner he wanted her in and tied her up neatly with a bow.

She'd sat there like a good girl, smiling and applauding and worrying over him. It infuriated her to remember how compliant she'd been, and all because he'd pressed her against that wall and made her remember what it had been like between them.

Heat crawled up her spine, settled between her legs and in her core. In spite of it all, her body still wanted his. It angered her to be so out of control of her own reactions, to feel so needy around a man who clearly didn't need her.

Lia went to the French doors and pulled them open, hoping the night air would help to cool her down.

A mistake, because it was summer in Virginia and the night air wasn't precisely cool. Oh, it was far cooler than it had been in the heat of the day, but it was still quite warm.

There was a breeze, however. Lia stepped outside

and walked barefooted across the stone terrace to the railing. The strong scent of lavender rose from the pots set along the wall. She ran her fingers over the blooms, brought them to her nose. It made her think of home.

If she could add lemon to the mix, she'd be transported to Sicily. Except that Sicily didn't quite feel like home any longer, she had to admit. Since the moment she'd fallen into Zach's arms at the wedding, she'd felt a restlessness that hadn't gone away. Sicily had seemed too small to contain her, too lonely.

But coming to the States was no better. She was still alone.

She could hear the river gurgling over boulders in the distance. The moon was full, its pale light picking out trees and grass and the foaming water where it rolled over rocks.

It was peaceful. Quiet, other than the river and the sound of a distant—very distant—dog barking. She leaned against the railing and tried to empty her mind of everything but sleep.

It was difficult, considering her body was on another time zone. Not only that, but she also had a lot on her mind. She'd fled Sicily because she'd been scared of what her family would do, but she'd never considered what Zach would do. Or what her life would become once she was with him.

Was it only yesterday that she'd stood in a hotel and

told him their arrangement would be in name only? And now here she was, aching for his touch, and simply because he'd kissed her tonight with enough heat to incinerate her will.

She was weak and she despised herself for it. She didn't fit in, not anywhere, and she wanted to. Zach had held out the promise of belonging on that night in Palermo—and she'd leaped on it, not realizing it had been a Pandora's box of endless heartache and trouble.

There was a noise and a crash from somewhere behind her. Lia jumped and spun around to see where it had come from. It seemed to be from farther down the terrace, from another room. Her heart was in her throat as she stood frozen, undecided whether to run into her room and close the door or go see what had happened. What if it were Zach? What if he needed her?

But then a door burst open and a man rushed through and Lia gasped. He was naked, except for a pair of dark boxer shorts. He went over to the railing and leaned on it, gulping in air. He dropped his head in his hands. His skin glistened in the night, as if he'd just gotten out of a sauna.

The moonlight illuminated the shiny round scar tissue of the bullet wound in the man's side. Zach.

As if it could be anyone else. Her heart went out to him.

"Is everything okay?" she asked softly.

He spun toward her, his body alert with tension. Briefly, she wondered if she should run. And then she shook herself. No, she would not run.

Zach wasn't dangerous, no matter that he'd told her he was in Palermo.

"You're okay, Zach," she said, moving cautiously, uncertain if he was still caught in the grips of a dream or an episode like the one in Palermo. "It's me. It's Lia."

He scraped a hand through his hair. "I know who it is," he said, his voice hoarse in the night. The tension in him seemed to subside, though she knew it was still right beneath the surface. "What are you doing outside in the middle of the night?" he demanded.

She ignored his tone. "I could ask the same of you."

He turned toward the railing again, leaned on it. It was such a subtle maneuver, but it warmed her because it meant, on some level, at least, that he trusted her. After what he'd been through in the war, she didn't take that lightly.

"I had a dream," he said. The words were clipped and tired.

Lia stepped closer, until she could have touched him if she reached out. She didn't reach out. "And it was not a good one," she said softly.

He shook his head. Once. Curtly. "No."

"Do you often dream of the war?"

He swung to look at her. "Who said I was dreaming of the war?"

She thought of the wild look in his eyes when he'd first looked at her, at the way he'd seemed to be somewhere else instead of here, and knew she was right. Just like that night in Palermo, though he had been wide awake then.

"Is it the same as what happened when I first met you? Or different?"

He didn't say anything at first. He simply stared at her. The moonlight limned his body, delineating the hard planes and shadows of muscle. She had an overwhelming urge to touch him, but she clenched her hands tightly at her sides instead.

She would not reach for him and have him push her away. She'd done that too many times in her life, when she'd reached out to family and been shunned instead.

"You don't quit, do you?" he asked.

"You can deny it if you like," she said. "But I think we both know the truth."

"Fine." He blew out a breath. "It's different than Palermo. When I dream, it's much worse."

"Do you want to talk about it?"

He laughed suddenly. A broken, rusty sound. "God, no. And you don't want to hear it, Lia. You'd run screaming back to Sicily if you did. But thanks for trying."

Lia bristled at his presumption. "I'm tougher than I look."

He shook his head. "You only think you are. Forget it, kitten."

Kitten. She didn't know whether to be insulted or warmed by that endearment. "The photographer did bother you."

"Yes."

There was a warning in his tone. But she couldn't leave it, not now.

"Why do you do these things if you're worried about your reaction?"

He growled. "Because I have no choice, Lia. I'm a Scott, and Scotts do their duty. And you'd better get used to it because soon you'll be one of us."

It suddenly made her angry. Why should people do things that hurt them just to please other people? "So you're saying I must put myself in situations that cause me stress for the sake of the Scotts?"

His eyes flashed. "Something like that."

She lifted her chin. "And if I refuse?"

"Too late to back out now, babe. I told Elizabeth Cunningham you were my fiancée. Tomorrow, the papers will be filled with you and me. The whole city will be interested in the woman who captured my heart. And you will be at my side for every damn event I have to attend. Like it or not."

A tremor slid through her. "You're no different than my grandfather was," she said bitterly. "It's all about appearances. The family. What will people think? What will they do if they know we're human, too?" Lia cursed in Italian. "We can't have that, can we? Because the family reputation is everything."

So long as you didn't shame the family, so long as you kept your mouth shut and your head down, you could stay. But, oh, don't expect them to care about you.

Don't ever expect that. She put her hand over her belly and vowed with everything in her that her child would never for one minute think public façades were more important than feelings. It was untenable, no matter the importance of the family.

She started to turn away, but Zach gripped her arms. She tried to pull out of his hold, but he wouldn't let her go. His face was so close to hers. And, in spite of her fury, her body was softening, aching. She hated that he did that to her. Especially when she did no such thing to him in return.

"Some things are bigger than our own desires," he said. "You know that."

Lia sucked in a breath that shook with tears. "And some things are more important than appearances."

She thought of him at the podium, of the way he'd looked when he'd started to fight the demons in his head, and then of the way he'd rushed out onto the terrace tonight, and she couldn't stand that he would have to face the same issue again and again, and all for the sake of his family reputation. "Maybe you should talk to someone—"

He let her go and shoved back, away from her. Then he swore. Explosively.

A second later he was back, one long finger inches from her nose. It trembled as he pointed. If not for that single detail, she would have been frightened of his temper.

"Leave it, Lia. It's none of your business," he growled. The finger dropped and he spun away, put both hands on the railing and stood there, drawing in breath after breath after breath.

She didn't know quite what to say. She hadn't thought her suggestion would cause him such pain, but clearly it had. She hated that it did. And she hated that he wouldn't share with her. That he lost his cool, but wouldn't tell her what she so desperately wanted to know to help him.

She closed her eyes and swallowed, and then closed the distance between them until she was beside him. He didn't move or speak, and neither did she.

"I'll do my duty, Zach," she said softly. "I'll be at every event you are. And I won't let them get to you."

No matter what she'd said about refusing to go along, she wouldn't leave him to face those situations alone. Not after tonight. He needed someone with him, and she would be that someone.

He turned toward her, his brows drawn down in a question.

She lifted her chin and tumbled onward. She felt silly, but it was too late to turn back.

"The photographers. The flashes. The crowds. Whatever it is, I won't let them derail you or trigger a reaction. You can count on me."

His expression didn't change, but his nostrils flared. "You're offering to protect me?"

Oh, it did sound so ridiculous when he put it like that. On impulse, she reached for his bare arm, squeezed the hard muscle encouragingly while trying to ignore the heat sizzling into her.

"Whatever it takes," she said. And then, because her cheeks were hot with embarrassment and she didn't want to hear what he might say in response, she turned and walked away.

"Lia."

She was to her door when he called out. She turned to face him, her hands at her sides, trying for all the world to seem casual and calm. "Yes?"

"Grazie, cara mia."

Her heart skipped. "You're welcome," she said. And then she stepped into her room and closed the door with a quiet, lonely click.

The day did not promise to be a good one. Zach turned up the speed on the treadmill, forcing himself to run faster. He needed to reach that Zen moment of almost total exhaustion before he could consider himself in any shape to deal with everything coming his way today.

The sun hadn't yet peeked over the horizon, and the sky was still gray and misty from the river. Soon, however, all hell would break loose.

As if the hell of his dream hadn't been enough to endure. He squared his jaw and hit the speed button. He'd been back in the trench, immobile from the drugs the medic had given him, and listening to the shouts and rat-a-tat-tats of gunfire. The marines had been cool, doing their job, but they'd known air support wasn't coming in time.

He'd wanted to help so badly. He could still see the last marine, still feel the pistol grip in his hand as the man gave him a weapon. He'd lifted it, determined to do what needed to be done—

But he always woke at the moment he pulled the trigger.

Terrified. Angry. Disgusted.

Sweat poured down his face, his naked torso. He ran faster, but he knew from experience he couldn't outrun the past.

No, he had to focus on today. On what was coming his way after last night.

First, there would be the papers. Then there would be an angry phone call from his father, Senator Zachariah J. Scott, demanding to know who Lia was and what the hell was going on.

Zach almost relished that confrontation. Except he didn't want Lia hurt. He should have chosen a better way to announce her role in his life, but he'd been too angry to think straight once Elizabeth Cunningham had looked at her like she was another piece of flotsam moving across his orbit. He'd simply reacted. Not the way he'd been trained to deal with things, but too late now.

She would handle it, though. He pictured her last night when he'd cornered her before his speech. She'd been fierce, angry, determined.

Sexy.

God, she was sexy. Something about Lia's special combination of innocence and fierceness was incredibly sexy to him. Addictive.

She wasn't like the women he'd been linked with in the past. They had always been polished, smooth, ready to step in and become the perfect society wife. Oh, he'd had his flings with unsuitable women, too. Women who were wild, fun, completely inappropriate.

Lia fit none of those categories. She wasn't smooth and polished, but she wasn't inappropriate, either. He doubted she was wild, though she'd certainly been eager and willing during their two-night fling.

Zach gritted his teeth and resolved not to think about that. Not right now anyway.

But he couldn't stop thinking about last night on the terrace when she'd said she would protect him. He'd wanted to laugh—but he hadn't. It had been incongruous, her standing there in her silky pajamas, looking all soft and womanly, staring up at him and telling him she would be at his side, making sure he didn't have a meltdown because of a camera flash or a nosy reporter.

He'd been stunned and touched at the same time. Yes, he'd nearly growled at her. He'd nearly told her she was too naive and to mind her own business. But her eyes had been shining up at him and she'd looked so grave that he'd been unable to do it.

He'd realized, looking at her, that she really was serious. That she cared, on some level, and that if he was nasty to her, she would crumple inside.

So he'd swallowed his anger and his pride and he'd

thanked her. It had been the right thing to do, even if the idea of her protecting him was ridiculous.

Except that she had intervened during his speech, coughing when he'd stumbled on the words. At the time, he'd thought little of it, though he'd been grateful to have something to focus on besides the photographer.

Now he wondered if she'd done it on purpose.

Zach finished his workout, showered and dressed, and went into his office to read the papers. The phone call came at seven. He let it ring three times before he picked it up.

"Care to tell me what's going on, Zach?" His father's voice was cool and crisp, like always. They'd never had a close relationship, though it was certainly more strained since Zach had come home from the war.

He knew his father loved him, but feelings were not something you were supposed to let show. They made you weak, a target to those who would exploit them.

And there wasn't a single aspect of his father's life that hadn't been thought out in triplicate and examined from all angles—except for one.

The only thing he hadn't been able to control was falling in love with his wife. It was the one thing that made him human.

"I'm getting married," Zach said, his voice equally as cool.

He heard the rustling of the newspaper. The *Washington Post*, no doubt. "I see that. The question is why."

"Why does anyone get married?"

His father snorted softly. "Many reasons. Love, money, comfort, sex, children. What I want to know is which reason it is for you. And what we need to do on this end."

A thread of anger started to unwind inside him. It was his life they were talking about, and his father was already looking at it like it was something to be handled and packaged for the world to digest. "For the spin, you mean."

"Everything needs to be spun, Zach. You know that."

Yes, he certainly did. From the time he was a child and his father had decided to step away from Scott Pharmaceuticals and put his hat in the political ring, their lives had been one big spin job. He'd grown sick of the spin. He'd thought going into the military and flying planes would be authentic, real, a way to escape the fishbowl of his powerful family's life.

He'd been wrong. It had simply been another chance for spin. Hero. All-American. Perfect life. Doing his duty. Father so proud.

How proud would his father be if he knew Zach hated himself for what had happened out there? That he wished he'd died along with the marines sent to rescue him? That he was no hero?

"But your mother and I love you," his father was saying. "We want to know what's going on in truth."

Zach's jaw felt tight. "She's pregnant," he said, and then felt immediately guilty for saying it. As if he were betraying Lia. As if it were her secret and not his, too.

He could hear the intake of breath on the other end of the phone. No doubt his father was considering how to minimize the embarrassment of his only son making such a foolish mistake.

Except the idea it was a mistake made him angry. How could it be a mistake when there was a small life growing inside Lia now? A life that was one half of him.

"You are certain the baby is yours?"

Zach ground his teeth together. An expected question, one he'd asked, too, and yet it irritated him. "Yes."

His father blew out a breath. "All right, then. We'll do what we need to do to minimize the damage."

"Damage?" Zach asked, his voice silky smooth and hard at the same time.

And yet had he not thought the very same thing? Had he not proposed this arrangement to Lia in order to minimize the damage to their families—most specifically his?

He had, and it infuriated him that he'd thought it for even a moment. What was wrong with him?

"You know what I mean," his father said tightly.

"I do indeed. But Lia is not a commodity or a project to be managed. She's an innocent young woman, she's pregnant with my child and I'm marrying her just as soon as I get the license."

His father was silent for the space of several heartbeats. "Very well," he said softly. "Your mother and I will look forward to meeting her."

It was the same sort of cool statement his father always made when he wasn't pleased but knew that further argument would result in nothing changing. Zach felt uncharacteristically irritated by it. He knew how his father was, and yet he'd thought for the barest of moments that his parent might actually have a conversation about Lia and marriage instead of one based on how Zach's choices would impact the family.

Zach didn't bother to waste time with any further pleasantries. "If that's all, I have things to attend to," he said in clipped tones.

"Of course," his father said. "We'll be in touch."

Zach ended the call and sat at his desk for several minutes. He'd never once had a meaningful conversation with his father. It bothered him. Instead of telling the older man what kind of hell he'd been through in the war, and how it really made him feel to be treated like a returning hero, he smiled and shook hands and did his duty and kept it buried deep inside.

Because that's what a Scott did.

The gardener rolled a wheelbarrow full of something across the lawn outside. Zach watched his progress. The man stopped by a winding bed of roses and began clipping stems, pruning and shaping the bushes. He was whistling.

Two days ago, Zach had been going about his life as always, attending events, making speeches and feeling empty inside. It was the life he knew, the life he expected.

Now, oddly enough, he felt like those bushes, like someone had taken shears to him and begun to shape him into something else. They were cutting out the dead bits, tossing them on the scrap heap and leaving holes.

He felt itchy inside, jumpy. He stood abruptly, to do what he didn't know, but then Lia moved across his vision and he stopped in midmotion. She was strolling down the wide lawn in the early morning sunshine, her long hair streaming down her back, her lush form clad in leggings and a loose top.

He watched her move, watched the grace and beauty of her limbs, and felt a hard knot form in his gut. She went over to the gardener and started to talk. After a moment, the man nodded vigorously and Lia picked up a set of pruning shears. Zach watched in fascination as she began to cut branches and toss them on the pile.

He suddenly wanted to be near her. He wanted to watch her eyes flash and chin lift, and he wanted to tug her into his arms and kiss her until she melted against him the way she had last night in the art gallery.

CHAPTER NINE

"YOU DON'T NEED to do that."

Lia looked up from the rosebush she'd been pruning to find Zach watching her. She hadn't heard him approach. He stood there, so big and dark and handsome that her heart skipped a beat in response.

He was wearing faded jeans and a navy T-shirt, and his hands were shoved in his pockets. He looked… delicious. And somehow weary, too.

Lia frowned. Larry the gardener had moved farther down the row. He was whistling and cutting, whistling and cutting. If he knew Zach had arrived, he didn't show it. Except that he moved even farther away, presumably out of earshot, and she knew he was aware of his boss's presence, after all.

Lia focused on Zach again. "I know that," she said. "I want to."

Zach's gaze dropped. "You don't have any gloves. What if you scratch yourself?"

Lia glanced down at her bare hands holding the pruning shears. "I'm careful. Besides, I'm not in a race."

She thought he might argue with her, but instead he asked, "Did you work in your grandparents' garden?"

She lopped off a spent bloom and set the shears down to carefully extract it from the bush. "Yes. I enjoy growing things. I'm pretty good at it, too."

"I don't doubt that. But you shouldn't be out here. It's hot, and you're pregnant."

As if in response to his reminder about the heat, a trickle of moisture slid between her breasts. "It's hot in Sicily, too. And the doctor said I should get some exercise. It's not good to sit indoors and do nothing."

"I have a gym, and a perfectly good treadmill. You can walk on it."

"I want to be outside, Zach. I want to be in the garden."

He frowned. "All right, fine. But not more than half an hour at a time, and not after nine in the morning or before five at night."

Lia blinked at him. "Why, thank you, your majesty," she said. "How very generous of you."

"Lia." Zach reached for her hand, took it gently in his. Instantly, a rush of sensation flooded her. She would have pulled free—except that she liked the feeling. "I'm not trying to be difficult. But you aren't used to the heat here. It's oppressively muggy in the summer, and it'll get to you before you realize it. Besides, we have a busy schedule and I don't want you to exhaust yourself."

Lia reached for another bloom with her free hand, only this time she was rattled from his touch and she grasped it too low on the stem. A sharp thorn punctured her thumb and she cried out. Zach swore softly and grabbed her hand. Now, he held both her hands between his.

Blood welled in a bright round bubble on the fleshy pad of her thumb.

"It's fine," she said, trying to pull her hand away.

Zach's grip tightened. "You're coming inside and washing it."

Lia sighed. She knew she wasn't going to win this battle. Besides, it was kind of nice that he was concerned. She shook herself mentally. There was no sense reading more into his concern than there was.

"Fine."

She called to Larry, who waved and smiled after she explained why she had to go. Then she followed Zach up to the house. He led her into the kitchen and slid on the taps. When the water was hot, he poured soap in her hand and made her wash.

"It's a rosebush, Zach, not a used hypodermic needle."

"Better safe than sorry," was all he said.

She finished washing, and then frowned while Zach put a dab of antibiotic ointment on her thumb and covered it with a Band-Aid.

When she looked up at him, his dark eyes were intent on her, his brows drawn down as he studied her. Her heart skipped the way it always did. Angrily, she tamped down on the rising tide of want within her.

"Did you eat breakfast yet?"

"I had a cup of tea and some toast," she said a touch breathlessly.

Zach frowned. "That's not good enough," he muttered, turning away from her and grabbing a pan off the hanging rack. "You need protein."

Lia crossed her arms, bemused suddenly. "Are you planning to cook for me?"

He glanced up at her, still scowling. And then he grinned and she had to catch her breath at the transformation of his features. "I can, actually. I had to learn when I entered the service. The air force frowns on hired help in the bachelor officers' quarters."

A man from a rich family who'd grown up with chefs and servants suddenly having to cook for himself? What an adjustment that must have been.

"Allora," she said. "It's a wonder you didn't starve."

He winked. "I'm a quick learner."

He retrieved eggs and cheese from the refrigerator. The housekeeper came in, took one look at the pan and him and shrugged. She retrieved whatever thing she'd come for—Lia didn't pay attention—and was gone again.

Lia didn't actually think she could eat anything else right now, but she was too fascinated to stop him from cracking the eggs and whipping them.

"So why did you join the air force? Couldn't you have learned to fly plancs anyway?"

His back was to her. She wasn't sure what was on his face just then, but he stiffened slightly, the fork ceasing to swirl the eggs for half a second before he started again. She berated herself for injecting a note of discord into the conversation when it had seemed to be going so well.

"I wouldn't have been able to fly fighter jets, no. I could have bought one, I suppose. The older ones come up for sale sometimes—but it's not quite the same. Besides, I wanted to serve my country."

"A noble cause."

He shrugged. "Yes." Then he stopped again, his broad shoulders tight. A moment later, he turned to her. His expression was troubled. "No, that's not why I did it," he said softly. "I joined the military because I wanted to get away from life as Zachariah J. Scott

IV. I didn't want the career at Scott Pharmaceuticals, the governorship of a state, the senate run and then maybe the presidency. Those are my father's dreams, not mine. I wanted to do something that mattered."

Lia's heart felt as if it had stopped beating. Dear God, he was sharing something with her. Something important. She didn't want to screw it up.

"You seem to have done that," she said. She thought of the medal in her room and knew he'd gotten it for good reasons. But why had he thrown it away?

He sighed, his shoulders relaxing a fraction. "You'd think so, wouldn't you? But here I am, and all that my time in the military did for me was set me up for even greater success if I were to follow the path my father wants."

"I think those things matter, too, Zach. It takes a lot of sacrifice to serve your country in any manner, don't you think?"

He glanced at her. "You're right, of course. Still…"

"It's not the path you want to take," she said when he didn't finish the sentence.

He slid the pan onto the stove and added a pat of butter. Then he turned on the burner. "No, I don't."

"What do you want, then?"

He looked at her for a long minute. "I want to fly. But I don't get to do that anymore, no matter that I want to." The butter started to sizzle. Zach poured in the eggs and swirled them in the pan.

"Surely there's something else," she said softly.

His gaze was sharp. "I want to help people returning from the war. It's not easy to go back to your life after you've been through hell."

Lia swallowed. He was talking from experience. And it suddenly made something clear. "Which is why you speak at these fundraisers."

"Yeah."

Yet he wasn't comfortable doing it. That much she knew from watching the effect on him last night. Oh, he was good at it—but it took a toll on him each and every time. "That's a good thing, then. I'm sure it makes a difference."

He shrugged. "It helps fund programs to return vets to a normal life. It also keeps the public aware of the need."

The eggs set in the pan, and Zach added the cheese. Soon, he was sliding the omelet onto a plate and carrying it to the kitchen island. He turned to look at her expectantly.

"Coming?"

How could she say no? She was ridiculously touched that he'd made her an omelet, and ridiculously touched that he'd shared something private with her. She walked over to the island and hopped onto the bar stool. Zach retrieved a fork and napkin, poured her a glass of juice and sat across from her, chin on his hand as he watched her take the first bite.

The omelet was good, creamy and buttery, with just the right amount of cheese. But it was hard to eat it when he was watching her. She could feel her face growing hot as she slid a bite between her lips.

"You have to stop staring at me," she finally said when her heart was thrumming and her face was so hot that he surely must see the pink suffusing her skin.

"I want to make sure you eat it all."

"I won't be able to if you don't stop watching me."

He sighed. "Fine." He sat back on the bar stool and turned to look out the window. "Better?"

"Yes. *Grazie.*"

Though she hadn't thought she was hungry, the omelet was good enough that she took another bite. Lia glanced up at Zach, and her heart pinched in that funny way it did whenever she realized how very attractive he was. And how little she really knew him.

"Thank you," she said after a minute. "It's very good."

"Hard to mess up an omelet," he said. "But I'm glad you like it."

"I could," she said. "Mess up an omelet, that is."

He turned to look at her. "You can't cook?"

She shrugged. "Not really, no. Nonna tried to teach

me, but I'm hopeless with the whole thing. I get the pan too hot or not hot enough. I either burn things or make gelatinous messes. I decided it was best to step away from the kitchen and let others do the work. Better for all involved."

"How long have you lived with your grandparents?"

"Since I was a baby," she said, her heart aching for a different reason now. The old feelings of shame and inadequacy and confusion suffused her. "My mother died when I was little and my father sent me to my grandparents. I grew up there."

"I'm sorry," he said. "I don't know what it's like to lose a mother, but I can't imagine it was easy."

Lia shrugged. "I don't remember her, but I know she was very beautiful. A movie star who fell in love with a handsome Sicilian and gave up everything to be with him. Unfortunately, it didn't work out." She moved a slice of omelet around on the plate. "My father remarried soon after she died."

She could see him trying to work it out. Why she hadn't gone to live with her father and his new wife. Why they'd left a baby with her grandparents. Bitterness flooded her then. She'd often wondered the same thing herself, until she was old enough to know why they didn't take her back. She was simply unwanted.

The words poured out before she could stop them. "My father pretended like his new family was the only family he had. He did not want me. He never sent presents or called or acknowledged me the few times he did see me. It was as if I was someone else's child rather than his."

Zach reached for her hand, enclosed it in his big, warm one. "Lia, I'm sorry that happened to you."

She sniffed. "Yes, well. Now you know why I had to tell you about the baby. I didn't have a father. I wanted one."

"Yeah," he said softly, "I understand."

Ridiculously, a tear spilled down her cheek. She turned her head, hoping he wouldn't see. But of course he did. He put a finger under her chin and turned her back again. She kept her eyes downcast, hoping that if she didn't look at him, she wouldn't keep crying. She didn't want to seem weak or emotional, and yet that's exactly how she felt at the moment.

Thinking of her childhood, and the way her father had rejected her, always made her feel vulnerable. Another tear fell, and then another.

Zach wiped them away silently. She was grateful he didn't say anything else. He just let her cry.

"I'm sorry," she said after a minute. "I don't know why..." Her voice trailed off into nothing as she swallowed hard to keep the knot in her throat from breaking free.

Zach let her go and scraped back from the island.

Another moment and he was by her side, pulling her into the warm solidness of his body.

She pressed her face against his chest and closed her eyes. Her arms, she vaguely realized, were around his waist, holding tight. He put a hand in her hair, cupping her head. The other rubbed her back.

"It's okay, Lia. Sometimes you have to let it out."

She held him hard for a long time—and then she pushed away, not because she didn't enjoy being in his arms, but because she was enjoying it too much. Her life was confusing enough already.

"I haven't cried over this in years," she said, not looking at him. "I'm sure it's the hormones."

"No doubt."

She swiped her palms beneath her cheeks and wiped them on her leggings. *Dio*, how attractive she must be right now, with puffy eyes and a red nose.

"It won't happen again," she said fiercely. "I'm over it."

He lifted an eyebrow. "I wonder—do we ever get over the things that affect us so profoundly? Or do we just think we do?"

Lia sniffled. "I'd like to think so. Not that the past doesn't inform our experience, but if all we do is dwell on it, how will we ever have much of a present?"

She felt a little like a hypocrite, considering how often she'd felt unwanted and out of sync with her family. But she didn't let it rule her. Or she was determined not to. Perhaps that was a better way of saying it. It crept in from time to time, like now, but that didn't mean it was in charge.

His eyes glittered in the morning light. "Precisely. And yet sometimes we can't help but dwell on a thing."

She knew what he meant. "Your dreams."

"That's part of it."

Lia closed her eyes for a moment. She was in over her head with this. How could what she'd been through compare to his ordeal? Shot down, injured, nearly killed, watching others be killed before your eyes. It made her shiver.

"I think maybe there's something in our psyches that won't let go," she said. "Until one day it does."

He looked troubled. "There were things that happened out there, things—"

He stopped talking abruptly, turned his head to look out the window. His jaw was hard, tight. But he swallowed once, heavily, and her heart went out to him.

"What things?" she whispered, her throat aching. When he turned back to her, his eyes were hot, burning with an emotion that stunned her. Self-loathing? It didn't seem possible, and yet…

He opened his mouth. And then closed it again. Finally, he spoke. "No," he said, shaking his head. "No."

* * *

Jesus, he was losing his mind. She'd been here for two days and he wanted to tell her everything. He wanted to take her to his bed, strip her naked and worship every last inch of her body. Which she would not allow him to do if he told her his darkest fears. His deepest secrets.

If she knew how flawed he was, she'd run far and fast in the opposite direction. She'd take that baby in her womb and get the hell away from him. Hell, she'd probably get a restraining order against him.

Her eyes were wide and blue as she sat on that bar stool and looked up at him. Innocent.

God, Lia was so very innocent. She would never understand what he'd been through, or what he'd almost done out there in that trench. Hell, he didn't understand it himself. He lived with the guilt every minute of his life and he still didn't understand it.

She was at a loss for words. He could see that. She dropped her gaze again, and he stepped away from her, breathed in air that wasn't scented with her intoxicating lavender and vanilla and lemon scent.

His body was hard. Aching. He hadn't needed a woman this much in…well, he couldn't remember. The last time had been with her. He wanted her again.

Now wouldn't be soon enough. But she was sweet

and delicate and pregnant. She did not need him making sexual demands of her just yet.

Zach rubbed a hand over his head. He couldn't think straight. His entire plan had been to protect his family from scandal—but really, was that the reason? His father had been in office for over two decades now. Would the news his son had knocked up a girl really shock anyone enough that they might not vote for him if he ran for president?

But what if Zach knocked her up and abandoned her to raise the child alone? Yeah, that might raise some heads. But so what?

It was his life, not his father's. Besides, his father had people who spun these things for him. Any scandal of Zach's, unless it involved criminal activities, wasn't likely to touch his father's career—or the funding for the veterans' causes that Zach worked so hard to obtain.

His plan, such as it was, had little to do with protecting anyone, if he were truthful.

And everything to do with the odd pull Lia Corretti had on him.

He wanted her, even if his brain had had trouble figuring that out at first. He'd nearly sent her away. He could hardly credit it at this moment.

"I'm sorry," she finally said. "I shouldn't have asked."

His gaze slewed her way. She was toying with the remains of her omelet. He had a sudden, overwhelming urge to tell her what she wanted to know.

But he couldn't. How could he say the words? He'd never said them to anyone. And if he did, what would she think of him? Would she look at him with terror or pity in her expression?

He couldn't bear either.

"It's not you," he said, because he didn't want to see that hurt expression on her face. She had so much to be hurt about, he realized, now that he knew about her father and what he'd done to her.

Rotten bastard. If the man was still alive, Zach would love to get his hands on him.

He blew out a harsh breath. "It's just…I don't talk about what happened out there. Not to anyone."

"It's okay. I understand."

She wasn't looking at him. He walked over and tilted her chin up with a finger. Her eyes were liquid blue, so deep he could drown in them.

"Do you?" he asked.

"Yes." Her voice was firm. "I know what it's like to have things that hurt you. Things you can't talk about."

The idea anyone had ever hurt her made him want to howl.

She reached up and wrapped her hand around his wrist. It was a soft touch, gentle—and he felt the ricochet effect all the way down to his toes. If he kissed her now, here, would she kiss him back?

"But if you ever want to talk about it," she was saying, "I'm here."

Here. His. He lowered his mouth, brushed his lips gently across hers. Her intake of breath made a current of hot possession slide into his veins. He wanted to hold her closer, kiss her harder.

Instead, he lifted his head and walked away.

CHAPTER TEN

LIA CAREFULLY BRUSHED her hair and donned the dress she'd chosen for this afternoon's cocktail party. Her reflection in the mirror looked the same as always, but she felt as if she'd been changed somehow. Her lips tingled at the thought of Zach, at that light brush of a kiss that had not really been a kiss.

She'd wanted more. She'd wanted to reach up and pull him to her and not let him go until he'd thoroughly kissed her.

And then some.

But he'd walked away without a word. He'd had no trouble doing so. He'd left her sitting there with a half-eaten omelet and a fire inside her that wouldn't go away.

She was mortified. And angry. He might not want her, but he had no right making her want him. If he tried that again, she was going to sock him.

Because her heart couldn't take it. He smiled and laughed and fixed her an omelet, and she wanted to sigh and melt and bask in his presence.

Pitiful, Lia. Just like Carmela had accused her of being. She'd spent so many years wanting to belong to a family that shunned her, and now she was up to her same old tricks with Zach. When would she ever learn? She had her baby now, and that would have to be enough. This thing with Zach was temporary.

He'd told her as much in her hotel room, hadn't he?

Except, dear heaven, when she thought of him this morning, telling her why he'd joined the military and why he continued to book public appearances even though they were difficult for him—well, she wanted to know him. Really know him.

She didn't want this to be temporary when he said things like that. She wanted this to be real. She wanted a chance. They'd gone about it backward, no doubt, but there was something about Zach that hadn't let her have a moment's peace since the instant she'd seen him in that ballroom in Palermo.

She wanted him in her life, and she wanted him to want her.

Lia picked up her perfume and dabbed a very little behind her ears and in the hollow over her collarbone. Then she grabbed her phone to check her email one last time before slipping it into her bag.

There was another email from Rosa. She opened it and read carefully, her heart rising a bit with every line. She had, after careful deliberation, answered Rosa's initial email. Now she had a reply. One that was friendly and open and even a little curious.

Lia sighed. Just when she'd given up on ever having a relationship with any Corretti other than her grandmother, this happened. She was pleased, but she was also baffled. It was as if so long as she wanted a connection, it would always elude her. The moment she stopped caring, or stopped wanting what she wasn't going to get, it happened.

If she could force herself not to care about Zach, would he suddenly be interested?

Lia frowned. If only it worked that way. She dropped her phone into her bag and went to meet Zach. He was waiting for her in the grand living room that overlooked the lawn and the river beyond. He looked up as she walked in, his dark eyes sparking with a sudden heat that threatened to leave her breathless.

His gaze drifted over her appreciatively. Tiny flames of hunger licked at her skin wherever he looked. Then he met her eyes again. The fire in her belly spiked. For a moment, she thought he might close the distance between them and draw her into his arms.

He did not, of course. Zach was nothing if not supremely controlled. Disappointment swirled inside her as they drove to the Lattimores' cocktail party. She kept her gaze focused straight ahead, but she was very aware of Zach's big hand on the gearshift so near her knee.

It was insane to be this crazy aware of a man, and yet she couldn't help it. Zach filled her senses. The more she worked to keep it from happening, the worse it got. He was the sun at the center of her orbit when he was near, no matter how she tried to ignore him.

The event was in a gorgeous mansion in Georgetown. After leaving the car with the valet, Zach escorted her into the gathering, his hand firmly on the small of her back. Lia's stomach vibrated with butterflies. Last night, she'd simply been the woman on his arm at an event. Tonight, she was his fiancée, and the media would take a more pointed interest in her now.

She'd seen the papers in his office, and read the stories about all-American hero Zach Scott and the mystery woman he was suddenly engaged to marry. Of course there was speculation as to why. That didn't surprise her at all.

The story basically went that Zach had traveled to Palermo for a wedding, met the groom's cousin and had a whirlwind romance. They also speculated that she and Zach had conducted this affair over the phone and through email until they simply couldn't stand to be separated any longer.

It was a lovely hypothesis, though laughably far from the truth.

Zach, however, seemed determined to play his role to the hilt once they entered the party. He was the besotted fiancé. He stayed by her side, fetched her drinks, kept a hand on her arm or her waist or her shoulder. Lia took a sip of her nonalcoholic cocktail and tried to calm the racing of her heart.

Zach's touch was driving her insane.

She could hardly remember half the people she met, or half the conversations she had. Her entire focus was on Zach's hand, on his warm, large presence beside her. On the butterflies that hadn't abated. Oh, no, they kept swirling, higher and faster, each time Zach touched her.

It was all she could do not to climb up his frame in front of everyone and kiss him senseless.

Her senses were on red alert, and her body was primed for him. Only him.

It irritated her, but she couldn't stop it. She watched him as he spoke with a gray-haired woman, watched the curve of his mouth when he laughed, the sparkle in his eyes and the long, lean fingers of his hand—the one she could see—as he held his drink.

Lia closed her eyes, tried to blot out the visual of that hand tracing a sensual path over her body. It didn't work, especially since she knew precisely how it would feel.

His arm went around her and she shuddered. "Darling, are you all right?"

Lia looked up at him, into those dark beautiful eyes that seemed full of concern for her. It was an act, she told herself. An act.

Her heart didn't care. It turned over inside her chest—and then it cracked wide-open, filling with feelings she didn't want.

"I—" She swallowed and licked her suddenly dry lips. "I need to freshen up," she blurted.

Without waiting for his reply, she turned and made her way blindly through the crowd until she found an exit. It didn't take her down a hall toward the restrooms, as she'd hoped, but spilled out onto a covered patio that gave way to a manicured garden with a tall hedge. Lia walked right down the path and between the hedges before she realized it was actually a maze.

Her heart beat hard as she breathed in the clean air, hoping to calm down before she went back inside and faced all those people—and Zach—again.

What was the matter with her? Why had she come unglued like that?

Because she was Lia Corretti, that's why. Lost little girl looking for love, for a home, for someone who needed her. She'd been staring at Zach, letting her mind wander, letting her fantasies get the best of her.

And she'd realized, boom, that she felt far more than she should be feeling. That she'd let herself fantasize him right into her heart.

How could you love someone you hardly knew? How could your heart make such a catastrophic mistake?

She hadn't seen it coming. How could she? Of course, she'd thought about him for the past month, thought about their blissful nights together and the way everything between them felt so right—but that was lust, not love.

When did love enter the equation?

When he'd made her an omelet and told her he wanted to do something meaningful with his life? Or earlier, when he'd pulled her against his hard body in Palermo and told her she was beautiful?

"Lia."

She turned at the sound of his voice, her heart thrumming, her skin flushing hot. She didn't want him here, and yet she did. He moved toward her, so tall, dark and gorgeous that he made her want to weep inside.

How had she let this happen? Panic flooded her as he approached.

But then she had a thought. Maybe—just maybe—it

wasn't love, after all. Maybe it was simply a deep in-
fatuation. Yes, she could certainly be infatuated with
him. That was far less pitiful than falling in love with
a man who was only marrying you because you were
pregnant.

Zach came closer, his brows drawn together. "Is
everything all right?"

"I needed space," she said. "The crowd was too
much."

It wasn't entirely untrue. She wasn't accustomed to
so many people. Her life in Sicily had rarely involved
crowds or massive gatherings. Her grandparents en-
tertained, and quite frequently, but she hadn't been
expected to attend. Now she'd been to three events
in as many days, and it was tiring.

"Do you feel well? Should we sit down somewhere?"

"I'm fine," she said quickly.

"Lia." He stopped in front of her, so close she could
feel his heat. Her head tilted back to stare up at him.
Her breath shortened in her chest as their eyes caught
and held. His hands came up to settle on her shoulders, and she felt a deep throbbing note roll through
her at that simple touch. "Don't lie to me, *cara mia*."

She loved it when he spoke to her in Italian.

"Fine, I will tell you," she said. "I feel overwhelmed,
Zach. I feel as if I don't really know you, and I won't

know you so long as we are constantly putting on a public face. I miss the man I spent time with in Palermo, the one who didn't say or do anything he didn't mean. There were no masks there, no appearances to maintain."

She dropped her gaze, focused on the buttons of his deep blue shirt. He'd worn a gray pinstripe suit, no tie, and Italian loafers. His jacket was open, and his shirt molded to the hard muscles of his chest. It was custom fit, of course—and the effect was mind-blowing on her already addled brain. He was perfect, beautiful.

For the life of her, she still didn't know what he'd ever seen in her. Or what he ever would see.

"This is my life," he said. "The way it really is. Palermo was an anomaly."

"Yes, well, I choose not to believe that is entirely true. You were more you because you weren't worried about being Zach Scott. You were freer there. You know it's true."

His head dropped for a second. And then he was looking at her again, his gaze dark and mysterious. "Yes."

"That's it? Just yes?"

He sighed. His hands on her shoulders were burning a hole in her. He slid them back and forth, back and forth, and the tension in her body bent like a bowstring. When he slid them to her upper arms, it wasn't a relief.

"You're right. What more do you want me to say?"

She couldn't believe he'd admitted it. But it made something inside her soar that he had. "About which part?"

"That I felt freer in Sicily. I wasn't the main attraction, and I knew it. The press might hound me here, they might follow me if I make a well-publicized trip abroad, but Sicily was unexpected. And too quick to matter much, though of course, they now wish they'd pursued me."

"Why?"

He laughed softly. "Because of you, Lia. Because the confirmed bachelor went to Sicily and came back with a fiancée."

"Thank heavens they didn't," she said, imagining a photographer lurking outside the Corretti Hotel. Or, worse, somehow learning they'd spent two nights together and contriving to get a photo through the open window. Lia shuddered.

"If they had, I doubt any of this would have happened," he said, and her heart twisted in pain. She knew what he meant.

"Perhaps you wish that had been the case." She lifted her chin, trying to hide the hurt she felt deep inside. He was so close. Too close. All she could smell was his delicious scent—a hint of spice and hard masculinity. She wanted to step in, close the distance between them and wrap her arms around him.

Her body ached with the need to feel him inside her again. To be needed by him.

Dio, she was pathetic.

She expected him to agree, to step away, put distance between them and tug her toward the house and the party.

He did not do any such thing. Instead, he slid one of those electric hands up to her jaw, cupped her cheek. The other went to the small of her back, brought her that short step closer, until her body was pressed to his, until she could feel the heat and hardness of him emanating through the fabric of his clothes.

"I should wish it," he said. "But I don't."

Her head was tilted back, her eyes searching the hot depths of his. "I don't know what that means, Zach."

His gaze dropped to her mouth, lingered. And then his lips spread in the kind of wicked smile that made her heart flutter. "I think I'm about to show you, *bella mia*...."

His mouth claimed hers in a hot, possessive kiss that stole her breath and her sense. Lia threaded her arms around his neck without hesitation, melded her body to his. She could do nothing else. She simply wasn't programmed to respond any other way.

The answering hardness in his groin sent a fresh blast of desire ricocheting through her. Had it been this incendiary between them the first time? Had she felt this sweet, sweet fire raging in her belly, her brain, her core? His tongue against hers was nirvana. She couldn't get enough. She kissed him back hotly, desperately, her tongue tangling with his again and again.

He groaned low in his throat, pulling her closer, one hand splayed over her hip, the other sifting into her hair, cupping her head, holding her mouth against his.

She was being swept away on a tide of heat and deep burning feelings that ached to get out. If he kept kissing her like this, she wouldn't survive it. She would not be the same Lia Corretti when it was over.

She would be his creature, his to do with as he wanted. His slave. His, his, his…

With a cry, she pushed him away. She didn't know why, except she knew it was necessary to her sanity, her survival. She could not be any less in control of herself and her emotions than she already was. She could not allow him to own her like this when he gave her nothing of himself in return.

Because she was certain, as certain as she was breathing, that she had no claim on his heart or his emotions. It was physical, this need, nothing more.

For him anyway.

And that was a kind of servitude she did not need.

She knew what it was like to be unnecessary—and she could not bear to be so in his life.

He let her go, his hands dropping to his sides. He looked angry, desperate—and then he looked cool, unperturbed. He wiped a thumb across his mouth, across that gorgeous mouth that had been pressed so hotly to hers only moments ago. Then he straightened his shirt, and she was mortified to see that she'd pushed it askew in her desire to touch him.

"Forgive me," he said coolly. "I forgot myself."

Her heart beat hard and swift, and nausea danced in her stomach. She took a step back, collided with the hedge. Tears filled her eyes, threatening to spill free. What was wrong with her? Why was she so emotional?

"I want to go home," she said.

His head came up, his eyes glittering hard as diamonds. "Home?"

She was confused at his reaction, at the tightness in his voice. "Yes, back to my room. I have a headache, and I want to sleep…."

She wasn't quite certain, but she thought his stance softened, as if a current of tension had drained away. He seemed remote, a gorgeous automaton of a man who stared back at her with cool eyes. He stepped to the side and swept a hand toward the entrance to the maze, indicating that she should precede him.

"Then we'll go," he told her.

They returned to the house in silence. Once there, they played the game again. Lia smiled, though it shook at the corners, as they moved through the gathering. Their leave taking was tedious, but then they were outside and the valet was bringing the car around. There were people clustered together on the mansion's grand portico, waiting for their cars or simply finding another place to take the party.

The lawn was wide, sweeping and, though the property was gated, the gates were opened to the street as cars came and went. A valet pulled up in Zach's BMW while another opened the passenger door for Lia with a flourish. Zach stood by her side. Ordinarily, he would hand her into the car, but this time he didn't touch her. She reckoned he was angry with her.

She took a step toward the car when something bright flashed in her face. It took her a moment to realize they'd been photographed. At first she thought it was simply someone taking a picture they'd ended up in by accident, but when she glanced at Zach, his taut expression told her it was more than that.

He stood there a moment, fists clenched at his side, but then he started around the car when nothing else happened.

The moment he was gone, the photographer took the opportunity to approach again, this time focusing in on Lia. Zach was halfway around the car when he turned to swing back toward the photographer, his face twisted in rage. The valet tried to put himself between Lia and the other man, but the man bumped against him and the car door swung into Lia, knocking her off balance. Before she could save herself, she landed on her hands and knees on the pavement.

Zach was at her side in a second, helping her up, his face tight with fury as he pulled her into the protective embrace of his body. He held her as if he were shielding her from another onslaught. She clung to him, breathed him in, though she told herself she should push away and tell him she was perfectly fine. Her body was still so attuned to his touch that her nerve endings tingled and sparked like fireworks on a summer night.

"Madame, I am so sorry," the valet said. "I tried to stop him—"

"It's not your fault," Zach said, cutting him off abruptly.

"Is the photographer still there?" Lia asked.

"He's gone." Zach pushed her back. "Are you okay?"

Lia nodded. "I think so. My palms hurt, but…"

Zach took her hands and turned them over, revealing scrapes on the heels of her palms. His expression grew thunderous.

"If I ever get ahold of that bastard—"

"I'm fine," Lia said quickly. "It was an accident."

"Your knees," Zach growled, and Lia glanced down. Her knees were scraped and bloody. A trickle of bright red blood ran down the front of her leg.

"I'll be fine," she said. "But I need to wash up."

Zach didn't look convinced. "Maybe we should have a doctor look at you. What if something happened to the baby?"

Lia smiled to reassure him. The scrapes stung, but they weren't life-threatening. She'd had worse the time she got stung by a nest of bees while working in the garden. That could have been life threatening, had she not ran and dived into the pool. "Zach, honestly. I fell on my hands and knees. If babies were hurt by such minor accidents, no one would ever be born."

He frowned, but he ushered her back inside. Their host and hostess were mortified, of course, and they were shown to a private sitting room with an attached bath where Lia could clean up before they went home.

The photographer had disappeared as quickly as he'd arrived. No one could seem to find him. Zach paced and growled like a wounded lion while she sat in the bathroom with a warm wet towel and cleaned the bloody scrapes. He would have done it for her, but she'd pushed him out of the room and told him she could take care of herself.

Once she cleaned the scrapes and stopped the bleeding on her knees, she reemerged to find Zach prowling, his phone stuck to his ear. He stopped when he saw her. He ended the call and pocketed the phone before coming over to her. He looked angry and worried at once.

"I think we should get you to a doctor to be sure," he said.

"Zach, I fell on my hands and knees. I didn't fall off a roof."

He looked doubtful. "I think I'd feel better if someone examined you."

Lia sighed. "Then make an appointment for tomorrow. Tonight, I want to soak in a hot bath and go to bed."

He raked a hand through his hair. "Fine," he said, blowing out a frustrated breath.

This time when they went out to the car, there was no photographer lurking nearby. The gates to the property were closed, opening only when Zach rolled to a stop before them and waited for them to swing open.

It was still light out, because it was summer, but the sun threw long shadows across the road. Zach didn't say anything as they drove, and Lia turned to look at the trees and rocks as they glided down a wide parkway that could have been in the middle of nowhere rather than in a major city.

"We're leaving," Zach said into the silence, and Lia swung to look at him.

"I beg your pardon?"

He glanced at her. "We're not staying here and enduring a media frenzy. I won't have you hurt or scared."

Lia frowned. "Zach, I'm not six years old. I'm not scared, and the hurt is minor. It's annoying, and I'm angry, but I won't break."

"I should have realized this would happen. I should have taken you somewhere else and married you first, then brought you back once they'd had time to get used to it."

Lia didn't know how that would help, considering he was still a Scott and still a media target no matter where he went. "It was an accident. Celebrities get photographed every day, and rarely do any of them fall down when it happens."

Not that she was a celebrity. In fact, that was the problem. She wasn't accustomed to the attention and she hadn't reacted quicker. She'd been surprised, and she'd let her surprise catch her off guard when the valet had tried to help.

"Vegas," Zach said, ignoring her completely. "We'll marry in Vegas, and then we'll go to my house on Maui. They won't be able to get close to us there."

CHAPTER ELEVEN

ZACH DIDN'T KNOW what he was doing. It was a difficult thought to grow accustomed to. He was always sure of his choices, always in charge of his actions. Even when he didn't want to do a thing, like stand in front of a crowd and make a patriotic speech about his time in the service, he did it. And he did it because he'd made a choice. There was an end goal.

Always.

What was his end goal now?

He ran a hand over his face and tried to focus on the computer in front of him. Less than twenty-four hours ago, he'd been at the Lattimores' cocktail party, mingling and schmoozing the guests for contributions to his causes.

Now he was on a jet to Hawaii, having taken a side trip to Las Vegas where he'd stood in a seedy little chapel and pledged to love, honor and cherish Lia Corretti until death do them part.

Which, of course, was a lie.

They would not be together until death.

There was a purpose for this match, a reason they had to join forces. He was protecting her from her family's wrath, first of all. Second, he was avoiding a media scandal that would be troublesome and inconvenient were it to erupt.

Except those reasons no longer felt like the whole truth.

Zach closed the computer with a snap. He couldn't concentrate on business right now. All he could think about was Lia, asleep in the bedroom, her body curled sweetly beneath the sheets, her hair spread out in an auburn curtain he wanted to slide his fingers into.

This need for her was like a quiet, swelling tide. The more he denied it, the stronger and more insistent it grew.

And now he was taking her to a remote location, where the distractions would be minimal. How would he keep his hands off her?

Did he even need to? She'd certainly kissed him back yesterday in the garden. Until that moment when she'd pushed him away, she'd been as into the kiss as he had. He'd forgotten where they were, why he couldn't have her the way he wanted then and there.

He'd been ready to lift her skirt and push her back on the grass if it gave him the release he needed.

But she'd been the one to say no. The one to remind him this wasn't normal between them.

Zach snorted. Hell, what was normal anymore? He'd left normal in the rearview the moment his plane disintegrated beneath him and he'd hit the eject button. Nothing since had been the same.

But, for a few minutes yesterday, he'd felt like it had. And, he had to admit, for those blissful few hours in Palermo, too. When he'd been with Lia, he hadn't forgotten—but he'd felt as if he could accept what had happened, what his life had become, and move on.

Why did she do that to him? Why did she make him hope for more?

Lia Corretti—Lia Scott—was a dangerous woman. Dangerous for him. It had taken time, but he'd learned how to live with himself in the aftermath of his rescue.

She threatened to explode it all in his face. To force him to face the things he kept buried. If he told her, would she understand? Or would she recoil in horror?

He got to his feet and paced the length of the main cabin. A flight attendant appeared as if by magic.

"Did you need anything, sir?"

"Thanks, but no," he said, waving her off again. She disappeared into the galley and he was alone once more.

He was restless, prowling, his mind racing through

the facts, through the possibilities. Since he'd met Lia, nothing had been the same. And now they were married, and he was feeling shell-shocked—and hungry.

Hungry for her. He'd thought he could keep it at bay, that this arrangement between them would be tidy. But he'd been wrong. So very wrong.

Soon, he had to do something about this hunger— or go mad denying it.

Maui was bright and beautiful, with a rolling blue surf—which changed from deep sapphire to the purest lapis, depending on the depth—impossibly blue sky and green palm trees that stood in tall clusters, their lush foliage fanning out from the top like a funky hairdo.

Except there were other kinds of palm trees, too, Lia noticed, palms that were short and looked like giant pineapples jutting out of the ground. The tropical flowers were colorful, exotic and so sweetly scented that she fell in love with the island's perfumed air immediately.

A car was waiting at the airport when their private jet landed, and a dark-haired woman in a brightly patterned dress greeted them with leis. Lia's was made of fragrant tuberose and plumeria, while Zach's was open on the end and made from kukui nuts and green ti leaves and tiny puka shells.

They got into the back of a Hummer limo and drove across an island that was flat in the middle and ringed by mountains. On one side was Haleakala, the tall volcanic mountain that could boast more than one climate. At the bottom, the weather was warm and tropical, but at the top, Zach informed her, it was often windy, rainy and cloudy. It was also bare and cratered, like the surface of the moon. But, before you got that high, there was an Alpine region, with chalets and misty cool air.

It was the oddest thought when all she could see were tall jagged peaks, fields of sugarcane and ocean.

Soon, however, they were on the coast again and driving up a road that led to a stretch of beach dotted with sprawling homes. Eventually, they arrived at one and were met by a man who came and got their bags and took them into the house. Zach lead her into the house and over to the stunning floor-to-ceiling windows that were actually sliding-glass doors. Once the doors were completely open, the house gave way to a sweeping lanai, which was tiered so that part of it sat in the infinity pool. Beyond was the beach, so white and sugary and inviting.

Lia could only stare at how beautiful it was. She came from an island, but one that was completely different from this island. They were both stunning, but Maui was a new experience.

"It's gorgeous," she said when Zach came up beside her again and stood there in silence.

She glanced up at him, and her heart flipped. They were married. *Dio*, she had a husband. She could hardly credit it. Even though he'd told her only a few days ago they would marry, she'd never quite gotten accustomed to the idea it would really happen. She'd been waiting, she could admit now, for that moment when he would decide he didn't want her, after all. When he would send her back to Sicily and the wrath of the Correttis.

Her family might be angry with her when they learned the truth, but at least they would be satisfied she'd gotten married and wouldn't be bringing scandalous shame onto the family by having a baby without a husband.

She wondered if Alessandro knew about the marriage by now. She'd sent a quick email to Rosa when they'd left Las Vegas, and then she'd sent another one to her grandmother. Nonna wasn't online for endless hours, like so many people, but she was technologically proficient and would get the missive soon enough. And she would surely tell the head of the family the news.

Lia decided not to worry about it. What was done was done.

"We won't be bothered here," Zach said. "It's too

far out of the way for your typical paparazzi. They'll find easier quarry to harass." He stood with his hands in his pockets—he was wearing khakis and a muted aloha shirt—and looked gravely down at her. "How are you feeling? Do you need to rest?"

He was still hung up on the fact the doctor had said she needed more rest and less stress in her life. Everything had been fine with the baby, as she'd predicted. But the doctor had given him something new to worry about.

"I slept on the plane. I'm fine."

"Then you should eat," he said. "I'll go see what we have." He started to turn away, but she put a hand on his arm to stop him. Sparks sizzled into her nerve endings, as always, when she touched him.

She wanted to melt into him, like butter in a hot pan. He looked down at where her hand rested on his arm, and she remembered that she'd meant to say something. That it was odd and awkward if she did not.

"You work so hard to avoid me," she said. "It's not necessary."

That wasn't what she'd intended to say, but it was too late to take the words back. They hung in the air between them, hovering like candle smoke.

His eyes were dark, fathomless, as he looked at her. Studied her like something he'd never encountered before. Her pulse skittered along merrily, and she forced herself to drop her hand away from the bare skin of his arm.

"You noticed," he said softly. "And here I thought I was so subtle."

Her head snapped up as pain sliced into her. Yes, she'd known he was avoiding her—but to hear him admit it dragged on the same nerve that had made her question her worth since she was a little girl. It should not hurt so much, but it always did.

She knew her worth was not determined by others, and yet she could never quite appease that lonely little girl inside who was still looking for acceptance.

"I noticed." She dropped her gaze, swallowing against the ridiculous lump in her throat, and his fingers came up to slide along her cheek. His touch made heat leap and tangle in her veins. If this heat were a light inside her, it would glow wherever he touched her.

"You pushed me away, *cara*. I was respecting your wish."

"I—I don't know what my wish is," she said truthfully. "I just know that you confuse me."

His gaze sharpened. "Why are you confused, Lia? I think you know what I want."

It took her a minute to answer. "I do," she finally said. "But I don't know why."

He blinked. And then he laughed. The sound burst from him, loud and rich and unexpected. Lia stared at him, her cheeks heating. A tiny thread of irritation began to dance through her. She crossed her arms and stared him down.

He stopped laughing at her, but he was still smiling. "Damn, I needed that." He put his hands on her upper arms. He didn't pull her in close like she thought he might. Like she hoped he might.

Yesterday, she'd pushed him away. Today, she wanted to pull him to her. Maybe it made no sense, but now that they were married, she felt more…secure. And her need for him had amplified since the moment he'd pushed a diamond—a large, family heirloom, it turned out—on her finger and said, "I do."

His fingers dug into her arms. Not painfully, but possessively. "Hell, Lia, you really don't know why I want you? Are you that blind?"

"I am not blind," she said defensively.

"You must be if you can't figure out what's going on here. You're beautiful, lush and perfect, and I ache with the need to touch you the way I did in Palermo."

His words made her soften, melt. Want. She wanted what they'd had in Palermo—except for the part where she woke up and he was gone.

"I…" She swallowed as her heart beat a tattoo against her rib cage. Her throat was as dry as baked sand. It was a frightening thing to say what she wanted. But he was looking at her as if he was dying to touch her, and so she took a chance. "I think I want that, too."

He made a noise of relief. Then he slid his hands down her arms and around her back, cupping her buttocks as he pulled her fully into his embrace.

"Grazie a Dio," he said then in a throaty purr, and a liquid shiver danced down her spine. Her hands went up to clutch his shirt as his head descended.

Their mouths touched and a shudder went through Lia. All those feelings she'd felt in the maze yesterday came rushing to the fore. They were almost too much, too overwhelming.

But she wouldn't push him away again. She couldn't.

He was big and hard and strong, and she pressed herself against him, her hands running over the hard muscles of his chest and shoulders. Her body was on fire as liquid heat gathered in her core. She could feel the dampness in her panties, the instant response that she couldn't have prevented even if she'd wanted to.

This thing between them was hot and bright and uncontrollable. It was a need that had to be assuaged, or she would be as restless as a spirit condemned to roam the earth for all eternity.

"Wait," he said, pushing her back, breaking that delicious contact.

Lia's stomach fell. If he was rejecting her now…

"Not yet," he said, his voice sounding tortured enough that she relaxed infinitesimally. "We just arrived, and you need to rest first."

"I told you I slept on the plane…."

He slid a hand into her hair, cupped her head while he traced a path over her collarbone with the fingers of his other hand. "I know, but it was a long trip and the doctor said—"

Lia cursed. "I wish you would allow me to make my own decisions without all this argument! We're going to get off to a very bad start, Zachariah Scott, if you constantly tell me what I should be doing."

He looked at her for a long minute. One corner of his mouth turned up in a grin.

"What's so funny?" she asked crossly.

"You. Such a temper from a little thing."

Heat suffused her. "I am not a little thing and you know it. I'm too tall and I'm only going to get fatter—"

He put a finger over her lips, silencing her. "You are not fat, Lia. You're lush and gorgeous and you make me hard."

The tops of her ears were on fire. She didn't consider herself to be a prude by any stretch—she'd read plenty of books where people had sex, sometimes even raunchy sex—but the idea she affected him that way,

and that he had no problem saying it, both embarrassed and thrilled her.

"Allora," she said, resisting the urge to fan herself
with both hands. "The things you say."

"Makes you hot, doesn't it?"

Lia put a hand over her eyes. *"Dio,"* she said.

Zach laughed and drew her hand away from her
face. Then he took both her hands in his and held them
in front of his body. "I like that you're still so innocent," he told her. "I like the idea of corrupting you."

A shiver washed over her as she imagined all the
ways in which he might corrupt her. She'd had a taste
of it, certainly, for two blissful days—but she knew
there was more, knew they hadn't even scratched the
surface of their need for each other.

"There's no time like the present," she replied, and
then felt herself blushing harder than before if that
were possible.

He led her through the gorgeous house with the
soaring ceilings, the koa wood floors and overstuffed
couches and huge open sliding doors, to a bedroom
with a king-size bed and a breathtaking view of the
ocean, with its white sand beaches, jagged black volcanic rocks and rolling surf.

The bed was on a platform, clothed in pristine
white, and there was a television mounted on the op-

posite wall. She wondered who would ever want to watch television in a house like this, but then Zach stopped and tugged her into his arms again.

He kissed her softly, sweetly—too softly and sweetly to mean he was actually planning to make love to her, she realized, and then he stepped away.

"Take a bath, Lia. Have a nap. We'll have dinner on the lanai and watch the sunset. After that—" he shrugged "—anything goes."

Anything goes.

Lia couldn't get that thought out of her mind as she bathed and dressed. In spite of her insistence she'd slept on the plane, she had managed to fall into that giant king bed and drift off to sleep after she'd stared at the ocean for several minutes. It had surprised her to wake sometime later, when the sun was sliding down the bowl of the sky.

The doors to the outside were still open, and the ocean rolled rhythmically against the shore. A gentle trade wind blew through the room, bringing with it the scent of plumeria trees.

Now, Lia gazed at the ocean again as she stood in the open doors and gathered her courage before she went to meet Zach. Why, when she'd been ready earlier, did she suddenly feel as if a thousand humming-birds were beating their wings in her belly?

Finally, she turned and strode from the bedroom, down the stairs and into the main living area. Zach wasn't on the lanai, and he wasn't in the living room. She continued to the kitchen, a huge room with koa wood cabinets and stainless-steel appliances. Zach was standing at the kitchen island, slicing fruit.

Lia blinked. It was such a domestic picture, and a surprising one. He looked up and smiled, and her body melted.

"You are fixing dinner?" she asked.

"It's nothing terribly exciting," he told her. "My repertoire is limited. But I can broil a fish, and I can make salad and cut up some fruit for dessert."

"You are a man of many talents," she said.

One eyebrow lifted. "I am indeed. I look forward to showing you some of those talents in detail."

Lia blushed and a grin spread over Zach's face. "You like embarrassing me," she said.

He walked over with a piece of pineapple and handed it to her. She popped it in her mouth, nearly moaning at the juicy sweetness.

"Not at all," he said as he went back over to the island. "I find it charming that you blush over such things."

"Charming," she repeated, as if it were a foreign

word. Her family had never found her charming. They'd never thought she was anything but a nuisance. Except for Nonna, of course.

He picked up the platter. "Come out to the lanai and I'll bring everything," he told her.

"I can take the fruit."

He handed it to her and then went back for the salad. When they reached the table on the lanai—a table set with simple dishes and silverware—he set the salad down and took the fruit from her. Then he tugged her into his arms and kissed her.

"Yes, charming," he said. "I've never known anyone as innocent about such things as you are."

He let her go and pulled out her chair for her. As she sat, she looked up at him, her chest tightening at the emotions filling her. Emotions she really didn't want to spend much time analyzing. She already knew she cared too much. Did she need to know more than that?

"I don't like blushing like a nun in a locker room," she said. "It's ridiculous."

He laughed. "Like I said, charming."

He went and retrieved the rest of the food, and then they sat on the lanai with a view of the blue, blue ocean, and a big orange ball sinking into it. They ate fresh fish and talked about many things, none of them singularly important, but all important in the bigger picture of getting to know each other.

Lia learned that Zach liked to read biographies and military treatises, and that he'd defied his father by going to the Air Force Academy rather than Harvard. She also learned that he managed his family's charitable foundation, and that he'd met Taylor Carmichael in his work supporting veterans' causes.

"Why did you drop the medal?" she asked, and then wanted to kick herself when he stiffened slightly.

But he took a sip of his wine and relaxed. "It's something the military does automatically, writing you up for medals when you've been in combat. But I didn't want it. I didn't want any of them."

Her heart pinched at the darkness in his tone. "But why?"

He kept his gaze on the ocean for a long time, and her pulse thrummed hot. She berated herself for pushing him, and yet she felt like she would never know him if she didn't ask these things. He was her husband, the father of her child, and she wanted to know who he was inside.

He turned to her, his dark eyes glittering hot. "Because six marines died saving me, Lia. Because I was drugged and I didn't do anything but lay there while they fought and died. They worked so damn hard to save me, and I couldn't help them. They died because of me."

Lia swallowed the lump that had formed in her

throat. "I'm sorry, Zach," she said. She reached for his hand, squeezed it. She was encouraged when he didn't snatch it away. "But I think they died because they were doing their job, not because of you."

"You aren't the first to say that to me," he said, rubbing his thumb against her palm. "Yet I still have trouble believing it. I'm treated like a hero, and yet I haven't earned the right to be one. They were the heroes."

She hurt for him. He looked stoic, sitting there and staring out at the ocean beyond, and she wanted to wrap her arms around him and hold him tight. She fought herself, fought her natural inclination not to reach for him because of her fear of being rejected. In the end, the fear won.

"I doubt anyone thinks they weren't heroes," she said hotly, because she was angry with herself and angry with him, too. "They had jobs to do, and they did them. But they died because the enemy killed them. No other reason."

His expression was almost amused when he turned it on her. Except there was too much pain behind that gaze to ever be mistaken for amusement. "How fierce you are, *cara*. One wonders—do you have a limit? Would you, for instance, stop defending me if I crossed the line?"

CHAPTER TWELVE

SHE WAS LOOKING at him curiously, her brows drawing down over her lovely eyes. He could tell she was grappling with herself, with the things he was saying. Did she want to run? Did she want to lock herself in her room, away from him?

He almost wished she would. It would make things so much easier.

Because he was enjoying this too much, sitting here on the lanai with her and talking about their lives while they ate and watched the sun sink into the sea. He couldn't remember ever enjoying a woman's company the way he did hers. He loved women, loved sex, but companionship? He'd never thought of that before. Never cared. The old Zach changed women the way he changed clothes—frequently and as the situation dictated.

But, with Lia, he enjoyed the simple pleasures of

spending time with her. It was a dangerous thing. Because she made him feel as if he could be normal again, when he knew he never could. He'd changed too much to ever go back to what he'd been before.

In the beginning, he'd thought it was possible. He'd thought the dreams would go away with time. That's what everyone said he needed: time. Time was the great healer. Time made everything better. Time, time, time.

He'd had time. More than a year's worth, and nothing was the same. He had to accept that it never would be. He might always be plagued by dreams and fears, the same as he was plagued with unpredictable headaches. Those had changed his ability to fly forever, so why did he think time could fix the other stuff?

It couldn't. She couldn't.

"What line?" she asked, her voice soft and strong at once. As if she was challenging him. As if she didn't believe him. His chest felt tight as emotions filled him. This woman—this sweet, innocent woman—had faith in him. It was a stunning realization. And a sobering one.

He didn't want to fail her. And he didn't want to fail their child.

Another paradigm-shifting realization.

"It's nothing," he said, surprised at the trembling in his fingers as he reached for his wine. "Forget it."

She kept staring at him, her eyes large and liquid. "You are a man of integrity and honor," she said. "I do not doubt that at all."

"I tried to pay you off and send you away, Lia. Or have you forgotten?"

She picked up her glass. "I have not. But I understand why you did it."

"Because I'm an arrogant bastard with an unhealthy sense of self-importance?" He meant it to be self-deprecating, but he recognized the truth in it, too. He'd had his family consequence drummed into him from birth, after all.

"I wouldn't have put it that way," she said carefully, and he laughed.

She looked at him in confusion, and he didn't blame her. Just a moment ago, the conversation had been so serious, so dramatic. Now that it had moved away from the deeply intense and dark things residing in his soul, he could find humor in her reaction.

"Because you are too sweet," he said. He reached for her hand. The heat that sparked inside him was always surprising.

She frowned. "I don't feel particularly sweet. I feel quite cross at the moment, actually."

He brought her hand to her mouth, nibbled the skin over her knuckles. "I think I know how to change that," he murmured.

* * *

Lia's insides were melting. She didn't want to melt just yet, but she realized she had no choice in the matter. Sparks were zinging and pinging inside her like a fireworks display on New Year's eve.

She was still concerned about the things he'd said, about the self-loathing beneath his mask, but it seemed the subject was now closed. She'd been allowed a peek at the raw, tormented nature of Zach Scott, but now he was wrapped up tight again and she wasn't getting in.

She wanted to know the man who dreamed, who worked hard to make those speeches and ignore the triggers that could send him spiraling out of control. She wanted to touch the heart of him, she realized.

The way he'd touched hers.

He tugged her toward him until she got up and went to his side. Then he was pulling her down on his lap, tilting her back in his arms. His eyes gleamed with heat, and a hot wave of longing washed through her with the same kind of relentless surge of the ocean beyond.

"No more talking, Lia," he said, his fingers gliding over the skin beneath her collarbone.

When his lips replaced his fingers, her head fell back against the chair. His mouth moved over her, teasing, tormenting. The ocean pounded the shore a few yards away, and the trade winds blew, and Lia shuddered and gasped and knew she'd found heaven.

Her heart hurt with everything she felt: passion, hot and bright; fear, cold and insidious; and love, warm and glowing, like the sun as it had been right before it sank into the sea. There was a rightness about this, a rightness that felt like destiny and perfection.

She was meant to be here, and Zach was meant to be the man she shared her life with. She shivered again as he unbuttoned her shirt and peeled it back to reveal her shoulders and the soft swell of her breasts against the silk of her bra.

"Bellissimo," he said, his voice a silky purr. *"Ho bisogno di te, Lia."*

I need you.

Lia shivered again, her entire body on fire from tip to toes as his gaze raked her with that naked hunger she'd come to crave.

"Yes," she said. "Oh, yes."

His mouth came down on hers, and she was lost to anything but this molten hot fire between them. She wrapped her arms around him and shifted in his lap—and felt the hard evidence of his arousal pressing against her bottom.

His body tightened beneath her—and then all that beautiful power was lifting her, carrying her into the house while she clung to him and pressed kisses to his jaw, his neck, the delicious skin of his collarbone.

Soon, she was on her feet in the master suite. The doors were still slung open to let in the breezes, but they were completely alone out here on this remote stretch of beach. Zach stripped away her silky top and tailored trousers until she stood before him in nothing but her bra and a tiny scrap of silk that covered her sex.

His eyes darkened as they drifted over her, and a thrill shot through her.

"You look good enough to eat, Lia," he purred.

A fresh wave of heat pulsed inside her. She was wet, hot, and she wanted him.

But she couldn't move. She couldn't take those three steps to him, couldn't wrap her arms around him and be a wanton, seductive woman. Always she feared she wouldn't do it right, that he'd disapprove, or that he'd push her away and tell her she wasn't good enough, after all.

She knew better, she really did. But when you'd believed something your entire life, it was difficult to suddenly stop in a moment where every gesture, every touch, every look, set off firestorms inside. You'd do anything to keep the storm happening, anything to keep feeling the sweet heat. You would not take a risk.

He took a step toward her, his big body menacing—

but in a good way. In a hard, protective, thoroughly delicious way.

"Do you want to touch me?" he asked.

She could only nod her head.

"Do it, then," he told her. "Touch me wherever you want. However you want."

"You have too many clothes on," she said, and blushed.

His laugh was deep, sexy, sinful. "Take them off, then."

She moved toward him, her fingers fumbling with the buttons of his shirt until she could finally push it free. It fell off his shoulders and landed in a pile at his feet. The shorts he'd changed into hung low on his body, revealing ridges of hard muscle and the perfect slash of hip bones.

She wanted to run her tongue along those bones. Wanted to dip it into the hollow of his abdomen, and then slide it down to the thick, hard length of his penis. But she didn't. She just stood and gaped like a kid in a candy store.

Zach swore, and then he was unbuttoning his shorts and shoving them down. His underwear went with them until he stood before her gloriously naked. His penis jutted out proudly, and his warrior's body made her mouth water.

She forgot herself. She reached for him.

But he reached for her, too, and soon they were lost in each other, kissing and touching and feeling what they'd missed for the past few weeks.

Lia wrapped herself around him until he put his hands on her bottom and lifted her. Her legs scissored around his waist as he carried her the few steps to the bed and tumbled her backward onto it.

"I wanted to seduce you slowly. But I can't wait, Lia," he managed finally, the hard ridge of his erection riding against the silk of her panties.

"Me, neither," she said—panted, really.

He rose up above her, jerked her panties down her legs and discarded them—and then he was back, pushing inside her until they were joined completely.

This, she thought, eyes closed, back arched, this utter perfection of his body so deeply within hers. This was what she wanted. What she needed.

His mouth fused to hers as he began to move. He wound his fingers into hers, pushed her arms above her head and proceeded to devastate her utterly with his lovemaking.

Days passed. Glorious sex- and sun-drenched days. They didn't talk about the military again, didn't talk about Zach's dreams. He slept with her at night, though she hadn't believed he would. The first night, when they'd made love and she was so thoroughly languid that she couldn't have moved if her life depended on it, he'd alarmed her by climbing from the bed and gathering his clothes.

When she'd asked him where he was going, he'd informed her he was going to his room. She'd sat up, the sheet tucked around her still-naked and glowing body, and wanted to cry. He'd told her it was best for them both, and that it wasn't her. It was him. She knew what he meant, but it still hurt to see him willing to walk away when she would have gladly walked across a room of broken glass just to be by his side.

He'd left her alone, and she'd turned to stare out at the ocean glowing beneath a full moon. The waves crashed against the shore, broke against the jagged rock cliffs that dotted the shoreline, and she felt as if her heart was broken and jagged, too.

Fifteen minutes later, Zach had returned. When he'd slipped into bed with her, she'd been unable to contain the small cry that erupted from her. He'd pulled her close, his mouth at her throat, and told her he wanted to try to stay with her.

She'd put her arms around him, threaded her fingers into that silky hair and nearly wept with relief and fierce joy.

They had not slept. Not at first. No, within minutes, Zach was inside her again, his body taking hers to heights that made the peak of Mount Everest look like an afternoon trek up a tiny foothill.

Finally, they crashed to the bottom again and fell asleep, entangled in each other's arms.

The days began to pass, each one as perfect and heartbreaking as the last. They spent hours making love, hours in the sunshine—floating in the pool, lying on the beach—and didn't leave the house to go anywhere. A service did the shopping and cleaning for them, so all they had to worry about was fixing their meals.

Zach did a great job at that, so there was nothing lacking in their self-imposed isolation. He'd been right, too, about the paparazzi. There were none on this lonely stretch of beach. They were opportunists, and opportunity was easier elsewhere.

The papers were filled at first with news of their hasty marriage and tropical honeymoon. Zach merely laughed and said it had all gone perfectly to plan. Eventually, though they were still news, they weren't on the front pages of the gossip rags anymore. Some Hollywood starlet and her latest drunk-driving conviction were taking center stage at the moment.

Lia spoke with her grandmother. The older woman seemed happy for her, though sad as well that she hadn't been at the wedding. Lia gave her some story about wildly beating hearts and true love being impatient, and her grandmother accepted it. Her cousin, apparently, was currently preoccupied with his own issues and wasn't inclined to worry about her fate at all.

She'd married a rich, influential man and that was good enough for the family. As for Rosa, Lia had been emailing back and forth with her sister quite frequently. They were both still wary, but there was a budding relationship that Lia thought might eventually grow into something she cherished.

Right now, however, she cherished Zach. She looked up from her book and let her gaze slide over him where he stood in the infinity pool, having just emerged from his swim. He was so very beautiful, hard and lean and fit in ways that made her mouth water.

And virile. She couldn't forget that one. The man did not tire out in the bedroom, or not until he'd exhausted himself pleasing her.

It was a good trait in a husband, she thought wickedly.

She was growing bolder in her experiments with his body. At first, she'd been afraid to try anything, afraid she would get it wrong and he'd not tell her because he didn't want to hurt her feelings.

But if she was getting it wrong, then he was a superb actor, because his gasps and groans and urgent touches and kisses spurred her to even greater experiments.

Like last night, when she'd taken him in her mouth as they sat out here on the lanai in the dark and listened to the ocean.

"Lia," he'd gasped as she'd freed him and then swirled her tongue around the head of his penis. And then he'd grabbed fistfuls of her hair and held her gently but firmly while she took him into her mouth. Her heart had beat so hard, so loud in her ears, but she could still hear him making those sounds of pleasure in his throat.

Before he'd orgasmed, however, he'd pulled her up and made her straddle him. She'd been wearing a silken nightie, no panties, and she'd sunk down on him while he held her hips and guided her.

She didn't remember much after that, except for the frantic way she'd ridden him until they'd both collapsed on the chaise longue. Much later, he'd carried her to bed and repeated the performance.

"What are you reading?" he said now, arraying his splendid form on the lounge beside her.

She held up her book. "I'm learning about the flowering plants of Hawaii. And how they make leis. Quite fascinating."

He groaned. "Please don't let me find you out pruning the plumeria one morning, searching for the perfect blooms."

Lia looked across at the single plumeria tree near

the side of the house. It was tall, at least twenty feet, and filled with blooms whose perfume wafted over to her even now. "Don't be ridiculous," she said. "It's huge, and I'd need a ladder."

"You are definitely not getting on a ladder," he growled.

She laughed. "Of course not. I wouldn't dream of it."

His expression softened, his gaze raking over her. She got that warm glow inside that she always did. The words she'd not yet said to him welled behind her teeth, threatened to burst out into the open if she didn't work to contain them.

How could she tell him she loved him when that would be the ultimate soul-baring act she could perform? She'd be naked before him, naked in a way she could never take back. And he would have the ability to crush her. A single word. A single look.

He could crush her beneath his well-shod heel and she'd never recover.

Dio.

His brows drew down. "Are you feeling all right?" he asked. "Do you need to see a doctor?"

Lia rolled her eyes. It was a screen to cover all her raw, exposed feelings, but it was also a true reaction. He was incessantly worried about her health, which was sweet, but also managed to exasperate her.

"Zach, I'm fine. I have an appointment with the doctor on Oahu next week, remember?"

He continued to study her like she was a bug under a microscope. "Would you tell me if you were unwell? Or would you hide it?"

She blinked. "Why on earth would I hide such a thing?"

He looked at her for a long minute. And then he shrugged. "I have no idea. I just get the feeling that sometimes you aren't being completely honest about what you're feeling."

Her heart skipped a beat. Wow, he'd nailed it in one. But not for the reason he supposed. She reached out and grasped his hand. His skin was still cool from the pool. "I'm not used to sharing my life with anyone," she said truthfully. "I'm used to being self-reliant in many ways, but if I felt truly ill, I would tell you. I don't want anything to happen to this baby."

"Or you," he said, and her heart seemed to stop beating in her chest. A moment later, it lurched forward again, beating in triple time. She told herself not to read anything into that statement, but, oh, how her heart wanted to.

He turned away and reached for his tablet computer while her pulse surged and her heart throbbed. She wanted what he'd said to mean something. Wanted it desperately. But he sat there scrolling through his tablet so casually, and she knew that it hadn't meant a thing. Oh, he didn't want her to hurt herself, certainly.

But not because he didn't know what he'd do if she weren't here. Not because the air he breathed would suddenly grow stale without her. Not because his life would cease to be bright if she were not in it.

Lia turned away from him, her eyes pricking with tears, and picked up the virgin mai tai he'd fixed for her before he slipped into the pool. The trade winds blew so gently across her skin, and the sun was bright in the azure sky above. It was so perfect here, and she'd let herself be lulled by it.

But she had to remember there was nothing about this situation that was permanent. It could all end tomorrow, if he so chose. Lia shivered and tried not to imagine what would happen when it did.

In the end she didn't need to imagine a thing.

There was a storm in the middle of the night. It was a rare occurrence on Maui, because the trade winds and the air pressure didn't usually allow for it, but tonight there was thunder and jagged lightning sizzling over the ocean.

Lia woke with a jerk when a crack of thunder sounded close by. Zach was beside her, sitting up, his eyes wide.

"Zach?"

He didn't move. She reached for him. He jerked, then spun and pinned her to the bed. His eyes were wild, his skin damp. He growled something unintelligible.

"Zach, *caro*, it's me," she said. "It's Lia."

He was very still. "Lia?"

"Yes."

The tension in his body collapsed. He rolled away from her with a groan and lay on his back, an arm thrown over his eyes. "Jesus," he breathed. "I could have hurt you."

She propped herself on an elbow and leaned over him. "You wouldn't," she said, utterly convinced.

The arm fell away and his dark eyes gleamed at her as he drew in deep lungfuls of breath. "How can you be so sure? I'm a mess, Lia." He choked out something unintelligible. "A damn mess."

Fear was beginning to dance along the surface of her psyche. He frightened her, but not physically. "I don't believe that."

He laughed bitterly. "You're too damn trusting. Too naive. You have no idea what goes on in this world."

He threw the covers back and got out of bed while she sat there with her heart pinching and her chest aching. He yanked on a pair of shorts and stalked outside, onto the balcony, oblivious to the rain coming down.

Lia's first instinct was to stay where she was, to let him cool off. But she couldn't do it. She loved him too much, and she hated when he was hurting.

She climbed from the bed and put on her robe. Then she went to stand in the open door and look at him.

The rain washed over him, soaking his hair, running in rivulets down his chest. He looked lonely and angry and her heart went out to him. She knew what it was like to be lonely and angry. She wanted nothing more than to fix it for him.

"Zach, please talk to me."

He spun to look at her. "You don't want to hear what I have to say."

She took a step toward him.

He held a hand up to stop her. "Don't come out here. You'll get wet."

"It doesn't seem to be hurting you," she said, though she stopped anyway, folding her arms around her body. "And you're wrong. I do want to hear what you have to say."

He shoved his wet hair back from his face, but he didn't make a move to come inside. Thunder rolled in the distance. A flash of lightning zipped along the sky, slicing it in two for a brief moment.

"I should have known better," he said. "I should have known it was a mistake to think this could work between us."

Her chest filled with chaotic emotion, tightening until she thought she wouldn't be able to breathe. But she held herself firmly, arms crossed beneath her breasts, and refused to let him see how much he hurt her. He thought she was naive, trusting. Unworthy.

It stung. But, worse, the idea she was a mistake threatened to make her fold in on herself.

"You can't mean that," she said tightly, though her brain gibbered at her to be quiet. To detach. To roll into a ball and protect herself. "These past couple of weeks have been perfect."

"Which is why it was a mistake," he snapped. "There's no such thing as perfect, not where I'm concerned."

"Because you don't deserve those medals?" she threw back at him, anger beginning to grow and spin inside her belly. "Because you have bad dreams and think you're so terrible?"

He took a step toward her, stopped. His hands clenched into fists at his side. He was close enough he could have reached out and touched her. But he didn't.

"You want to know the truth? I'll tell you," he grated. "The whole, sorry story."

He turned his back on her, walked over to the railing. The rain was lessening, but it was still coming down. When he turned back to her, his expression was tight.

"You've heard part of it. I broke my leg during the ejection. It hurt like hell, and I couldn't move much. But I'd landed near a protected ravine and hunkered down to wait. I expected the enemy to find me first. But they didn't. The marines did. Only the enemy wasn't far behind."

Lia imagined him alone like that, imagined him waiting, and fear crawled up her throat, no matter that she'd heard him say this part before. She wanted to go to him, but she knew he didn't want her to. It made her desperate inside, but all she could do was listen.

"The medic drugged me," he said. "And I couldn't help them defend our position when they most needed me. Hell, I think I drifted in and out of consciousness. I have no idea how long it went on, but it seemed to take forever. They hit us with grenades, small-arms fire. It was ceaseless, and air support wasn't coming no matter how many times the marines called for it. One by one, the enemy picked off the marines, until it was one sergeant and me."

He didn't keep going, but she knew he wasn't finished. He turned away again, and she could see the tightness in his jaw, his shoulders. Zach was on edge in a way she'd only ever seen him when he was in the grips of a dream.

"Zach?"

He turned his head toward her. "Here's the part you

don't know. The part no one knows. He gave me a pistol. Put it in my hand and removed the safety. And then he told me it was my choice when the enemy came. Shoot them, or shoot myself."

"No," she breathed as horror washed over her.

Zach's gaze didn't change, didn't soften. "Obviously," he said, "I didn't shoot myself. I didn't shoot anyone. Sometime in the night, the last marine died. And I wanted to shoot myself. I wanted it pretty badly."

"Oh, Zach…" Her eyes filled with tears.

"What you need to know, Lia, is that I tried to do it. I put the gun under my jaw." He put his finger just where he would have stuck the gun. Her heart lurched at the thought of him lying helplessly like that with so much death and destruction all around him. "But I couldn't pull the trigger."

The words hung in the air between them, like poison.

"I'm glad you didn't," Lia said fiercely, her throat a tight, achy mess. How close had he come? How close had she been to never, ever knowing him? It didn't bear thinking about.

"I can't forget that night. I can't forget how they all died, and how I could do nothing about it. I can't forget that I should have died with them."

Lia put a hand over her belly without conscious

thought. "You weren't meant to die, Zach. You were meant to live. For me. For our baby."

His laugh was bitter, broken. "God, why would you think that? Why, after everything I just said to you, after the way I attacked you tonight, would you want me within a thousand miles of a child?"

She was starting to quake deep inside. Something was changing here. Something she couldn't stop. She was losing him. She'd begun to believe, over the past couple of weeks, that something was happening between them. Something good. She'd let herself be lulled by the sun and sea and the fabulous sex. Hadn't she had a glimmering of it earlier today by the pool?

"You didn't attack me. I startled you, but you have to remember that you let me go."

"What if I hadn't? You can't trust me, Lia. I can't trust myself."

"Then get some help!" she yelled at him. "Fight for me. For us."

He was looking at her, his chest rising and falling rapidly, and her hopes began to unfurl their wings. He could do this.

"It's not that easy," he said between clenched teeth. "Don't you think I've tried?"

"Then try again. For us."

He looked almost sad for a moment. "Why are you so stubborn, Lia? Why can't you just accept the truth?

I told you I couldn't be a husband or a father. Now you know why."

Fear and fury whipped to a froth inside her. "Because I—" *I love you.*

But she couldn't say the words. They clogged her throat, like always, the fear of them almost more than she could bear. She'd worked hard not to love people who wouldn't love her back. She'd hidden inside her shell and shut everyone out.

Until Zach. Until he'd walked into her life and opened her up, exposing her soft underbelly. He'd made her love him. He'd made her vulnerable to this horrible, shattering pain again.

"Because what?" he said.

Lia swallowed the fear. She had to say the words. If she expected him to face his fear, then she had to face her own.

"Because I love you," she said, the words like razor blades. They weren't supposed to hurt. But they did.

Raw emotion flared in his eyes. And then his face went blank. He was shutting down, pulling up the cold, cool, untouchable man who lived inside him. She wanted to wail.

"That," he finally said, his voice so icy it made her shiver, "is a mistake."

"I don't believe that," she said on a hoarse whisper. "I refuse to believe that."

He came over to stand before her. She wanted to touch him, but she knew better than to try. Not now. Not when he was pushing her away. Not when her heart was breaking in two.

He put a finger under her chin and lifted until she had to look him in the eye. What she saw there eroded all her hopes.

"You're a good woman, Lia. You deserve better than this." His throat moved as he swallowed.

She feared what he would say, feared the look in his eyes. "Zach, no…"

He put his finger over her lips to silence her. "That's why I'm letting you go."

CHAPTER THIRTEEN

SICILY WAS JUST as Lia had left it, though she was not the same as she'd been when she'd left Sicily. She was bitterly angry. Hurt.

But one thing she was not, not ever again, was pitiful. She'd told her grandmother about the baby, because she couldn't hide it for much longer—and because she was no longer afraid of her family's reaction. Yes, it helped that she'd married the father. But she was still having this baby alone, regardless of what her family thought about that.

Far from being scandalized, Teresa had been thrilled to have a great-grandchild on the way. If the head of the family was upset about it, Lia didn't know it. Nor did she care.

Lia snipped lavender from the garden and dropped it into the basket sitting on the ground beside her. Then she wiped the back of her hand across her brow to remove the sweat before it could drip into her eyes. It was hot outside, crackling. Perhaps she should be inside, but she was going a little crazy just sitting there and reading books.

She was still in her cottage on her grandparents' estate, but she was in the process of purchasing an apartment of her own in Palermo. Once she'd returned to Sicily a month ago, she'd marched right into the family lawyer's office and told him she wanted her money. He'd blinked at her in a slow, lazy way that she feared meant he was about to deny her request or refer her to Alessandro, but instead he'd turned to his computer and began bringing up the family accounts.

She'd discovered that she had far more money than she'd thought. She would not need Zach's money to take care of their baby. It wasn't a fortune, but it would do.

It gave her great satisfaction to refuse a meeting with Zach's local attorney when he'd called to say he'd set up a bank account for her and needed her signature on some papers.

She would not take a dime of Scott money. Not ever.

The thought of Zach still had the power to make her feel as if someone had stabbed her with a hot dagger. She was so angry with him. So filled with rage and hate and—

No, not hate. Bitter disappointment. Hurt.

Her worst nightmare had come true when she'd given him her heart and he'd flung it back at her. He'd rejected her, just as she'd always been rejected by those to whom she wanted to mean something.

And it hadn't killed her. That was the part she'd found amazing, once she stopped crying and feeling sorry for herself.

She was hurt, yes, but she was here. Alive. And she had a life growing inside her, a tiny, wonderful life that she already loved so much. Her child would have everything she had not had. Friends, love, acceptance.

But not a father, she thought wistfully. Her baby would not have a father. Oh, Zach didn't want a divorce. He'd been very clear that she was still a Scott for as long as she wanted to be one, and that their child would have his name.

She'd met Zach's parents before she'd left. They'd been nice, if a bit formal, and they'd told her they wanted to be involved in their grandchild's life. So, her baby might not have a father, but he or she would have grandparents. She had agreed to return to the United States at least once a year, and they had indicated they would come to Sicily as often as she would allow it.

It had seemed far enough in the future that she figured she would have learned how to deal with her memories of Zach by then. She kept seeing him as he'd been that last night in Hawaii. Dark, tortured, dripping wet and so stubborn she wanted to put her hands around his throat and squeeze until he would listen to sense.

But there was no talking to Zach when he made up his mind. And, in his mind, he was a dangerous, damaged man who had no hope for the future. They'd boarded a jet the next morning after the storm on Maui. By nightfall they'd been back in D.C and then he'd disappeared.

Finally, on the fifth day, she'd decided she'd had enough. She'd made travel arrangements to Sicily and then she'd informed Raoul when she was leaving for the airport.

Zach had appeared very quickly after that. It had been an awkward meeting in which he'd told her he didn't want a divorce and that he would support her and their child. She'd sat through it silently, fuming and aching and wanting to throw things.

In the end, she'd left because it hurt too much to stay. Before she'd walked out the door the final time, she'd gone into his office and dropped the medal on his desk. He wasn't there, but she'd known he would see it. If it made him angry, so be it. It was the final tie she needed to cut if she was to move on with her life.

Apparently, her leaving hadn't fazed him in the least. It had been a month and she'd heard nothing from Zach, though she'd heard plenty from his local attorney. A man who was beginning to leave increasingly strident messages. Messages she had no intention of returning.

She clipped off some rosemary a little more viciously than necessary and dropped it in the basket. Then she got to her feet and put her hand in the small of her back. Her back ached quite a lot these days, but the doctor said everything was normal. She hadn't really started to show yet, though she'd had to get expansion bands for her pants and wear clothing that was loose around the middle. Soon, it would be time for maternity wear, but right now her maxi dress and sandals did just fine.

In the distance, the sea sparkled sapphire. It looked nothing like Maui, but it made her wistful nevertheless. She often found herself sitting on her little secluded terrazzo and gazing at the sea. She thought that if she did it enough, she would anesthetize herself to the pain.

So far, it hadn't worked. It was like reopening a wound each and every time.

She turned to make her way back to her cottage. The grounds sloped upward and the walk in this heat made her heart pound until she began to feel lightheaded. She stopped for a moment, the basket slung over her arm, and wiped her forehead again. Her vision was growing spotty and her belly was churning.

She groped in the basket for her water and came up with an empty bottle.

She could see her destination, see the terrazzo through the pencil pines and bougainvillea—and a man standing with his back to her. He had dark hair and wore a suit, and a swift current of anger shot through her veins, giving her the impetus she needed to keep putting one foot in front of the other.

She'd told Zach's lawyer that she didn't want to meet him. Yet he'd dared to come anyway, no doubt to try and force her to sign the documents that would make her the owner of a bank account with far too much money in it. She was not about to let Zach assuage his guilt that way. Let him choke on his millions for all she cared.

The man should not have made it through the estate's security, but he'd obviously sweet-talked his way inside. A red mist of rage clouded her vision as she trod up the lawn. Her stomach churned and her vision swam, but she was determined to make it. Determined to tell this man to take his briefcase full of papers and shove them where the sun didn't shine.

He might have sweet-talked Nonna into letting him onto the estate, but he wasn't sweet-talking her.

She stepped onto the tiles, her heart pounding with the effort. "How dare you," she began—but he turned around and the words got stuck in her mouth.

Her vision blurred and started to grow dark at the edges as bile rose in her throat. Too late, she recognized what was happening. Then everything ceased to exist.

Zach was miserable. He paced the halls of the local hospital where Lia had been taken. Her grandmother had promised to let him know what was happening, but she'd disappeared into the room with Lia and the doctor and hadn't come out again.

Zach shoved a hand through his hair and contemplated bursting through the door to Lia's room. This was not at all what he'd expected when he'd arrived today. He cursed himself for not being more cautious, for not calling her first. If he'd caused any harm to Lia or the baby, he would never forgive himself.

He stood with his fists clenched at his sides. He'd been such a fool, and now he couldn't shake the feeling he'd come too late.

That night, when he'd stood in the rain and told Lia about what had really happened—what had nearly happened—in that trench, he'd felt like the lowest kind of bastard. The kind who didn't deserve a sweet wife and a happy ending. He'd hated himself for turning on her during the storm—and earlier, in Palermo. He couldn't control the beast inside him, the slavering animal that reacted blindly, lashing out in fear and fury.

When he'd shoved her back on the bed, he'd known he couldn't take that risk ever again. He hadn't hurt her, as she'd pointed out, but he didn't trust that he was incapable of hurting her. He'd known then that he had to end it between them, and he had to do it immediately.

Letting her go had been the hardest thing he'd ever done. For days after she'd left, he'd walked around his house like a ghost, looking at the places she'd been, imagining her there within reach. Dying to touch her again and aching so hard because he couldn't.

He told himself he'd done the right thing. He was a beast, a monster, a man incapable of tenderness and love. He'd sacrificed himself for her safety, her happiness, and he'd felt honorable doing it.

But he'd also been miserable. And once he'd walked into his office and found the medal she'd left, he'd had a sudden visceral reaction that had left him on his knees, his gut hollow with pain, his throat raw with the howl that burst from him.

That's when he realized what he'd done. He'd sent her away, the greatest gift to come into his miserable life. In that moment, he knew what the hollowness, the despair, deep inside him was. He was in love with his wife. And he'd sent her away.

He'd wanted to go to her immediately, to beg her forgiveness—but he couldn't. He had to get himself straight first. He had to work on the things he'd shoved down deep. She'd told him to fight for her, and he'd been a coward.

Well, no more. He wasn't ready to quit. He wasn't going to quit. He'd done everything he could to come to her a changed man. Everything he could to deserve her.

He stared at the door to her room, ready to burst through it and see if she was all right. It was taking too long and he was about to go crazy with fear. But then the door opened and the doctor came out.

"How is she?"

The man looked up from the chart he was holding. "Signora Scott will be fine. But she needs rest, *signore*. A woman in her condition should not be working outside in the heat of the day." He shook his head, then consulted the chart again. "She is dehydrated, but the fluids will take care of that. I want to keep her for observation, because of the baby, but she should be able to go home again in a few hours if all remains stable."

Shuddering relief coursed through him, leaving his knees weak. He put a hand on the wall to hold himself upright. He was about to ask if he could see her when Teresa Corretti came out of the room. She was an elfin woman, but she had a spine of steel. He'd seen that the instant he'd met her. Right now, she was looking at him with a combination of fury and concern.

"She will see you," she said. "But don't you dare upset her, young man. If you do, I will not be responsible."

He took her meaning quite well, especially since it was accompanied by a hard look that said she'd like to rip his balls off and feed them to him if he harmed a hair on her granddaughter's head.

She jerked her head toward the door. "Go, then. But remember what I said."

"Sì, signora," he replied. Then he took a deep breath and went inside.

His heart turned over at the sight of Lia in a hospital bed. She was sitting up, but her normally golden skin was pale, and her head was turned away from him as she gazed through the window at the parking lot beyond.

"Lia." His throat was tight. His chest ached. He'd been through so much this past month, so many emotions. He hadn't thought seeing her again would be so hard, but he should have known better. He'd done his best to destroy her feelings for him, hadn't he?

"Why are you here, Zach?" she asked, still not looking at him.

He went over to the bed and sat in the chair beside it. He did not touch her, though he desperately wanted to. "To say I'm sorry."

Her head turned. Bright blue-green eyes speared

into him. "You have come all this way to say you are sorry? For what? Breaking my heart? Abandoning your baby?" She waved a hand as if to dismiss him. "Take your apologies and leave. I do not need them."

His chest was so tight he thought he might start to hyperventilate at any moment. But he swallowed the fear and looked at her steadily. He could do this. He *would* do this.

"I'm ready to fight," he said.

She blinked. "Fight? I don't want to fight, Zach. Go away."

He took her hand this time. He had to touch her, needed to touch her. She flinched but did not try to pull away. Currents of heat swirled in the air between them, like always. It gave him hope.

"No, I want to fight for you. For us."

She turned her head away again, and his heart felt as if someone had put it in a vise and turned the screws. Her lip trembled, and something like hope began to kindle again inside his soul. If she was affected by his words, maybe it wasn't too late.

But it was a fragile hope. He'd done too much to her to deserve a second chance. He'd taken her love and thrown it away. He knew what kind of life she'd had, how she'd been deserted by her father and ignored by her family, and he'd pushed her away just the same as they had.

He'd discarded her when he should have fought for her. He'd figured it out finally. He just hoped it wasn't too late.

"You come here now and say this to me," she said, her voice thready. "Why should I believe you? What has changed in the past month? Do you dare to tell me you realized you cannot live without me?"

She'd turned back to him then, her voice gaining in intensity until he could feel the heat of her anger blistering through him. Her eyes flashed and her red hair curled and tumbled over her shoulders and he was suddenly unsure what to say. What if he got it wrong? What if she sent him away?

He couldn't let that happen. He'd do anything to prevent it.

"Yes," he said firmly. "That is exactly what I intend to say."

Lia's chest ached, and not from her fainting episode. She'd gotten overheated, her grandmother had told her. She'd fainted on her terrazzo, though Zach had caught her before she'd hit the hard marble. And then he'd carried her up to the house and ordered someone to call an ambulance.

Now she was here, feeling like a fool for getting too hot and fainting. She was also getting flustered by Zach's presence. By the words she could hardly believe he'd uttered.

They made her heart sing. But she was also afraid.

"I want you to come home," he said. "I want to be with you."

Lia swallowed. "I'm not sure I can do that," she said softly.

His expression was stark. Terrified.

"Leaving was hard," she continued, resolutely ignoring the ache in her heart, "but I've started to live my life without you. And if you drag me back, if you pull me into your life and then decide you can't handle a wife and child, I'm not sure I will survive that heartbreak a second time."

"I went to see a doctor," he told her quietly. His hand was still wrapped around hers, and she felt the tremor shake him as he said those words.

"Oh, Zach." There was a lump in her throat.

"I can't guarantee I won't have dreams. I'm pretty sure I will have them. But I know how to deal with them now."

He stood, moved until he was so close she could reach up and touch him if she wanted to.

He pressed her hand to his heart. It beat hard and fast beneath her palm.

"I told the doctor about the gun and how I couldn't pull the trigger. And I'm taking medicine, Lia. It helps with the fear and anger. I didn't want to take it before. I thought I could handle it myself. But the truth is I can't. No one can. We aren't meant to handle these things alone."

Her vision blurred again, but this time it was due to the moisture in her eyes. "I'm glad you got help, Zach. Really glad." She turned her hand in his and squeezed. "But I'm still not sure coming back is the right thing. You hurt me when you sent me away, and I can't be hurt like that again. I can't let our baby be hurt, either."

He looked suddenly uncertain, as if he'd come across a roadblock he hadn't expected.

"And if I said I love you?"

Her heart went into free fall before soaring again. She told herself to be realistic, practical. To not simply accept what he said at face value because she'd wanted it for so long. She'd been disappointed so many times by her need to be loved. She would not let it rule her now.

"Why do you love me, Zach? Why now?"

He sank onto the chair beside the bed again. His eyes were intense, burning, as they caught hers and held.

"I love you because you give me hope. Because you see the good in me instead of the bad. Because you believe in me. Because you made me believe in myself." He sucked in a breath, his nostrils flaring. His voice, when he spoke again, was fierce. "I'm glad I lived, Lia. I'm glad I'm here with you, and even if you send me away, even if you never let me back in your life again, I won't regret a single moment I spent with you."

She felt a tear spill free and slide down her cheek. She dashed her hand over her face, as if she could hide her tears from him.

But he saw them, of course.

"It kills me when you cry," he said softly. "And it kills me to think I caused it."

Her heart squeezed. "I'm not crying because I'm unhappy. I'm hormonal."

It wasn't the truth, of course, but she stubbornly didn't want to admit she was crying because of him. She'd cried too much over him this past month already.

"I love you, Lia. I don't want you to cry. I want to make you happy. Always."

She was trembling hard now, but she turned away from him and tried to focus on the cars moving in the parking lot outside. How could she cross this bridge again? How could she make herself vulnerable once more to all the vicissitudes of a relationship with this man?

"I—I want to believe you. But I'm not sure I can."

"You can," he said. "I know you can. Isn't that what you said to me?"

She dropped her chin to her chest and sucked in a huge breath. She had said that to him. She'd said it and she'd been angry when he hadn't listened. When he'd denied it and sent her away.

How could she do the same thing to him? How could she be a coward, when he ultimately had not? He was facing his fears, finally. How could she be any different?

"I will try," she said softly. "That's the best I can do."

She left the hospital that evening. She'd thought she was going back to her grandmother's house, but when Zach turned a different direction, she could only look at him. He glanced over at her.

"I'm taking you to our home," he said. "It will be more private for us."

She lifted an eyebrow. "I wasn't aware we had a home in Sicily."

He shrugged. "Actually, it's a rental. If you like it, I'll buy it for you. And if you don't, I'll buy you another one somewhere else."

A little thrill went through her, in spite of her resolve to take this slowly and carefully. She'd agreed to try to believe he loved her, and that this could work between them, but she hadn't actually thought about what that would entail. Of course they would go to a home they shared. And of course they would be alone together.

So much for her resolve when her pulse picked up at the thought.

Zach took her to a large, beautiful villa with a view of the sea. She could tell because the lights of homes carpeting the island below them gave way to a vast inky darkness. The lights of a ship moved alone on that black surface, isolated from civilization.

She stood on the balcony and let the sea breeze ruffle her hair, feeling like that ship, adrift on an immense sea of uncertainty and fear.

"You should be sitting," Zach told her. "You've had a rough day."

"In more ways than one," she replied.

"Yes."

She felt bad for saying it then, for making him quietly accept her lingering animosity. But it was the only thing standing between her and complete capitulation, so she nursed it in wounded silence. Until it burst from her, like now.

"I'm sorry," she said, turning to him. He stood so near, hands in pockets, dark eyes trained on her.

"Don't be. I deserve it."

She sighed. "No. I'm just afraid, Zach. Afraid it won't be real."

"Maui," he said, his voice so quiet, and her heart pinched because he knew.

"Yes, Maui." She took a deep breath. "We had such a perfect time there. I thought there was something between us, and then it stormed and you became a stranger to me. You showed me that I didn't matter, that nothing we'd shared mattered."

"I'm more sorry for that than you know. But I was damaged, Lia, and I was afraid of that damage some-how spilling over onto you. You, the sweetest, most innocent woman I've ever known. How could I tarnish that brightness of yours with my darkness?"

"You can't be undamaged now," she said, shaking her head. "Not in a month. Not ever. So how do you propose to reconcile what you think of as damage—which I think of as life, by the way—with our rela-tionship now? Will the first dream or episode send you running again?"

He sighed. "I deserve every bit of your condem-nation. No, I am not undamaged. But none of us are, are we? I'm learning to cope with that." He paused for a moment. "I found the medal you left behind. I put it with the others. And they're in my desk drawer at home, where I see them every day when I open it. I earned them with my blood and sweat and tears. And

I owe it to those who gave their lives for me to honor their memories by not running from my own."

A chill slid down her spine as he spoke. And she knew, deep in her heart, that what he said was true. That he'd turned a corner somewhere in his journey and he was finally on the way to healing.

She took a step toward him, reached up and caressed the smooth skin of his jaw. "Zach," she said, her heart full.

He turned his face into her palm and kissed it. "I love you, Lia Corretti Scott. Now and forever. You saved me."

A dam burst inside her then. She went into his arms with a tiny cry, wrapped herself around him while he held her tight. This was what it meant to love and be loved. To belong.

"No, I think we saved each other."

"Does this mean you still love me?" he asked, his voice warm and breathless in her ear.

She leaned back so she could see his face. His beautiful, beloved face. "I never stopped, *amore mio*. I never could."

"Grazie a Dio," he said. And then he kissed her as a full moon began to rise from the sea, lighting their world with a soft, warm glow.

EPILOGUE

LIA WOKE IN the middle of the night. She sat up with a
start, certain she'd heard a cry. It was raining outside,
a typical summer storm. A jagged bolt of lightning
shot across the sky, followed by a crack of thunder.

The bed beside her was empty, the sheets tossed
back. She grappled on the nightstand for the baby
monitor, but it was gone. Sighing, she climbed from
bed and put on her robe. Then she padded out the door
and down the hallway to the nursery.

Zach looked up as she entered. He was sitting in the
rocking chair, cradling their son in his arms while the
baby cooed and yawned. Zach smiled, and her heart
lurched with all the love she felt for the two men in
her life.

"I believe it was my turn," she said tiredly.

"I was awake," he said, shrugging.

"A dream?" she asked, thinking of the storm and worrying for him.

"I was dreaming, yes," he said. "But not about the war."

"You weren't?"

He looked down at their baby, his sexy mouth curling in a smile. "No. I dreamed I was flying. And then I dreamed I was on a beach with you."

"What happened then?"

"I could tell you," he said, slanting a look up at her. "But I'd far rather show you."

Heat prickled her skin, flooded her core. "I'll look forward to it," she said softly.

"Give me a few minutes." His gaze was on his son again.

Lia pulled a chair next to the rocker and sat down beside him. Zach reached out and took her hand in his, and they sat there with their baby until his little eyes drifted shut. Gently, Zach placed him in his crib— and then he took Lia by the hand and led her back to their bedroom.

Later, as she lay in his arms and drifted off to sleep, she knew she'd gotten everything she ever wanted.

Love. Family. Belonging.

* * * * *

*Read on for an exclusive
interview with Lynn Raye Harris!*

BEHIND THE SCENES OF
SICILY'S CORRETTI DYNASTY
with Lynn Raye Harris

It's such a huge world to create—an entire Sicilian dynasty. Did you discuss parts of it with the other writers?

Oh, yes! We started an email loop and discussed where to set the Corretti estates and whether the wedding, which kicks off the whole thing, would be in a chapel or a cathedral, etc. We also discussed character interactions and how they felt about their histories.

How does being part of the continuity differ from when you are writing your own stories?

Well, one of the hardest parts of writing a continuity is finding connection with the characters. When they are your own creation it's much easier to find that connection than when you are given a brief about them. But it eventually happens, and then you have fun!

What was the biggest challenge? And what did you most enjoy about it?

This time, for me, the biggest challenge was writing an American hero. That's probably an odd thing to say, since I am an American, but I found Zach far more difficult because of it. Add in his military service, and I really had a difficult time. Not because I don't know anything about the military—but because I know too much! My husband was in the air force, though he didn't fly planes, and I'm pretty familiar with military life. It was a challenge to balance that element in the story, probably because I was too concerned with making it correct.

As you wrote your hero and heroine was there anything about them that surprised you?

Zach told me something that surprised me. He tells Lia, too, so you'll get to see what it is. It's a very dark thing, and we both ached for him that he's been living with this guilt and self-loathing.

What was your favorite part of creating the world of Sicily's most famous dynasty?

The research! Who doesn't like looking at pictures of Sicily and reading about the culture? Regrettably, my characters don't spend a lot of time there, but it was still fun!

If you could have given your heroine one piece of advice before the opening pages of the book, what would it be?

Chin up, babe.

What was your hero's biggest secret?

I can't tell! It's in the book.

What does your hero love most about your heroine?

Her sweetness and strength. She believes in him and that means a lot.

What does your heroine love most about your hero?

He's honorable and he cares a great deal about doing the right thing.

Which of the Correttis would you most like to meet and why?

Oddly enough, I think I'd like to meet Teresa Corretti! She's the matriarch who kept the whole thing together when it should have failed long before. She's a strong woman used to dealing with lots of arrogant men. I imagine she's the strength behind the family throne, really, though they don't quite know it.

Please read on for a sneak peek at the next book in
SICILY'S CORRETTI DYNASTY,
A Scandal in the Headlines by Caitlin Crews,
which features in
The Correttis: Scandals
available in August 2013.

A SCANDAL IN THE HEADLINES

Caitlin Crews

She understood that she would have to live with this. That this was a defining moment. That her life would be divided into before and after this scorching hot dance, and that she would never again be the person she'd believed she was before this stranger pulled her against him. But his eyes were locked to hers, filled with wonder and fire, and she didn't pull away. She didn't even try—and she understood she'd have to live with that, too.

And then he made it all so much worse.

'You cannot marry him,' he said, those dark green eyes so fierce, his face so hard.

It took her longer than it should have to clear her head, to hear him. To hear an insult no engaged woman should tolerate. It was that part that penetrated, finally. That made her fully comprehend the depths of her betrayal.

'Who are you?' she demanded. But she still let him hold her in his arms, like she was something precious to him. Or like she wished she was. 'What makes you think you can say something like that to me?'

'I am Alessandro Coretti,' he bit out. She stiffened and his voice dropped to an urgent, insistent growl. 'And you know why I can say that. You feel this, too.'

'Coretti…' she breathed, the reality of what she was doing, the scope of her treachery, like concrete blocks falling through her one after the next.

He saw it, reading her too easily. His dark eyes flashed.

'You cannot marry him,' he said again, some kind of desperation beneath the autocratic demand in his voice. As if he knew her. As if he had the right. 'He'll ruin you.'

Elena would never know what might have happened then, had she not jerked her gaze away from Alessandro's in confusion—and seen Niccolo there at the side of the dance floor, glaring at the two of them with murder in his black eyes.

Elena was amazed that it was possible to hate herself so much, so fully. And that the shame didn't kill her where she stood.

'How dare you?' she hissed at Alessandro, all her horror at her own appalling actions in her voice. 'I know who you are. I know *what* you are.'

Special thanks and acknowledgement are given to Caitlin Crewes for her contribution to *Sicily's Corretti Dynasty* series

The Correttis

Introducing the Correttis, Sicily's most scandalous family!

On sale 3rd May

On sale 7th June

On sale 5th July

On sale 2nd August

Mills & Boon® Modern™ invites you to step over the threshold
and enter the Correttis' dark and dazzling world...

Find the collection at
www.millsandboon.co.uk/specialreleases

*Visit us
Online*

0513/MB415

The World of Mills & Boon®

There's a Mills & Boon® series that's perfect for you. We publish ten series and, with new titles every month, you never have to wait long for your favourite to come along.

Blaze
Scorching hot, sexy reads
4 new stories every month

By Request
Relive the romance with the best of the best
9 new stories every month

Cherish™
Romance to melt the heart every time
12 new stories every month

Desire
Passionate and dramatic love stories
8 new stories every month